California Smoke

California Smoke

Hank Shaeffer

ISBN: 0996636323
ISBN 13: 9780996636322

CHAPTER 1

PLAYER

Scanning the crowd at the Eco-Resistance demonstration down in South County, dressed up in his Injun outfit, Russell George motioned toward the mill gate.

"See the woman?"

She was standing next to the flatbed truck they had set up like a stage. Tall, with long red hair that fell over a cropped leather jacket, wearing skintight jeans and hand-tooled cowboy boots. Could he see her? How could he fucking miss?

Eddie Fuentes said, "Wait. You said she's a *lawyer*?"

Russell nodded. "So, what would a lawyer like *that* be doing in a place like *this*, right?" He smiled. "Lemme know when you ask her."

Now a skinny kid standing on the flatbed was leaning down, handing the woman what looked like an envelope; the woman nodding, putting it in a jacket pocket.

Watching, Eddie said, "When does that happen?"

Russell said. "When she circles in, I'm guessing over drinks. ... The fish, don't chase the shark, *hombre*; the shark comes after the fish."

It started that morning, Eddie in bed at the old Motel 6 up in Redwood Bay. This was back in the glory days, before the Redwood Casino upped the ante and Prop 64 turned Redwood County into a Technicolor tourist attraction. Russell called, said he wanted Eddie to meet him, wanted to hook him up with someone, a player.

Eddie asked him, what kind of player.

"The kind's gonna turn you upside down and shake out the nickels, you know some other kind? … What happened to you, dude? I think your brain went to sleep in the cradle of syphilization."

Did he mean Anbar or Oakland? Eddie worked Oakland ten years as a vice cop after the tours in Iraq. This while Russell was up here playing big shot and, before that, hanging around Berkeley, getting a "higher education". Now, they were both back in Redwood County—for different reasons. Or, anyway, that's what Eddie thought.

Russell told him the woman's name was Shanna Black, and she was going to be at a demonstration at the Liberty Mill. He said Eddie should meet him, ten o'clock, at the VFW lot, but he wouldn't say any more on the phone. "Fucking NSA, man. Don't you read the papers?"

Eddie Fuentes knew Russell George his whole life, and Russell hadn't changed much. Nobody really changed, did they? They grew up at Cold Flats, the Rancheria, what people who weren't Indians called 'a reservation'. In those days, Russell's old man was Chairman of the Mynot Tribe. When he died, they elected Russell, about as pure blood Indian as you could get. Eddie was maybe twenty-five percent. They were near the same age, Russell a few months older, so they were pretty tight back then. They played high school football, got stoned, watched old movies on TV. Or they might hang at the pool hall in Juanita, and maybe tool around the county looking for a game, Eddie the shooter, Russell the shill. Eddie would stall till there was money on the table. Then, he'd have a run of luck. Over fifteen years ago. Jesus.

Liberty was an old mill town twenty-five miles south of Redwood Bay. It was a short hop on the 101, a four-lane road that snaked through forested hills people from the city called mountains. Today the fog was in. It usually was, summer mornings, draped on the trees like that fake spider web shit people put up at Halloween. Eddie never cared for the fog, the morning, or Halloween, for that matter.

He was driving Matty's truck today, his only transportation since Karen took the Mustang. Eddie didn't much miss the Mustang, a woman's ride, nothing like the muscle car McQueen drove back in the day. But even the Mustang was better than this—a '77 F-150, with no radio, no heater, a blown engine, and a worn-out clutch. Gears grinding, coughing on the grades, blowing smoke, barely making thirty-five in a sixty-five zone. It was Matty's all right. It even smelled like him—gasoline, fertilizer and sweat. Eddie would have rolled down the windows, if they worked.

Driving down the 101, he could just about see the old man, that ruined dude, kneading the wheel with grimy palms, wild hair flying, flannel shirt stained with chain oil. People would honk; he'd give them the finger. "Kiss my ass. … Like I give a fuck."

In fact, it occurred to Eddie now his old man maybe gave too much of a fuck. So it twisted around like a knife in his gut. So he never cut his hair or fixed his teeth or took a bath or worked on his truck. And that cabin he lived in, out past the Divide. He didn't have to live out there, or anyway let it turn into a slum. It was like some kind of a statement he was making, a protest. But against what?

Shit, Prior Road! Eddie woke up, yanked the wheel hard right to make the ramp. Exits came up fast in the fog.

Russell said the Liberty ramp would be jammed. Get off at Prior, take the old forest highway south, park in the VFW lot. They could walk in from there. Eddie remembered the place from when they were kids, and set it on fire one time, flipping cigarette butts on the roof, not thinking the pine needles might catch.

The lot wasn't paved or striped or oiled against the dust, and the old building wasn't painted, either. Nothing looked like it changed in all those years, except Russell put on weight, and Eddie saw some gray mixed into that long, heavy hair. He was standing by an old Ford Ranger, the truck scoured the color of worn-out denim by that hard salt wind that blew at Cold Flats. Russell George, tall, high cheekbones, strong jaw, dressed up in his official Injun outfit today, with the canvas pants, the abalone beads, and the authentic deerskin jacket.

Eddie pulled in next to him and got out. Seeing Russell eyeing Matty's truck, then his ratty fatigue jacket, he shook his head and chucked a thumb at the beads. "What's up with that?"

Russell said, "My wardrobe for media appearances, maybe some protection when the batons come out." Eddie squinted to show he didn't like the sound of it. Russell said, "I'm just fucking with you."

It was a good half-mile along the access road to the overpass, another quarter mile to the top. They'd park up here sometimes when they were in high school, drinking beer, looking out at the Liberty Draw. It was a nice view, the old mill town, set in that perfect three-sided valley. A valley the Mathesons never logged 'cause they didn't want to spoil the view out of their executive offices. The Mathesons were gone, but Eddie was pretty sure whoever was looking out those windows today wasn't liking what they saw. A mile-long line of semis with redwood logs the handlers couldn't unload, the conveyors couldn't convey and the band saws couldn't rip into finish lumber—trucks stacked all the way from the mill gate, back through town, and up the ramp to the 101 Freeway.

Looking at it now, Eddie said, "So, they shut the mill down, I guess the kids get bragging rights. You want to tell me what the Indians get?"

Russell said, "Don't worry about it."

They started walking, down the other side of the overpass toward town. Russell said, "See, I know what you're thinking. If they stop the logging, so what? Maybe the government buys a few more trees, puts them in a park. Some *turistas* get lost trying to find them, blow a tire at the Rancheria, and maybe an Injun makes a buck."

Eddie said, "Okay—"

"What you see down here?" Russell shook his head. "It's a show. ... Like I told you, don't worry about it."

They walked on awhile. Eddie said, "This show I'm not worrying about, you gonna tell me what it is?"

Russell put his hands in his pockets. "I'm doing you a favor, *hombre*."

"A favor."

"Your old man's truck runs worse than it did in high school."

"You gonna buy me a truck?"

"I'm *doing* you a *favor*." He smiled. "Fast Eddie, ease off. The play is gonna come." He took a beat. "This could be good for you. Be cool. Can you do that? Clock it? Wouldn't want to see the *hombre* get eaten *before* lunch."

The sound of rotors came up now, beating the air, as a news chopper flew in low over the freeway then, banking above them, headed for the mill at the far end of town.

The Liberty Mill was a relic, the only place left with equipment big enough to handle the old growth. Not that it mattered; there wasn't much old growth left to cut. Still, Russell said, that's why they picked it. It was a symbol. Liberty was a company town. A shrine to the golden age of logging. Not that there ever really *was* a golden age of logging. It was always a dirty, dangerous business. But the Mathesons liked to pretend, and they had the money to rewrite history. So, they kept it up—paved the roads, kept the wooden sidewalks clean, painted the little bungalows on the side streets, and kept the stores along Main Street looking like Frontierland.

Today, though, it looked like the aliens had landed—city kids hanging around; green and white sheriff's cruisers at the intersections, lights flashing; yellow crime scene tape along the sidewalks—God knows what that was for. There were locals in logger gear standing around, drinking coffee out of Styrofoam cups, some talking, others with arms folded, just watching, waiting to see what might happen.

Russell told him how they set it up on the way into town. Some guys from a group he called "The Coalition" drove in, middle of the night, ran a tow chain across the truck gate, padlocked to the gate posts at each end. Then, they got a bunch of mentally defective college kids—his words—to hook themselves onto the tow chain with bicycle locks. By the time company security realized something was up, the first semi was at the gate with a full load. There was no way in, and the kids had a flatbed parked in the turnaround, so there was no way out either. A few minutes later, a second truck came, and a third truck and so on. The kids wanted a mess big enough to draw the media, and they got what they wanted.

They walked passed the post office, and now the old bar, a general store, and up to the outdoor equipment display in front of Foley's

Hardware. The closer you got to the mill gate, the louder the chanting got, and the younger the crowd.

> *Logging kills!*
> *Logging kills!*
> *Save the trees!*
> *Shut down the mills!*

From Foley's you could see the turnaround, the crowd waving signs—*Loggers Kill, Save the Watershed, Wall Street Out of Redwood County*—and behind the crowd, the "heroes" locked up to the tow chain, accepting congratulations and plastic bottles filled with mineral water.

Eddie nudged Russell, pointed up a side street where you could see a row of tour buses. Russell motioned to the sign above the gate. It was supposed to read:

WEST COAST LUMBER MILL NO. 1
LIBERTY, CALIFORNIA

But the demonstrators had a banner hung over the top part, so now it read,

FREE REPUBLIC OF
LIBERTY, CALIFORNIA

"Telegraph Avenue," Russell said.

Telegraph, sure, Berkeley's version of the street life, but this was better. You had a beefy set of twins with shoulder length hair dressed up like redwood trees. You had a good-looking brunette in a bird outfit with a sign on her back that said "Marbled Murrelet". You had a shiny new flatbed truck, still sporting dealer tags, the truck set up like a stage, with mics and amps and speaker stacks, left and right. In front of it, a blonde was selling tee shirts out of a wicker basket.

Now, a news crew jogged by, elbowing through the crowd—the female producer running interference for a cute Asian reporter in her navy blazer, bow tie blouse bouncing, followed by an overweight cameraman in a fatigue jacket. On the back of the flatbed, Eddie could see a short, skinny kid watching them, probably waiting till they got set up before he bothered talking.

In the meantime, Eddie's eyes drifted back to the blonde with the tee shirts. She was a pretty girl, but heavy, like pretty blondes can be, big butt, wide in the hips. It reminded him of some girls in West Oakland he knew. Blondes working for dudes like De Marius Williams. De Marius, king of the coat hanger, Eddie seeing it now, the blonde bare-ass across the bed at the Sage Brush Motel, purple welts starting to swell. They found out later she was fifteen, a runaway from Chico, not that far from here. What was her name?

His gaze wandered, back along the street to the girl in the bird suit with the sign. He said, "What's a 'Marbled Murrelet'?"

Russell followed his gaze. "It's a bird, *hombre*. Lives in the old growth trees." Then, he motioned ten minutes right of the bird. "You see the woman?"

CHAPTER 2

HOMBRE

"**M**ay I have your attention please? Attention? Thank you. Thank you very much." A skinny kid took the mic out of the stand, up on the flatbed truck, a practiced move, like a game show host. " My name is Eric Ross, and I'm northwest regional coordinator for the Eco-Resistance Coalition."

The system started to screech, and Eric waited while a kid ran over to adjust the volume. The screeching stopped, but the sound out of the speaker stacks was still loud enough to damage your eardrums.

"First of all," Eric Ross said, "I want to thank everybody for coming out this morning. We've all got things to do, I know. But we're here for a very important purpose. We're here today, in the town of Liberty, California, to STOP THE KILLING!"

There was some cheering. Not much, but Eric held his hand up like the crowd was going wild. You got the feeling he'd done this hundreds of times, telling the people how they were part of a historic movement, a vanguard calling attention to the plight of the ninety-nine percent. He told them they were hapless victims preyed on by a "conniving corporate culture that objectified everything it touched" —turned animals into 'livestock' and people into 'human resources'. It was a rapacious, all-consuming greed, he said, motioning dramatically to the hills, "That looked at these majestic redwoods, and saw so many board feet of lumber."

The kid was pretty good. though apparently not good enough for Shanna Black. She had apparently have taken off.

"We are here, my friends—" Eric was saying, motioning now toward the mill behind him, then back again to the crowd. "—But, I don't have to tell you why we're here, do I?"

A few people called out, "No!" and Eric flashed a friendly smile.

"Okay, why don't you tell me? Why are we here?"

Somebody yelled, "Shut the mill!"

Eric put his hand to his ear. "What?"

A few people yelled, "Shut it down!"

"I still can't hear you!"

More people joined in, and it turned into a chant, "Shut it down! Shut it down! Shut it down!" Then, "Logging kills! / Logging kills! / Save the trees! / Shut down the mills!"

Meanwhile, Eddie was thinking about Shanna Black. There was something familiar about that name, but he couldn't think what it was. Remembering her standing, one hand resting on the truck, the other sweeping long red hair back out of her eyes, he was thinking she was the kind of woman people noticed. The kind that was used to it, didn't mind the attention, didn't get embarrassed. The kind that maybe got off on it.

Karen was that kind of woman. Karen in the past tense, Karen who took off with the furniture the day the arbitrator's ruling came down. Karen, who cleaned out the checking account, took the Mustang, and didn't bother to leave a note. Not that Eddie needed a note. What bothered him was the furniture. He didn't mind that she took it. He hated the stuff—big, heavy pieces she got off one of Bluestein's clients before they filed the chapter proceeding. Sectional sofa, matching cocktail and end tables, armoires. A bedroom set with a Sleep Number mattress that weighed a fucking ton. Karen was only five six, and Bluestein was maybe three inches taller. So, who carried all that shit down the hall to the service elevator and out through the garage? Somebody with muscles ... and a van. Knowing Karen, she wasn't going to write a check to the first bozo out of Craig's List. She got estimates. And the question was, how long did she plan it? When did she decide to take off? Was it after the night she made love to him on the kitchen floor and told him she'd stand by him forever? Or was it before?

Meanwhile, on stage, Eric was explaining how Americans had been seduced by the boomerang evils of modern materialism. "You think slavery ended with the Civil War?" he was saying. "Look at your situation. Student loans, car leases, credit card bills, the mortgage on your house—if you have one. Look at what you owe and what you own." He motioned with a sweep of his hand. "This town. They call it Liberty. I got news for you, people. This isn't Liberty. This is servitude."

He could be right, but Eddie was also thinking what a shot of bourbon would feel like right now, the sweet taste of sour mash whiskey, the slow burn going down. Thinking now about that bar they passed on the way in, Eddie tapped Russell on the shoulder and motioned with his thumb. "I gotta take a piss."

Eddie remembered the inside of the bar from when they'd score quarts of beer growing up. It was a real logger dump, long and narrow, wood paneled walls hung with old time pictures—hard-eyed men, leaning on long handle axes around muddy landings, or sitting on old growth logs bigger than subdivision houses. They didn't look happy, these men with haunted faces, and turned down moustaches. They reminded Eddie of his father.

There was a rose colored mirror behind the bar, the kind that makes you look like a movie star with a suntan, even if you've been living in a hole. But sitting there, waiting for his whiskey, Eddie didn't see a movie star. He saw a guy in an empty apartment, sitting on the floor where the sofa used to be, looking at himself in a sliding glass window somewhere in Oakland with a view of other sliding glass windows. The sky getting dark, the landline ringing. Eddie letting it go to voicemail, and listening to a man tell the machine he was calling from the Redwood County Public Administrator's Office. Eddie didn't really hear anything after that 'cause Eddie was a cop, and knew the PA was the guy at the Coroner's Office who notified the next of kin when a body came in. If Eddie was the next of kin and the body was in Redwood County, it would be his father's. The news was a shot to the gut, but not exactly a surprise. Mattias Fuentes wasn't the kind to live a hundred years, or pass away peacefully in his sleep. When he went, it would involve a mess of one kind or another.

The bartender set down Eddie's drink now; Eddie set down some cash, and asked for the men's. The bartender pointed toward the back. That's when Eddie saw them, sitting in a booth. Shanna Black, facing away from him, but unmistakable—the tangle of red hair, the way she held her head, the expensive jacket. Sitting across from her, facing in Eddie's direction, was a man he hadn't seen before. A light colored African American in gold designer shades and a tan designer suit. The man seemed about as much at home in a logger bar as the bottle of mineral water in front of him or the ring on the hand holding the cell phone he was talking into. The way Eddie read the dude, he could be many things, but if he had to bet, the choices were down to three. A dope dealer, a pimp, or a cop. But, you know, that was Eddie.

As he walked past on his way to the john, he thought he felt her eyes on him, but maybe not. On the way back, she barely looked, talking to the black dude about sports cars. The dude telling her he didn't like Corvettes. The woman saying something about Lamborghinis.

Back at the bar, Eddie found himself wondering what Shanna Black would be doing with a guy Eddie could see running a stable of girls on San Pablo Avenue. Probably a client. Up here, Redwood County, she'd have to do criminal work. What else was there? Then found himself thinking, okay, she represents the guy. That doesn't mean she has to have drinks with him, does it?

Eddie ordered another round and sitting there, looking at his reflection, started thinking about last night, the bar in Juanita. Russell told Eddie it was a sign, he got bounced from the Oakland P.D.

"You didn't belong down there, *hombre*," he said, "You're Indian."

Eddie told him how he saw it, with the blue eyes and light brown hair, he didn't look much like an Indian. Plus, he was only a quarter blood, which meant he was three-quarters something else

"You're Indian enough," Russell told him. Then he started talking about an old sixties movie they watched a couple times at the Rancheria, one Eddie happened to like a lot, about a half breed Apache who got caught up in a stage coach robbery. Back then, Russell told Eddie he looked like the Apache, and started calling him, *Hombre*, the title of the film.

Last night, feeling the Jim Beam, Eddie said the movie didn't prove shit. The guy who played the Apache wasn't Indian. "That was Paul Newman," he said. The man was Jewish."

Russell shook his head. "Half Jewish, *hombre*. The reason they say he was Jewish? That's what *he* said he was."

They paved paradise
Put up a parking lot
With a pink hotel, a boutique
And a swinging hot spot

Standing outside Foley's, Russell could hear the Anglo girl with her expensive guitar, trying to look Appalachian in her Doc Martens and puff sleeve granny dress. What he was thinking, whoever wrote that song—which he had heard a thousand times at least—didn't live on food stamps or work for minimum wage at Wal-Mart. People who lived that life would suck shit off a stick to work in a pink hotel, a boutique *or* a swinging hot spot. Fucking middle class values, man, they infected everything. Environmental movement ... what environment did they think they talking about?

Russell checked his watch. Eddie gone close to an hour now. What kind of piss takes an hour? Not even noon yet. Jesus, what happened to the old *hombre*? That slow smile he had when he walked into a room. Russell felt like it might still be in there somewhere, and maybe he'd get it back, if he hung around long enough.

There were a lot of things Russell did—like the thing with Eddie Fuentes—where the benefits weren't immediately obvious. Actually, most of what he did fit in that category. Russell was not what you would call a Type A personality. Sure, he might consider a possible outcome—how he might relate if things turned out like that. He might even consider, in a general way, what he could do to nudge events in that direction. But in terms of working up a sweat? Based on decades of dicking around, trying to get dudes to do things they *ought* to do, but for some reason, or no reason, didn't *want* to do, Russell's attitude was—chill the fuck out. The secret to getting along in this big, wide, wonderful world was, let the big time assholes make the waves. Then, go get your board.

The girl with the guitar was gone now, and the kid, Eric, was back.

"Did you ever *listen* to these people?" he was saying. "Our so-called leaders? These self-congratulatory assholes, running around the world bragging about private enterprise? Private *enterprise*? I'm sorry. A Federal Reserve System that's *owned* by the banks it's supposed to regulate. Drug companies in bed with the FDA? Military contractors slopping at the Pentagon trough? Wake up, people! What we have isn't capitalism. It's a fascist state hiding behind a democratic façade."

Russell was wondering what the guy was so upset about? Did he just figure this out? Anyway, nobody was listening. There was a buzz, yeah, people talking, pointing in Eric's general direction, but what Eric didn't realize, they weren't pointing at him. They were pointing *behind* him, on the other side of the truck gate, where private security was forming up in a sort of a wedge formation. At the tip of the spear, as the warriors say, was a thin, hard-eyed type. Man, this bad boy was perfect, fatigue pants and a commando sweater. A little old for operations, but he could have played CIA brass in one of the Bourne pictures.

"We have to look at the entire concept of *ownership*," Eric was saying. "The Mathesons sell out to some Wall Street *asshole*. And he wants to crank out more cash flow to—oh, I don't know—add onto his house in the Hamptons, so he decides to *redeploy* some assets. Don't you love it? *Redeploy assets*? This is the code they use for cutting down two thousand year old redwood trees."

Eric went on talking, totally clueless about the security wedge, moving through a narrow man-gate behind him, marching over to the flatbed truck. Now, the bad boy was hopping up on the truck with surprising agility for a guy his age, snatching the microphone right out of old Eric's hand.

"This will only take a minute," he said. Then, turning to the crowd, "I need your attention up here for a minute, ladies and gentlemen. Attention? My name is Walter Hellman, head of security for West Coast Lumber. I have a brief announcement to make."

The guy had a funny voice, Russell thought. Like he wanted to *sound* military, but came off a little like a dork.

Now he pulled out a folded piece of paper, shook it to get it open. "If you don't mind, I'll just read this thing, to make sure I get the wording right." He cleared his throat. "'The City of Liberty, California, including, without limitation, the mill and yards, all municipal facilities, and all means of ingress and egress thereto and therefrom, constitute the sole and exclusive property of West Coast Lumber Company, and the right of any person to come upon, use or occupy said property, exists solely by permission, and subject to the control of the owner. Section 1008, California Civil Code. That permission is hereby withdrawn until further notice.'"

He lowered the paper. "What that means in English, ladies and gentlemen is, this is a company town. The town is closed, and you are hereby ordered to leave. You have fifteen minutes to begin making an orderly exit. Any unauthorized personnel remaining after that time will be subject to arrest and prosecution. ... Okay, that's it. Let's move it out, people."

Russell heard Eddie's voice now, behind him. "Well, Chief, looks like you missed your speaking opportunity. Now what?"

Russell sniffed the air. "Sour mash, huh? You pissing drinks or half pint bottles?"

Eddie ignored the remark. Up on the flatbed, the ex-military type guy was gone and the kid, Eric, had the mic back. "Everybody? ... Hold on a minute ... Be cool, okay? The *Gestapo* over here, they're just playing with your heads. This is a *public place*. We have a *right* to be here. So let's just chill for a few minutes. Let's go back to some entertainment. "

He motioned to a tall girl with a guitar, but she didn't look too excited about the idea. Nobody did. Some of the people were already starting to drift back up the street, or onto the sidewalk. A kid ran up to the truck, motioned to Eric, said a few words, then Eric talked into the microphone again. "Uh, Shanna Black? Shanna, if you hear this? Could you please head back up to the stage area at this time? Shanna Black?"

Now, you could see a huge diesel fork lift bouncing through the mill yard, headed toward the truck gate. From the size of the thing, it wasn't going to have much trouble moving a flatbed truck, or anything else for that matter. But it wasn't going to *get* to the flatbed truck until they got the humans out of the way—probably why a private security detail was putting on gas masks.

Eddie pointed. "Looks like they're going to use OC. Pepper spray. Burns like a sonuvabitch, if you never tried it."

The security guy was getting back up on the flatbed now, but with a bullhorn this time. "This area is now closed. I repeat, the street is closed. Security! Clear the area!"

The signal for things to get started. Uniformed private security spraying the chain kids—getting right up in their faces with the OC. Chain kids screaming. Kids in the crowd jumping the uniforms. Uniforms spraying the crowd kids. Crowd kids grabbing spray canisters from the uniforms, picking up picket signs, trash cans, breaking up traffic barricades. The news cameraman managed some close-ups near the mill gate, then beat it back to the sidewalk with the reporter in the nick of time, as a dozen mill hands with two by fours, headed through the personnel gate, and out into the crowd. It was getting ugly fast. People were really moving now, most of them away from the gate, crowding the sidewalks, or heading out of town past the semis parked in the street. The interesting part? For some reason, the sheriff's deputies weren't doing shit, just hanging by their cars, while the news chopper dropped down to get some close-ups.

Eddie said to Russell, "What do you want to do?"

Russell didn't answer, holding his hand up, like he was listening to something. And now, Eddie could hear it, too. A sound coming from the far end of town, a low, rumble, the pitch rising and falling, like—what?

A truck, yeah, the engine revs going up and down as somebody shifted through the gears.

Now an air horn blasted. And like it was a signal, the fighting stopped, and you started to hear the voices.

"You see that?"

"See what?"

"The truck."

"The truck? Oh, shit, Jesus!"

And turning now, Eddie could see people moving to the sidewalks on either side of the street, and beyond them, a bright red Peterbilt log truck roaring up the wrong side of the street, dual stacks smoking. Only the truck couldn't exactly *fit* on the wrong side of the street, so it was hitting things along the way—mowing down street signs, knocking over trash cans, side-swiping the occasional sheriff's car, finally taking out a fire hydrant, sending a stream of water shooting thirty feet in the air.

The truck wasn't coming fast, and it wasn't coming slow, but it was sure as hell coming. Headed straight for the mill gate with the tow chain strung across it, headed straight for ... what? Jesus, the kids.

And the announcement, again, "Shanna Black to the *stage* area. Shanna, *please* if you hear this, we *need* you! It's an *emergency!*"

Locking themselves to a tow chain did not put the kids in line for a genius award. But Eddie didn't see it was a reason for dying, either. So now he was moving, through the crowd, down toward the sidewalk. And getting a better feel for the situation, breaking into a jog, and then a dead run, racing the Peterbilt back toward the mill. The smoke was clearing out of his head as the adrenaline kicked in, he dodged a pile of debris scattered in the brawl, blew through a crowd clogging the sidewalk.

"Asshole!" a girl's voice called after him.

On a pivot now, Eddie scanned the row of semis jamming the near side of the street. No way through there. His eyes moved to the turnaround, thirty yards from the mill gate. Could he get there ahead of the Peterbilt?

Figuring the angle without thinking—where the truck was, where it was going to be. His head was empty and clear and he was feeling—what? Alive. Like he woke up from a dream. Like he'd been sleepwalking, rope-a-doping, taking punches. And now, he was awake. Rolling. Feeling his rhythm. Getting in stride. Jesus, for the first time since — forget the first time since. He was rolling, end of story.

The crowd thinning out … now gone. Passing the last truck … into the turnaround. Whirling to see, on top of him … the Peterbilt … the running board … the door handle.

He leaped.

CHAPTER 3

THE SQUEEZE

Shanna Black caught a glimpse of the truck as she came out of the bar, her eyes still adjusting to the light. A second later, she heard her name echo over the loudspeakers, "Shanna, *please* if you hear this! It's an *emergency!*"

She felt the keys in her pocket, Jesus, and tried to move, but the sidewalk was jammed. There was nowhere to go. She stood, frozen, watching as bright red steel flashed into the turnaround. Then, a blur. A man? She couldn't tell. Jostled in the surging crowd, she lost her balance, and saw nothing more, then she heard the crash. And felt the bottom drop out of her stomach. Thinking, fuck me, my life is over. People are dying, and they're going to pin it on me. They are going to come after me guns blazing. They are going to sue the living shit out of me for this. I'll get disbarred and still be in court the rest of her my—as a defendant.

Darryl Waters—man, what she wouldn't give to shove those designer shades where the sun did not shine.

It started a month ago. Shanna's assistant apparently gone to the bathroom, the cool dude strolled into Shanna's office up in Redwood Bay, skin tone a shade darker than his tan double-breasted suit. The outfit finished with a black silk turtleneck and gold designer shades. He looked things over, nodding his head.

"All *right*. Looking *good*. Seem like the country life agree with *some* people, anyways."

Shanna watched him, wondering where this was going, the man wandering around her office, touching things. "My *goodness*, would you look at the size of that vase? Is that *Italian*? Shit, I bet that is *hand painted*. ... And that piece over there, that's an antique, isn't it? ... Wet bar. Oriental rugs. Plate glass desk, call that a racetrack shape, I believe, with the waterfall edge. Very *nice*." Then, pointing to the floor. "What do they call that, sugar, how they did the floor? Designs in there and everything?"

Shanna, looking at the man, said, "Parquet."

"Par*quet*. Mmm *hmmm*. Got to remember the term, write it down for future reference."

But he didn't write it down. Instead, he made a broad circular motion with his hand. "Now tell me, this impressive house we in here—not just the office, but the structure, too—my guess is, that would belong to you."

"That's right."

"So, what would you call it? The style, I mean. Would that be Victorian?"

"Victorian."

"Very *nice*."

"You could say. I inherited it. I'm partial to mid-century myself."

"Mid-century. You mean like, 1950s. That's interesting. I come up here, it reminds me more of the seventies. Tie die tee shirts and hippy shit vans." He sat down in a client chair, began rolling around on the castors, Shanna standing there, arms folded, watched him. "Now, as I understand it," he said, "you're primarily engaged in criminal defense work, am I correct in that assumption?"

"More or less."

"Good, good. Make it easier, you to understand what I'm 'a say to you. See, the thing is, Ms. Michelle Thomas—" He shook his head. "— Very attractive lady, though she could be a pain in the ass time to time, 'tween the two of us—*her* boss, Ms. Sarah Breckinridge, U.S. Attorney, Northern District of California—*that* woman is in *love* with Title 21, United States Code. 'Real property used to facilitate commission of a felony drug offense.' 'Proceeds traceable to a felony drug transaction.' Know what I'm talking about? Civil forfeiture provisions?"

Shanna didn't say anything.

Darryl went on. "Shit is music to the woman's ears. Specially now, with the budget cuts and all. Now—you not gonna believe this—they got us on a point system. One point for every dollar of value seized. Agent in the task force with the most points at the end of the year gets two weeks, all expenses paid, in Honolulu, Hawaii."

He looked around. "So, rough numbers, what would you say a place like this might bring? I mean, if you had to move it quick? Have to be a couple million dollars, am I right?"

Shanna said, "Oh, I get it, you're a real estate broker."

He started to laugh. "Shit! I'm supposed to do that part first." He pulled a card out of his pocket and handed it to her. "Darryl Waters," he said. "U.S. Drug Enforcement Administration." The card identified him as a Special Agent with an address in Oakland.

"So, Darryl," Shanna said, looking at the card. "Are you lost or what? The freeway's straight down, half mile east. You get on, drive south a couple hours, there's a turn off for San Quentin. Pass that, cross the Richmond Bridge, first thing you know, you're in Oakland. Well, depending on the traffic."

Darryl was smiling. "Very cool. Giving me directions. I like that." Then the smile faded. "How about I give you some? Lose the attitude, ease your designer ass into that fancy leather chair, lets the two of us have a friendly legal consultation. How would that be?"

Shanna took her time, but moved to the chair.

Darryl seemed to be enjoying himself, rolling around with his shades on. "Good old Redwood County. Yeah, I imagine criminal work produce quite a nice cash flow up in here, seeing as the drug trade's what? About half the economy?"

"We do all right."

"I'll just bet you do," Darryl said. "Still, I could see where you might do a whole lot better, you willing to step over the line, time to time, take a more active role in the criminal enterprise so to speak."

"I imagine that would depend on how active."

"Well, how about, say, bribery of a public official. Conspiracy to obstruct justice. How would that pencil out?"

Shanna said, "Gee, Darryl, I don't know. You'd need to tell me how much the bribe was, how many times it got paid and who got the money." She smiled. "But then, I don't see where that would concern you. Bribery's public corruption, FBI jurisdiction. You're DEA, right?"

"Mmm," Darryl was nodding, "But see, sometime, situation involve what we call effective administration of justice, they put a task force together. DEA, IRS, DOJ, and so on." He stretched his legs, looking down at a pair of shiny loafers. "Biggest industry in Redwood County ain't redwood, everybody knows that. But somehow, year in, year out, nobody up here gets busted for weed except a few long hair hippies happen to crop a little too much bud in there with the chard and vine ripe tomatoes. Ever wonder why that might be?"

"Why the hippies grow weed? Or why they bother with chard and tomatoes?"

"Why the *cops* don't bust the big time growers."

"I wouldn't know, Darryl. I'm not an expert in law enforcement priorities. But seeing as weed's going all out legal in a couple years, I suspect they think they've got better things to do."

"Maybe they getting *paid* to think that way, too."

"If they are," Shanna said, "You'd have to prove it."

Darryl chuckled. "Oh, we can prove it all right. That ship's gone down, Counselor. Only question is, how many *rats* going with it."

Shanna got up now, took a stroll over to the window that had a view out to the harbor. It was a nice enough day, the fog sitting on the horizon, but still out there, like smoke from a distant fire. "And this *ship* that's going down. Does it have a name?"

He turned to look at her. "How about, Norville E. Petty, Jr. Do anything for you?"

Turning, Shanna whistled. "Norville? The Sheriff? Wow!"

"Mmm hmmm. We got a lawyer there, too, holding the bag."

"A lawyer, too? Well that sounds serious." Shanna said. "What I'd say, though, Darryl—if this is a legal consultation— it's always tough, going after a lawyer." She folded her arms, pacing. "For example, let's say a lawyer delivers a package on behalf of a client. How are you going to prove the lawyer knew what was in it? Any communication with the client would be privileged."

Darryl looked at his fingernails. "I wouldn't get too smart, Counselor," he said. "I wanted to *bust* your ass, you be wearing an orange jump suit by now." He waved her back to her desk. "Go on, sit down."

She did, and he went on. "Norville E. Petty, Jr. Man living the lifestyles of the rich and famous on sixty-eight thousand five hundred dollars. We take his ass down anytime we want on tax fraud, man gonna sing like the Metropolitan Opera."

"Why don't you do it?"

"Could be we will. But for the moment, we interested in a song ain't in the classical repertoire." He chuckled. "DEA, they all white boys from the eighties, like that song from the Eagles, *Life in the Fast Lane*. You know that song?"

Shanna caught herself smiling. "Where are you going with this, Darryl? You gonna hold me for ransom in the heart of the cold, cold city?"

He laughed, just a little. "No, they interested in the *other* part. Where the man coming down, he say, 'Call the Doctor, I think I'm gonna crash.'"

Shanna played along. "Doctor say he's coming, but you gotta pay him in cash."

Darryl was nodding. "What some folks say, that song's referring to a client of yours."

Shanna took her time with this. "So, Darryl, *that's* what this is about? Seriously?" shaking her head now, "I mean you would think, with the Sinaloa boys, littering the national forests with body parts and tortilla wrappers, you could find something better to do than harass a refugee from the Woodstock Nation."

"That how you see it, we harassing the man."

"You've been after him forty years, Darryl. What would you call it?"

"Me? I call it determination. Dude's a legend of the drug trade."

"Along with a lot of other people."

"Yeah, but see, those dudes—Lucas, Escobar, Freeway Ricky Ross—they all dead or done hard time. The Doctor, on the other hand, living the good life somewhere up in here. Growing weed, cooking up Molly, he need a little cash. Think no one gonna touch him."

Shanna lit a cigarette. "Tell me this, Darryl. How the fuck do you know what he's cooking? I mean, really. You got him under surveillance? You said it yourself. He's a legend." She got up from her desk again, went back to the window. "You can't believe what you hear about legends, Darryl, don't you know that? This is the wild, Wild West up here. We got a million of them. Black Bart, Pecos Bill, Joaquin Murrieta." She smiled now, drawing out her words. "You heard of him, Joaquin Murrieta?"

Darryl didn't say anything, so she went on.

"Seems like some Anglos ran Joaquin off his claim. This was back in the gold rush days. So what he did, old Joaquin, he tracked them down, one by one. Cut their ears off, took their gold, and gave it to the poor. They called him the Robin Hood of El Dorado."

"Robin Hood of El Dorado. God damn." Darryl was nodding. "Then what?"

"The State Rangers went after him. They *claimed* they shot him and his partner, Three Finger Jack, in the mountains east of Salinas. Put his head in a jar of brandy, took it around the state, and charged a dollar to see it."

"No shit."

"Printed up posters and everything. You can still get copies on eBay. The head wound up behind the bar at the Golden Nugget in San Francisco. That was before the earthquake. But see, the thing is, Darryl, the people who knew Joaquin, they said the head wasn't his."

She walked slowly across the room to where Darryl was sitting. "They said it didn't have a scar where he had one, on his left cheek, right here." She traced a line on his face with her finger, then moved to sit on the side of her desk, facing him. "Later on, folks said they ran into him here and there. And *some* people say his ghost still rides the hills when the moon is full. I heard a woman swear she saw it."

The two of them were close now, facing each other. Finally, Darryl got up and moved toward the door. When he got there, he turned. "I like the part about charging money to see the head," he said. "We'd have to raise the price, though. To adjust for inflation."

And that was the last Shanna saw of Darryl Waters until this morning, when he turned up behind her at the demonstration, telling her he had "some information could impact her decision-making process." He said to meet him in the bar in fifteen minutes. When she got there, he was stretched out in a back booth, talking on a cell phone, the urban dude with his Revo's on.

He motioned. "Sit down, counselor, have a drink. Wouldn't think they'd have Perrier in a shit hole like this, would you? Guess you don't know till you ask, though, do you?"

Shanna went to the bar while he finished his call. When she got back, Darryl was smiling. "Damn, double Stoli, not even lunch time. Seem like you under some serious pressure, counselor."

Shanna told Darryl to kiss her ass, and sat down while he made small talk about how impressed he was, she was representing the protestors. "*Pro bono publico.* Means you don't get paid, right?"

Shanna told him to get to the point.

"Let's talk about legends."

"Legends." Shanna felt a man brush past the booth, headed toward the back. He was facing away from her, so she couldn't be sure. But she had a feeling it was the man standing with Russell before, who would be Eddie Fuentes.

"Yeah, seem like we got us a sighting, down the East Bay. Busted a rave, you'll never guess where the many say the Molly come from."

Her eyes still on the man going into the restroom, Shanna said, "How about the Robin Hood of El Dorado."

Darryl laughed. "Shit! They put that man's head in a jar. No, we talking about the other legend. The one you carrying the bag for."

Shanna took her time. "So this guy you busted—I'm sorry, what did you say his name was?"

"I *didn't* say," Darryl smiled, looking at her,

She shrugged. "I'm curious—this unnamed suspect—what did he tell you? The legend was making retail deliveries? He's ready to pick him out of a lineup, testify the man sold him a controlled substance at a specific place, date and time?"

Darryl kept looking at her, but didn't say anything.

"What I think, Darryl?" Shanna said, keeping it light, taking a sip of her drink. "Is that you are one hell of a guy. Bright, slick, ambitious. And you have this feeling you ought to be moving up in the world. But when you step back, take a look at it, what you see is, a Corvette stuck in the mud. High performance potential in a dead-end situation. Any of this ringing a bell with you, Darryl?"

The man—Eddie Fuentes—was coming out of the restroom now, headed toward her, while Darryl watched her with the shades on.

"I had a Corvette one time, Counselor," he said, "but I got rid of it. Know why? The *feng shui* was for shit. Way you sat, low down there inside the car. Like driving a bathtub, you understand? No sense of control in the situation."

Fuentes was closer now, his eyes on hers, steel blue in a hard, chiseled face. He reminded her of someone, an actor from the fifties, but she couldn't think of his name off the top of her head.

Lighting a cigarette, Shanna said, "I can see what you're saying about the Corvette, Darryl. But that doesn't mean you wouldn't like a Lamborghini."

Darryl took his Revo's off. "Damn if you ain't a piece of work," he said, "Sitting there in your thousand dollar cowboy jacket with that solid gold watch on your wrist. Know what I think?"

Taking a drag, she said, "I'm just dying to."

"I think that starchy food out there at Tucson's not gonna do a god-damn thing for your figure. And that jump suit?" Shaking his head, "Orange definitely ain't the new black, feel me? That color don't go with the shade of your hair *or* your petal pink complexion."

Shanna had to admit, the guy was good.

"Let me give you a piece of advice," he was saying now. "See, I am bright, and I am ambitious. And one time I took a webinar, know what that is? On the Internet? Subject was 'Marketing Strategy'—account of I was thinking of getting into real estate at the time. And you know, the dude on there, what he said the first principle was?"

Shanna shook her head, taking a drag. "You're going to tell me, though, aren't you?"

"He said, you got to understand the value *to the buyer* of the item you got for sale. Now, see, applying that to your own situation, at the present time you got something to sell. And the value is, we prepared to let you walk on public corruption. *Nolle prosequi,* you understand? File no charges. But say we get old Doctor Feelgood some other way? You need to ask yourself what you got left to sell."

He took a sip of his Perrier. "Now, let's turn it around, talk about what you got to lose. We got the *cholo* down there in the East Bay, possession with intent. He can't give us the Doctor, no. But we can use his ass, understand? Work our way up the food chain. The *cholo* roll on the dude does deliveries for the Doctor. That gives us conspiracy to distribute. See, I know what you thinking. Bribery of a public official, Level 8 offense. Good-looking woman like yourself, no prior convictions, you probably get probation. But see, if I can tie you in on a conspiracy, you could be looking at Level 40, twenty years mandatory. Hard time, understand? Something you need to think about."

CHAPTER 4

EDDIE'S STORY

Eddie was sitting on a cheap metal chair in the hallway of a doublewide security trailer, waiting to make his statement. The kid in the Peterbilt was sitting across from him in plastic handcuffs, head down, with a bandage on his head and gauze plugs in his nose. He was young, early twenties, and reminded Eddie of kids he knew in high school—big, baby faced, beer belly. He smelled like a bar on a Sunday morning, with a hint of urine.

Next to the kid, an office door was open. Inside, looking down from a dull green wall was a photograph of George W. Bush. It was the one with Bush standing on the deck of the aircraft carrier with a "Mission Accomplished" banner behind him, giving the world a big thumbs up. The first time Eddie saw that picture was in the CO's office in the Green Zone, Baghdad, Iraq. At the time, Eddie had assumed the Green Zone was the only place you'd find a person dumb enough to hang a picture like that. But he had been proved wrong since then on more than one more occasion.

Now, the military type, Hellman, and the Sheriff were arguing about jurisdiction. Hellman said the kid was the Sheriff's problem because the incidents occurred in Redwood County. The Sheriff, a barrel-chested, red faced man wearing aviator sunglasses and a solid gold Rolex watch, whose name was Petty, said the kid was Hellman's problem because the incident occurred inside the city limits, on West Coast Lumber Company property.

Hellman said Liberty wasn't an incorporated city. Petty said, if it wasn't a city, what did Hellman think he was doing, ordering people off the street and operating his own private army?

"You got your cub scouts running around in riot gear, playing war games, whatever the hell it is you do down here. Seems like you got your own operation," he said, sitting back in his horsehide aviator jacket with his feet up on the desk.

"What I do is no concern of yours," Hellman told him. "This is private property."

"That's what I'm saying," the Sheriff said. "Could be a lack of jurisdiction. No, I think where I'm coming down on this, I'm not arresting anybody till I have a talk with Tommy Garrett."

So, they put in a call to Tommy Garrett, who was the District Attorney, but they couldn't reach him because he was on vacation, and it turned out his assistant was in San Francisco, at a seminar of some kind or other.

Now, Hellman was getting angry. "What the hell kind of bullshit is this? You're an elected official, goddamn it. You don't get to pick when you enforce the law and when you don't. You had a half dozen felonies committed right in front of your eyes. I want to know what you're going to do about it."

The Sheriff thought a minute. "Felony's a legal term," he said, finally. "I wasn't aware you was a lawyer. And by the way, you're not in the Rangers anymore, case you haven't figured it out, so you can step down off your high horse any time. I don't see anybody taking orders."

He kicked his feet off the desk. "Now, the way I analyze the situation, the only one I saw get hurt out here to speak of was little Billy. And what did the boy do? Drive on the wrong side of the street, scrape up a couple of cars, knock over a hydrant, maybe scare a few people. Come to think of it, I don't see more than a couple misdemeanors. And I'll tell you something else. Those kids out there? They shut down your operation. Had your ass in a wringer is what they did. Now, it's back to business as usual." He chuckled. "Hell, maybe you ought to give little Billy a medal, is the way I see it."

Hellman was really hot now. "The way you see it?" He leaned closer. "Let's get something straight, you fat fuck. I am not interested in the way you *see* it. Those *kids* out there are probably gonna file *lawsuits*. You know who they're gonna file 'em against? West Coast Lumber. You know why? Because I had to have *my* men go out there and do what *your* men should've been doing. Now I'm finished talking." He motioned over his shoulder. "Either you put that moron out there under arrest *right now*—or I'm getting on the phone to Mr. Duncan and we're gonna figure out who's got the best chance to take you down in the next election. Then, we're gonna make some campaign contributions. Am I getting through to you, *Sheriff?*"

The way they worked it out, Petty had a couple deputies escort Little Billy up to Redwood Memorial to get him looked at and, in the meantime, Petty was going to track down Tommy Garrett to see what he said about filing charges.

The Commando wasn't exactly satisfied with that. "The kid gets charged, Norville," he said. "You tell Tommy, he gets charged and he gets put on trial unless he pleads guilty to one or more felony charges. Tell him I said that. And tell him if he's got a problem, he can join you on the list of folks who file for unemployment come November."

A few minutes later, two deputies came in and hauled Little Billy to his feet. As they were taking him out, the kid stared at Eddie, trying to look ornery.

"Bill Odom," he said, pounding his chest. "Remember my name," then, pointing at Eddie with his shackled hands, "I'm coming after you, motherfucker."

"Wait," Eddie said, getting up now to face the kid. "If you want to come off like a bad ass, you need better lines. What you just said? That doesn't even make any sense. If you're coming *after* me, *you* need to re-member *me*. Why would *I* need to remember *you?*" He patted the kid on the shoulder. "Work on it."

*　*　*

The sun was starting to break through the fog when Eddie headed out the mill gate. They were still shooting news footage. The Five-Alive reporter was standing in front of the yellow crime scene tape. Behind her was the jack-knifed Peterbilt, trailer load tipped over, logs scattered. As Eddie came out, the producer ran up and wanted to know if they could ask him some questions.

The reporter asked him why he decided to do what he did.

Eddie said he didn't decide. He saw a situation.

The reporter asked him if he knew what he was going to do ahead of time.

Eddie said, no, he didn't.

"But, you knew *what* to do. I mean, you had experience driving a truck."

Eddie said, not really.

"Did it occur to you, the driver might be armed?"

Eddie said, "Yeah, but I thought he was more likely on speed or PCP, maybe drunk. Or he could have been nuts. Not that those things are mutually exclusive."

The reporter wanted to know what he was doing at the demonstration.

Eddie said, "I came with a friend."

"So, would you say you support the goals of the Eco-Resistance Coalition?"

"I don't know," Eddie said, "Maybe you could tell me what they are?"

Strolling up the street from the gate now, Eddie noticed a black Range Rover parked outside the hardware store. It wasn't there before, and it wasn't the kind of car he would have missed. It was the tricked out kind—tinted windows, heavy-duty shocks, powder coated brush guards and wheels—a lot of money invested. But the thing was filthy, like it just went through a thousand mile race. Eddie's eyes moved to the driver's door now, and noticed it was open, someone sitting inside. As he came closer, Shanna Black got out, and stood there watching him. Not pretending she wasn't. Watching him, like a cat.

Shanna was one of those rare women who are better looking close up. Her hair was red yeah, but with some gold highlights in there, falling in waves around a runway model face—strong jaw, high cheekbones, and wide set green eyes. As her eyes met his, she smiled just a little, looking right at him.

"How does it feel to be a hero?"

He said, "Compared to what?"

"There it is," she said, "It's all about the options." And holding out her hand, said, "I'm Shanna. Shanna Black."

"Eddie Fuentes."

"So … you're an Eddie, not an Ed."

"It depends on who's asking."

"Eddie, then." She looked at him thoughtfully. "Let me guess what you do for a living, Eddie. …You're a cop."

"Past tense, was a cop." Now, Eddie gave her the same thoughtful look. "So Shanna, let me guess, if you made me for a cop … that would make you—a lawyer."

It stopped her a second, then she laughed. "What else did Russell tell you?"

"He said you're a player."

"He didn't."

"In fact, he told me if I didn't watch out, you'd eat me for lunch."

She raised an eyebrow. "I don't eat lunch." Then, glancing up the street, added, "I *have* been known to have a drink, though."

They sat in back, in the same booth where she was sitting with the black dude before. When the bartender got around to asking, Shanna ordered vodka, Eddie ordered bourbon over ice.

He watched her take out a pack of those long, thin, cigarettes, and offer him one. He shook his head. "I quit."

"Mmm." She lit one, took a drag, and blew out some smoke. "Me, too."

She was looking at him now, like she was trying to make up her mind about something. She said, "I'm trying to think who you remind me of. There's this actor, I can't remember his name, he was in a bunch of movies, back in the fifties. There was one with Elizabeth Taylor."

He said, "Mickey Rooney? No, I guess that was the forties. Spencer Tracy? Liz was in a lot of movies."

"You like the movies."

"I love the movies," Eddie said. "Especially the old ones."

"Really."

"Something about the style. Karen—my *ex*-wife, I guess you'd call her— she said I'm the old fashioned type. Actually, I think the word she used was *throwback*."

"Hmm." She took some time playing with her drink. "Well, this movie I'm thinking of was kind of steamy. You know, set in the South, Liz is married to this guy, he's under his old man's thumb, used to be a football hero, and he drinks too much...."

Eddie said, "Paul Newman."

Shanna smiled slowly. "And nobody told you that before. That you look like him."

"They said it about my father, before he stopped shaving. With me it was more Richard Gere." She was looking at him with her head tilted to one side. He said, "Okay, a few people might have said Newman. I rented a bunch of his movies. But, to tell you the truth, I never saw the resemblance."

"I think it's the eyes," she said. "I mean, if you don't see the resemblance, you need corrective lenses."

Watching her now, Eddie decided Shanna didn't remind him of Karen after all. Shanna had more of an ease about her. With Karen there was always an edge, a self-consciousness, thinking how she looked, the impression she was making, working at it. Eddie got the feeling Shanna wasn't working. Her smile reminded him a little of an actress who was in a bunch of Tarantino pictures, Uma Thurman or no, with the hair, more like the one where these people playing are playing a long con in Atlantic City. What was her name?

He said, "Actually, you remind me of someone, too. You know the movie about these fraud artists? Christian Bale was in it, but you can't tell it's him."

"Amy Adams." She said it just like that, without a pause. "But that was the only picture I liked her in. I mean, some of the parts …. Who would want to be Lois Lane? She made some strange career choices." She seemed to think about, then added, "So, maybe they weren't choices."

"But, nobody ever told you, you look like her."

"You mean the player, or the girl in the Disney picture?"

He felt himself smiling now, looking in the eyes of this beautiful woman, having to remind himself what Russell said, she was a player. He said, "I'll tell you one thing—" shaking his head, "— you don't look much like a lawyer."

She said, "My clients don't look much like clients, either."

"You do criminal work."

"Murderers, rapists, wife beaters, child molesters. That's in addition to the drug stuff. It's a full service office."

"And the guy. The one you were in here with before? Was he a client?"

She seemed to think about it. "No," she said slowly, "he wasn't."

She finished her drink, motioned to the bartender, holding up two fingers, then turning to Eddie, said, "You're ready, aren't you? I can always tell when a man's ready." She ran a hand through her hair, brushing it back off her face. "That was quite a show you put on today."

"You saw it?"

"Some of it. I caught the Batman act, jumping on the running board. A few seconds later, the truck jackknifed and the trailer flipped. Saved my ass — I figured the kids were history."

"Dumb luck they weren't," Eddie said, remembering it. "You should have seen it in the cab. Kid was in the bag, beer cans everywhere. He had a bottle, must've used it when he was on the road, filled with piss. It was spilled all over the place. I don't know what he thought he was doing. I guess they'll sort it out."

"Or they won't. … So, what happened, I mean, when you were in there?"

Eddie shrugged. "I sucker punched him, probably broke his nose. That's what he said. He was screaming, hands up on his face. He wasn't doing any good where he was, so I opened the driver's door, and gave him a shove. After that—I got lucky. I don't know all that much about driving a truck."

She seemed curious. "How come you did it?"

"Call it a notable lack of impulse control. Coupled with a consistent disregard for the accused." He thought a minute. "So, you know him?"

"Who?"

"The kid in the truck."

"Why would I know him?"

"Everybody else seems to."

"Well," she said, "I didn't say I never *heard* of him. Everybody's *heard* of him." She waited while the bartender set down another round. "His father was murdered—I can't remember the details. There were two, no, three brothers. One of them disappeared. There was something about the mother being involved, but she was never brought up. Do a Google search. It was in all the papers."

"But you weren't involved."

"No, I missed out on that one."

It hung there a minute. "Tell me about the demonstrators."

"What about them?"

"You represent them?"

"Not in a formal sense."

"They gave you the keys."

She hesitated. "So?"

"Why would they do that if you don't represent them?"

"I didn't say that. I said, not in a formal—" She stopped. "You know, officer, you're gonna have to read me my rights if this is an interrogation."

"That's what my wife used to say when I asked her why she was working late at the office."

"So, you're suggesting what? ... I'm fucking the demonstrators?" Eddie couldn't help laughing. She said, "You know what? I don't want to talk about the demonstrators."

"What do you want to talk about?"

She looked straight at him "You. ... Russell said you two were brothers."

"He says a lot of things."

"You mean you're not?"

"It's an Indian thing. I'm maybe a quarter Mynot. My old man was a half-breed; my mother was a white girl. Came up from Marin County, had her little fling, and ran back home to Mama. Anyway, that's what my Grandma said. I never met the woman."

"You never met her?" She seemed surprised. "You weren't ... curious?"

"Maybe I was. But I figured, if I saw her ... I don't know ... she'd probably try to act like she cared. Or maybe she *would* care, feel guilty about it. I didn't know which was worse. Anyway, I didn't see a happy ending, and it wasn't going to change what happened."

"So, what? ... Your father raised you?"

Eddie laughed. "I'm not sure that's the word I'd use. My father wasn't what you'd call the child-rearing type. He was always drunk or stoned on something or other. They say it was different before he went to Vietnam, but I wouldn't know about that. My Grandma's the one raised me. When she died, Russell's folks took me in till I finished school."

"Then what?"

He shrugged. "I took off. Day after graduation. Did a tour in the Army. When I was discharged, I couldn't see coming back here, so I became a cop."

"But not anymore."

Eddie took his time. "I got canned. Or I guess the correct term is, re-signed in lieu of termination." He thought a minute. "Come to think of it, you're lawyer. I'd be interested to hear your opinion."

And he told her the story. How he was working a buy and bust in West Oakland, a motel called the Sage Brush. How he ran into a pimp by the name of De Marius Williams, a guy he knew before. De Marius was known for beating his girls across the butt with a coat hanger when they got out of line, his idea being they'd feel it on the job, make sure to avoid future transgressions. This time, he took it a little further. The room was a mess when Eddie got there, girls screaming, blood splattered on the sheets.

That day, that place . . . or situation, something snapped, all the bullshit he had to deal with, the red tape, plea deals, evidence problems. So, he decided to take things into his own hands, escorted De Marius out front, laid him bare-ass across the hood of his Mercedes, and let the girls take turns with whatever struck their fancy.

Shanna seemed to like the story. She said, "That must have been a real Kodak moment."

He said, "KKOL Eye in the Sky. Somebody must have called it in. They got the whole thing live, broke into their regularly scheduled programming."

"Sure beats a car chase. Then, let me guess, social media?"

"Somebody put it on YouTube. The guy at the union said it logged three million hits. Everybody thought it was kind of a joke—until Al Whitaker got involved."

"The *Reverend* Al Whitaker."

Eddie took a drink. "He said it was ... racially motivated."

She thought a minute. "And the union?"

"They would have stone-walled it, except I was already on probation—that's another story. I guess they figured it was easier to just ...."

"Cut you loose."

"There was a hearing in front of an arbitrator."

"And they gave you a choice. Get fired or quit."

"Yeah. ... So, what do you think?"

She lit a cigarette. "You mean, do you have a case? I'd need more information."

"Like what?"

Blowing out smoke, she said, "Like whether you're paying cash, or you're expecting somebody to take the case on a contingent fee basis."

Eddie said, "You haven't heard the rest of the story." And Eddie told her how he went out for a drink after the hearing. Well, a couple of drinks. And when he got back to the apartment, Karen was gone, along with the furniture, the car and the money.

"And that's when you decided to come up here."

He shook his head. "Later that night, somebody called from the P.A.'s office up in Redwood Bay. He said my dad was dead. There were things I needed to take care of."

Shanna didn't say anything. She finished her drink, and motioned to the bartender for refills. Then, she looked at Eddie with those beautiful green eyes. "Eddie," she said, "I'm going to level with you."

Russell had told Eddie to let it come to him, but that wasn't Eddie's style, so he heard himself say, "I just hope you're not going to tell me you're after me for my money, cause after all we've been through together, I'd hate to see you walk away disappointed."

She laughed. "Actually, Eddie? Your money is exactly what I'm after."

It was a long story—another three drinks before Eddie lost count. West Coast Lumber. Everyone in the County knew something about it. Their old lady worked in the office, or they had a cousin drove a truck, or an uncle worked in the mill. Even Eddie's dad worked there for a while as a topper, or that's what he heard. That was before he hired out logging off five and ten acre stands for small landowners who had run out of money.

But Shanna had a different story. It started with Chrissie Matheson, twice-divorced lumber company heiress and former tabloid party girl, who sold the business off a few years back so it wouldn't interfere with her social schedule. The man she sold it to, a New York financier by the name of Harriman Saul, was what Shanna called a "liquidator", a guy who bought businesses with borrowed money, broke them up, and sold off the pieces. In the case of West Coast Lumber, the pieces were the pension fund, the timberland, and some undeveloped real estate along the 101 Freeway. By now, the pension fund and most of the real estate was gone, and Saul was cutting the timber as fast as the State of California would let him do it. The most valuable piece left was something called the Watershed Grove, which also happened to be the largest privately owned stand of old growth redwood in America.

"The environmental groups think Saul hasn't cut the Watershed because of the bad publicity." Shanna shook her head. "Saul doesn't give a shit about publicity. The reason he hasn't cut the Grove is, he thinks the only way to get the timber out is with helicopters; and that would cost too much money. ... If there's one thing Harry Saul dislikes more than public relations, it's spending money."

Eddie took some time digesting all this. Finally, he said, "You said, 'he *thinks* the only way to get the timber out is with helicopters."

Shanna said, "West Coast Lumber Company owns a lot of land in Redwood County, Eddie, but they don't own it all. It turns out there is another way to get the timber out of the Watershed. But Saul wants to do it, he's going to have to build a road through a piece of land he doesn't own."

He looked at her. "Okay? So, who owns it?"

She said, "As a matter of fact, you do."

CHAPTER 5

DICK DUNCAN

Dick Duncan was flipping through the emails on his iPhone, reading important messages from the Auto Club and Leland Fly Fishing, trying to look busy. But what he was really doing, was waiting. Waiting was the main thing Dick got to do when Harry Saul came to town. Waiting and, oh yeah, answering stupid questions.

Right now, Dick was sitting next to Harry in the company helicopter, en route from Redwood County Municipal Airport to Company headquarters, waiting for Harry to go through the financial reports. This was Harry's favorite game, going through the financial reports. He did it in excruciating detail, asking questions about obscure line items that not even a controller would know the answer to without drilling down to a sub-ledger. He would do this in any setting, but he seemed to prefer moving vehicles. Harry with the battered leather case balanced on his lap, a stack of printouts on top of that, utterly absorbed in his numbers.

Dick glanced around the cheesy vinyl interior of the base model Bell 206, wondering what Harry Saul was going to ask about next. The little fart always found something he didn't like, some number that seemed too high or too low, some ratio a little out of whack, some slight variance from the results projected. Then he would ask questions and keep asking them until he found one Dick couldn't answer. Dick would have to call Farley. Farley generally wouldn't know either, at least not offhand. But he would eventually track it down, and Dick would try to explain it to Harry. But Harry wouldn't seem to care about the answer; either that, or he wouldn't acknowledge there had been an answer at all. Instead, he would just look at Dick like he hadn't said anything, or he would ask another question—about some other number he didn't like, some other ratio or variance. And so on, and so on, and so on.

Harriman Saul was reportedly worth somewhere close to seven *billion* dollars, but he wore dumpy flannel suits off the rack. He wore ankle socks that showed patches of pale, hairy flesh whenever he crossed his legs, as he was doing now. His cap toe oxfords were run down at the heel, and in desperate need of a shine. His briefcase looked like it had been run over by a truck. So the question, Dick was thinking, just this once, *he* would like to ask *Harriman Saul* was this: "Where's the fucking money, Harry?"

But he didn't ask. Instead, he waited. Waited until Harry pounced.

"What's this?" Harry pointing now to the printout, he said,

"What's what?"

"Under G & A. Public Relations Expense. Fifty-five thousand three forty three. I thought Michaels was only charging us thirty grand a month."

"Let me see that." Dick leaned over, buying time, pretending to study the number. Finally he said, "They probably put the Visitor's Center in there. You know, public relations, same category."

Harry looked at him. "Visitor's Center?" As though he had never heard the words before.

Dick looked back at him, not about to explain it further. Harry Saul knew there was a Visitor's Center. He'd been through it at least once, probably twice, around the time he bought the Company. It was right next to the corporate headquarters building. But of course, Dick couldn't tell him that. Instead, he waited, while Saul stared at him for a while, not saying anything, then finally returned to the printouts.

Dick glanced across the cabin. Saul's secretary, an officious New York type by the name of Ina Jaffe was trying to get someone on a cell phone. Occasionally, he'd noticed hints of a promising figure peeking out from under her unrevealing suits. Come to think of it, Ina might be interesting, if he could find a way to extract the gigantic bug she had up her ass.

"Mr. Saul?" She raised her hand now and, when he looked at her, held up one finger, speaking into the cell phone. "Mr. Crawford? Yes. Hold one moment please for Mr. Saul." Then, she handed the phone to Harry and said, "Trace Crawford."

More waiting. Dick looked around the cabin again—brown nylon fabric seats, beige plastic paneling, matching beige pattern carpet. Everything about it said, cheap. When Saul finally agreed they needed a new helicopter, Dick put in an order for a 407 with the local distributor. Saul told him to cancel it, told him he knew the President of the company in Dallas. Apparently, he thought he could get a discount. When that didn't pan out, he had Dick order the cheapest model available, with no interior options. If there was one thing Dick hated more than a man who was cheap, it was a *rich* man who was cheap. That, in a nutshell, was Harriman Saul.

"Trace? … Hello, Trace? Hold on a minute." Now Saul was saying to Dick. "Can't they run this damn thing any quieter?"

Dick wanted to tell him it would run quieter if it had the quieter engine and the upgraded passenger compartment with better sound insulation. But instead, he got up and went into the cockpit. "Ted? Throttle back a minute. Mr. Saul's on the telephone."

Dick stood there then, looking out the flight deck window. Twenty-seven years working for West Coast Lumber, cow-towing to the Mathesons, working his way up the ladder, all the way to the top, only to become— what? A fucking errand boy. Dick looked out the window, across the mountainous terrain—the crazy quilt of clearcuts, second and third growth stands, the ribbon of freeway snaking through the hills. The sky was blue, but the fog hung over the Pacific, extending inland through the valleys like the fingers of a large, malevolent hand.

"Missed by how much? … Jesus Christ! When do you report?" Harry was still on the phone as Dick wandered back into the cabin. "Yeah, but you're really hanging me out here, Trace. I'm sitting on thirty-five million shares with another thirty parked. Those guys aren't in it for their health, you know." He glanced at Dick for a moment, shooing him away. "When we announce, sure, but we have to get there. In the meantime, the algos take the stock down and I get margin calls."

Silence, Harry was listening, then, "The long run? Well, Trace, you know what Keynes, said about the long run. We're all dead." He listened again. "Look, I'm not going to argue with you on the telephone. What I'm telling you now, if you see some action in the options market, I need to protect myself, if you get what I'm talking about." He waited. "What's that? .... The Citation. No, I haven't pulled the trigger on it, but ... Right, I'm thinking about it. ...." He laughed, a brittle laugh. "I think you told me that already. .... Right, I'll see you in Tampa."

Harry disconnected, handed the phone to his assistant. "He wants me to buy a $25 million airplane. If it weren't for the upgrades, I'd fly coach." Then, he looked at Dick. "You didn't hear that conversation."

Dick said, "What conversation?"

Harry took a minute, staring out the window. Then suddenly, he turned to Dick. "So, this Visitor's Center that's costing me twenty-five grand a month."

"I never said twenty-five—"

"This Visitor's Center," he cut Dick off, opening his briefcase. "The purpose is, what? Entertain the socialists when they shut down my operations?" He held up a couple articles that had apparently been printed from Google Alert, waving them in the air.

Dick said, "I told you that was going to happen."

"You told me?"

"I told you, yes. Old growth is an issue. People are upset about it."

"They're upset about it." Saul snorted. "Well, I'm upset about a lot of things, including the fact that the chairman of an airline, in which I am a significant shareholder, doesn't seem to think he has to earn a return on my investment. The difference, Dick, is that return on investment is something I have a *right* to be upset about because it's *my money*. I don't suppose any of these morons who are so *upset* about the old growth are willing to step up and *pay* for it."

"Not that I know of."

"Because it's for sale, you know. Like I told that mannequin they've got for a governor out here. This is America. Which means that everything is for sale, at a price. But until somebody is willing to write me a check for half a billion dollars, the Watershed Grove belongs to *me*, and I'll do whatever the hell I want with it."

Duncan smiled. "I'm not sure Alan Michaels would recommend going out with that as a talking point in our public communications."

"Alan Michaels can suck my dick. Thirty grand a month, and this—" tapping the articles, "— is what I get for it." He shook his head. "Demonstrators. You think any of them ever actually earned a dollar? I'll tell you something. People with *jobs* don't chain themselves to a mill gate. They're too busy delivering packages, or preparing food or ringing up sales on a cash register. If you don't believe me, turn on the television. It's a bunch of kids out there with nothing better to do."

Saul took a minute. "I'll tell you something else about demonstrators, which I found out with the land-fills in Jersey," looking at Dick now, "They don't go away. As long as there's something to demonstrate about, they demonstrate."

"So, what are you saying?"

"What I'm saying is, the sooner we cut the damn trees down, the sooner we see the back of these people."

Dick was thinking, finally, this could be going somewhere. But it had to be the man's idea. He had to lay back, let it play out. He said, "I hear what you're saying, Harry. But like I've explained to you, they won't give you a permit to cut the trees until you submit a plan that shows how you're going to get them out, and what you're going to do in terms of remediation."

"So?"

Trying to be patient, Dick said, "Harry, this isn't rocket science. Like I said before, there are only two options. Either you build a haul road, or we've got to use helicopters."

Saul banged the top of his briefcase. "No helicopters! What is it with you? You have a brother-in-law in the helicopter business?" His expression soured. "I hate renting things, I told you that. You pay out good money, and when you're done, what have you got to show for it? Nothing. Besides, I saw the numbers. Helicopters cut your margin in half."

Dick said, "You're saying we're back to the road …."

Harry shook his head, fuming. "Fucking Mathesons. How could they own half a billion dollars in prime saw timber, and *not* own a way to get to it?"

Dick said, "We've been through that, Harry. I don't *know* how. It's before my time. All I can tell you is, we had the engineers look at it, we had the lawyers look at it, and we just don't own a right-of-way that makes any sense. We'd have to buy it. And you specifically told me you'd burn in hell before—"

"No," Harry interrupted him. "I did not say that. … Maybe I did. It doesn't matter. What I meant was, I don't write blank checks. I'm not saying yes or no till I hear a number."

Dick tried not to smile. "You're not going to like it," he said.

"My daughter is anorexic and my son has what I call the new ADHD—ambition deficit hostility disorder. There are a lot of things I don't like. … What is this, a game show? I have to guess? Give me a number."

Dick was nodding now, rubbing his eyes with his fists. "Okay," he said, "Construction, three million a mile, plus another couple for the landing, so figure a total of eight. The tricky part is the land. As far as comparable sales, there isn't much out there we don't own, and it doesn't change hands that often. Obviously, if people find out who the buyer is, the sky's the limit, so I've been working through a local attorney to keep it quiet. But the fact is, until we're in a position to step up and make an offer, there's no way to give you a hard number."

Saul turned, looked him in the eye now. "We got people laying down in front of the log trucks, Dick, chaining themselves to the mill gate. We got tear gas, fist fights, people jumping onto moving trucks. My kids are watching this on YouTube, Dick. My son who is living in a tent, my drama queen daughter, they don't talk about anything else. They're texting about it, following it on Twitter. You're the President of the company, what do you conclude from this? What's the takeaway, Dick?"

Dick waited.

"It's the new reality entertainment. And the show goes on as long as the trees are there. But like I told you before, I'm not giving you a go-ahead until I hear a fucking number. So, are you going to give me a number? Yes or no?"

"Okay. For the right-of-way? Rough numbers? Twelve million."

"Twelve million," Saul repeated it, deadpan, like he was playing poker.

Dick said, " I told you, you weren't going to like it."

"You were right." Saul rocked a little in his chair, taking some time, looking out the window. "So here's the question, Dick. You have a third of a billion board feet of redwood at a buck and a half gross, and you have a haul road that's going to cost you twenty million dollars. You're the President of West Coast Lumber Company. You tell me, what do you do?"

Dick said, "You build the road."

CHAPTER 6

THE LETTER

L ate afternoon, the fog starting to drift in across the hills, Eddie was headed south, nursing Matty's truck up the Divide. He was headed out to the old man's cabin to look for a will. He'd been out there once before after he talked to the Public Administrator, the guy telling him it would be easier to process the paperwork if he could find a will. But the place was a mess, papers in piles all over the place. Eddie just couldn't see going through it. Now, after what Shanna told him, he could see he was going to have to do it.

Thinking now about Shanna, and the piles of shit out there, putting the two together, he suddenly remembered. The thing about her name. He thought he'd *heard* it before, but that wasn't it. He'd *seen* it. It was printed on an envelope lying in a pile of junk mail in the kitchen. *Shanna Black, Attorney-at-Law.* He remembered it because it wasn't a window envelope like an unpaid bill or a sweepstakes offer and Matty's name wasn't on a label. It seemed to be typed right on. So, he'd picked it up to have a look. But it was empty. Now, he was thinking he'd like to know what was in it.

The Divide was an east-west ridge that cut a jagged path across the center of Redwood County. The north side drained to the Wild River; the south side drained to the Rappold. The ridgeline split in places, with steep canyons between. Matty owned what they called a quarter-quarter section in one of those canyons—40 acres of steep, unyielding land, along a stream that snaked to the south.

Most of the land out that way had been logged over two or three times since the white man came. The redwoods were mostly gone now, the slopes grown back to chaparral, some tanoak and madrone, and the bottomland to alder. They grew dope up here, and Matty grew his share. When Eddie came out, as he did sometime in the summer, Matty always told him if he wanted to wander around, stick to the canyons, stay away from the hills. The growers didn't like visitors, especially close to the harvest. Eddie did do some wandering those summers—there wasn't much else to do—so he knew that if you hiked the canyon south from the Matty's place, you eventually got to a stand of redwood that looked like it had never been logged. It didn't have a name as far as Eddie knew, but apparently, somewhere along the way, somebody started calling it the Watershed Grove.

The road narrowed as you headed up the Divide, two lanes, hardly wide enough for trucks to pass, even if they weren't log haulers. The F-150 was struggling, coughing and bucking, threatening to stall. But what did he expect? The truck was older than he was. Matty was gone. What he ought to do, park the thing in a barn somewhere, pull the battery, and let her go. Everything deserved a rest sooner or later, even a truck.

Wisps of mist were already blowing over the top of the Divide by the time Eddie got up there. The wind had come up, like it did most late afternoons, the sun still shining, but the fog getting set to roar back in. Soon as the sun was gone, the fog would boil through the canyons like horror picture smoke. In Redwood County, the night belonged to the fog.

The road up here was hard, even when it was clear. It wasn't much more than a logging track, narrow, with sheer drops to the east of at least a thousand feet, six hundred to the west, and not much shoulder. Heading south past the crest, the road dropped a quick two hundred feet before it climbed to another ridge. Matty's cabin was at the bottom, on a turnoff to the west that led into a draw. He built it himself out of log timber he milled on the site with a saw rigged to run off an old VW engine. It wasn't much to look at—one room with a sleeping loft. There was an old gas generator in an open shed that ran the lights. And there was a pump that moved water from the stream up to a tank on the hill; a gravity feed from the tank passed for plumbing. There was no hot water.

Matty wasn't one for luxury, or even comfort. His basic food groups were meat, bread and alcohol and, in his later years, he seems to have cut back on the first two. Anyway, the place gave that appearance. Karen used to complain Eddie was a slob. Obviously, she never met his father. The stove was filthy, the chimney was probably clogged, the pump was broken, and the roof leaked. There was no other explanation for the smell—a combination of mildew, smoke and urine, not necessarily in that order.

Eddie never liked this place. It did not bring back memories of joyful childhood, and he was not real eager to be here now. The P.A. and Shanna had both told him the same thing about the land. Since Eddie was the sole heir, it probably belonged to him, but the process of getting into his name would go easier if there was a will or a trust showing Matty intended him to have it.

When Shanna told him this, Eddie asked her, "Suppose I find a will, and it shows he didn't want me to have it? Like if he left it to someone else?"

Shanna seemed surprised. "You think he'd do that?"

Eddie shrugged.

She took a minute, then reached into a jacket pocket, "Here," she said, "Just in case." And handed him a pack of matches.

She'd told him the land could be worth a million bucks. Half for him, after she took a "contingent fee" of fifty percent. To a guy with a negative bank account balance, half a million dollars looked pretty good, even if the "contingent fee" was twenty percent too much. Russell said, clock it. That was hustler talk. It meant keep your eyes open, get a sense of the situation, see what's going on. Now, that's what Eddie had to do. Go through his father's things, use what he found to put Matty's life together like it was a case. Make some sense out of it, if he could.

It wasn't easy. The place looked like it'd been tossed. Papers everywhere—on a table near the stove, in piles on the counter, scattered on the floor. Even more in the loft. Eddie needed a system,. He should have brought trash bags along; that's what most of the stuff was anyway. The fog was in now, giving the place a chill, so he decided to get rid of the trash by burning it. But the chimney was clogged, and the air quickly filled with smoke.

The buff-colored envelope with Shanna Black's name on it was easy enough to find, still on the floor where Eddie left it. The letter came later. He found it upstairs, in the sleeping loft, in a pile near the bed. It read:

Dear Mateo:

It was a pleasure meeting with you last night to discuss the sale of your property on Ellendale Road extension. This will confirm our agreement in principle for you to sell your property to me (or my nominee) for the sum of $200,000 cash, escrow to close in sixty (60) days or less. The only contingency would be verification that you hold clear title.

I have opened an escrow with North Coast Title Company. Please call my office at your earliest convenience so we can schedule a time to sign the papers. I hope to hear from you soon.
Sincerely,
SHANNA BLACK
Attorney-at-Law

The letter was dated a week before Matty's death.. So he had to wonder, if Shanna wasn't telling him she tried to buy the old man's land before he died, what else wasn't she telling him?

* * *

Shanna's dreams tended to exhibit certain recurring features, a fact originally brought to her attention by a shrink by the name of Marty Whitman, some years ago—this was after the divorce, but while she was still living in Reno. As Marty pointed out, all the features weren't in all the dreams, but they tended to be there more often than not, thus providing insight, he thought, into the gestalt of her psychological constellation.

In Marty's view, the most salient feature of Shanna's dreams was that she was naked. Admittedly, this was not … revealing … standing alone, because Shanna liked to sleep in the nude, but it was a recurring motif, and not to be ignored in his professional opinion. A typical example of its contextual significance might be the dream in which Shanna was delivering her summation before a mixed gender jury in a criminal case and, in the dream, found herself thinking, "I'd better wrap this up before these people notice I'm not wearing any clothes." Another example might be a dream in which she was attending a Halloween party at the estate of an important client. The client, dressed as a rabbi but, for some reason, wearing a Moroccan *djellaba*, asked her who she was supposed to be. Realizing she was naked, Shanna found herself saying, "Holly Sampson? I don't know. Am I wearing a costume?"

A second recurring feature of Shanna's dreams was that often, she would be performing an ordinary action, but the results weren't ordinary. In a recent example, she was playing an old fashioned slot machine at the Three Bears Casino, the cherries lined up, and actual cherries came out the shoot. In another version, silver dollars came out, but since—combined with another salient dream feature—she wasn't wearing any clothes, she had nowhere to put them. Recently she had been having variations on this dream a *lot*.

After a couple sessions— Marty Whitman listening attentively, but not saying much— Shanna asked him his opinion. He said, "If you think about it, Shanna, from a psychological perspective, the question isn't really what I think of your dreams, but what *you* think of them."

Shanna took some time considering this, then said, "So, tell me this, Marty. If I'm not paying you for your fucking opinion, what am I paying you for?"

Now, lying in her two-story bedroom overlooking the fog-draped Pacific, Shanna was dreaming that she was swimming naked in a pool of incredibly beautiful, blue water. In her dream, she realized she was underwater, and wondered if she had been breathing, or if she had somehow learned to breathe underwater. As she was wondering this, she heard a sound coming from above her, and found herself swimming toward it, higher and higher, through lighter and lighter blue water, until finally, the water was gone, and she realized the sound she was hearing was the telephone.

A man's voice said, "Shanna?"

She sat up in bed, holding the phone, while looking for the clock. "What time is it?"

"Shanna, it's Dick."

She found the clock. "Shit, shit, shit!" It was nearly ten o'clock

"What's the matter?"

"Nothing, nothing." She rolled out of bed, carrying the phone into the bathroom.

"Okay, are you ready for this?" Dick said, "The asshole's in town, and ...."

"Dick? Shut up, okay? Where are you?"

"At the Wagon Wheel, but ...."

"I'm coming there."

"How long will it take you?"

She looked at her naked body in the mirror, running a hand through her hair. "Jesus, I don't know Give me an hour."

The Wagon Wheel wasn't hard to identify. In addition to the cursive on the sign, there were neon wheels with spokes that lit up in a clockwise pattern. There were wagon wheel-shaped windows on either side of the front door and a miniature covered wagon on an overhang above it. Inside, there were wagon wheels on the walls and chandeliers that hung by chains from the ceiling that were made from genuine antique ... you guessed it, wagon wheels.

Driving in, the place was reminding Shanna of her first husband. She was eighteen then. This was Reno, she married a guy by the name of Rex King, his real name. Rex, who owned a Cadillac dealership called, what else? King Cadillac, used to drive around in a gold Sedan de Ville with an actual crown on top of it. He'd go on television a dozen times a day in his king outfit, telling people from Elko to Tahoe—about his 'regal deals' and 'courtly customer service'. After that, they'd cut to an aerial of the dealer-ship, and the voice-over would say, "So, come on down to King Cadillac, 1800 Mill Street, Reno, where every day, in every way—" Then, they'd cut back to Rex for the closer.

"We treat *you* like a King."

They went to Tahoe on their honeymoon. Rex had them booked into a place called Valentine's. It had pink walls, a heart shaped bed with a blood-red cover, hot pink carpeting, and a heart shaped tub. Rex thought this was terrific. And one thing you had to say for him, right up to the end, he was consistent. Trying to patch things up before the divorce, he took her to Maui, booked them into a suite at a place called the Seashell Lodge, where everything from the ashtrays to the sink was made of sea-shells. And the divorce settlement itself was fit for a king. No prenuptial agreement.

The Wagon Wheel did a decent breakfast business, but it was desert-ed now, nearly eleven thirty as Shanna drove in. Dick's smoke gray Lincoln looked like a beached whale in the gravel lot. The only other cars—beat up Hondas and Toyotas parked around back—belonging to the help. Shanna pulled the Range Rover in back next to a Corolla, took a minute to check the little voice activated recorder she kept in an inside jacket pocket—a professional model with better pickup than the cell phone kind— then walked around front and went inside.

Dick was sitting in a back booth, a coffee mug in front of him with a wagon wheel on it. As she walked over, he got up. "You're late."

"So sue me," she said.

He pulled her to him, a s clumsy move. She looked around. "What are you, nuts?"

"They're all in the kitchen," he said. "I haven't seen a waitress in twen-ty minutes."

She looked around some more. "Twenty minutes, huh?"

This time, she let him kiss her, his beefy hands moving on her body. Dick saw himself as a hunk and maybe, once upon a time, he was. A big man with thinning blonde hair, regular features, pale blue eyes set wide apart. He was probably solid once, but now he was going soft, settled into his life of corporate frustration. Dick was a dresser, a man who favored double breasted suits and custom tailored English broadcloth shirts. A man who wore cologne.

Shanna pulled away now, but not entirely. "So, Dicky," she said, "Remember what I told you? About calling on your cell phone?"

He tried to kiss her neck. "What can I tell you, baby? I forget to bring quarters."

She pushed him off. "A common feature of the people I see at sentencing hearings, Dick? They forgot to bring quarters."

Sitting now, Shanna lit a cigarette, giving Dicky her full and undivided attention so he could tell her about his conversation with Harriman Saul.

"So, it's definite?" she asked. "Twelve million?"

"It's *definite* when the little turd signs the check." Dick took a sip of coffee, managing to spill a few drops on his shirt. "Shit! ..." He dipped his napkin in a glass of water, then dabbing at the stain, added. "I tell you one thing. The bastard absolutely cannot stand helicopters."

"It sounds like he isn't wild about signing checks, either."

Dick was smiling now. "He'll sign. I can always tell him we're getting held up by a shyster lawyer who put herself in the middle of the transaction. The only thing he hates worse than helicopters is lawyers."

Dick lifted the cigarette out of Shanna's hand, and took a drag. "It was beautiful. Really, you should've been there. The thing with the demonstration? It was perfect. Harry says, 'You got people laying down in front of the log trucks, Dick, chaining themselves to the mill gate. People jumping onto moving trucks. It's the new reality entertainment.'"

"That might not be a bad idea," Shanna said. "I hear they're desperate for new ideas."

Dick wasn't listening. "I tell you, though, every day it gets harder putting up with the sonuvabitch. I'm supposed to be president of the company. The guy comes to town, his goddamn *secretary* treats me like a secretary. And with Jenn, we don't actually *talk* to each other anymore. We deliver monologues." Dick was getting into his "poor me" routine now. "She's got Jason and Jody on her side. I go home, I'm thinking, what the fuck am I even doing here? I might as well be in Cincinnati. And the way she spends money. It's unbelievable. Speaking of which—"

Shanna pulled an envelope out of her shoulder bag, put it on the table. Dick picked it up, weighing it in his hand. "By the way," he said, "It occurred to me we might up the ante a bit. You know, help make ends meet?"

"You really want to go there, Dick? Piss the man off?" She narrowed her eyes. "If he finds out what we're up to, you want to guess what happens?"

"He's not going to find out," Dick said. "Anyway, what does he care what we do, as long as he gets his crop in? He's a dope grower, the same as the Mexicans."

Shanna paused. "Tell me this, Dick. Have you ever actually met the man? Gone out to the Coast? Been to one of his little Halloween parties?" Shanna smiled, getting up now. "Let's just say this. The Doctor isn't the Mexicans. In fact," she said, brushing lightly at his shirt, where a coffee stain was still visible, "There are ways in which I'd say he has a lot less in common with them than you do."

CHAPTER 7

THE DOCTOR

The Doctor lay on the massage table in his physical therapy room, face down, stark naked. It was never easy carrying on a conversation like this. But one does what one must.

"You say he owns the place?"

"Right. It's a condominium," Wayne Mehana stood over him in his black silk shirt and matching karate pants, bearing down with a gigantic forearm, ironing out the Doctor's calf muscles.

"Argghh," the Doctor grunted, making a supreme effort to let go of the solid body, and relax back into the penumbra of multi-colored lights circling in the transparent Jell-O.

"I'd never been there before, but it's a nice spot, right on the bay," Wayne was saying now, his Kiwi accent somehow odd, issuing from a huge Polynesian body with Marshall Island tattoos. "I don't think I'd want to live there 'cause of the wind, but it's a really special view. You know, with the lights? It's like Kowloon, looking at Hong Kong across the water."

"Mmm." The Doctor saw it now, standing on the ferry with Roger, stoned on Thai stick, watching the lights dance on the glistening black harbor. Thinking of it, he felt a wave of nostalgia. A simpler time, before the fall. "But you're saying he hasn't been there."

"Unh-uh," Wayne was working his way up the back of the knee and thigh with his elbow, sending searing bolts of pain up the Doctor's right leg.

Breathe. Relax. Exhale into the pain. "Who did you talk to?" he managed to ask.

"I knocked on some doors, no luck," Wayne said. "But then the birds that clean the place turned up. They come every week. I gave one of them a twenty. She said the guy's a real dongo, but this time there was nothing to clean. The bed hadn't even been slept in. So she thinks he must be out of town."

"Drongo?"

"A loser, kind of a slob. Leaves shit all over the place."

The Doctor rolled himself over. "The guy's a *slob*, you said?"

Wayne looked at him, apparently surprised. "No, no, that's what *she* said."

The Doctor clasped his hands behind his head, angling it up, so he could see Wayne better. "And *how* much is he into us for?"

"A couple hundred, two I think."

"A couple hundred!" The Doctor repeated the number, "And the guy's a *slob*?" Holding out a hand, he signaled for Wayne to help him up. Now, sitting on the side of the massage table, he looked the big Maori in the eye. "Character, Wayne!"

Wayne looked away.

"*Character is the collateral!* Didn't Roger tell you that?"

No answer.

"It doesn't matter if the person owns the condominium, Wayne. It doesn't *matter* if he owns the Burj Khalifa, Wayne. What are we going to do? Take him to court?"

No answer.

"You know what character is, Wayne? *It's what you do when no one's looking.* So, if the guy is a drongo, what does that tell you? He's disorganized, lacks self-control. He has no respect for himself or his property. You get it?"

The Doctor tried to get Wayne to look at him. Still no luck with that. "Wayne," he said, "Listen to me. Are you listening?"

Wayne finally nodded.

"We're in a business. The way the business works is very simple. If a customer stiffs us, we have to hit him. We don't *want* to hit him. It's a waste of time and money *and* its bad karma. So, if we *think* he's going to stiff us, we don't do business with him. Tell me you understand that."

Wayne finally looked over, nodding. "Right," he said. "I get it."

The Doctor patted Wayne on the back. "Good." He sank back on the table now as Wayne went back to work, trying to let go of the body, floating back into the transparent Jell-O, the blissful realm of a forty-seven microgram maintenance dose, pure lysergic acid diethylamide.

The trouble with a life outside the law was, you got mixed up with violence. Like everything else, the law was a transaction. You agreed to let them tell you what to do. In return, they agreed to protect you. That's why they carried guns. They protected you with violence. If you lived outside the law—dealt in psychoactive substances, for instance—then the law didn't protect you. If someone didn't pay, you couldn't sue them. If they robbed you, you couldn't call the police to get your property back. You had to do it yourself. You had to provide your own violence. And in this way, even a nonviolent and peace-loving man like the Doctor, had been coerced by a repressive, adolescent society into a life of violence. But frankly, if the choice was eternal adolescence or occasional violence, he'd have to vote for the violence.

It seemed obvious to him now, as the masters said, that duality was imbedded in the structure of the created worlds. That there could be no up without down, no light without dark. That every beginning implied an ending, and that everything gained brought a fear of loss. Change was woven into the fabric of creation. Patterns dissolved before new ones formed. Shiva had to dance destruction before Brahma could arrive on the back of his swan. The world was incessant change. There was no use resisting. And yet, we resisted.

Roger went away. Beautiful Roger—their life together so completely realized, now so completely dissolved. Dissolved in the Jell-O. Attachment was blinding, the wise men said. And the Doctor had been blind. Holding on to that perfect life, now gone. *Sinsemilla* for example. They were growing it in tract houses, in suburban gardens, storage units, warehouses. It was absurd dealing in a product that was becoming legal. He might as well be selling razor blades. Especially now that the Mexicans had moved in, setting out hundreds of thousands of plants, killing wildlife with D-Con, polluting the rivers with fertilizer, paying rock bottom wages, ignoring quality, and destroying the brand.

When Wayne was finished, he asked the Doctor what he wanted him to do about the customer. The Doctor thought a minute. "Where did you say he was from?"

Wayne thought a minute. "El Salvador, I think."

"El Salvador," the Doctor said it in the Spanish way. "Named for the Savior."

"One dude said he mighta gone down there to see his Mom. They're having some kind of festival or other."

The Doctor thought about it. "And he's a friend of yours?"

Wayne shrugged.

"But you don't want me to give it to Lon."

Wayne took a minute. "I don't see why you keep him around to tell you the truth. Martial arts are based on spiritual principles. Lon's a pig. That tat on his neck? It gives me the creeps. His vibration—" He waved his hand as though shooing away a bad odor. "Phew!"

The Doctor was visualizing the tattoo with the flying skull and bloody daggers. "Not that I disagree about the tattoo," he said, "but I'd appreciate your keeping your opinions to yourself."

"Why? You don't think I could take him?" Wayne got into his fighting stance. He was Maori, a big boy, not much over six feet, but two sixty, and solid.

"Well, it would be an interesting match," the Doctor said. "Unfortunately, darling, one of you would die, and I can't afford to see that happen."

He was quiet a minute. "Let's give the Salvadoran a week. Let him work out his own salvation. If he doesn't pay up by then, he won't have to visit his mom. Lon will introduce him to his ancestors."

* * *

TA-TA-TAT-TA! TA-TA-TAT-TA! Lon Odom let off a few bursts of the weapon to get their attention, then held it above his head. "Okay, listen up! This here is your basic Heckler & Koch UMP45 submachine gun." Lon turned around a few times so the bean patrol could get a good look, while the *jefe* did the Español translation. Then, he brought the weapon to shoulder, ripped up some tan oak with a burst of .45 caliber rounds. Shit, the thing had a kick to it.

"Forty-five caliber ammunition, twenty-five shot clip. Light in weight, easy to use, and highly reliable." Lon squeezed off a few more bursts into the chaparral. "Weapon fires from the closed-bolt position during all modes of operation. Very accurate, high stopping power."

The amigos listened to the *jefe* doing his translation, looking like deer in headlights. Lon felt like a moron, lecturing a bunch of dirt farmers from Sinaloa on the operation of a sophisticated firearm. These guys wouldn't know delayed blowback roller lock action from a fucking bag of *frijoles*. The thing with the Doctor, whatever it was, had to be state of the art. He must've seen the H & Ks in *Shotgun News*, went out and bought a few cases 'cause he thought they were cool. Cool was wasted on the *braceros*. Shit, they didn't need to hit anything with the guns anyways, just rip up some brush, make some noise with them.

How Lon had them lay out the irrigation, the farm was nicely set up as a death trap. All the lines spiraled down to a single point—a big old snag at the bottom of the draw where he'd set up in a blind. Hounds would come in from the canyon, follow the irrigation, working their way up the lines, picking the bud until a sensor fired. Then, all the beaners had to do was fire off some rounds. The hounds would crawl back to the bottom— right to where Lon would be, set up with a 12 gauge. Shit, he'd done it a dozen times. Why you needed the beaners wasn't for hitting anything. It was digging the graves. That was the hard part of the operation.

"Yo, dude!" Ike Rampas was motioning now, the longhair hippy sticking his dirty old Giant's cap out the door of the tarpaper shack they used for a bunkhouse. "C'mere a minute." Ike was the farmer out here, best around at what he did. Problem was, he was his own best customer.

Lon waved to Rampas, then motioned to a box of H & K's, and said to the *jefe*. "Pass out the weapons, let them squeeze off a few rounds," he said. "And try to make sure they don't kill each other."

Lon walked up to the shack. As he came in, Rampas held out a joint, gave him a big, gap-tooth grin. "THC's starting to come up. Got a good clear stone to her. Give her a go."

Lon shook his head. "Cannabis and gunpowder don't mix. What's up?"

Motioning toward the police scanner, Rampas said, "Man, you ain't gonna *believe* this."

"Try me."

Rampas took a hit, "Your fucking brother, man," he said, voice squeaking.

"Is he dead?"

Ike cracked up, exploding smoke, then started coughing. "You wish. Got his ass in jail down Manzanita." He started laughing again. "Shit, I thought he was still in jail from the last thing he did."

Lon ran a hand across his head. "What he do this time? Jerk off on the sidewalk? Sass a cop, what?"

Ike shook his head, "Hell no, dude. Billy hit it big time. They got him on felony counts. DUI with injuries, assault and battery. Few other things."

Lon didn't say anything.

"You going down there, bail him out?"

Lon said, "I'm thinking, let him sit there awhile. Maybe he'll get depressed and hang his self with a bed sheet. Or I'll get really lucky. He'll piss off some Nazi skinhead, get himself gutted in the shower."

*   *   *

Russell was sitting with his Birkenstocks up on the old wooden desk in his storefront office in Juanita, talking to the tribal gaming consultant, a guy out of Sacramento by the name of Robby Martinez. He said, "Robby, listen to yourself. You think I don't know where the Rancheria is? I fucking grew up here."

"Well, then—"

Russell cut him off. "It's near a wildlife refuge. So what? Maybe it's a plus. You watch the birds while you roll the dice. If people who watch birds roll dice. Maybe they don't. Forget about that. I don't see where it's a problem."

"They told me it's on the Pacific Flyway."

"Robby," Russell said, "Half of California is on the Pacific Flyway. So what?"

"No, what I'm saying, they stop there. The birds. Millions of birds on an annual basis."

The Cold Flats Rancheria was adjacent to the Redwoods National Wildlife Refuge—two hundred square miles of tidelands and estuaries that ran into the Pacific Ocean. This was not a breaking news headline. Russell said, "I'm not getting the point, Robby."

"The point is appropriate land use. It's part of the legal requirement. There has to be a finding that the casino isn't detrimental to the surrounding community."

Russell said, "What surrounding community? The ducks? What are you saying? The ducks are offended people are playing the slots?"

"Hey, I didn't make this up, okay?" Robby said, "I'm just telling you what they told me in the Governor's Office."

"Who told you?"

"Legal Affairs. A gal by the name of Joy Ramirez."

"So how about you tell Joy Ramirez sixty-one *other* tribes in the State of California already have gaming compacts, and so far, the ducks never said a word about it."

"You think she gives a shit? She's just taking orders. It's not the ducks man. It's the environmental lobby. Kennan owes them big time. Anyhow that's how they see it—they put him in office. You think he cares about the Pacific Flyway? He probably thinks it's a fucking restaurant."

Russell looked out the window, coated with salt film like everything else in this God-forsaken place, toward the park across the street. There was a patch of grass, a block-long section of track from the old San

Miguel-Juanita line, maintained for historical reasons, but without a sign to tell anybody that. There were five cypress trees, three picnic tables, and two trashcans. Next to the patch of grass, there was a gravel parking lot with a sign that said, "Parking." The parking lot was empty, but two pickup trucks were parked on the grass *next* to the parking lot. For some reason, Russell found this depressing.

He said, "Robby, listen to me. The Mynot Tribe got restored in 1990. We're a sovereign nation. We're asking for permission to build on our own land."

"I didn't make the rules," Robby said. "The magic date is eighty-eight. I told you that. If you got restored before, all you need is the Feds. If you got restored *after*, you also need approval from the Governor."

Russell kicked his feet off the desk, sat up in his chair. "Let's cut the shit, Robby. What are you telling me? Cold Flats isn't going to happen?"

Robby said, "To be honest with you, man? I don't see it. Not unless you got an in with the Sierra Club. Or you got some serious cash to throw at the Governor."

* * *

The town of Juanita sat at the edge of the Cold Flats Rancheria, 100 acres of wind-swept coastal plain held in trust for the Mynot Indians by the United States Department of the Interior. Driving in, the place looked like a movie set, built on a back lot for some old western—dusty streets with tumble down wood frame storefronts, most of them vacant. The pool hall closed down before Eddie left for the Army. The same for the Pharmacy. Maya's Hair Force Salon, a new arrival, was closed (temporarily, according to a sign in the window). The Post Office was on a list to get closed, Russell had told him. The only other things left were the Juanita Market, the Juanita Bank, the Gilded Age Bar, and a little office squeezed between Maya's and the Post Office with black letters painted on a grimy plate glass window that read:

Mynot Tribe
Cold Flats Rancheria
Cold Flats Gaming Commission

Eddie pulled up in the F-150 and got out.

Eddie's father never lived on the Rancheria. Most of the Mynot didn't. But they all knew the story of the Lost Treaties; they all knew what happened to the Indians. There were eighteen treaties signed in 1851, giving the California tribes eight million acres of the Golden State. But the senators in Washington were white men. They decided not to ratify the treaties. Instead, they hid them under a seal of secrecy and pretended they never happened. Then they passed the Land Claims Act, stripping the Indians of whatever rights they had left. When California came into the union, the legislature more or less legalized the kidnapping of Indian children, turning them into slaves. The population numbers told the story. In 1848 there were a hundred thousand white men in California and three hundred thousand Indians. Fifty years later there were a million and a half white men and twenty-five thousand Indians—all of them homeless.

In 1905, a Senate clerk found the Lost Treaties in a dusty archive. This got into the newspapers, and Congress had to do something. So it set up the Rancherias. Originally there were sixty, scattered around the state on land no one wanted, a total of nine thousand acres. Nine thousand instead of eight million. It didn't help all that much, so a few years later, Congress decided things would be better if the tribes simply went away. It voted to revoke their legal status, and split up the Rancherias. But the Indians didn't want to be split up, so they filed lawsuits. Eventually, they won. But it took decades, and by that time, the tribes had been scattered to the winds. Eddie's people were like that. Scattered.

Russell's office didn't look like much—one room with a lavatory in back, some old metal file cabinets, two wooden desks, one empty. Russell was sitting in the other one, reading the sports section of the Redwood Bay News. When Eddie walked in, he looked up.

"Fast Eddie Fuentes," he said, pushing the front section of the paper across the desk. "Here, sign this for me. Maybe I could sell the autograph."

Eddie picked up the paper and there he was, right on page one, dressed in his old fatigue jacket, with mussed up hair and a crooked grin. The picture next to him showed a bleary eyed Billy Odom, face forward, apparently a booking photo. The headline read, "Ex-Cop Makes the Collar."

Eddie shrugged, tossed the paper on the desk, then dropped into a chair, motioned to the sign in the window. "What's the Cold Flats Gaming Commission?"

"A name on a window." Russell got up. "You want coffee? It's stale, but the burnt out taste has a way of hiding the poor quality."

"I'll pass." Eddie shook his head. "But with the Commission, you're trying to set up something."

"The casino, sure." Russell walked to a coffee maker on top of a file cabinet. "I've been trying to hustle that one ever since the old man died. Actually, before. I tried to explain it to him, you know, the economics, how it works. I told him everybody was doing it. He said, 'The rest of the tribes can fish in a sewer if they want to.'" His voice trailed off, pouring coffee—two cups. He put one on the desk in front of Eddie, then sat down and was quiet for a minute.

Finally, he said. "My old man … he hated doctors, right? Hospitals even worse. He wasn't afraid of dying. What scared him, maybe he'd wind up on a machine. So he asked me to get one of those forms—"

"Health care directive." Eddie said, "I did one when I was a cop."

"Right. … I had to go over it with him, make sure I got it right. We're sitting there at the kitchen table. That's when I figured it out."

"Figured what out?"

Russell looked up. "He couldn't read, *ene*. He couldn't read. You believe that? My whole life, I lived with him, it took me that long to realize what was going on. It's crazy, you know? But then, I looked at it—it was like, it explained a lot of things. Like he never read the papers, never answered letters, never wanted to get the tribe involved in anything where he'd have to deal with—you know, paperwork. He was afraid somebody would figure it out."

They sat there for a while, drinking coffee, not saying anything. Then Russell said, "Coffee sucks, right?"

Eddie grimaced. "Right. So, what's the problem? Money?"

"With the casino? You want to hear something funny, money is the one thing that's not a problem. There's a lot of people with money. The boys from Nevada are running around with suitcases full of it."

Eddie looked at him. "Okay ...."

"Politics, man. The environmentalists. These people? Their values are so fucked up. You know those tee shirts they were selling down at the mill? Save the Old Growth? From Bangladesh. That's how they think. Save the plants! Save the animals! What about the people? They don't give a shit." He motioned across his chest. "Plants first. Animals second. People—get fucked."

Russell took a minute. "So what can I tell you? Everybody's on disability, back trouble, one thing or another. Glory's pregnant—you remember her, my sister—she's pregnant. Again. She's up to like, one fifty. Don't know who the father is. ... We got cable now, Suddenlink, she sits around all day watching this shit, *The Biggest Loser, The Real Housewives of Orange County.* I said, Glory, don't you get it? The biggest losers aren't the girls on the show, it's the morons watching. No answer. ... There's a new community center, you might have seen it on the way in. We got a dartboard, card tables, Ping-Pong converts to a pool table. You could shoot on it if you got a sense of humor...."

Eddie waited a minute, then put down his coffee. "So?" looking Russell in the eye now, "You gonna tell me who she's working for?"

Russell smiled. "And all along, I'm sitting here thinking how nice it is the *hombre* dropped by, catch up on old times at the Rancheria. We don't get that many visitors out here at the Cold Flats, you know. Time to time, somebody gets lost. Or comes to see some shit washed up from Fukushima."

Still waiting, Eddie said, "So—"

"Who's she working for?" Russell shrugged. "She's a lawyer, man. She works for herself."

Eddie took out the letter he found at his father's cabin, flipped it across the desk.

Russell took a minute to read it. "And this pisses you off. But I'm not getting why exactly. She offered you less for the land than she offered him?"

"No, she offered me more." Eddie thought about it. "Let's talk about who she's going to sell it to."

Russell said, "Okay. Let's talk about that."

"She wants to sell it to West Coast Lumber."

Russell shrugged. "Who did you think she was going to sell it to, Henry David Thoreau?"

Eddie frowned. "Tell me what I'm missing. I thought she was representing the people trying to *stop* the logging— in the exact same place the road is supposed to go."

Russell raised an eyebrow. "And your analysis is, perhaps she's not being completely honest with you." He got up, poured himself more coffee, held up the carafe. Eddie shook his head. Russell said, "What did I tell you at the demonstration? You remember what I said?"

"She's a player."

"And I also said, the whole thing's a show. Didn't I tell you that?" He came back and sat down. "Okay, here's what I know. A few months back, the woman calls me up, asks me if I know somebody by the name of Mateo Fuentes."

"Why would she call you?"

"My guess? She found out he owned the land, asked around, somebody told her he was an Indian. Anyway, I told her I didn't know him that well, but I had a mailing address, you know the post office box he had. So, I gave it to her. Why not? I figured, hey, if he could make a few bucks, more power to him."

"What about me?"

"After he died, it was in the papers. I guess she found out you were the next of kin. She called me again, I said I'd hook you up. But, as far as who she's working for? You're asking the wrong question."

Eddie looked at him.

Russell said, "Stop me if I get any of this wrong. You lost your cop job. Your wife took off on you, cleaned you out, stole your stuff. Matty fell off a fucking bridge. You're living in a cheap motel, driving a 35-year-old truck that don't run too good. With me this far? So, now a beautiful woman comes along, picks you up, offers you a pile of cash for a piece of land that's not worth the gas to drive out there unless maybe you want to grow dope on it. But you think there's a problem with this on account of the woman's a player and you feel like she's running some kind of con."

Eddie said, "Okay …." Nodding now. "So what's the question?"

Russell raised an eyebrow.

"You said I was asking the wrong question. What question am I supposed to ask?"

"Well, seeing as you got no skin in the game, *hombre*, if I was you, I'd ask, where do I sign? Or I guess you could ask around for someplace to get your head examined."

CHAPTER 8

BILLY ODOM

Coming into the back of the courtroom, Shanna heard the judge say, "Are you sure he's not indigent, Mr. Cooper? If he's indigent, I'll continue, pending referral to a public defender."

Walking up the aisle, Shanna said, "No need, your Honor."

The judge and a young assistant D.A. both looked up. Shanna knew the judge, a no-nonsense African American lady by the name of Mildred Clark Robinson.

"Shanna Black, your Honor. Appearing for Chris Cox? He got called into trial in Division Six. Sort of a last minute thing. He sends his apologies, your Honor." Well, not exactly. The guy she had representing Billy Odom before wasn't returning her calls; Chris said he'd do it, but couldn't handle the arraignment.

"Let the record show that Ms. Black is appearing on behalf of Mr. Cox. I take it that's acceptable to you, Mr. Odom."

Shanna leaned over and whispered in Billy's ear, "Say 'Yes, your Honor'."

Little Billy gave the redhead lawyer a big smile. "Yes, your honor," he said, trying to sound sweet, but thinking man, oh man! This honey could hog-tie his ass to a truck bumper anytime she had a mind. Mmm, yeah, would he like to give this girl a dance on top of the old one-eyed trouser snake. Looking at her out of the corner of his eye, Billy slid over, angling to maybe sneak a feel up under that skinny little skirt she had on.

But now the nigger lady judge was looking up at him from a piece of paper. "In the present information, Mr. Odom, you are charged with violations of sections 23153 and 38316 of the Vehicle Code, and sections

245(a), 588b, 590, 664 and 834a of the Penal Code, to wit, felony drunk driving causing injury, malicious destruction of highway and related property, assault with a deadly weapon, resisting arrest and attempted murder. How do you plead to the within described charges?"

"Not guilty on all counts, your Honor," the redhead said.

"Let the record so state. Does the prosecution have a bail recommendation?"

"This defendant has a history of increasingly serious offenses and represents a demonstrated threat to the community," the little Jew prosecutor said. "For this reason, we're requesting bail be set at two hundred fifty thousand dollars."

"Two hundred and fifty what!" Billy said to the redhead.

The redhead told him to keep his mouth shut.

The judge looked at Billy some more, then started reading from another paper. "DUI 2006; DUI, reckless driving, 2007; aggravated assault, 2009; drunk and disorderly, malicious mischief, 2010; assault and battery, 2011,; breaking and entering, carrying a concealed weapon, 2012." She looked at Billy. "What happened in 2008, Mr. Odom?"

"He was in the military, your honor," the prosecutor said. "Discharge Other than Honorable."

"I was AWOL was all that was," Billy told the redhead. "It's not like I actually *did* anything."

The judge looked at the redhead. "Ms. Black? Anything?"

"The defendant may be a threat to the court's patience," she said. "But I don't see where he's a flight risk or a serious threat to the community. We'd like the defendant released on his own recognizance."

The judge seemed to think that was funny. "Recognizance?" she said. "You mean as in 'recognition of responsibility'? Nice try, Counselor. Bail's at $75,000. On the Master Calendar for a week from Thursday. Prisoner is remanded into custody pending bond."

And the next Billy knew they was moving him back to jail and the redhead lady lawyer was gone.

* * *

Two days after the bail hearing, 1900 hours, Lon had Little Billy in the Yukon headed up the 101 from the South County Annex to Wild River. What happened, Mama got hold of Lon on his cell, out on an ammunition run, and laid a trip on his head. How could Lon leave his little brother in jail like that? Billy might be a fuck-up, but he was still an Odom. And what would people think of the Odoms if they didn't look out for blood? Christ, it was enough to make him vomit.

It took one entire day to get the little fart-bag out. Get the cash together for the bond, fill out the paperwork, wait around to get it issued, then wait around some more while they processed the release. Then, finally, he got that done, the little asshole didn't want to go. Deputies laughing their fucking heads off; they couldn't believe it! Lon would've left the little weasel in jail, but he knew Mama'd be up his ass like a case of diarrhea, so he told Barry Stroh, bring him out front, grabbed him by the ear and, dragged him out to the Yukon.

Now, twenty minutes later, the little pork winkle was whining his sorry ass off, and Lon was about ready to put his head through the windshield.

"I ain't *going* home." he said. "I told you that already. Shit. Lee Ann, blowed up like the Goodyear Blimp. Glued down to the armchair with her Rottenbugger popcorn, whatever the hell they call it. Watching her TV shows with her fat fucking friends. Lynette screaming her head off, snot running down her nose. I tell you, I can't stand that fucking place."

"Is *that* so."

"You think I'm kidding, but I'm telling you right now. You can drop me off up there, walk me in the door, you want to. But I ain't gonna stay there. You get in your truck and take off, I am fucking gone."

Lon had about enough. He said, "What makes you think I give a shit what you do? You don't want to go home?" He jerked the wheel hard right, pulled to a skid stop on the shoulder. Then, he leaned over, and snapped open the passenger door. "Go on, get out." Lon kicked at him. "Get!"

Billy wasn't moving, though, looking straight ahead.

Lon said, "I don't give a shit what you do. You got that? I don't care where you go or don't go. Only one thing I care about." Lon turned, pointing at him now. "You get your sorry ass to court the time they told you. Are you listening to me?" Billy wouldn't look at him, staring straight ahead. "I said, are you *listening* to me? 'Cause if you take off? On my col- lateral? Boy, I'm'a tell you, they won't need a bounty hunter. I will go out and bring you back myself. And if I do, you ain't gonna enjoy that experi- ence one little bit, I guarantee you."

Little Billy sat there, rocking in his seat like he was four years old. Next thing you know, he'd be sucking his thumb. "Mama wouldn't like you talk- ing to me like that," he said. "We're flesh and blood, you know. I'm your goddamn brother."

"Half-brother," Lon said. "Jesus, you think I'd put up bail if you wasn't?" He threw the truck in gear, stomped the gas, and jerked her back on the freeway.

They drove a while, neither one saying anything. Finally, Billy gave him a grin. "Hey, I got an idea. How about you take me out to the garden? I ain't never been there before."

Lon smiled. "You gonna work with the Mexicans, that it? Pull weeds and haul fertilizer?"

Billy laughed a nervous little laugh. "No, not like that. I just thought I'd go out, chill awhile, you know. Maybe learn a few things from Rampas."

"Rampas is busy. It's a fucking art what he does. You got no idea." He shook his head. "Jesus, you are a piece of work. Don't you get it? It's a business, turning out the best field grown weed in North America. What do you think the man's running out there, a goddamn resort?"

Billy sat there a minute, got this pissy look on his face, "Well, *excuse* me," he said. "And all this time I thought, *you* was running things out there. I thought *you* was the boss. You could do what you want to do."

"I get it. You're saying, the man that *makes* the rules can *break* the rules, that about the way you see it?"

"God damn right!"

Lon powered down his window, and spit. "Shit. No wonder they kicked your ass out of the Corps. What you don't know about leadership would fill a fucking encyclopedia."

"I got drunk. Took a Humvee. Was a mistake is all that was."

"The Marines don't make mistakes, you moron; they make *men*. Why they kicked you out, they saw that wasn't what you was. You was a little fairy boy, had to have what you want the minute you want it."

Lon drove on for a while. Finally, he said, "You're afraid of her, aren't you?"

"Afraid of who?"

"Lee Ann." Shaking his head. "Jesus Christ, I can't believe my own brother'd be scared of a goddamn woman."

Billy looked out the window. "I ain't scared of her," he said. "Shit, I split her lip, almost broke her nose last Christmas."

"That don't mean you're not afraid of her."

"Well, I'm not," Billy said.

"So how come you don't want to go home, then."

"'Cause I'm sick of that place, that's why. I'm sick of my goddamn life, same thing day after day. Ain't no goddamn fun to it, no excitement." He shook his head, looking out through the windshield then. "I wasn't gonna hit those kids, you know," he said. "I just had to take a piss was all. Thought maybe I'd scare 'em. I don't know how many times I gotta say it."

"That what you told Petty? You had to take a piss?"

Billy nodded. "Said it was outta his hands, didn't make no difference." He took a deep breath, blew out. "Piggott's gonna fire my ass for sure, then what? How am I gonna make the payments? Got the doublewide, furniture, the goddamn pickup. Shit, we're gonna lose the medical. What're we gonna do with Lynette? And Lee Ann's goddamn yeast infections? Jesus!" Billy threw a punch at the dashboard. "It's that fucking cop. Wasn't for him, none of this woulda happened."

Lon glanced over. "What cop you talking about?"

"The one threw me outta the truck. Barry said he was a cop in Oakland."

Lon wasn't following. "A cop threw you out of the truck? What's that got to do with anything?"

"'Cause *that's* why they say I was gonna hit those kids. If I missed 'em on my own, wouldn't be more than DUI, maybe destroying public property … I'm gonna *kill* the motherfucker done this to me. I told him I was, too."

"You told him, huh?"

Billy was nodding his head. "At the guard shack down the mill. I said, 'I'm coming after you, motherfucker.' Just like that."

"And this cop, what did he say?"

"I don't recall. I guess he don't talk that much. Barry said he's part Indian."

Lon thought about that for a minute, wondering if it could be more than a coincidence. "This cop from Oakland, he have a name?"

"Yeah, he has a name," Billy said. "It was in all the papers. Name's Fuentes. Barry said he lived up around here, but he croaked or something."

Lon couldn't believe it. "Matt Fuentes? Was that his old man's name?"

"How the hell would I know? All I know is, that motherfucker's gonna pay for what he done to me."

Lon thought some more, and decided when you got right down to it, it didn't really matter if the cop was a relation or not. He said, "And you're gonna take this cop out, huh? Get yourself a big time reputation?"

"Goddamn right," Billy said. "I know how I'm gonna do it, too."

"Uh-huh. How's that?"

"Gonna run him down with my truck," Billy said. "Follow the motherfucker till he stops someplace where no one's looking, then I'm gonna run his sorry ass over a couple of times."

Getting off the freeway now, headed down the ramp toward Wild River, Lon pretended to think it over. "That's one way to do her, I guess," he said. "Of course, there could be some problems with it."

"What problems," Billy asked him.

"Well," Lon said, "If there's somebody around you don't know about, they could get your license number. Or the cop might spot you tailing him, bring down the law. Or if he's fast, he could jump out the way at the last minute. And if you did hit him, you'd have his DNA on your bumper. Could be some damage on there, too. Have to think how you'd deal with that. You'd be a suspect, on account of, you have a motive."

They drove on awhile, Billy seeming to think about what Lon told him. Finally, he said, "And I guess you have a better way to do it."

"Maybe." They were outside Billy's double wide now. Lon could see the lights on in there, the big screen TV flashing through the window.

Lon said, "Tell you what I'm gonna do. I'm gonna give you a chance to redeem yourself." He reached in his pants pocket, peeled off three C-notes, handed them to Billy. "Go on down to Wal-Mart, get you a Stevens pump and a box of 12 gauge shells. Okay?"

"Yeah—"

"Ask around where this Fuentes lives, but don't ask Barry Stroh. Find out some other way. Then, you go out there. Time it so it's dark outside, but not so late he might get suspicious. Understand?"

Billy was nodding.

"You're still in your truck, you rack the pump, get ready. Then you go up and knock on the door. When he opens it, you shoot him" He tapped on his chest, demonstrating. "Right here." He paused. "Now, if he don't open it when you knock—say he asks who's there— you shoot him right through the door. Just like that. Go for the sound, understand? Then, you blast the latch, move inside, and shoot him again. Make sure he's dead."

Billy was looking at him, wide eyed, like he could not quite believe it.

"Now here's what you *don't* do," Lon went on. "You don't make no threats, engage in no trash talk. Understand what I'm saying? You get the job done. You don't say a fucking word, not to him or nobody else. Then, when you're finished, you come and tell me about it. Okay?"

Little Billy was still looking at him, not saying a word.

Lon said, "You want to redeem yourself? That's how to do it. You get the job done. Then, maybe we can find a place for you in the operation."

What Lon was thinking, shit, Little Billy kills the guy or the guy kills him or they kill each other, any way you looked at it, this was what you called a no lose situation.

CHAPTER 9

THE DEATH OF MATTY FUENTES

Matty Fuentes' truck died at a '76 Station right off the freeway with a sign that said "Mechanic On Duty." Wandering into the bay, Metallica pumping from a powerful set of speakers, Eddie saw a pair of legs sticking out from under a Toyota pickup.

All roads they lead to shame
All drowning in the blame
All reflections look the same
In the shine of the midnight revolver

He leaned down and yelled, "You the mechanic?" Nothing. He repeated it. Still nothing. Finally, he tugged on the legs until a nose ring, ear studs, and a shaved head rolled out in that order, and tried the question again.

"That's it, amigo."

Eddie pointed outside. "Mind taking a look?"

The kid picked up a towel, wiped off his hands. Looking at the truck as they walked outside, he said, "That's a Ford, right?"

Eddie finally got the engine started while the kid looked under the hood, the engine running rough, black smoke pouring out the back, until it died and wouldn't start again.

"Could be a vacuum leak," the kid said finally. "Or dirt in the fuel lines. Where's the injectors at?"

Eddie said, "It has a carburetor."

The way they worked it out, Eddie left the truck, so the kid's boss could take a look when he got back from a parts run. This was supposed to be sometime after lunch. In the meantime, it was a half-mile up to the Coroner's Office, and there was no other way to get there, so Eddie started to walk.

The '76 Station was about a mile south of downtown Redwood Bay, in an area of shabby one-story industrial buildings and equally shabby shotgun bungalows with barking dogs lunging at rusty chain link fences.

Redwood Bay was the seat of Redwood County, and the only collection of buildings within a couple hundred miles could lay honest claim to be called a city. The Mynot had lived here for thousands of years before the European seal hunters and Russian fur traders showed up. But things didn't really change till they discovered gold in the Trinity Alps. The mountains were a hundred miles inland, but Redwood Bay was the closest way in. The Trinity Gold Rush was over by 1865, but San Francisco had become a boomtown by then. It needed timber. Timber was a lot easier to find than gold, and the area around Redwood Bay had timber.

There was a lot of money around in those days. You could still see it near the waterfront—big Victorian houses owned by lumber barons and shipping magnates. There were still dozens of them there, well maintained, or recently restored, some still lived in, others converted to restaurants or offices. That was the public face of Redwood Bay. The rest of it was a dump.

The Coroner's Office was part of the dump—located on the back side of a beige stucco building that housed a mix of County offices. The building didn't have a sign on it, but three of the parking stalls did. One said, Coroner, one said Public Administrator, and one said Medical Examiner.

Morgues didn't really work the way you saw it on television. They didn't bring folks in with a lot of drama to ID a body unless there was a reason. If they knew who it was, and the death looked it was accidental, or from natural causes, their main interest in the next of kin was getting him or her to pick up the body. If it went unclaimed, the County had to spring for the cremation. When the PA's office got hold of Eddie in Oakland, they gave him a list of undertakers, and he called one. At the time, all he wanted was a quick cremation. Now he was thinking he'd like a few answers to go along with it.

Inside the beige stucco building, down a beige stucco hall, there was a glass door that said "Coroner" with a counter behind it. Behind the counter there were some desks, and above the desks, there was a clock. Beneath the clock, there was a sign that read, "We Are Grieved by Your Loss." A heavy set strawberry blonde sat behind the counter wearing an angora sweater set and a gold necklace formed into letters that said "Connie." As Eddie walked in, she was looking for something in her purse.

"We close for lunch at noon," she said, not looking up.

Eddie looked at the clock, which indicated ten to twelve. He said, "Well, Connie, lucky for me, it isn't twelve o'clock yet."

Connie looked at the clock, then at him, but didn't say anything.

Eddie said, "I need a file. Fuentes, Mateo." And told her the date of death.

Connie returned to her purse. "The body is the property of the next of kin," she said. "Are you the next of kin? We don't deal with anybody else."

Eddie took out his wallet, dropped a driver's license on the counter. "I'm his son."

Connie picked up the license, looked at him, then looked at the license, then at him again. Then she pulled a form out from under the counter. "Fill this out."

He filled out the form, and handed it to her. This took about a minute.

She looked at the clock again, then sighed dramatically. "Wait here." She dragged herself out of her chair, flounced to the back, and reappeared a few minutes later with a thin, manila folder. "You have to read it at the counter," she said, looking at the clock. "If you want a copy, it's two dollars and fifty cents."

Eddie opened the folder. There was a single piece of paper inside. It was a form, filled out on a typewriter, or it could have been a printer that looked like a typewriter, giving details of the death of one Mateo Fuentes. The deceased was identified as a male, age 63, with a residence address of Ellendale Road Extension, Redwood County (unincorporated). According to the form, the body of the deceased was discovered at 0830 hours on Union Pacific Railroad property under Abandoned Alder Creek Bridge No. 2, near the town of Wild River. The approximate date and time of death was put at 2100 hours the previous evening. The investigating agency was identified as the Redwood County Sheriff. The next of kin box was checked as notified. Under the heading, "Autopsy", the box for "Yes" was checked on the form.

Eddie looked up. "Where's the autopsy report?"

Connie stared at him.

Eddie pointed to the paper. "It says here there was an autopsy. Where's the report?"

"If there was an autopsy, the report would be in the folder," she said.

Eddie held up the empty file folder. "But it's not."

Her eyes narrowed. "If it isn't *in* there, there wasn't an *autopsy*."

Eddie showed her the form. "The form says there was."

Connie gave him a thin smile. "Maybe the form is *wrong*," she said. "I *get* the files. I don't have anything to do with what goes in them."

Eddie said, "Who does?"

She looked at him. "Are you trying to make trouble? 'Cause if you are, there's a sheriff's station right down the hall."

"Connie?" Eddie shook his head, "If you call the Sheriff, you'll be late for lunch. One last question. The Medical Examiner's Office, where do you suppose that might be?"

The office was around the corner, but already empty when Eddie got there. He was about to leave when a door behind the receptionist's desk opened, and a thin, dark skinned man in a lab coat came out.

He smiled pleasantly. "May I help you?"

"I'm looking for the Deputy Medical Examiner."

"That would be me. V.J. Satyanarayan. You can call me Dr. Veejay. Everybody else does."

He held out his hand; Eddie took it. "Eddie Fuentes."

Dr. Veejay thought a minute. "We had a Mateo Fuentes a week or so ago. Age 63. Are you his son?"

"You ought to be a detective."

Doctor Veejay tilted his head back and forth. "That's exactly what I am. A detective of the medical variety."

"You performed the autopsy on my father."

"An autopsy is required by law in cases reported as accidental death."

"The report isn't in the folder at the Coroner's Office."

Doctor Veejay didn't seem surprised. "Perhaps it hasn't been written up yet. I dictate the reports, but sometimes there are delays in transcription. Especially with the budget cuts. Government barely grinds along. In any case, I remember your father's case fairly well. If you want, I can tell you about it. ... But I need to warn you, pathology can be an unpleasant subject. The name comes from 'pathos', it's Greek for suffering, you know."

Eddie told him he was used to unpleasant subjects because he used to be a cop. Dr. Veejay seemed to accept this. Then he asked, "Were you ... close ... to your father, Mr. Fuentes?"

Eddie shook his head. "No."

"The reason I ask, his body showed the effects of long term alcohol abuse. Multiple focal necroses in the brain, early laennec liver cirrhosis."

"He drank a lot. That much I know. But ... that wasn't the *cause* of death."

"We're charged as pathologists to determine a cause of death. But in my experience, Mr. Fuentes, an individual's manner of living is seldom unrelated to his manner of dying. In the case of your father, the medical cause of death was respiratory arrest resulting from an acute pontine infarction."

"Respiratory arrest. You mean he died because he stopped breathing."

"Actually, yes. But the suppression of respiratory function was due to compression in the brain stem. Infarcts were also present in the midbrain, left thalamus and left hippocampus, as I recall. In my opinion, this was a result of ethanol poisoning. His blood alcohol level was close to point five percent."

"I thought he fell off a bridge."

"Apparently, he did. The remains showed multiple cranial fractures, hematomas of the scalp and neck, fractures of the right tibia, ulna, femur and so on."

"But you're saying that wasn't the cause of death."

Dr. Veejay shook his head. "Not in my opinion. Disorientation would have been consistent with the brain infarction, of course. He could have lost balance, lost consciousness, or even died prior to the fall—that's speculation. But, from a medical point of view, there's no doubt in my mind your father would have died whether he went off the bridge or not. He was killed by alcohol."

* * *

Sitting in a client chair in Shanna Black's office wearing an Eco-Resistance tee shirt and a Thomas collar, Eric Ross said, "It's not *about* us."

Sitting next to him, Rhonda Myers nodded her agreement—stiffly. The girl, about twenty-two, was a veritable health food poster, with long brown hair, a flawless complexion, and perfect white teeth glowing above her tee shirt and Thomas collar, identical to Eric's.

Shanna said, "Of course not," making it unanimous.

"It's the principle of the thing," Eric said.

"Motherfuckers think they can corn hole the world and get away with it," Rhonda added. "We're gonna cut their nuts off, make 'em pay. That's all these billionaires understand is money."

"I understand the sentiment," Shanna said. "But in terms of expectations, I think you need to realize, the people you'd be suing aren't exactly billionaires."

Rhonda didn't seem to believe it. "That lumber company? They're huge. And, that bastard, Harriman Saul has more money than God. I read about him on the Huffington Post."

"Mmm. But from a legal perspective, they're not the ones you'd sue. You'd sue the guy driving the truck, and probably the company that hired him. I assume they have insurance."

"So," Eric said, "We go after them, right?"

Shanna pursed her lips. "Well, *we* wouldn't. As I said, I don't take these … kinds … of cases. But in terms of insurance, I'm guessing a couple million per occurrence would be pretty much standard."

Rhonda said, "Okay, a couple million dollars. What's wrong with that?"

"Of course, it might be a little tricky proving that kind of damages, with a limited history of employment, but—" Shanna got up. "Like I said, it's not really my area."

Eric said, "You're saying it wouldn't be you representing us."

"That's what I'm saying. I ... don't take contingent fee cases. But I can provide referrals to a couple local attorneys who would."

Rhonda turned to Eric. "Fucking lawyers are all the same." Then, to Shanna, "You bet your ass we want a referral. There's no way we're walking away from this."

"Mmm," Shanna said. She turned. "Eric, there's something I need to discuss with you for a minute—in private." Then, back to Rhonda, nodding toward the door. "We'll just be a minute."

When she was gone, Shanna took an envelope out of the top drawer of her credenza, and handing it to him said, "I assume ... recent events ... won't undermine the resolve of the Eco-Resistance Coalition to oppose this indiscriminate and environmentally insensitive logging?"

Eric told her he didn't see why it would.

It was half a mile from the Coroner's office to Shanna Black's, but it could have been a million. Up near the waterfront, the streets were wide, with manicured lawns and beds of colorful flowers. Shanna's office turned out to be in a three story Victorian with plenty of gingerbread—spindles and scrollwork, gothic windows, even a turret, the whole thing painted a muted green, with silver and white accents. Out front a simple brass sign read, "Shanna Black, Attorney-at-Law." Apparently she didn't need to share the building.

Inside, beyond a wrap-around porch, and a heavy wooden door, Eddie found himself in a big entry hall—oak paneled, with a massive stairway and Oriental rugs on the floor. A small desk at the foot of the stairway was empty, except for a sign with an arrow pointing to a doorway to the right that said "Reception".

Through that door was another oak paneled room, this one with a fireplace, client chairs, and a reception desk. At the desk, a pretty young man, was talking to a good-looking brunette in overalls, a tee shirt and a Thomas collar. As Eddie approached the desk, another door opened and the fellow from the demonstration walked out.

His face broke into a smile above his matching Thomas collar. "Hey, man, how you doing?" He held out his hand. "That was awesome, what you did at the mill. ...A lot of people owe you big time."

Shaking hands, Eddie said, "I can provide an address for contributions."

"Uhhh, right," the kid said. "Hey, it said in the papers you were a cop. That's far out." He seemed to be searching his memory. "I don't think I've seen you around. You get to a lot of demonstrations?"

"Nothing lately," Eddie said. "I kind of ... burned out on them, you might say."

"I heard that." The brunette was walking over now. "Demonstration is masturbation, man. If you want traction, take action!"

"Not to mention," Eddie said, "You can't really hear the speeches with a gas mask on."

The girl's jaw slacked a little, as she maybe got what he was saying.

Then, Eddie turned, and saw Shanna standing in the doorway, arms folded, watching him.

Eddie had been in a few high rent law offices before—Bluestein's for one, when Karen worked there—and they tended to give you the impression that whoever decorated them had a lot more money than taste. Shanna's office was different. Not just the size of it, or the old time details—carved wood ceilings, big arched windows, Grecian columns, parquet floors. Or the furnishings—the big glass table, glove leather swivel chairs, Oriental carpets, twelve foot palms in hand painted ceramic pots. It was the way the whole thing worked together.

Eddie could feel Shanna watching him. She was a little dressier today, in an emerald velvet jacket the color of her eyes, cream silk under the jacket, but still keeping it casual with a pair of faded designer jeans and cowboy boots. She said, "What do you think?"

"I think ...you have expensive taste."

"I've been told that before."

"By your clients?"

"By my husband ... ex-husband. But he meant it in a good way. That was before the divorce." She dropped into a swivel chair, motioned, "Sit down. You want something to drink? Donald makes a pretty good latte. Or, we could go cold and alcoholic."

"No, I'm good." Eddie wandered to the window, looked out at the bay. It was afternoon now, the fog offshore, the sky a powder blue. "The guy that was here—I forget his name ...."

"Eric. Ross."

"Right. He a client of yours?"

"Eric?" She shook her head. "I help the Coalition out. But, Eric wanted to file a personal injury lawsuit, and I don't handle those sorts of things."

He said, "Strictly cash in advance."

She said, "Not always."

He said, "Not always cash, or not always in advance?" She didn't answer, watching as Eddie moved to the big, glass desk, and sat down. "So, what's the matter with him? I didn't think you could get whiplash running *away* from an accident."

"We didn't get into it," Shanna said. "Eric and Rhonda—that's the girl, she wears the bird costume—they think somebody should pay for what happened. Given the situation, Eric believes it's his ethical responsibility to pursue the matter." She paused. "Eric is a master of what you might call 'situational ethics.' Give him a situation, and he'll come up with the ethics."

Eddie said, "He should have been a lawyer."

Shanna smiled slightly. "Aww. You don't like lawyers."

"No, I love lawyers. Sure, they're corrupt. But I don't agree with the people who say they have no imagination. Take the *Canon of Ethics*—a list of the things lawyers are *required* to do. And it turns out, they're exactly the same things lawyers *want* to do. They *have* to have a written fee agreement. They *have* to represent a client, even if he tells them he's guilty. They *can't* testify against a client, even if he tells them he committed a crime. I mean, how could you come up with something like that if you lacked imagination?"

Her expression had turned a little wary.

"Of course," he went on, "there *are* lawyers who can't even manage to follow their *own* rules. Lawyers who lie, for example, or fail to disclose material facts, or represent people when they've got a conflict of interest." Eddie pulled out the letter he found at his father's cabin, dropped it on the table.

Shanna looked at the letter, but didn't pick it up. "I never represented your father," she said. "I tried to buy the place from him. That was the extent of our relationship."

"Tried to buy it for a fraction of what it was worth."

She took out a cigarette, lit it with a match. "Okay, I tried to get it cheap. So what?" She tossed the match in an ashtray. "You're forgetting, when I made him the offer, I wasn't sure Saul was going to build the road. And I'll tell you something else. It was a reasonable offer. I would have paid him more than anybody else."

Eddie was quiet a minute. "But you didn't buy it. Why not?"

She took a drag. "I was supposed to meet him the night he died, but he never showed."

"That didn't seem strange to you?"

"Strange?" She shrugged. "Look, I'm probably not telling you anything you don't already know, but your *father* was strange, and that's being nice about it. I had a friend at the title company do a search, so I knew he owned the property before I called him up. But when I got hold of him, he said he didn't own it. So I asked him, if he didn't own it, who did? He said, nobody did. Then, he asked me, just out of curiosity, if he did own it, how much would I be willing to pay. When I gave him a number, he said he wanted more. Then, we haggled around, and finally he said, okay. He was a pain in the ass, to tell you the truth."

Eddie listened, not about to deny it.

"You know in a way, I was kind of surprised he decided to sell in the first place. They tell you, when you're buying property, try to get the seller focused on what he's going to do with the money. Play on the desire to go somewhere else. With your dad, I couldn't figure out where he'd go. He wasn't exactly a candidate for a Caribbean cruise, or assisted living."

Eddie hesitated. "Did you ever ask him?"

She shook her head. "I don't think he knew."

Eddie took some time, digesting it. "Let me ask you something else. The letter said you met with my father. When you were with him, how did he seem to you?"

"What do you mean?"

"Start with, was he drunk?"

"What do you want me to tell you? We met in a bar."

"I guess I'm asking if he was *on* a drunk."

She seemed to consider it. "He wasn't incoherent if that's what you mean. I'm not sure where you're going with this."

"I talked to the medical examiner. My father didn't die falling off a bridge. He died of alcohol poisoning." He thought a minute. "If I ask you a question, what are the odds you'll give me a straight answer?"

She fixed him with those green eyes. "If I give you a straight answer, what are the odds you'll believe me?"

CHAPTER 10

SHANNA'S STORY, PART I

Fucking Garth Piggott was leaning back in his big, red leather swivel chair, candy ass cowboy boots propped up on the desk. "I hope you understand now, Billy," he was saying, "ain't nothing personal about this."

"There ain't, huh?" Billy said, getting the thought he ought to bash the fat fuck over the head with that polished bulldog paperweight he kept on his desk.

"Hell no," The Pig shook his head. "Boy, to my mind? This county owes you a debt of gratitude for what you done. Damn communists come up here from the People's Republic of Berkeley, shut the mill down. I tell you what, that mill shuts down, I'm shut down. You understand that. I get paid by the load." He shook his head. "No, believe you me, this is not personal. It's purely a matter of insurance."

Billy looked at him. "Insurance."

"It's the DUI," the Pig said. I don't give a damn about the rest of the charges. DUI, driving a commercial vehicle? They gonna pull your license, boy, I can tell you that right now. Even, say you get you a lawyer, dodge that bullet, all the property damage up at Liberty? My carrier's probably gonna pay right up to the policy limit. Shit, even without personal injury, my rates going through the roof. And say somebody files a lawsuit?" The Pig made a face. "Well, nothing I can do about that. It's a cost of doing business. But if I try and keep you on the schedule?" He snorted. "They'll cancel the whole damn thing, and that puts me out of business. Can't haul for West Coast or anybody else."

Billy was thinking the goddamn situation was like wrestling Mama when he's a kid, she's there holding his arms down, sitting on his chest. There wasn't no options to it. He heard himself kind of whining then, not even liking the sound of it himself, "Well, Jesus Christ, what about me? I got a wife and kid. I got bills to pay. What the hell am I supposed to do?"

The Pig nodded thoughtfully, "Well Billy, what I would do, if I was you? I'm gonna be real honest with you now, son. I'd go out and find myself another line of work. I really would."

The fat fuck was saying some more stuff now about how Billy was a fine young man and he was sure everything was going to work out just terrific. Then, he kicked his cowboy boots off the desk and motioned toward the door. "Now Michelle out there, she's got your check. We put a little extra in there for you, 'cause I know you're gonna have expenses to meet."

The Pig stuck out his hand. "Best of luck to you, son," he said. "And make sure you give my very best regards to your mother."

Later that afternoon, Billy was at the Wharf Rat with Danny Villa, happy hour up at Sanchez Landing, the two of them doing shooters. They knew each other since high school. Danny, little guy, not over five ten, but not bad looking if you liked that Mexican kind of appearance, and he had a way with the women—anyway, if you believed half of what he said.

Danny climbed for West Coast Lumber, topping the big trees, and could be a pain in the ass, telling logger tales of one kind or another. At the moment, though, he wasn't telling tales, the two of them sitting at the bar, watching Lana Janich work her backside toward the rear of the bar with a tray of drinks.

"Yeee-haw!" Billy said. "I'm gonna get me a piece of *that* local motion."

"Yeah, man," Danny said. "All you need's an Escalade, a cigarette boat, and a sheriff badge. That'll land you second place for a hand job."

Billy looked at him, having trouble following the conversation. "What're you talking about?"

"What am I talking about? The Sheriff, dog? Don't you know about that?" Danny pointed to the back of the room where the Sheriff was sitting with some people Billy didn't recognize. Lana was dipping down, back there in her little pirate girl outfit with the micro-mini skirt and the low cut ruffled top. And now Billy could see Lana was letting the Sheriff reach in, give a little squeeze underneath her skirt. Giving the man a little extra holler for the dollar, you might say.

"God *damn*," Billy said.

Danny nodded, "She a piece of tail, all right. ... Way she's built and all, know who she reminds me of?"

Looking at Lana, Billy said, "Who's that?"

"Your Mama." Danny held up his hand, smiling. "Hey, man. I'm just saying."

Billy punched him in the arm, hard as he could. Rubbing his arm, Danny said, "Hey, fuck, man, that hurt!" But a minute later he was smiling again, looking at Lana. "Yeah, your Mama? I'll munch her carpet anytime."

Billy punched him again. Danny winced, but he was also laughing. "That's a fucking compliment, dog. Don't you get it. See, *I* don't go around jumping every snaggle-tooth skank walking down the street, like *some* people I know."

Billy said, "Yeah, it's gotta have two legs with a hole in the middle for you to get interested."

Danny laughed, "Hey, *I* wasn't the one fucked Wilma Turley."

"Who said I fucked Wilma Turley?"

"Dude. Everybody *knows* you did it."

"Yeah, well that's a goddamn lie is what that is."

Meanwhile, both of them were watching Lana fool around with the Sheriff.

Danny said, "What I'm wondering? Is all of that natural, or you think she got some cosmetic assistance?"

Billy tossed down a shooter and said, "Soon as I get my hands on 'em, I'll give you my expert opinion." Billy motioned to the bartender. "Walter?" But Walter didn't see him.

Danny said, "You better lighten up, dude. You're shit faced already."

"You think I don't know my limit?" Billy emptied his pockets out on the bar. He was maxed out on his Home Depot MasterCard, speaking of limits—found that out when he went to buy gas. It was too late to cash the severance check he got from Piggott. Two of Lon's three C-notes went in Lee Ann's pocket to shut her up, and now there wasn't one whole hell of a lot left.

While he was trying to figure out just how much, Danny said, real casual like, "Oh yeah, I meant to tell you. Guess who I saw today?"

Billy asked him who.

"The guy kicked your ass outside the mill the other day. I can't remember his name."

Billy looked at him. "You sure it was him?"

"It was him alright. He had that old rust bucket truck I used to see up at the Chain Saw, belonged to that crazy som'bitch was his old man. It was at the '76 Station. You know, the one right off the freeway ramp down Redwood Bay. Looked like he was having car trouble."

"When?"

"Couple hours ago." Danny thought a minute. "Hey, you hear about that? His old man? He fell off a bridge." Danny was laughing.

"What's so funny about that?"

"What's funny is, he used to do what I do. He was a topper. They say, he was good, too. Dance a jig on top of a spar, a hundred fifty feet in the air and he wouldn't even bother to tie on. You ought to try *that* sometimes."

Billy said, "Yeah," not giving it much.

"The guy's a topper, get it? Gets drunk enough he falls off a goddamn bridge." Danny was shaking his head. "That dude, man, he was one insane motherfucker."

"You know where he lives?"

Danny looked at him. "He's dead, man, I just told you that."

"Not the old man, jerk-off, the other one, at the mill."

Danny shrugged. "How am I supposed to know? I think the old man used to live somewhere south of the Divide. Maybe he's staying out there." Then, he smiled. "I don't think he's going out there real soon, though."

Billy asked him why not.

"'Cause his truck's broke down, you dumb fuck."

*   *   *

Sitting in her office with Eddie Fuentes—the big, orange sun already sunk in the harbor now, the light quickly fading to blue—Shanna decided there were three main things she didn't like about the man. The first thing was, he looked too damn good. It seemed like Shanna always wound up with big men, men that skated on the edge of sloppy. Her father was like that, which could have had something to do with it. This guy was ripped, but compact, probably no taller than she was in spikes. Well, maybe a little taller. And he had these smoky blue eyes she liked, that could flash at times. High cheekbones, a full mouth, and a square jaw with a chin that had just the hint of a crease in it when he smiled …. Okay, enough of that.

The second thing she didn't like was, he had this easy way about him that made her want to tell him stuff. And what made it worse, when she told him stuff, it felt good, even though she knew she'd probably regret it later. He had this way of looking at her, it made her feel like he knew her, like they knew each other, even though they didn't really know each other at all.

And the third thing she didn't like, which was maybe the most important, he could hold his liquor better than she could— and that was saying something.

Shanna's original idea going into this thing was, keep it simple, tell the guy enough to bring him along, leaving out unnecessary details. Later, when the hook was in, and he was dreaming about how he was going to spend the money, she could explain the other parts or, anyway, as much as he needed to know. But now, without really thinking about it, she could feel the plan starting to change. Like maybe there could be a bigger part for him in this.

"Who are you really working for?"

When he asked her the question, she said, "Eddie, what would you like to drink?"

And after she poured the whiskey, holding his eyes with hers, she gave him an answer. "Look at me, Eddie, right here," she said, pointing to her eyes. "Who do you think I'm working for?"

He took some time, then smiled with those blue-gray eyes of his, not really saying anything. And Shanna could have left it there, probably should have left it there, but heard herself go on, telling him her fucking life story for Christ sake. How she'd been working for herself since the day she walked out the ranch gate in Pinehurst, Wyoming, hitchhiked down to Rock Springs, and caught a Greyhound bus. How she met a man, working in the VIP lounge at the Giddy-Up Club off of East Fourth in Reno, Nevada—Shanna taking her clothes off to Tammy Wynette doing *Stand By Your Man*, if you could believe it—and wound up married to Rex King of King Cadillac. How she lost most of her money after the divorce, managed to put herself through school, and landed the job with Jimmy Kennan when he was still Attorney General.

Eddie raised an eyebrow at that point, and said, "That's quite an accomplishment."

She said, "Yeah? Which part? Working for Jimmy Kennan, stripping to Tammy Wynette or being married to a guy who wore a cape and drove a Cadillac with a fucking crown on top of it?"

Eddie said he wasn't sure.

She went on, told him the job with Kennan as fun in a way. They called it "public affairs" but it mainly meant figuring out ways to get positive press coverage for the boss. She'd arrange for him to appear at a courthouse when somebody won a big case, or to show up at a drug bust—as if he had anything to do with drug busts.

Eddie smiled. "*You* were the one who did all that stuff."

"I was good at it, too."

"I'll bet you were."

She took a minute. "Public Affairs, yeah. But, then somebody did a background search, came up with a little personal history, and Jimmy got the idea the job description might include some *less* than public affairs on the side."

He said, "Sounds like sexual harassment to me, forcing himself on you under circumstances less than consensual, should be a pretty easy lawsuit." Saying it with an edge, telling her she couldn't bullshit him, but then smiling, like he wasn't judging her, either.

"It happened, okay? Anyway, it didn't get very far before Megan found out."

"That would be the wife."

"She didn't miss much. She was connected, too. They had one of those political partnership arrangements, the two of them. But she wouldn't tolerate playing around if it was more than casual. Next thing I knew I was transferred out of Public Affairs into Legal Opinions, then Cyber-Safety, finally Crime Statistics. A few months after that, I was out the door. Situations like that, they don't fire you all at once, they do it in stages."

"As opposed to situations like mine." Eddie grinned. "Where they kick you out the door from the fifty yard line. What happened next? You came here?"

"Not right away." She finished her drink. "When I think about it, I must have been looking for a place to hide. I grew up in a small town, you know...." Then, pouring refills, added, "Of course, growing up, I didn't have to earn a living ...."

Eddie looked around the room, then at her. "You seem to do okay ... earning a living."

"I do okay."

Their eyes held; he said. "It's not easy, getting by in Redwood County. I know. I grew up here."

She took a minute, then smiled, "You used to hustle pool when you were in high school. Russell said, you were pretty good at it."

Looking around, he smiled. "Not *that* good."

She said, "Maybe you weren't playing the right game."

He seemed to consider it. "Maybe I wasn't."

*   *   *

Danny told Billy he was in no condition to walk, let alone drive, and Billy didn't see the point in arguing about it, so they left the Dakota at the Wharf Rat and took Danny's tricked out Silverado down to Redwood Bay.

It was maybe twenty minutes on the freeway, and sure enough, the old Ford was still at the '76 when they got there, parked off to one side of the office, just like Danny said it was.

Billy said to Danny, "Pull in and get some gas."

"I don't need any gas," Danny said.

"Jesus, would you just do what I tell you?" Billy said, "Get a couple dollars worth. I'll pay for the damn gas."

Danny pulled up to the pump, and Billy told him to wait while he went in to talk to the kid in the office, who turned out to be a little pimple ass metal head, reading *Penthouse*.

Billy pulled a couple of singles out and put them on the counter. "Two dollars Number 4," he said.

The kid looked out at the Silverado. "Where you going, around the corner?" He took the money, punched it into the console.

Billy wanted to yank the fucker over the counter, put his head through the door of the beer cooler, but made himself smile instead. "That old F-150 out there. You know who it belongs to?"

"Why, you want to buy it?"

"Maybe."

The kid laughed. "I wouldn't, if I was you."

"Why not?"

"'Cause it's a rusted out piece of shit, that's why not. Got to flush the whole thing out, replace the fuel lines and the gas tank, among other things."

Billy stood there another second or two, then he said, "The guy that owns it. When's he coming back?"

The kid shrugged. "He was supposed to be here an hour ago."

Billy thought a minute. "Hey, glad I asked about that truck. I guess I ain't interested after all."

A few minutes later Billy and Danny were sitting across the street in the Silverado, Billy trying to convince Danny they weren't getting into anything illegal.

"I'm telling you, there's nothing more to it than that," he said. "The man picks up the truck, you tail him out of town. When he gets going up the Grade, you call me on my cell phone. That's all I'm asking you to do."

"You're not going out there with me?"

"How could I do that? I told you, you're dropping me at Piggott's first. Then, you're coming back and wait for him."

"Yeah? Where you gonna be?"

"No, no, see I can't tell you that."

"Why not?"

"Because you don't want to know."

"Why not?"

"Man's going to be here any time. Would you please start the damn truck so we can go?"

Danny shook his head, but he did start the truck.

"Go on, hang a Huey," Billy motioned. "Head toward Piggott's. Up on 12th"

Driving, Danny said, "Man, I don't get it. What's this thing about, anyways?"

"It's a joke, I told you."

Danny asked him what kind of a joke.

Billy said, "No, see, that's ... I can't tell you that. The man takes off in the truck, you make the call. That's all you know. That way, if somebody was to ask you, you wouldn't have any more information."

Danny asked him who was gonna ask.

"Shit," Billy said, getting a little impatient now. He pulled the cash he had left out of his pocket, counted it out. "Look, I'll give you seventeen—no, wait a minute," He pulled out the change, counted that out, too, slapped the money down on the center console. "Eighteen dollars and twenty-seven cents, man. I will give you eighteen dollars and twenty-seven cents to stop asking questions and make one fucking phone call."

Danny looked at the console. "Hey, shit, man, *pennies*?" Then, shook his head. "Look, I don't want your fucking money, okay? I just wanted to know what was going on."

Billy said, "No, see, you don't *get* it. I *want* you to have the money, okay? Piggott, that fat fuck, he fires my ass. I ask him what the hell am I supposed to do? He says, 'Well, if I was you boy, I'd find myself another line of work, I really would.' So that's what I'm doing. Finding myself another line of work, and you're helping me get started. So I got to pay you, see, to keep things on a professional basis."

And Danny said, "I thought you said it was a joke."

CHAPTER 11

SHANNA'S STORY PART II

Sipping Coronas, munching salsa and chips in a back booth at *El Habanero*, the question was still out there. Just how much was Shanna going to tell this man? She could feel herself sliding into it. Slipping into a situation, and not feeling bad about it; actually feeling pretty good, but without a clear idea in her mind exactly where it was going. On the one hand, the guy had weight. He was a cop; he knew the system. He could talk the talk, man up if he had to. She could use somebody like that right now. On the other hand, if she brought him into one part of the thing, it could open doors that led other places. But outside all that, there was something else. Looking at him now, sitting across from her, that hint of a smile in his eyes, she seemed to relax. There was an energy, like a wave, and it seemed to be carrying her, carrying both of them along. And even though she didn't know where they were going, she was pretty sure it was someplace she wanted to go.

The waiter came with the food order now—Chile Colorado for her; Carne Asada for him—and he asked her, in a casual sort of way, how she got into doing criminal work as a lawyer. So, she started off with a casual sort of answer.

"What can I tell you, Eddie? I guess I relate to people who have trouble controlling their impulses."

He smiled, and she heard herself telling him how she started out renting space from Harley Rosenthal in Manzanita. Harley, an aging civil rights lawyer, handled the cases that interested him and referred everything else to her.

"He didn't like divorce or custody fights—so he gave me that kind of stuff. I got the wills and trusts. And real estate bored him to tears, which meant it was my bread and butter."

"In other words, nothing you wanted to do."

"That was the problem. I went to work for the guy because he had a reputation for doing criminal defense. But that was also what he *liked* to do, and he didn't want to give it up. ... If I stuck with Harley, I would have wound up comatose, or in some other occupation."

Eddie said, "Maybe an honest occupation."

"Mmm. Or maybe not. Anyway, it never came to that. I got lucky, and ran into Roger Bachman."

"He was a criminal lawyer?"

"That's how he started out, yeah." Shanna took some time now, eating chili. She needed a quick reality check. She could stop here, but somehow didn't want to. She felt good talking about this stuff. She'd never really talked about Roger with anyone, so she kept going. "But by the time I met him, he was more of an ... entrepreneur. He owned pieces of things—apartment buildings, motels, car washes, an airplane dealership. He owned a bar in San Francisco," and watching his expression, added. "A lot of the stuff, he was partners with a ..;. client ... of his. A man by the name of Philip Doctor."

Eddie stopped eating. "*The* Philip Doctor?"

"*The* Phillip Doctor." Shanna said. "They weren't just business partners. They were ... life partners or, anyway, that's how Philip saw it."

"They're gay?" He seemed surprised.

"Roger went both ways. He was open about it. I don't know about Philip. I never saw him with a woman. ... Roger was the front man. The public face. He was good at it, too. But then, Roger was good at everything. ... He could sing, dance, shoot skeet, ride a horse, play a harmonica. He could juggle." She smiled at the thought. "I remember one time at a party, I heard him play old Cole Porter songs on the piano. He was good. I never met anybody even a little bit like him. He was one off ... incomparable."

Watching her now, Eddie said, "It sounds like ... you're ... in love with him."

Shanna seemed to be considering it, maybe trying to get a handle on how she really did feel, or how to put it into words. Finally, she said, "I don't know. Maybe I *was* in love with him. I would have jumped him in a minute if he showed any interest. ... Even though he *was* old enough to be my father."

Eddie caught it then. "You said, '*Was* old enough?'"

"He died three years ago." Shanna said, picking at her food absently.

"I'm sorry."

"Yeah." She took some time, and there might have been a mist in her eyes, or maybe not. "The thing was, he never said a word. No note, no good-bye. He just disappeared." She shook her head. "It was just like him. That's how I got the office. It was his. He put it in my name. Recorded a deed, left a copy on the desk, and disappeared. That was Roger."

Eddie looked at her. "It didn't seem ... sudden?"

She shrugged. "Well, he played around. Had a reputation. People said maybe it was AIDS related ... I don't know." She shook her head. "I heard he went back to Connecticut; that's where he was from. But some people said he died at a hospice in Colorado. Then, I heard he shot himself at a hotel in Las Vegas. There were a lot of rumors. I even heard he went off to live in the south of France someplace, that he didn't die at all. Who knows?"

It hung there awhile, Shanna quiet, frowning, deep in her thoughts. Finally, she went on. "Philip was pretty torn up about it. After a while, he started asking me to do things for him ... you know, here and there."

Eddie looked at her. "You mean, you took Roger's place?"

She said, "No, no, nothing like that. I handle a few things for him. From time to time. You know."

"What kind of things?"

Shanna ate some of her food, chewing it slowly, and Eddie could feel her trying to decide whether to tell him something or not. And he could feel himself wanting her to, wanting to know more, to get involved, wanting to take the next step, even though he had no idea where it would lead him, just going with the feeling that it was someplace he wanted to go.

*   *   *

Little Billy dropped two twelve-packs of Coors Light on the counter at the 7-Eleven down at the Ellendale off-ramp and asked the guy if they took credit cards. He would have rather paid cash, avoiding a paper trail, but he gave Danny his last eighteen bucks to make the phone call, and the credit card was all he had left.

The guy behind the counter, a big, dark skin motherfucker, with a scruffy black beard and a light blue turban, said, "MasterCard or Visa. We don't take American Express."

Billy handed over his Visa debit card and watched the dude swipe it. Well, shit, he'd just have to pay the overdraft fee if he didn't have the money. Waiting for the machine, he pointed to the turban, "Hey, I always wondered, what's them fucking things for anyways?"

The guy's eyes got narrow. He pointed to the Raiders cap Billy had on "The same as those fucking things are for. Any more fucking questions?"

Billy was thinking he ought to say something cool like, "Yeah, I got a question. How come you assholes don't wear a hat like a normal human being?" Only the way the dude was looking at him, the odds looked good he might just come over the counter with a baseball bat, and that would be the end of the operation.

It was a piece of cake getting the wrecker, the way it worked out. What give him the idea, when Billy was counting his money up at the Wharf Rat, he saw he still had the gate key on his ring. Seems like Piggott never asked for it back, the fat fuck. So, all's Billy had to do was waltz into the yard, jimmy an office window, and take a key out of the cabinet behind the dispatch desk—any truck he wanted. Billy knew right away which one it was gonna be. The big Mack wrecker, an RD 800, fire engine red, five hundred horses with a diamond steel push plate. Whoo-eee! A man could do some serious damage with that kind of equipment.

Now, coming out of the 7-Eleven, Billy set the twelve-packs on the passenger seat, turned the Mack out on the Ellendale Road, and headed up toward the Divide. It was a long, straight grade to start, then you came into some bends, sweeping turns tightening into switchbacks the higher up you went and, shit, the road got narrow up here. Dark as hell, too, and foggy toward the top, before she dropped down into that first canyon. The road was way too skinny to turn around up here, but Billy knew a turnoff a half-mile past the top of the grade. He was pretty sure he could get the tractor turned around over there, then head back up top to wait.

That's what the beers was for.

*   *   *

"You have to understand," Shanna was saying now. "I was the only one in the office. The files were a mess. Record keeping wasn't Roger's strong point. That and his handwriting. It was notorious." She smiled. "Of course, I'd met Philip before. He has this place out at the Costa Perdida where he gives Halloween parties. It's … different. Anyway, he asked me to go out there, and we … came to an agreement."

"An agreement."

She lit a cigarette. "Well, I sort of … inherited Philip. I was in Roger's office, sitting behind his desk. I got his mail. I got his calls. There were things that … came up. There were people who had … relationships. People with … expectations …"

Eddie was nodding. "You mean payoffs."

And just like that, it was out there. Shanna looked at him now, trying to get a reaction, but didn't see any. His eyes said, he understood. He wasn't judging. Shanna felt herself exhale, a weight lift off her chest, almost a physical thing, like she could breathe better. She stubbed out her cigarette, even though she hadn't taken more than a few puffs.

"You're not surprised," she said.

"A county sheriff with a twenty thousand dollar wrist watch? He's either taking payoffs, or he married well." He took a minute, then looked
back at her. "So, is that what this is about?"

"What?"

"The land."

"What you're asking, am I buying it for Phil Doctor?" She laughed.
"You don't know the dope business. No one with any sense grows on their
own land. It's too risky. Ties you to the operation, number one. Plus, if you
get busted, you forfeit the property." She shook her head. "Not a good
idea. You know the saying, don't shit where you eat? It's the first rule in the
dope business. Plus, I'll tell you something else. People with risky occupa-
tions? They tend to like safe investments."

Shanna ate some chili then, tasting it for the first time tonight. She was
relaxed now, and it tasted good. But she could still feel him watching her,
and knew he wanted her to say more, and that she wanted to. Finally, she
found his eyes. "Eddie," she said, "Listen to me, okay? What I told you
about the land. That I'm in it for myself? That was the truth. One hundred
percent. ... But there's something else."

He said, "Okay," making it easy.

She hesitated, "How about a cup of coffee?"

And while they drank it, she told Eddie about Darryl Waters or, anyway, most of it.

When she was done, Eddie thought it over. "So, humor me," he said.
"If the DEA's offering you immunity, why not take it?"

"You're kidding, right?" He looked at her, not saying anything, so she
went on. "Let me ask you a question. State and federal law enforcement
have been after Philip Doctor for forty years, and they haven't even caught
him speeding. Why do you suppose that is?"

"He's a careful driver?" He smiled. "How about, he has a sexy lawyer."

"I'm being serious."

"So am I."

For a second, their eyes met, and she smiled in spite of herself, then
got serious again. "Think about it, Eddie. Forty years. Phil Doctor isn't just

careful, *or* lethal, *or* smart. Though he is all those things. He's a piece of work, if you meet him. My point is, he has people on the inside. He has to."

"And you know this how? You pay them off?"

"Not the ones I'm worried about."

"What about protection? The DEA guy didn't offer you that?"

"What good is it if he has somebody inside? Let me tell you something. If I agree to cooperate, you know what happens? I disappear. Just like that. … This thing with the land? It's a way to make money, sure. But I got to tell you, it's a hell of a lot more than that. It's my fucking exit strategy."

In the Range Rover, driving down to the '76 Station, the cold, mercury vapor lamps turning everything to black and white, Eddie thought about Shanna's story, and decided he believed it. Or anyway, as much of it as she told him. After all, it wasn't exactly the sort of thing you'd make up. But there was still a piece missing so now, as they rolled through the neighborhoods, changing from offices to strip malls to rundown warehouses, he said, "What I wanted to ask you, you know, you were talking about people on the inside …."

She said, "Yeah."

"This deal with West Coast Lumber. How come you happen to know so much about the road?"

She took a second. "Okay, I might as well tell it all. There's this … guy." And told him about Dick Duncan, how she met him at a party. "A big, good looking fella, but you could tell right away he wasn't happy."

Eddie said, "He *had* been happily married, but he and his wife had grown apart."

She looked at him sideways. "There *was* that. But see, it's also, Dickey's been with the company his whole life—finally worked his way up to the top, and what happened? They sold the business out from under him. Dicky feels like he got the shaft. This guy, Harriman Saul's been taking the company apart, piece by piece, and Dicky sees his future disappearing."

"And so, unfulfilled at work, and misunderstood at home, he takes comfort in the arms of a beautiful woman."

"Fuck you!"

"Am I missing something?"

"I *could* be in love with him, you know."

"But you're not."

She sighed. "It would be a hell of a lot easier if I was. He's got this idea in his head, the land deal is the answer to all his problems. He thinks, when he pulls it off, he leaves his wife, flies off into the sunset, and lives happily ever after."

"And you fly off with him. ... But that isn't how you see it."

"I don't believe in happily ever after. I told him that."

Eddie thought a minute. "The thing with the land, whose idea was it, his or yours?"

"A little bit of both. See, Dicky can't get involved directly, because he has a conflict of interest. The original idea was, I'd buy the land and double-escrow it to West Coast Lumber. You know what that is?"

Eddie wasn't sure, but nodded anyway. "More or less."

"It's a little more complicated now, but the idea's the same. Dick tells Saul he needs somebody in the middle because if the seller finds out the buyer is West Coast Lumber, the price goes up. But if we put a few layers in the middle, there's no way Saul knows what the *real* price is. Dick has all the numbers, how much it costs to helicopter log the Watershed, how much it costs in hard dollars to build the road. All you need to do is subtract, and it gives you the number—how much the company can afford to pay for the land."

Eddie wasn't sure he understood that one either, but it seemed to make sense. As they pulled into the '76 now, Eddie motioned for Shanna to park next to the old F-150, and said, "I guess I still have one more thing I need to ask."

"Yeah?"

"How much *can* the company afford to pay for the land?"

Shanna took some time, then finally turned in her seat to face him. "You know, if I tell you that, it makes us partners."

Eddie said, "I thought we *were* partners."

"Well, here's the thing, Eddie ...." Shanna ran a hand through her hair. "There's all kind of partners. See, I'm already splitting 50-50 with Dick. If you come in for half of my half, my share goes down to twenty-five percent."

"Are we negotiating?"

"Well ... it's just, you know ... a lot of money."

Eddie said, "Yeah, well, see, that's my question. How much money?"

She held him with those emerald green eyes of hers. "Our half? I was hoping, after expenses, a couple million."

"A *couple* million?"

"Okay, three million, all in."

"*Three* million."

"Yeah, three million. ... Don't you believe me?"

Eddie wasn't sure. But he couldn't think of a way to find out either. "Is there some reason I shouldn't?"

"Not that I can think of. ... If you want to be partners." She was smiling now. "You do want to be partners with me, don't you, Eddie?"

There was an electricity between them now, like a magnet, pulling them together. Without thinking about it, they were in each other's arms. Was it just a play? Eddie didn't think so, or maybe that's just what he wanted to think. But then, it didn't matter, because his mind shut down, and everything was feeling. A wave, and they were riding it, the two of them moving together, riding that wave. And somewhere in the midst of it, her hands on his body, her lips on his, he thought he heard her whisper, "Partners, right Eddie? "

CHAPTER 12

A LONG WAY DOWN

Danny Villa had to take a wicked piss. He'd been sitting in the Silverado watching the SUV at the '76 Station, could be an hour now, the man still in there with the woman. Good for the man, but not so good for Danny. With the fucking shooters, now he had to go, and the station was closed. Worse than that, with the cars getting off the freeway, he couldn't just go out and do it in the road. Danny was a big fan of the buddy cop pictures, and now he could see why, the cops in the movies, they never went on the stakeouts alone.

It was bad now, he couldn't sit still, teeth grinding, squeezing on the wheel. Fuck little Billy, man, with his eighteen dollars. He had to go! But then, Gracias Jesus! When he made up his mind he was going to turn the key, finally, the door on the SUV opened up! Now, the man was getting out. A couple minutes more maybe, tail him down to Ellendale, give Billy a call. Or better yet, make the call right now!

* * *

Damn! It was so quiet up the top of the grade, Billy's cell phone scared the shit out of him, even though he left the damn thing at the truck. Now with the old beef bayonet in hand, watering the weeds, he wasn't exactly able to stop things right there in the middle of it to take the call.

But he called back as soon as he got up to the cab. "Danny?"

"Shit, where the hell you been?"

"Never mind that. Where's he at?"

"You know that little road heads east off of Ellendale before you start up the grade?"

"Yeah, I know it."

"I'm pulled off there."

"Damn, I didn't ask where *you* was. I asked you, where's Fuentes?"

"That's what I'm trying to tell you, okay. He pulled off at the 7-Eleven by the freeway. I couldn't just pull in behind him or he might have got suspicious."

"Well, where's he at now?"

"I told you, the 7-Eleven, I guess."

"Shit!" Running somebody off the road wasn't as simple as it looked on television. "You call me as soon as you see him, okay?"

When he hung up, Billy checked the time on his phone. Quarter past eleven. He timed it on the way up, just under fifteen minutes to the top. About five minutes before you got there, the switchbacks started, and there was a sheer drop, had to be a thousand feet, went all the way to the river. Billy smiled. Give Fuentes about ten minutes after Danny called, then start down. A little nudge from the wrecker, and Eddie Fuentes was gonna enter aviation history.

Billy started thinking then, how he'd tell Lon about it. Never come out and say what happened exactly. Just sort of hint around about it. Real professional.

"Hear about Fuentes? Asshole I told you about, was in all the papers? Sonuvabitch went off the road the other day. A thousand foot down. Accident, is what they say. Man should have been be more careful."

"Is that right?" Lon would look at him with them blue-white eyes, hard to read, but enough in there so Billy would know he got the meaning.

Billy might nod his head some. "Mmm hmm. And how about old Garth Piggott, the fat fuck? You hear how somebody broke in his yard, took out a big Mack wrecker. Funny thing, whoever stole that truck brought it back the same night. Probably some kids, joy riding, is what the cops figure."

Lon probably wouldn't say much, just look at Billy. Then, he might say, "You didn't buy that shotgun, though."

And Billy would tell him, why bother? Just a waste of money.

And Lon might say, "Yeah, come to think of it, we might have some-thing for you. Working security. Why don't you and me take a ride out to the garden, I'll introduce you around, some of the folks involved in the operation."

Yeah, sweet Jesus. Finally, Billy was gonna get some excitement in his goddamn life.

* * *

It hadn't taken Eddie long to pick up the Silverado, parked across from the '76 with a little guy slouched down behind the wheel. The truck, gleam-ing black, lowered a good six inches, with a Godfather bumper, a chrome roll bar, and a spring whip antenna, wasn't exactly inconspicuous. Eddie saw it when he walked around to get the truck keys on top of the front wheel where the mechanic left them. When the Silverado followed him toward the freeway ramp, he thought it was interesting. When it got on, and stayed behind him, even though he wasn't going more than thirty-five, he thought it probably wasn't a coincidence. So, when it got off be-hind him at the Ellendale ramp, he took a quick right into the 7-Eleven, and watched it go past. Now, he figured it probably wouldn't hurt to get himself a Slurpee and figure out what to do next.

Inside, Eddie asked the big Sikh dude behind the counter which was better, the Berry Blaster or the Goji Berry Cherry?

The guy shrugged. "They all taste the same to me," he said. "And the red comes off on your tongue. My advice, unless you're into the *Vampire Diaries*, go with something else."

Eddie went with the Classic Coke.

Back outside, it was deserted. No sign of the Silverado, but that didn't mean it wasn't out there. Eddie got in the Ford with the Slurpee and stared at the road, thinking what to do. The truck was running rough, but it was running. The mechanic said he shot some Gumout in the carburetor, but didn't know how long it would last. When Eddie heard what it would take to actually fix it, he said, thanks but no thanks. Eddie still hadn't found the will, but that didn't mean he had to look for it now. It was tempting to head back to Redwood Bay and spend another night in the motel, even though he couldn't afford it.

With all that in mind, Eddie started her up, rolled the Ford out toward Ellendale Road, and sat there. A right turn would take him back to the Motel 6—an easy drive and a decent night's sleep he couldn't afford. A left turn would take him out to the cabin—a hard drive along a deserted road to restless night on a mildewed mattress. Eddie put the truck in gear, eased up the clutch, and hung a left. Maybe it didn't make sense. But the way Eddie looked at it, you had a choice—you could die one time when your turn came around, or you could die a thousand times in your head, worrying about it.

*   *   *

A few minutes later, Billy got the call.

The Mack was cold, but she started up, no problem. Billy checked his phone again for the time. Four more minutes. He snapped on the lights, feeling the excitement. Jesus, he hadn't had this much fun since the time he ran his dirt bike through the dance at the school gym. Now *that* was a goddamn memory. What was it about this life, the way it just closed down on you? You started out looking for a good time was all it was. Then, you got involved with a woman, and wound up with a wife and a kid and a job and a bunch of bullshit—loans and taxes and payments. And all the time, life was getting smaller and smaller, closing in on you, till there wasn't no room left to have fun anymore.

Billy engaged the clutch now, pushed into first, then hit the gas and got going. Moving through the gears, the big engine revved easy, building speed going down the grade. Billy couldn't help grinning now. The Mack was roaring like a bear in a beehive. Shit! Five hundred horses gliding through the nine-speed transmission like a hot knife through butter. *Damn*, it felt good! Billy let out a howl.

"Whoooeeee!"

Air was coming in through the windows now, night air, clearing out his head. Adrenaline kicking in, feeling strong. He gunned her into a short straightaway. Going pretty fast now, his mind went to how it was gonna be. Packing a chrome plated .45 auto. People looking at him when he went by. Saying, "Uh-huh, that's Bill Odom. Lon's brother. Whacked out that Injun cop. Yeah, they say he's a real professional."

Billy was laughing now, cold wind blowing in his face. No, he hadn't felt this good in a *long* time. The big Mack growling now, heading through a tunnel of trees. Took him back to one time he was high on crystal meth, headed south on the 101 toward the Golden Gate Bridge. Hit that tunnel, man, coming through the hills and out the other end into city lights, floating across the bay like a dream. Thinking yeah, only this time it wasn't gonna be *city* lights. It was gonna be *head* lights, *Ford* headlights with Eddie Fuentes behind the wheel.

Curve ahead, shifting down into a quick left bend, keeping the big Mack tight against the hill, hitting the gas a coming out, then—God *damn*! Headlights dead ahead. Bear down now, be cool … aim for the center of the lights….

Then, on the left, a shape flashed past the corner of his eye … a man. Holding up his hands? … And he was past, headed into the lights. But … they weren't headlights, they were flares! And they weren't in the middle of the road. They were toward the edge.

Billy jerked the wheel hard left, away from the flares, and WHAM! felt the big steel push plate ram a truck parked on the side of the road. And then, Jesus, felt the rear end starting to let go, the big wrecker going into a skid, hauling the other truck along with it. He yanked the wheel right, into the skid, but with the tow rig, there was too much weight. Everything was going too fast, the Mack going sideways now, the rear wheels headed for the edge. Sliding, sliding —

WHUMP! the angle changed. The big double wheels was over the side. Sweet Jesus! He was going down. Then—

ERRGHH! There was a groan, then a shudder, and the truck stopped! He wasn't going down after all!

A second went by. Two seconds. Nothing. All quiet, except for the Mack's big diesel engine running on idle. Billy turned, looked out the side window. The Mack was backwards, angled down, front wheels a little off the ground, half off the road and half on it, but stopped there. And Billy was thinking the old pickup could have got stuck on his bumper, or maybe it the Mack was caught on her under carriage. Either way, all he'd need to do was pop the door, and get his sorry ass the hell outta there.

But before he could, ERRGHH! a bigger groan. And Billy was thinking, fuck me! The truck's going down!

And it sure as hell was, over the edge now, the whole rig, going backwards, picking up speed. The road gone, but the headlights still on, lighting up trees flashing past. He thought there was a chance he might hit one, get hung up again. But then, WHUMP! The Mack hit a bump. WHUMP-WHUMP! A bigger bump, and he was airborne, backwards pinwheeling, end over end, snapping limbs, ripping through the treetops. And thinking, holy Mother of God, this is the end of me!

And oh shit! The Mack hit, real hard this time, and there was a CRACK! Something snapped at the base of his head, and a bolt of white lightning shot through him, like he was on fire everywhere at once.

Things got weird then. And the weirdest part, it wasn't even all that exciting. It was more like he was watching a movie on the big screen in the double wide with the sound turned off, only somebody slowed down the picture. And there wasn't nobody there watching. Shit, *he* wasn't there. Or maybe he was, but not in the truck exactly. Someplace else, only he didn't know where. All he knew, he was going lower, falling through space, into a place he didn't want to go. A place where there was no lights, no sound, no—nothing.

CHAPTER 13

HARRY SAUL'S PROBLEM

Leaning back in the glove leather interior of his new, twenty-five million dollar, twin-turbofan Citation X, talking on the telephone, Harriman Saul said, "Arthur? Hold on a minute, I'm moving the receiver to my *good* ear." He took a second, but didn't move the receiver. "Now, you want to repeat what you just told me. Because what I *thought* you told me, you're not financing Southeast Air, and I know that can't be right, because if it is—"

"Harry—" Arthur tried to interrupt him.

"If it *is*, every penny of my consolidated deposits is leaving that casino of yours and entering some other insolvent institution."

En route Tampa to New York at 47,000 feet, Harry was on the phone with Arthur Chasen, Executive V. P., First National Bancorp. An hour ago, Harry had finally signed a standstill agreement with Trace Crawford of Southeast Air, giving Harry the exclusive right to buy the company for 120 days. Now, he was trying to figure out how to pay for it.

Arthur was saying, "Harry, will you wait a minute? I didn't say I couldn't lend you the *money*. What I said was, I have a *collateral* problem."

"A collateral problem."

"An airline is not an asset play, Harry. It's not a liquidation. The equipment is hocked; the facilities are leased; the pension fund's been starved already; there isn't any room to maneuver."

"I never said it was a liquidation."

"I read the proposal."

"The plan is, we file chapter proceedings, void the union contracts, cut operating costs and pay out of cash flow."

"Harry, what did I just say? I *read* the proposal."

"Then maybe you missed the ratios—labor cost per ASM, debt coverage, projected operating margins ...."

"You're not listening, Harry. I'm not worried about *margins*. I'm worried about *collateral*. You take me into a chapter proceeding unsecured, I get thrown to the wolves."

"You get administrative priority."

"I don't know what lawyers *you're* talking to, but what *my* lawyers tell me is, I can't get priority over other creditors unless I come in *after* the filing. You want me to come in after, I have no problem. You want me to come in *before*, I need collateral."

Harry felt a sinking feeling in the pit of his stomach. "What about Steel Forge?"

"I have Steel Forge already."

"You're over-collateralized. We can rewrite it, increase the line."

Silence. Then, Arthur said. "It's not enough. Look, I'm not just talking about some *farkakte* loan committee. I've got to sell this to a syndicate."

Bankers, Jesus. Telemarketers, magazine salesmen, purveyors of slice and dice machines and magic cleaning compounds—they all contributed to the real economy. Even dope dealers and prostitutes provided in-demand goods and services for a fair compensation. But bankers? They were parasites, flimflam men who ran a Ponzi scheme called fractional reserve banking, and used the profits to buy legislation. The latest hustle? Get a bankrupt government to reduce interest rates to zero so they could pay the depositors nothing, then use the proceeds to buy Treasury bonds at two percent to prop up the bankrupt government. Harry didn't know who he pitied more, the politicians who sold their votes for a tiny fraction of what they were worth, or people like himself, who got rich, holding their nose, and playing along with the system.

"Okay, Arthur," he said now, "Tell me what it takes to make my little Shylock happy. How about my first-born son? You got the pound of flesh already."

"I *have* a first born son," Arthur said. "And if you know anybody willing to take him as collateral, I'll buy him dinner. In the meantime, you know what I need as well as I do. A downstream guarantee secured by liquid assets—no junk, understand? Investment grade paper, on deposit with the bank, single A or better."

"How much?"

"Give me two-fifty, I think I can sell it."

Harry could feel it in his stomach. "Is *that* all? Okay, I'll tell you what I'll do. A hundred and a half, and I keep the interest on the collateral."

Arthur Chasen laughed. "You should have been a been a comedian. Give me two hundred and I'll present it."

"One eighty -five and I keep the interest."

"Jesus. One ninety and I'll see what I can do."

Harry pressed the disconnect and spent a few minutes doing the math. How on earth he was going to put together a hundred ninety million dollars cash in a hundred twenty days or, more accurately, a hundred fifty days, giving himself thirty days to close the transaction. But come to think of it, given the options, it was an easy question. He checked his watch. Still only eight a.m. on the West Coast. He'd have to wait till he was back in his office. Then, it would be time to light a fire under Mr. Dick Duncan.

* * *

"It's all there is, dude. They got something going at Redwood State. Sorry." Pointing out the plate glass window to an electric blue glass and metal box, shimmering in the Global Rent-A-Car lot, the kid at the counter didn't sound overly apologetic. He'd already kept Eddie waiting ten minutes while he took a phone reservation for a wedding that apparently wasn't happening till September.

Following the kid's gaze, Eddie said. "What do you call that thing, anyway?"

"Nissan Cube," the clerk told him. "It's something, ain't it?"

"Interesting color."

"Bali Blue Metallic. ... But if you can wait till this afternoon, I think I got a Yaris coming in. I'm not sure what color it is, hold on a minute." He darted through a door behind the counter before Eddie could stop him.

A minute later, Shanna strolled in, wearing skintight ripped jeans and a fringed buckskin jacket, looking like a million bucks. She glanced at the empty counter. "What happened?"

"We started with the client welcome," Eddie told her, "Now we're into the vehicle selection process."

An hour and a half ago, Eddie woke Shanna from an interesting dream she was having. In the dream, she was rolling sevens and elevens in a casino she believed was the Bellagio. Someone put a big blue steel revolver on the pass line. She wanted to see who placed the bet, and was turning around to look when the phone rang. When she picked it, up Eddie told her he was calling from the South County Substation in Manzanita, and wanted her to pick him up. She asked him what happened to his truck.

"It flew off to its final rest," he said, "in that big junkyard in the sky."

Manzanita was a dozen miles south of Liberty on the 101 Freeway, a little town favored by hippies who moved up to Redwood County in the 1960s, deciding it was as far away from San Francisco as they cared to get. Now the town was an odd mix of Mill Valley and Cheyenne, Wyoming—liquor stores and head shops, barber shops and nail salons, French bakeries and chain saw repairs. There were two real estate brokers. There were also four law offices; two competing bail bond operations and a sheriff's substation, complete with a jail.

The substation was located in a squat khaki building at the end of a side street. When Shanna got there, Eddie was outside, talking to Norville Petty. They started walking over as she pulled up, and Shanna powered down her window.

"Hey, Norville," she called out "Everybody's talking about your boat."

He seemed pleased. "Is that right?"

"Yeah, they're all wondering how you're gonna pay for it on a sheriff's salary." She turned to Eddie. "Hey babe. Ready to go?"

Eddie sitting in the passenger seat on the way up to Redwood Bay, Shanna asked him what happened. He started with the guy following him in the

Silverado. When he got to the part where he pulled off at the 7-Eleven, then decided to go up the grade anyway, she said, "And your thinking was what? Your life was lacking excitement and you needed to turn up the volume?"

"What it is," he said, "I think I don't deal that well with anxiety. You know, waiting for shit to happen. I'd just as soon get it over with."

Shanna said she thought that was interesting, and asked him to go on. So, he did, telling her how the truck started coughing half way up the grade, and finally died in what was probably the worst possible place, a stretch of tight switch backs with a sheer drop and no shoulder on the downslope side of the road.

"There were a couple flares in the truck, so I laid them out at the edge of the road and started walking. It wasn't much, but I figured the first trucks in the morning would be headed up, not down, so it wouldn't matter." Then, Eddie was quiet a minute, remembering it. "But I was barely around the next bend before I heard a truck headed down. The road's so narrow up there, I was mainly hoping he didn't hit me. I tried waving him down, but …." He shook his head. "There was a crash, tires screaming, like he went into a skid."

"Do they know who it was?"

He hesitated "Not exactly. The truck's in a riverbed a thousand feet down. They flew over in a helicopter, but couldn't find a place to land. They'll hike in later today. What they do know is, a truck like the one that's down there was stolen out of the yard where Little Billy worked. I guess they fired him. His wife says he didn't come home last night. They found his car at a bar up in Sanchez Landing." He turned to look at her. "Why didn't you tell me the kid was a client of yours?"

"Because he isn't."

"That's not what Petty said."

"Oh, that," Shanna shook her head. "I just covered the bail hearing. Chris Cox, he has an office down the street, he was in trial, so I did him a favor."

"Who put up the bail for him?"

"Actually, I … don't know. Like I said, I just covered the hearing."

"What about his brothers?"

"What about them?"

"Petty asked me if I knew who Billy's brothers were. I said, my guess would be Harpo and Zeppo. He didn't seem to think it was funny."

He looked over, but Shanna didn't seem to think it was funny, either.

CHAPTER 14

LON AND HIS MAMA

Lon Odom was sitting on the sofa with Mama up at the trailer park in Tobago, the temperature in there ninety degrees at least, and humid, everything all sweaty, the way Mama liked it. Lon was flipping through the Yellow Pages looking for the listing, but couldn't find it.

He said, "I told you, Ma, it goes straight from 'umbrellas' to 'uniform rentals'. Ain't no 'undertakers' in there at all."

Next to him in her nightgown, hair still wet from the shower, staring at the TV screen, watching the *Bold and the Beautiful* with the sound turned down, but not completely off, Mama said, "Honey, you gonna tell me there's no undertakers in Redwood County? People die all the time around here, don't they?"

Lon knew they did, but didn't say anything.

"We had one took care of Albert after he had his accident, I recall."

"I don't remember about that. I think Big Billy did it."

Ma smiled, "Well, we burned his ass is what we done, honey. Scattered the ashes up at Wild River. I just don't remember who we got to do it is all." She thought a minute. "Marley, Morley, something with an 'm' in it. ... Look under coffins," Mama said.

Lon took a minute to look, then shook his head. "No coffins either. Coffee houses, then the next thing's coin dealers."

Mama patted him on his thigh. "Lemme see that, Lonny darling." She took the book out of his hands and paged through it, looking at the pictures. Mama didn't read all that good. She took off with a horse trucker when she was fourteen, and never had much education, is how she explained it.

"Got to be in here somewhere," she said, snuggling in close to him, wearing that lightweight bathrobe she had, you could more or less see through it, especially when it was wet, like it was at the moment. Most times, Mama didn't have a lot of clothes on. Didn't like being hemmed in is the way she put it.

"You should a seen me when I was your age," she used to say, strutting her stuff in front of her full-length mirror. "The men couldn't keep their hands off a me, and that's a fact, Lonny."

Lon got up now, headed for the kitchen. "Never mind, Ma," he said, "I'll go down the morgue later on. I'm pretty sure they got a list over there."

"Now, that's a real good idea, Lon honey." Mama was nodding now. "Ask for the prices before you make the arrangements, though. These undertaker types, they know how to fleece the loved ones in their hour of need. Son of a bitches more or less make a living at it."

Lon opened the refrigerator, brought back a couple of beers, handed one to Mama. "What do you wanna do about … you know, Big Billy?" he asked her. "Think we ought to send him a letter or something?"

Mama popped the tab and took a pull. "Big Billy will turn up when he turns up, sugar. I already got one boy to bury, that's enough for the present." She patted the spot next to her on the sofa. "Come sit down here a minute."

Lon sat down, Mama puts an arm around his shoulder, rubbed his back. "You're my big, blue-eyed boy, Lonny. Yes, you are. The Billys got them dark eyes like their no good daddy, but you was always blue eyed, like your Ma."

Lon felt his face flush.

"I just don't know what I'd do without you, if you was gone, baby."

Lon said, "I'm not going nowhere, Ma."

Mama sighed. "Well, that's what men say, Lonny. That sure is what they say. But then you catch 'em porkin' the pooch with some slut when they's supposed to be out changing a tire. Or you wake up one morning, the cereal box is empty, and they are flat out gone, honey."

Lon didn't say nothing. It didn't matter what you said when she got like this. She wasn't gonna listen anyway.

"This world's a cold, hard place, baby," she was saying now. "Even a rattlesnake will give you warning, but I'll tell you something, a man runs out on you? He won't give you no fucking warning at all."

She sat there awhile, curled up with her arms around his waist, staring at the TV screen, not saying anything, then finally got to it. "What I don't understand, Lon honey," she said, "is what Little Billy was doing running that truck up there in the woods, middle of the night. What do you suppose he was doing up there?"

Lon was quiet a minute, not exactly sure what he wanted to say. Finally, he shook his head, "Billy was a fuck up, Ma. You never knew what he was gonna do, 'cause *he* didn't know it either."

Ma didn't argue with that, just sat there watching the TV screen, but not really watching it. Finally, she said, "You think it had anything to do with the Piggott boys? How they fired him off his job? Maybe trying to get even?" Then, thinking about it, "I never did like the Piggotts. You know, there was a time, I knew their father."

"Yeah," Lon said it slow, not wanting things to go in that direction. There was an awful lot of Piggotts, "but they paid him out, Ma. He had a check on him. You know, severance?"

Mama didn't say anything for a minute, then turned to face him. "Is there something you're not telling me? You know I don't like secrets, Lonny."

Jesus, she was a piece of work. "What're you talking about, Ma?"

"You know what I'm talking about. He said something to you, didn't he?"

"No, Ma, he didn't say nothing," Lon shaking his head, and Mama giving him a sideways look like she knew he was lying. "Only—when he got out of jail, he did say something about … taking care of somebody."

"Taking care of somebody. Who was he talking about, Lonny?"

"I guess it was—" Lon rubbed a hand over his face. "You know, the fella put him in the hospital. The thing happened down at Liberty."

"What'd he say exactly. You know it's no sense holding out on me, Lonny."

Eventually, Lon wound up telling her what Billy said, how he was gonna take Fuentes out with his truck, though he didn't see any reason to tell her about the rest of the conversation.

Mama took some time with it. "Sounds like Billy all right."

"Billy was a jerk-off, Ma." Lon said, hoping she'd forget about it. "One damn thing after another."

Mama looked back at the TV. "It's not good to talk ill of the dead, Lon honey," she said. "Billy might have been wild, but he was a good boy. Like I always said, his problem was, he chased his damn pecker like a junkyard dog gone after a bone. Knocked up the first girl give him a hand job, wound up pussy whipped and nagged half to death. I told him not to marry that woman, as God is my witness I did. Her mama's a probation officer, what the hell'd he expect? But you know Billy, he wasn't gonna listen. He did what he did."

Ma seemed to be thinking. "You never did say what happened to the fella Billy was after. What'd you say his name was?"

"Fuentes."

"Fuentes," she repeated it. "He work for the Mexicans?"

"He's a cop," Lon told her. "Used to be, anyway. It was in the papers."

"How come there wasn't nothing on the news about him."

Lon drank some beer. "Wasn't nothing to tell. Billy totaled the man's truck up there, but I don't guess he was in it. That's what Barry Stroh said."

Mama took some time, staring at the TV. "Don't seem right, they had to scrape Billy up off of that river bottom, and the other fella just walked away from it," shaking her head now, "Don't hardly seem right, Lonny."

What Lon was thinking, he ought to buy this Fuentes a fucking case of sour mash whiskey. But of course, you couldn't say a thing like that to Mama.

* * *

Sitting behind the oversized redwood desk, custom built for R. T. Matheson, and surrounded by archival logging photos museum framed with UV glass and carefully hung on custom redwood paneled walls, Dick Duncan was listening as his wife, Jennifer, brought him up to date on the important events in her challenging and busy life.

"Jody has soccer practice after school, and she really needs my support," she was telling him. "I don't know what it is that makes her so insecure, I really don't, but Dr. Rosen says she's in a critical phase, so I don't see how I can *not* put in an appearance."

"Mmm." Dick put Jennifer on the speaker, and strolled over to the telescope, trained on the steep, evergreen hills across the freeway from his office.

"After that," Jennifer was saying, "I promised I'd take her to the mall. But I have to tell you, the odds we'll be able to find anything even remotely acceptable at that place, are slim to none."

"Mmm." Dick said again, pivoting the scope on its tripod, angling it down now to a white frame house on a cul-de-sac across the freeway. And there it was again, the low rider Silverado, parked out front while the man of the house, Lt. Colonel Walter J. Hellman, U.S. Army, Retired, was at a meeting on security response training issues at West Coast Lumber Company, a meeting to which Dick had been invited, but had declined.

"This place," Jennifer was going on, "Is a fashion wilderness. You have to go to San Francisco for anything at all decent. Speaking of which, Mother called."

At the telescope, Dick was panning the scene, moving past the Silverado to the walkway, past a sign warning that the property was monitored by 24-hour video surveillance. He was searching for a window, located in the L-shaped master suite recently added at the back of the house. Hoping against hope the love of fresh air previously exhibited by Hellman's young wife would once again overcome her desire for privacy, and ... he felt himself smile. Once again, fresh air had prevailed.

"She wants us to come down for Jason's birthday. They're taking the boat out. Can you believe it? In November? They'll have to scrape our frozen remains off the foredeck. But I don't see how we can possibly say no, do you?"

At the telescope, Dick said, "Mmm."

"What did you say? Dick, are you even listening to me?"

"Of course I am."

" Dick, did you put me on the speaker? You know I hate it when you put me on the speaker. Like it's too much effort to hold onto the goddamn telephone."

Jennifer went on.

And meanwhile, there it was. The young woman, tall, slim, but with amazingly big boobs, was there with the little Mexican, her dark hair flying, riding him like a fucking bronco. Dick was captivated by this woman, dying to know her story. Who was she? Married to the superannuated Hellman, living in a white frame house in a small town, but out there living life to the fullest. He tried to imagine Jennifer riding him like that. Christ, riding anyone like that. He'd like to see it—he didn't care who it was.

"I thought we'd take Jason," Jennifer was saying now. "There's some new kind of Nikes he has to have, and he's outgrown absolutely everything anyway. While we're there I thought we could stop for dinner."

Dick said, "Mmm hmm."

"It's Alicia's night off, so you'll have to fend for yourself. There's some Lean Cuisines in the freezer, or if you don't like that, you can pick something up on your way home from the office."

Suddenly the intercom went off, bringing Dick out of his semi-reverie. "Mr. Saul on line two."

"Right with him," he called out, then picked up phone, "Jen, gotta go. Boss is on the other line."

"I thought *you* were the boss," she said.

He pressed a different extension button, and was instantly talking to Harriman Saul. "Harry, how's the new airplane?"

"Expensive," Harry said. "Where are we on this Watershed business?"

"We're ... still putting the pieces together," Dick said, "But it looks promising."

"*Promising*," Harry said, "is a kid who hits .300 in Triple A, before they bring him up to the majors. We need to put this thing on a schedule."

Music to his ears. Dick said, "Don't worry. We'll get it closed. Give me a couple weeks."

"How long to build the road?"

"Two months."

"Wrong answer." Silence on the line for a few seconds, then Harry said, "Tell me something. On the helicopters, the number you gave me, you can't do any better than that?"

Dick felt his stomach tighten. "I thought you said no helicopters."

"I know what I said. Now I'm saying, call them back, tell them to sharpen their pencils, see if we can get a better number."

Dick took a deep breath, "Helicopter logging isn't janitorial services, Harry," he said. "There's only a handful of companies in the business, and they *talk* to each other."

That shut the prick up for a minute. Then he said, "Okay, Dick. I need to generate two hundred million cash in one hundred days. You're the boss, you tell me. How do we do it?"

Dick thought a minute. "Go 24/7 on the road. It's been done before. Probably shave a month off the schedule. You'll pay overtime, though."

"Put together the numbers."

Dick felt himself smiling again. "We'll ... need to file for the permits right away, to get the ball rolling. But I'll tell you, if these people find out we filed to build a road on property we don't own, the price is going to go up."

Harry Saul said, "Then make sure they don't find out."

*   *   *

The Doctor pulled a small set of pruners from the pocket of his long, white lab coat, snipped a bud spike and held it up for Russell to sniff.

"You smell the hints of lime and hibiscus?"

Russell said he wasn't sure.

"Waipi'o hapa," the Doctor said. "A window on the universe. Don't smoke it if you have anywhere to go." He dropped the spike in a little plastic baggie. "Don't forget to dry it when you get home. Mildew doesn't add a thing to the experience."

He moved to another bush, plucked another spike, his motions smooth, effortless for a big man. The Doctor was at least six-three, maybe two-twenty, but narrow in the shoulders, and wide in the hips, not fat exactly, but built like a woman. "This one is called Outer Space, but don't pay any attention to that. The effects are more cerebral than otherworldly." He smiled. "The people who come up with the names smoke too much of the product.."

Since it was the season, the Doctor had insisted on giving Russell a walking tour of his private greenhouse. People who knew the Doctor, knew he lived at the Costa Perdida, but even the people who'd been out there didn't really know exactly where it was. He'd send a car to pick you up in Manzanita and a beefy driver would put you in the back with a set of window shades pulled down. Still, Russell had been out here enough that he knew the turns. And when they hung a left, a mile from the coast, and drove into a canyon, he knew something was up. A few minutes later, the car pulled to a stop in front of what turned out to be the Doctor's experimental greenhouse. Apparently he was in for a tour.

A half hour later, getting dark now, Russell was trying to seem interested, nodding as they walked past rows of seemingly perfect plants, the Doctor pointing out the various varieties and their attributes, providing samples, each in a separate bag: Pineapple Train Wreck, Sour Diesel, Purple Haze, Green Goblin. It wasn't that Russell didn't like weed. He did. And, as everybody knew, the Doctor grew the best. But weed wasn't why he was out here, and he was feeling a bit antsy, trying to turn the conversation to something else.

"The dirty little secret of *sinsemilla* cultivation," the Doctor was telling him now, in one of his didactic moods, "is frustration of the reproductive function. The female of the species produces flowers, and secretes a thick, sticky resin to attract the pollinating bees. Unfortunately, *we* have destroyed all the male plants. So, there isn't any pollen. Since there isn't any pollen, there can't be fertilization. No fertilization, no seed. *Sinsemilla.* No seed, no reproduction." The Doctor smiled. "Of course, the female doesn't know that." He glanced at his bodyguard, Wayne, who smiled back at him, then looked at Russell, and winked.

"As the days grow shorter," the Doctor was saying, "she secretes more resin, trying to draw the pollinators. But we have made sure pollination never happens." He looked at Russell. "Sadistic in a way, isn't it?"

Russell said, "I've heard worse."

The Doctor raised an eyebrow. "Such as."

"Take away a man's land, rape his women, kidnap his children and turn them into slaves." Russell glanced at the Polynesian, but the guy just stood there grinning, probably stoned.

The Doctor sighed. "Native Americans, torn from the land, swindled, lied to, locked up on reservations, infected with the white man's diseases. Really, the Trail of Tears? I'm disappointed, Russell."

"You asked the question."

"You're right." The Doctor said. "I'm over-reacting. Every son with a Jewish mother has a history with guilt."

Russell shrugged, "I'm not into guilt. The winner gets to write the history, isn't that what they say?"

"That's what they say."

Russell saw an opening now. He took some time, "But you know, what interests me. The thing about writing history doesn't seem to apply to you."

The Doctor looked puzzled. "Apply to who?"

"The Jews. They were a tribe, right? Twelve tribes, the Bible says, but ten were lost. Scattered after the Romans destroyed the Temple. Outcasts, hounded everywhere they went, put on reservations."

"I'm not getting your point."

"They didn't win any wars. Anyway, none I know about. They got kicked out of Spain. Slaughtered in Russia. The Nazis almost wiped them out. But the thing is, they wound up controlling the narrative, know what I mean?

Writing the history. Got their own country, joined the middle class. They run Hollywood, the financial industry, the Treasury, the Federal Reserve."

"And you want to know their secret. ... Well, to start with, your premise is flawed. It isn't the people who *fight* the wars who win them. It's the financiers."

Then, the Doctor told him the story. How the Church told the Christians they couldn't lend money, and the Christians told the Jews they couldn't own land. And how the Jews made the best of it, lending money, which, in those days, meant gold. But the gold was heavy and people didn't want to carry it around. So, the Jews issued receipts. Whoever held the receipt owned the gold. The receipts became money. The great contribution of the Jews, according to the Doctor, was they discovered you could issue a lot more receipts than you actually had gold.

Russell told the Doctor that sounded like fraud.

The Doctor said, "Well, it was, but it was useful. There wasn't enough gold to finance the wars." He paused. "There never is—unless you constantly devalue your currency, and no one wants to do that 'cause it makes it obvious that you're broke. Things are more complicated now, but essentially they haven't changed. You deposit money in the bank and think it's yours, but it isn't. The bank keeps a few percent and loans out the rest. The equity requirement is four percent. And even that's just another form of debt. Take a twenty dollar bill to the Federal Reserve, tell them you want to cash it in, and see what you get. Another twenty-dollar bill. That's all it is. A piece of paper."

Russell was trying to keep up with this, all stuff he hadn't thought about before.

"Is it fraud?" The Doctor went on. "You bet it is. The greatest Ponzi scheme in history. But, like I said, it's useful. Let's them pay for things they can't afford." He looked at Russell now. "I assume this is about the Indians."

Russell nodded.

"You have tribal sovereignty."

Russell smiled. "I don't see us printing money."

"What about the casino?"

"Seems like we're late to the party. Being a sovereign nation, they can take our land and cram us into a Rancheria without paying compensation, but we still need their fucking approval to build a casino on the Godforsaken piece of shit we got left."

The Doctor put an arm around Russell's shoulder now, walking him toward the greenhouse door, past the lush rows of cannabis, ripe for the harvest. "You know, when we came up here from San Francisco, things were simple; people left us alone." He shook his head sadly. "Now, here we are, victims of the global economy with the Mexicans. Our lives thrown into turmoil because some Wall Street bandito wakes up with a new desire for the illusion of control."

He started to smile. "I'm told our friend, Harriman Saul, wants to buy an airline. Can you even imagine the level of self-deception involved in *wanting* to *own* an *airline*?" He chuckled. "Just between you and me, I think old Harriman could be riding for a fall."

Outside now, the driver with the back door open, ready for Russell to get in, the Doctor stopped and looked at him. "Has your friend decided to sell his land?"

"What else is he going to do with it?"

The Doctor raised an eyebrow. "He could always grow dope."

"The kids are running a con. I just hope old Eddie hasn't lost his edge. I'd like to see him wind up with a few bucks."

"Edge?" The Doctor seemed interested. "I thought he was a cop."

"Back in the day." Russell said, "he used to hustle pool."

The Doctor clapped his hands. "Fast Eddie! Like in the movies. Was he any good?"

Russell said, "The thing with Eddie, when you saw him shoot, he never looked that sharp. On the other hand, when it came time to count the money, he never seemed to lose."

Russell started to get in the car, but the Doctor hadn't quite finished. "About the casino," he said, "I think I have an idea. The secret of the Jews was, they gave the Christians something for nothing—well, nothing for nothing, it was kind of a scam, but most folks didn't know that. .... Your people used to *trade* with the white man back in the day, right?"

"Furs and shit, sure."

"Well, we need to keep up with the times. Give them an object of their desire, solve their problems for them." He broke into a smile, patting Russell on the shoulder. "You know, there *are* people who say, long before the white man came, the lost tribes of Israel settled right here in America."

* * *

Wayne Mehana loved everything about the Doctor's new Tesla Model S— the dark green color, the clean sleek lines, the tan leather interior, the awesome way it handled. The problem was the conditions he got to drive it in. At night, in the fog, on winding roads that led back and forth to nowhere—from small town Manzanita to the Doctor's deserted house at the coast. The problem was, Wayne thought, he was just like the Tesla— capable of doing so much more.

It was dark now, coming back from the greenhouse. Wayne had dropped the Indian in Manzanita, then gone back to the greenhouse to pick up the Doctor. The road was deserted, winding its way through the fog. And Wayne was thinking about the lights of San Francisco. A million miles from this deserted hole. Down there last weekend, Todd Manoa— his boyfriend—asked him what it was like working for the Doctor. Wayne told him, "Equal parts *Pulp Fiction, The Matrix,* and *The Big Lebowski*". Todd got a kick out of that, and it was true. But what Wayne didn't tell him, it wasn't his description. It was Roger's.

Wayne had met Roger Bachman four years ago at a place called Five Card Stud on Harrison Street, South of Market. Wayne was worried at the time he'd get sent back to Christchurch because he overstayed his tourist visa. Wayne's friend, Ahmadu, a Nigerian who tended bar at the place, pointed to a tall, handsome guy standing in the back. The man was dressed in the most beautiful suit Wayne had ever seen—light grey, double breasted sheer wool flannel—super 150s Loro Piana or anyway, something like it—a straight collar broadcloth shirt and a hand painted silk tie that looked like Joan Miro. Wayne asked Ahmadu who he was. Ahmadu said he was a lawyer, and Wayne should hook up, maybe he could help with the immigration problem.

It turned out Roger Bachman—that's who it was—was at least as magnificent close up as he was across the room. He had these perfect, chiseled features and sparkling eyes, almost black, that seemed to say, "Honey, nothing could possibly be worth worrying about. Why not lighten up and enjoy the show?" It made you relax just looking at him.

Wayne surprised himself, walked right up and came on with a line, asked if anyone ever told him he looked like Cary Grant. Roger raised an eyebrow, "Not Montgomery Clift?" Like it was a joke, like everything was. Then, "Do I hear an accent." When Wayne started to tell him, he held up his hand. "No, let me guess. New Zealand?" That was another one of his talents, he could tell by the way they talked where people were from. Not just different countries, but states, even parts of states. He'd say, "You're from New York. Don't tell me where. South Shore, Long Island. Five Towns, am I right?"

They hit it off right away. When Wayne told Roger about his immigration problem, Roger said, "Honey, if I were the ICE man, I'd lock you up myself," and winked, but then went on, "The Feds aren't going to pick you up unless you commit a felony. You wouldn't commit a *felony* ... now would you?"

When they got to know each other better, Wayne found out Roger didn't live in San Francisco. He split his time between a condo on Russian Hill and a few other places, commuting back and forth in an airplane he flew himself. Another thing Wayne found out, the bar where he and Roger met, belonged to Roger. He used it as a way of ... recruiting talent, he said.

"I wanted something that combined the Rainbow Room with the Bar from Star Wars." He smiled. "But this is close enough, don't you think?"

That was another thing Roger did—combining things. Like the job with the Doctor. Roger said it was "Part narco, part ninja, part nanny." Looking back, the way he described it, he was right.

"Turn the heat up, will you, Wayne?" the Doctor was saying now. "Just a little."

"No problem," Wayne nudged the passenger side thermostat up a couple of degrees.

In the beginning, doing the drops, handling the collections, it was an adrenaline rush. The money was great; he bought clothes, hooked up, tasted the party life, even bought a Lexus-IFS racer. It was like time travel after Christchurch, fucking place stuck in the 1950s. Yeah, it was all good. Until that one day it wasn't. That one day Roger was gone.

"What have you heard from the Salvadoran?" The Doctor asked him now, bringing Wayne back to the present.

"Nobody's saying anything much."

"And how's your boyfriend?"

"Todd? He's good. They're giving him more playing time. Say he'll probably start next time somebody goes down." Wayne's boyfriend, Todd, was an offensive left tackle with the 49ers, and got three million a year for playing one day a week, if that. With Roger gone, Wayne thought, it was too bad he never learned the sport. He picked up Karate down under, Qigong and Dim-Mak in Hawaii. But realistically, what was the market?

"Are they in town?"

"The Niners? Right. At home against the Seahawks Sunday."

"What's the line?"

"Seahawks by three and half. But Todd says, the money's on the dog."

"Well," The Doctor said, "He's prejudiced." His eyes narrowed in thought. "I'll tell you what. As long as they're in town, why don't you go down for the game? See if you can find anything out."

CHAPTER 15

DARRYL'S CASE

They had Ramón Delgado in an interview room on the fourth floor of the Federal Building, 1301 Clay, Downtown Oakland, Darryl Waters and Doug Vanowen, Vanowen senior on the case.

He said to Darryl, "What do you say we do this by the numbers."

Darryl glanced over at Ramón, the dude maybe five seven, one-forty, head shaved, diamond ear studs, bright red do-rag, black fatigue pants three sizes too big. Darryl shrugged. "Up to you, you want to take the time."

Vanowen said, "Ramón's never been busted federal, I think we owe it to him, you know, lay it out, give him the picture. Okay with you, Ramón?"

Ramón said, "Fuck you, asshole. I want my attorney. I told you that already."

Darryl said, "You showing your ignorance, Ramón, the man here trying to give you some information not gonna cost you nothing."

Ramón gave him the finger.

Ramón Delgado had been busted in San Leandro with 800 grams, pure MDMA powder and a couple thousand gel caps in the trunk of his electric blue Nissan GT-R. They were trying to roll him over, get him to identify his source.

Vanowen held up the pamphlet, "Ramón, this here is called the Federal Sentencing Guidelines, lays out the mandatory minimums for every offense chargeable under federal law. Judge has nothing to do with it. You got that? These are mandatory."

Darryl said, "Mandatory mean 'must happen', Ramón. Convicted on the crime, you do the time."

Ramón said. "I told you, I'm not talking."

Vanowen said, "Okay. How it works? It's real simple. You go to the book, look up the *crime*, it tells you the *time*. Simple as that. So, okay, first off, Molly—unfortunately for you, Ramón—see that is a Schedule I Hallucinogen. 800 grams puts you right up there at a Base Offense Level 38."

Darryl said, "Murder One's at 43, Ramón just to give you some idea. 38, you stepped up to the big time."

Vanowen said, "Okay the next part, after we determine the Base Offense Level, we calculate the *crime history points*. System gives you three points for every sentence longer than a year and a month. In your case, two felony priors, that's six points there, plus another two for commission of the present offense within two years after release on your last prior. Total, we got eight points, Ramón, puts you in Category IV." Vanowen showed it to him on the chart.

"Now see the way we do this, Ramón, we read *across* the chart here, get the Crime History Category, then we read *down* to the Offense Level. You see that? Category IV. Put it together with Offense Level 38, what do we get? You see the numbers there? 324 to 405? That's months, Ramón. 324 months. You do the math, divide by 12, you're looking at 27 years."

Darryl said, "Mandatory federal time, Ramón. Twenty-seven years."

The guy, Ramón, looked like somebody hit him with a hammer. Dude couldn't be more than twenty-four, twenty-five, looking at more time inside than he spent outside his whole life.

Darryl said, "You want your lawyer now, Ramón, you go ahead, make the call, we can arrange that for you."

Vanowen said, "I thought I'd tell him about the other part first."

Darryl said, "C'mon, didn't you hear the man? Ramón here already told us to fuck off, said he wants to talk to his attorney."

"I guess you're right, " Vanowen said. "Okay, Ramón, you got an attorney, or do you need a public defender appointed to represent you?"

Ramón said, "Hold on a minute. What other part?"

Vanowen said, "Well, the Guidelines have Part K, and there's a section in there, 5K1 called 'Substantial Assistance to Authorities.'"

Ramón said, "What's that part say?"

Vanowen read the part that lets the judge impose a lighter sentence if the government files a motion, saying the defendant provided substantial assistance in the investigation.

Darryl said, "What that means, Ramón, you cooperate with us, tell us where you got the Molly, we could put in the word, tell the court to go easy on you."

Ramón looked from Darryl to Vanowen and back again. Finally, he said, "How easy?"

*   *   *

You could drive from Redwood County to Oakland in four hours, if you set your mind to it—hang in the right hand lane except to pass, keep your eyes open for black and whites. The Cube wasn't a bad car to do it in, either— not the kind of high power vehicle likely to attract the attention of law enforcement. But Eddie wasn't up for pushing it today. He was up for letting it roll by, redwoods to live oaks, mountains to rolling hills, forests to ranches, orchards, dairy farms; into the housing tracts and big box retail, garden apartments, then into strip malls and freeway clutter. Traffic picked up in Santa Rosa, tightened into San Rafael, lightened heading east over the Richmond Bridge, and crawled into Oakland.

It was five o'clock when Eddie pulled into downtown, streets filling up, people getting off work. Eddie kind of related to Oakland: gritty step-kid looking across the Bay at the glitter of San Francisco, choking on the rich kid's smog, but not asking for apologies, and not giving any, either. Eddie lived in the city ten years, felt as much at home here as anywhere. Which wasn't saying much.

The Federal Building was on Clay, twin steel and glass towers with a bridge in between. Eddie cruised past, took a right on Broadway, and headed back under Interstate 980 toward police headquarters. A few minutes later he was walking into a bar called Seville's, a hangout for local law enforcement. Seville's was where Eddie met Karen when she was a secretary in the DA's office. That was before she went to paralegal school, got a job in criminal defense, and began working her way up to marital infidelity.

Walking in now, letting his eyes adjust to the warm, dim light, Eddie heard a familiar voice. "Damn! My man, Eddie Fuentes. How you doing?"

Eddie smiled. "Hey, Mack. How you doing?"

"Doin' all right, can't complain. Nobody listen if I did. Yeah, I didn't know if I'd see you again, moved on up there to *God's* country, busy with all the animals, and shit."

"You got it right about the animals," he said.

Mack McCutcheon was a big man, six-three, two sixty and black as coal, sitting on his usual stool at the end of the bar drinking what Eddie assumed was bourbon. Mack broke Eddie in at Vice, then he moved over to Homicide in the Criminal Investigation Division. He was about as tuned in to what's going on in town as anyone, which is why Eddie was here. Shanna had asked Eddie to have a talk with Darryl. He said he would, but wanted to talk to Mack first.

Eddie ordered Jack Daniels over ice and bought Mack a refill, Old Granddad neat, plain water back. "Blood pressure medication," he called it.

Mack took a sip of his drink, the big man delicate with his hands, picking the glass up with a sapphire pinky ring extended. "Heard about your father," he said. "I'm sorry. Shit can be hard, I know. Emotional ties among family members ...."

"Mack?" Eddie interrupted him. "We weren't that close."

"Mmm." Mack tilted his head to look over. "I *heard* that. *My* old man? Took off like a bluebird in a snowstorm before I's even born. Never even knew the man's name for sure." He took another sip of his drink. "So, what are we talking about? I figure you got some reason you're here."

"Darryl Waters."

Now Mack was smiling. "Dar-ryl Wa-ters." He said the name slowly. "What kind of business you got with my man, Darryl, you don't mind my asking?"

"Nothing personal," Eddie told him. "I have a friend Darryl's been talking to, knows I was in law enforcement, asked me to see check him out, see where he's coming from."

Mack nodded. "Well, I don't know what kind of business your friend has with Darryl, but generally speaking, where Darryl's coming from, is the 'hood, if you understand what I'm saying. Deep-C. Iron Triangle. City of Richmond. Not too many getting outta there alive. You got to hand it to the man on that. Cal State, degree in Law Enforcement. Landed a job working for the state, looking into workers' compensation fraud."

"I thought he was federal."

Mack took another sip of his drink. "We gonna get to that part, but you need to hear the other part first. See, what the state job was, say a claim's made don't look quite right, they send somebody like Darryl out to investigate. But the thing with Darryl was, when he went out, seemed like he'd hardly ever find fraud."

"Soft hearted," Eddie said.

"Thrifty, too. Quit a couple years later with a brand new wardrobe and a convertible Corvette. Thing is, it's a whole lot harder to take the *hood* out of a brother, than it is to take a *brother* out of the hood."

Eddie smiled. "And he's DEA now?"

"Fighting the war on drugs over there on Clay Street. Working with an old friend of yours."

"What friend is that?"

"Doug Vanowen."

Eddie looked at him, surprised. "Vanowen? I thought he was...."

Mack shook his head. "Let him finish his twenty."

Eddie said, "You mean ... he retired? I don't get it."

Mack chuckled. "Way the story goes, his old lady couldn't stand the man hanging around the house. Got in the way of her long established lifestyle. ... It wound up, she divorced ol' Doug, the way those things work, half his pension went with her."

Eddie grinned, not too torn up, hearing Doug Vanowen got at least part of what he had coming. Vanowen was part of the bad old days — shakedowns, takedowns, and breakdowns, the way Mack used to put it.

Now he said, "What's up with Darryl, though, you deal with the man, you got to understand, he don't see law enforcement in his future plans."

"No?"

Mack shook his head. "Darryl sees himself moving up in the world. Got himself a law degree out of Golden Gate University. Gonna be the next Johnnie Cochran, if you remember. Johnnie started off with the D.A., most folks don't know that."

"Darryl's a lawyer?"

"Not yet, " shaking his head. "Got to pass the bar exam first. Word is, he flunked the damn thing half a dozen times already."

"But he's playing it straight. With the DEA, I mean."

"Far as a I know." Mack thought a minute, then checked his watch. "I tell you what, though. It's getting on suppertime. How about we find a place, see if you find something you like on the menu."

Mmm. The Friday Night Bites—Fat Boy's, West Oakland, serving up the World Famous All-U-Can-Eat Bar-B-Q Buffet Supreme. Darryl liked to drop by when he was in the area, Fat Boy ribs with the Bar-B-Q beans being a little slice of paradise, far as he was concerned.

Except, fifteen minutes into it when old Mack McCutcheon shuffled in. The man headed his way, wearing his usual—the rumple ass sport coat over a funky plaid shirt, knit tie didn't match either one, no taste to the man at all. Man with him not much better, white dude in Levi's and an old leather jacket with a plain, white shirt underneath. Darryl was thinking the white dude looked a little bit like the guy played the lawyer in an old movie he saw once, only that dude was older at the time. Lawyer was a drunk, got in over his head, up against a big time law firm in a personal injury case. Darryl liked watching movies with lawyers in them, pick up on the attitude, mannerisms and so forth. The guy with Mack didn't look much like a lawyer, though. He looked more like a cop.

Now, Mack was at the table with that gorilla grin. He said, "Tell me that ain't your BMW parked by the fire hydrant out there."

Darryl wiped his mouth off with a napkin, "Why? You gonna give me a ticket?"

Mack turned to the white dude, "See, I knew it was his on account of the parking job, half on the sidewalk, half on the street. Man never did know how to drive." Then, to Darryl. "What happened to the Corvette. You crack it up?"

"Shit." Darryl shook his head. "Dog, you behind the times. Man's ride got to go with his lifestyle, you understand, reflect his occupational trajectory."

Mack turned to the white guy. "What Darryl's trying to say, he's an attorney, sees his career in law enforcement's temporary." Then, to Darryl, "But I don't suppose you passed the bar exam yet, did you? Otherwise, you'd be sending out cards."

"Don't hold your breath," Darryl picked up a rib. "I'll be sending my cards out soon enough. And when I do, one thing's for sure. You not on the list."

Mack said to the white dude. "Darryl be my man," then, to Darryl, "Uh, mind if we sit down?" Not exactly asking, Mack slid his big butt into the booth, shoving Darryl into the corner. The white guy slid in across. Mack motioned in his direction. "This here's Eddie Fuentes. He's an old friend of mine, used to work vice down here, till he retired to the country." Meanwhile, Mack was looking at the ribs. "Fat Boys! Damn, those ribs looks *good*. You don't mind, do you?" He picked one up, started gnawing on it.

Darryl looked at the white guy, then back to Mack. "You *gentlemen* got some business with me? On account of, otherwise, I'm eating my dinner."

The white dude said, "Couple of questions, Darryl, if you don't mind."

Mack was looking around, "You got a napkin? Oh, yeah, never mind." He reached across Darryl's plate, took a couple out of a holder, wiped his fingers. "Shit's *messy*, is the problem with it."

The white dude said, "You been talking to a friend of mine up in Redwood Bay, a lawyer name of Shanna Black?"

Darryl said, "Well, if I *am* talking, which I'm not saying one way or the other, that would be DEA business, and I wouldn't be discussing it with an ex-vice cop from Oakland, would I?"

Now, Mack was fumbling with his rib, like he couldn't hold on to it. "Man, this some slippery shit!" Suddenly, it flew out of his hand and landed in Darryl's lap.

"God *damn*!"

"Oh, I'm sorry. Did I mess up on your suit? Here, lemme fix it." Mack took a napkin, rubbing the bar-b-q shit around on Darryl's pants.

"Man, gimme that. Shit! You know how much this suit cost?" The suit happened to be a pin stripe Armani, thirteen hundred retail —but cost Darryl a hundred twenty from wholesale sources. He grabbed some napkins from the holder, dipped them in his water glass, dabbed at his pants, but not doing much good.

Meantime, Mack had another rib, waving it back and forth as he spoke. "See the thing is, Darryl," he was saying, "When the man ask you a question, you supposed to give an answer. How a conversation work."

Darryl didn't say anything, and the white dude went on, "This friend of mine, you offered her a deal. You said you got her making payoffs to law enforcement, but you're willing to let it go if she gives up one of her clients—the one she's making the payoffs for."

Darryl said, "If you know so much, what you bothering *me* about?"

"Uh-oh!!" Mack started juggling his rib again … and it wound up on Darryl's suit coat.

"Mother*fucker*!" Darryl picked the rib off his coat, tossed it back on the plate. "Man, you crazy, you know that?" What he wanted to do was get the hell *out* of here, but that gorilla, McCutcheon, had him boxed in.

The white guy was talking now. "Simple question, Darryl. If you got the sheriff, what do you need the lawyer for?"

Darryl was dabbing at his suit coat. He said, "Shit, man! I got to spell it out for you? Sheriff can't give us dick, on account of the client don't deal with the man direct. That's what the lawyer's for. Lawyer can't testify against the client, on account of it's a 'privileged communication,' you understand? But the way the Task Force worked it out, we gonna get the lawyer to wear a wire, get things digitally recorded, so all she got to say on the stand is, she wore the wire. Not providing testimony against the client, if you get the difference."

"Can you do that?"

Darryl smiled. "Case out of Miami, *United States* vs *Ofshe.*" He spelled it. "O-F-S-H-E, check it out."

"But the lawyer told you she won't go along."

"Won't say either way. Playing games, how it is. Folks on the task force getting tired, tell you the truth. USA's looking for headlines. Not interested in what she call some two-bit bust."

The white dude took a few seconds. "Suppose I could get her to go along."

Darryl shrugged. "We might be interested in that," he said. "And we might not."

The white guy looked at him.

"Things change, my man, hear what I'm saying? Let's say we busted a dealer, two-time loser, looking at thirty years in the slam. Say the dude could give us the mule does the drops, handles collections. We don't need the lawyer if we flip the mule."

Fuentes said, "He's probably got a felony sheet."

"Could be. We not that far into it."

"The lawyer's a better witness. ... Besides, without her, all you have on the sheriff is tax fraud. She could get you bribery."

Darryl thought about it, shrugged. "Bribery's FBI. Public Corruption Unit. They part of the Task Force, but I don't report to those dudes." Darryl looked at him. "What are you, her fucking lawyer?"

"No." The white dude said, giving him his deadeye look now. "I'm her fucking bodyguard. Tell your boss if he wants the deal, it's full use immunity ... and she'll need protection till the client is behind bars, and a new identity after."

He played with the saltshaker a minute. "Just one more thing and I'll let you get back to your dinner." Looking at Darryl now, "Roger Bachman— tell me what you know about him."

CHAPTER 16

AT SHANNA'S HOUSE

Late afternoon in her office, Shanna and Russell were sitting at the big, racetrack plate glass desk with Eric and Rhonda, the Eco-Resistors both wearing their Thomas collars today, but with subtle wardrobe differences. Eric had on a chambray shirt and Levis, both neatly pressed; Rhonda wore desert camouflage fatigue pants and a black tee shirt that said, "Fuck Harriman Saul" in big, red letters. Russell had just finished explaining a plan he and the Doctor had cooked up for the next phase of the demonstrations. Shanna wasn't wild about it, but couldn't really say anything under the circumstances. She was hoping Eric might do it for her.

Rotating his Thomas collar thoughtfully, he said, "Yeah, man. I don't know."

Turning in her chair, Rhonda said, "You don't *know*?"

Eric said, "Yeah, I'm … gonna have to think about it."

Rhonda said, "Think about what? What's there to think about?"

Eric tried to look at her without turning his head too much. "See, that's your problem, Rhonda. Know what I mean? You just … *do* … shit without thinking ahead, about the consequences."

"What *consequences*? It's not like nobody did it before. Remember, Julia what's her name? Look at the *coverage* she got. She got a *book deal* out of it, for Christ sake."

Eric fingered his Thomas collar, not saying anything.

"And that other guy?" Rhonda went on, "Nate something or other?"

"Whatever," Eric mumbled, "I don't see what that it's got to do with us. We gotta make decisions based on our own situation."

Rhonda said, "Well I think it's a great idea. Count me in."

Eric and Rhonda were both looking at Shanna now, hoping she'd agree with them, when Russell stepped in. He looked at Eric and said, "What is it, dude? You don't want to blow your lawsuit?"

Eric said, "Well, think about it. They introduce testimony, photographs. How's it gonna look. I mean, I am, obviously, you know, out there. You'd have to put up a website with a video feed, live chat, a Facebook page, an active Twitter feed. I'd be doing interviews. Extremely high visibility ...."

Russell interrupted. "Eric?" He waited for Eric to look at him, then said, "We weren't thinking about you."

Eric looked from Russell to Shanna. They both shook their heads.

"You mean?"

They both nodded, looking at Rhonda.

Just then, the telephone rang, and she hit the intercom button. "What is it, Donald?"

Donald said, "Can you speak to an Eddie Fuentes?"

Shanna held up one finger, picked up the phone, and walked to the window. "You're back."

Standing on the porch of Matty's cabin, talking on his cell, Eddie said, "Shanna? Can you hear me?"

Shanna said. "You're cutting out, but keep talking."

Eddie said, "Listen, I'm at the cabin. I found something. I want to show it to you."

"Mmm. I found something I want to show you, too." There was a smile in her voice. "When do you want to do it?"

"I can be there in an hour and a half."

She said, "Meet me at home and I'll make dinner."

Eddie asked her if there was anything she wanted him to bring.

The smile still in her voice, she said, "Yeah, bring desert," and gave him directions.

After they hung up, Eddie went back inside, sat down at the kitchen table, looking at a document, a printed form that said, "Quitclaim Deed" at the top. Under that, there was language indicating that "Mateo Fuentes" did hereby remise, release and forever quitclaim to "Mateo Fuentes and Edward F. Fuentes, as joint tenants," certain property in Redwood County, this followed by a legal description it was impossible to make any sense of. The deed was dated a couple years earlier, and had apparently been notarized, but there was nothing to show it had been filed in the public records. Joint tenants— Eddie wasn't sure what it meant. Did it mean his father wanted to give him half the property and, if it did, why would he want to do it?

Matt Fuentes wasn't the trusting kind. He didn't trust neighbors; he didn't trust the government; and he didn't trust banks. That's how Eddie found the deed. It was in a cache under a closet floor together with other stuff Eddie knew he'd have— guns and cash. There was an AR-15, a 12 gauge Mossberg, a blue steel .45 Colt, three thousand rounds of assorted ammunition and a thousand dollars in cash, Matty apparently expecting a war either before or after a run on the banks.

What Eddie didn't expect was in a green metal box under the guns, arranged in two manila envelopes. The first had legal stuff—an old Grant Deed and some escrow papers from when he bought the place, a mortgage, and papers showing the mortgage had been paid off. Then, there was the newer deed, the one that said, "Quitclaim" at the top.

The second envelope was thicker, and had papers in it going all the way back to when Eddie was born. A birth certificate stating that on a certain date, at a certain time, a child had been born at Redwood Memorial Hospital, the parents shown as Mateo Fuentes, and Robin Ann Watkins, with an address for the mother in San Rafael. It was the first time he had ever seen her name. There were also newspaper clippings describing football games Matty didn't show up for, letters from Iraq he never answered, a high school diploma, from a graduation he never attended, and a wedding invitation with a reply card he never sent back.

It was like the poor sonuvabitch was saving evidence of a relationship that never existed. And now it was too late. There was no going back.

*　　*　　*

Shanna's house was a few miles south of Redwood Bay, a mid-century modern set on a bluff overlooking the Pacific. Two-story entry, three-car garage, on the water. Eddie didn't know real estate, but figured on a bad day it had to be worth a couple million. He parked the Cube in the drive next to Shanna's black Rover, walked to the door, rang the bell a couple of times, waited, then rang it again. A few minutes later the door opened and Shanna was there, dressed in a torn sweatshirt and her ripped, designer jeans, hair still wet from the shower.

She kissed him on the mouth, letting her hands move on his body, then she stopped, looking past him toward the electric blue Cube. "It makes a statement," she said.

"Right," Eddie said. "I just can't figure out what."

They walked through an entry hall with palms and fichus, glass brick and abstract art, into a big, open living room with a few large canvases, bold splashes of color setting off a wall of glass leading to a deck that overlooked the Pacific.

"Wow." Eddie whistled. "Who says, crime doesn't pay?"

"It belonged to Lindy Matheson, Chrissie's mom. Had it built after the divorce. 1959. You like it?"

Looking around, he smiled.

"I thought you would. Being as it's out of the fifties, just like you."

She led him to a big, restaurant kitchen, with gleaming tile floors, granite counters, and heavy commercial appliances, and put him to work making a salad while she got a bottle of Jack Daniels out of the bar and a bottle of vodka out of the freezer. The salad stuff was ready to go. Greens, cut up in a bag, tomatoes, a cucumber, and some radishes, all neatly packaged in cellophane.

"I think there's some cocktail onions in the fridge," she said, pointing to a big, stainless steel model.

Looking inside, Eddie didn't see much else. Olives, capers, Dijon mustard, Italian dressing, Rose's lime juice, some Parmesan cheese, a couple bottles of Pinot Grigio. Handing her the onions, he said, "Looks like you don't eat at home a lot."

Taking them, she said, "I keep forgetting, you're were a cop." Shanna handed him a whiskey and poured vodka for herself. "That reminds me," she said, "I was thinking about that thing with the pimp. What was his name?"

"De Marius. Williams."

"De Marius, right. From the Department's point of view, I guess that kind of thing might *support* a termination. But I don't see why they'd want to come down that hard. Even with the Reverend Al what's-his-name on the case."

"Whitaker," Eddie said, then, motioning to a pile of tomatoes he'd been cutting, "Where do you want me to put this stuff?"

Shanna found a wooden bowl under the counter.

Eddie went on, "Like I said, I was already on probation."

"Probation for what?"

Eddie took a minute, not really wanting to get into it. "Mostly related to a liquor store holdup. I shot a guy coming out. They said it was excessive use of force."

"Why would they say that?"

Eddie hesitated, "Because he didn't have a gun."

And he had to tell her the story. How he was off-duty, going to pick up a pizza at Rizzoli's on his way home, he happened to glance through a liquor store window a couple doors down. Through the window, he saw the Korean guy, owned the place—Eddie knew him; he'd been in before—and a couple of kids, banger types with the hoodies and the pants down past their assholes, giving the Korean a hard time. They were knocking over counter displays, fucking up the merchandise, dropping shit on the floor, keeping the Korean occupied, while their buddies ripped off fortified wine from the cooler. Eddie was kind of wondering what he ought to do, when all of a sudden, the kids were coming out the door, so he didn't have time to think about it.

He said, "Oakland P.D., get on the ground."

The kids stopped. One of them, a tall, thin dude, who seemed to be the leader, looked at Eddie, "Whoa, now, Spiderman. You say you Oakland PD, but I don't see no uniform."

Eddie showed him a badge.

The kid examined it, then he said, friendly enough, but with an edge, "Excuse me, officer. Didn't mean anything by that. Just being careful, you know. See, my friends and I, we're just playing. We not armed or anything."

Eddie said, "On the ground, hands behind your head."

The kid said. "On the *ground*? No, no, man. We do that, we gonna mess up our couture, pick up germs and shit. God knows what all's down there, understand what I'm talking about?"

Eddie pulled his 9-millimeter. "I said, on the ground."

The kid took a step back. "Hey, now. I told you, we not armed. You gonna shoot us on account of a couple quarts of Cisco? Man, I don't see *how* that could be inside the use-of-force guidelines."

It hung there awhile, Eddie considering it. Finally, the kid grinned. "All right, then. Glad to see we getting somewhere. Job security prevail over the hard ass bullshit. You have a nice evening, officer." And turned to go.

Eddie said, "Hold it!"

But the kids didn't hold it; they started walking away, kind of slow, swinging their shoulders side to side, showing how cool they were. And it might have ended there, except the kid threw a few last words over his shoulder.

He said, just loud enough for Eddie to hear it. "Hold my dick, motherfucker. You wanna pop a cap in my ass? Go on, you got the balls to pull the trigger."

Explaining the situation to Shanna now, in the kitchen, slicing a cucumber, Eddie said, "For some reason, the way he said it, it just sounded like the right thing to do."

"You shot him."

"Nothing serious. He probably had trouble sitting down for a month or two."

Shanna thought it over. "The kid was right, you know. About the use of force. You should have let him go."

"Oh yeah," Eddie said, "I know that. But see, the 'shooting outside policy' wasn't really why I got in trouble."

"It wasn't?"

He shook his head. "When they ran the kid's name, it turned out to be Whitaker." Shanna looked at Eddie, he said, "Yeah, his son."

The dinner wasn't half bad—grilled salmon, some fancy kind of rice that came out of a box, Eddie's prepackaged homemade salad, a bottle of Chardonnay. Eddie really didn't want to talk any more about why he was not a cop, or how he felt about it, so he changed the subject and told her about his talk with Darryl Waters.

When he was done, Shanna said. "What I hear you saying, he's not going away."

Eddie said, "Not unless he passes the bar examination."

Shanna smiled slowly. "Maybe I should offer him a fucking job," only half kidding. Then, "And you think they've got Petty."

"Custom made uniforms, Rolex watches, that boat you were talking about. Where's he getting the money? It's a pretty simple, what they call an asset case."

Shanna said, "Maybe he got lucky at the track."

Eddie said, "Maybe he won the Mega Millions. It's taxable income, either way. If he didn't report it, they can take him down. Of course, that's not bribery. I told Darryl, if he wants bribery, he needs you."

"What did he say?"

"He said, bribery's FBI, he doesn't give a shit, but I don't believe him. They've got this task force set up. FBI, DEA, IRS. U.S. Attorney's in charge."

"Sarah Breckinridge," Shanna was nodding. "I read about her."

"Seems like they're getting antsy. They want something big. Headlines, Darryl said. I think they need you—unless they can roll this dealer they busted in San Leandro, get to the Doctor through him." He thought a minute. "This guy who works for the Doctor, handling the drops, any idea who that might be?"

Shanna nodded. "You think I should have a talk with him?"

"Jesus, you mean tip him? Tell him to take off? I can't believe I'm having this conversation."

She said, "Eddie, look at me," and when he did, held him with those eyes of hers. "You're not a cop anymore."

She was right, he wasn't. He'd been saying it himself all along, but realized now, maybe for the first time, it was true. What did he care if they busted the collection man or not? He played with his food a minute, drank some wine. Finally, he said, "There is one more thing. If it matters. You know your friend, Roger Bachman?"

"What about him?"

"Darryl told me Petty gave him up. They were trying to get him to wear a wire before he disappeared, just like they're trying to do with you."

She seemed shaken. "What are you saying …."

He shook his head. "I don't know. It's just …. you said yourself … they've been after this guy, Philip Doctor, since before the two of us were even born. It couldn't be an accident they never got him. If he finds out about *any* of this—you, me, Wayne, Duncan, Petty—it wouldn't surprise me if some *more* people started disappearing. "

*　*　*

When Philip Doctor was a kid, sometimes, after school, he'd tend the soda fountain at his father's drugstore in Ardmore, Pennsylvania. The Doctor loved that soda fountain— the gleaming stainless steel cabinets, rows of syrup dispensers, milkshake blenders, fountains dispensing plain and carbonated water. He loved the cleanliness of the place, the shininess. But mostly, he loved the science—mixing disparate ingredients in precise proportions to create unexpected sensory impressions. The problem with the soda fountain was, people didn't want the unexpected. They wanted the same goddamn thing repeated *ad nauseum* until the end of their pathetic, boring existence. That was not something the Doctor was interested in dispensing.

Nessun dorma! Nessun dorma!
Tu pure, o, Principessa,
nella tua fredda stanza,

Pavarotti soaring in the background, the Doctor was preparing his dinner, whisking mashed potatoes to go with the pesto chicken in his gourmet kitchen overlooking the Pacific.

A week ago, Wayne had come back from San Francisco for the second time, empty handed. So, twenty-four hours ago the Doctor put in a call to an acquainance in San Francisco letting it be known he would pay ten thousand cash for information as to the whereabouts of a certain Salvadoran national by the name of Ramón Delgado, Ramón having dropped out of sight owing the Doctor two hundred thousand dollars. An hour ago, the word came back from a law enforcement source proven in the past to be reliable, that Ramón was in federal protective custody in Oakland, cooperating in a major drug investigation. Now, the Doctor had to do something about it.

Einstein was often quoted as saying, "God doesn't play dice with the universe." To this, the Doctor would have replied, "He does play dice, but he loads them." Men and women had free will to choose—to roll the dice—but the dice were loaded—with consequences. Consequences. One always had to consider the consequences.

"Wayne, come in!" The Doctor waved this big, beautiful Maori boy in from the doorway. "Sit down. Pour yourself a glass of pinot. It's better than I expected." He found the remote, poked down the volume on the aria:

Ma il mio mistero è chiuso in me,
il nome mio nessun saprà!
No, no!

The Doctor motioned Wayne to a stool at the pass-through, where he could get a better reading on his portable RF detector. The possibility had to be considered that they had gotten to Wayne already; that even now, he was wearing a wire.

"Aoteroa," he said, glancing into his palm, but getting no RF reading. "The Land of the Long White Cloud. Isn't that what the Maori call it?"

Wayne looked at him without much expression. "That's what they call it."

"Springtime now. Cherry blossoms along the Avon, waterfront concerts, sand painting on the beach. What could be better?"

"I'm allergic to cherry blossoms," Wayne said. "If you want to know the truth about it."

"A lot of people are." The Doctor said. "I'd recommend an immune booster. Also a good over-the-counter nasal spray containing a mast cell inhibitor. The sooner you start taking it the better."

"Sorry, I'm not following," Wayne said.

"You're going on a vacation." The Doctor told him, placing an envelope on the counter beteween them. "This is for your expenses. I think you'll agree it's more than generous. You'll find a ticket in your name at the Air New Zealand counter at San Francisco International Airport. I suppose it's the time difference, but the flights all seem to be red-eyes. You leave tomorrow night at 11:55 pm."

Wayne slowly picked up the envelope. He started to say something, but the Doctor put a finger to his lips. "Stay as long as you like. No need to hurry back. In fact, I'd recommend against it." He smiled, "Bon voyage," he said.

CHAPTER 17

THE HUSTLER

After dinner, Shanna asked Eddie what he brought for desert. Eddie looked at her.

"You forgot *desert*?" She sounded disappointed, then got up from the table, held out her hand. "Maybe not. Come on."

"What's up?"

"We're about to find out."

They made love on the living room floor, not even making it to the couch. The vast blue Pacific was gone now, lost in the fog, and Eddie was gone with it, lost in the fog of this woman—her body, her voice, the subtle scent she wore. The fog of her hips and breasts, the irresistible excitement inside her. Feeling was all that was left, and for those few minutes, or hours, in a place without time, Eddie Fuentes was gone.

Later, Eddie went out to the car to get the stuff he found at the cabin. When he came back, Shanna was standing, barefoot, at the thermostat, turning up the heat. She'd thrown on a heavy plaid robe. Walking to the couch now, she sat down, and held out her hand. "Let's see."

Eddie handed her the envelope, and sat down next to her as she went through it. When she was finished, she kissed him on the cheek. "And you thought Matty didn't love you." She patted the envelope. "This is his Last Will and Testament," she said. "Actually, better." She held up the Quitclaim. "The beauty of what your father did, the property's already in your name. He even got his signature notarized."

Eddie didn't get it. "I thought it was in both our names. Joint tenants?"

"Yeah, but see, that's a legal term. It means there's a right of survivor-ship. When he died, the property went to you automatically. All we need to do is record the deed with a certified copy of the death certificate, and it's all yours. You can do whatever you want with it."

Eddie thought about it, "Okay? What happens then? I give Saul's company a deed and they give us the money?"

A short pause, and Shanna said, "Not quite that simple. But for let's say, five million dollars, you wouldn't expect it to."

"*Five* million?"

"Total, after expenses. Our share's two and a half."

The number seemed to keep changing, but it still seemed big enough. "So, what comes next?"

Now Shanna was smiling. "There's plenty of time for that. Right now, we're still doing show and tell. And it's my turn. But you have to come in the bedroom to see it."

She led him into another soaring space, open to the deck overlooking the Pacific. This one had a king size platform bed against one wall, and a big flat screen mounted on another.

"I like to watch movies in bed." She sat down amidst scattered pillows and patted the spot next to her, fiddling with a remote.

"I found this online," she said. "I never heard of it, but it gets 97% on Rotten Tomatoes, so how bad can it be?"

She punched a few buttons, the screen lit up with the old 20th Century Fox logo, and then, without any opening credits, they found themselves in a black and white 1950s world. Main Street, USA, a Packard coupe pulls into a gas station, two men get out and stretch their legs. The older man ambles across the street to a bar, while the driver, a younger man, hand-some, early thirties, says a few words to the attendant. Now, inside a small town bar with a couple pool tables, the two men order drinks. After a little conversation about a sales convention in Pittsburgh, the younger man challenges his pal to a game of pool. He clowns around, drinks too much, makes stupid bets, misses easy shots and loses a lot of money.

In the bedroom, Shanna looked at Eddie. "Is that how it's done?"

Eddie said, "That's one way to do it."

She said, "You really do look a lot like him, you know."

The plot moves pretty fast for a story written in the fifties. Fast Eddie (Paul Newman) hits the big time, challenges legendary hustler, Minnesota Fats (Jackie Gleason) to a game of straight pool, almost beats him, then gets drunk, and gives himself an excuse to lose. He gets involved with Sarah (Piper Laurie, a damaged woman, probably an alcoholic). He gets his thumbs broken in a busted hustle, and slowly heals. He signs on with Fats' manager, a gambler named Bert (George C. Scott), and travels to Lexington for the Kentucky Derby. There, he dumps Sarah when Bert convinces him she's holding him back from winning at pool. A devastated Sarah has sex with Bert in his hotel room, then goes into the bathroom and slits her wrists.

In the last sequence, Eddie shows up at the big time pool hall again, challenges Fats to a rematch and, this time, beats him cold, because now Eddie has nothing to lose. Bert tells Eddie he's still his manager, and demands his share of the winnings, but Eddie says no. Bert tells Eddie, if he walks out, he'll never play big time pool again. But Eddie walks out anyway.

Lying close to Eddie now, as the end credits rolled, Shanna said, "I don't get it. He went through so much to win. Why would he walk away?"

Eddie said, "He probably couldn't stand the idea of having that jerk, Bert, on his back for the rest of his life."

Shanna said, "But you heard what Bert said. He was willing to negotiate. Eddie could have had any deal he wanted."

Eddie said, "Yeah. … I don't know. Maybe he felt bad about the girl … maybe he proved what he needed to prove. … or, maybe that was just the kind of guy he was."

She looked at him. "What kind of guy is that?"

Eddie said, "The kind that walks away."

Next morning, Eddie and Shanna were wrapped in blankets, drinking coffee on the deck overlooking the Pacific. The fog was still in, but the air was fresh, the wind was calm, the birds were singing in the evergreen trees. All was right with the world, except Eddie didn't feel that way. There was still something hanging around in his head from that goddamn movie, something he wished he could forget.

"I'll be right back," Now, Shanna went inside, and came back with a stack of documents at least an inch thick, which she dropped on the table.

"What's that?"

Shanna said, "You wanted to know what comes next. I know, it looks like a lot, but it's really just a bunch of … you know, details. Let me walk you through it."

Which she proceeded to do. It turned out the first *detail* was, Eddie didn't actually *sell* the land to West Coast Lumber. In fact, he didn't sell it at all. He *contributed* it to a trust organized in a place he never heard of, an island called Nevis. The second *detail* was that he didn't get any *money*. He got *certificates*. And the certificates didn't mean he *owned* anything; they just gave him a share of the trust assets when it was terminated. In the meantime, Eddie had nothing to do with how the trust was managed, and neither did anyone else. That was all left up to a trustee, a lawyer in the Cayman Islands Eddie had never even heard of.

But that was only the start. There were a whole bunch of other *details*, too. For example, the property wasn't sold by the trust directly. It was sold by a California corporation owned by a Cayman Islands Corporation that was, in turn, owned by the trust. All of this made absolutely no *real* difference, Shanna assured him. It didn't matter what the papers said. You had to follow the money. When the land was sold, the money was going to get wired to a bank account in the Caymans, and Eddie was going to be able to do whatever he wanted with his share of it.

After Shanna was through explaining, Eddie said, "I'll tell you what," he said. If it's all the same to you, I'd rather just sell the land and get the money."

"Well, I know that seems easier, but it wouldn't work. You have to trust me on that," she said, sounding a bit condescending.

"Not that I don't trust you?" Eddie said, "But why don't you explain it to me?"

This led to an introductory course on the law of taxation. According to Shanna, Eddie wouldn't have estate taxes to pay because there was an exclusion of $5 million. And he also got something called a "step up in basis". That meant if the value was $5 million when his father died, and he sold it for $5 million, there wouldn't be any tax to pay. So, basically, Eddie didn't have a problem. The problem was the money going to Shanna and Duncan. All of it, from dollar one, would be what she called "ordinary income" rather than "capital gain", meaning at least a third of it would go to the government.

"Okay. But, I'm not seeing where that's my problem," Eddie said. "Why don't you just pay the tax."

Shanna said, well, for herself, she'd be all right with it. The problem was Duncan. "He won't pay taxes," she said. "He told me that from the start. And he has an even bigger problem. Selling land to his own corporation?" She shook her head. "It's a clear conflict of interest. He has to be totally invisible."

It turned out the rest of it—the layers of off shore trusts and corporations—all had to do with the same thing—taxes and invisibility. Even the part about the trustee. He asked her, "Why not let the people who *own* the trust run it? Why put this guy—what's his name—in the middle?"

"Colin Winsett," she said. "See, the thing is, the way the IRS looks at it, if you have the right to *control* a trust, you *own* the trust, and if you *own* the trust, you get taxed on trust income. So, you have to set up a situation where you don't control it, anyway, not on paper. The trick is, in real life, guys like Winsett don't do anything without asking. Setting up trusts like this is all they do. If they tried to pull a fast one, they'd be out of business in a minute. Trust me, Eddie, everybody involved in this thing knows exactly who's in charge, and who's giving the orders."

Eddie nodded, thinking that might be true, but also wondering who *was* giving the orders? And when you got to the bottom of it, who *was* in charge?

*   *   *

Sitting in the tribal office in Juanita, looking out the window at the fog, drifting down the empty street, Russell said, "Robbie, you're not listening. What I'm saying is, suppose we *had* the land."

Tribal gaming consultant, Robbie Martinez, said, "You're saying, the tribe *owns* the land."

Russell said, "I'm saying the tribe *controls* the land."

Robbie said, "*Controls*, meaning what exactly?"

"Meaning, we have the power to get it transferred over to the government."

"To the Department of the Interior? And they hold it in trust for the tribe."

"If that's what we need, yeah. Why not? We can make it happen."

Robbie was quiet a minute, then he said, "Obviously, we're not talking about the Rancheria, here. But, you're saying there's a historic tribal connection?"

Russell said, "The Mynot have a historic connection north to the Oregon border and south to the Rappold. It's not a problem."

Robbie said, "Okay. Then the answer is, assuming there's a historic connection and we get Interior to accept it for gaming purposes, and assuming we get the governor to sign off—and assuming the economics make sense, the answer is, why the fuck not? We create a gaming authority, issue construction bonds, get an operating loan from Vegas—"

Russell said, "Let's not get ahead of ourselves."

"You don't want an operating loan?"

Russell said, "Let's see what they're asking."

Robbie said, "Hey, that's up to you. Right now, what I need is the location. You give me the location, I can get going. You know, sound people out."

Russell said, "I'll get back to you."

Now Russell stared out the window, looking through the fog blowing down the street, to the park on the other side: the block-long section of railroad track, the five cypress trees, the three picnic tables, the two trash receptacles. On the far side of the park there was a pickup truck, parked on the grass, right next to the sign that said the gravel lot was for parking, but not parked in the fucking lot. Sometimes Russell wondered what he was doing with his life. Whether it was worth it, trying to make things happen for a bunch of people who couldn't read a goddamn sign, or maybe could read it, but just didn't want to do what it fucking said. A bunch of people that were *his* people. Jesus.

* * *

One o'clock in the morning at the Costa Perdida, the Doctor was sitting in his command center sipping wheatgrass juice from a cocktail glass, staring at his black and white photograph of Roger Bachman, Roger dressed in a tuxedo, looking back at him with his smiling eyes that seemed to negate the very concept of worry or judgment. The Doctor always felt better in Roger's company, and didn't exactly consider him absent, though his physical form was no longer in the vicinity.

"Hang on, baby," Roger seemed to be saying, "Just a little bit longer, and this part of the dream will be over. You will leave that dreary dream and come flying home to me. To my Technicolor world, where no clouds come, and golden dreams dwell." The Doctor felt himself relax. What a lovely thought!

Two o'clock now, Wayne would be high over the Pacific, winging his way to a new life in Kiwi land. Change was in the air. And to make things even better, Ahmadu had called from San Francisco, saying someone had come in—a young man just off the boat from Port Louis, Mauritius. Trained as a *chef du garde manger*, with excellent references, the poor boy had to depart the island quickly, having killed three men with a knife. *Quel dommage!*

The Doctor told Ahmadu to send him right up.

* * *

Two o'clock in the morning on Harrison Street, San Francisco, Lon sat in the Yukon across from a gay bar called *Five Card Stud*, looking at his watch. Jesus, six this morning down to the garden to swap the SID's, then out to the coast to talk to the Doctor, then all the way down to the fucking San Francisco airport, and back up here to sit on his ass for a couple more hours. He got out a little bottle of *yayo*, tapped a line on the top of his fist, and took a snort. Motherfucker, he needed *something* to pick him up.

Lon had been at it the better part of a week, trying to figure what was wrong at the garden, deer getting into the bud, but not tripping the alarms. First off, he checked the sensors, and the batteries was dead, all of them. He thought maybe it was a bad batch and put in new ones. But a couple days later, the deer was back and the sensors was dead again. He finally figured, it was bad sensor chips draining off the power and had to get new ones Fedexed out. What pissed him off, it wasn't even his job. Rampas was the farmer. Except Rampas was a fucking pothead, didn't know shit about technology, living in a different century.

Still, Lon didn't say nothing. He was cool with it 'cause he thought at least he could drop by Fuentes' cabin while he was out that way. His idea, get that taken care of before the weekend, so Mama wouldn't get on his case about it. Jesus, the woman not giving him a minute's peace since they cremated Little Billy, getting it in her head it wasn't fair her little boy was dead, with no harm coming to the asshole responsible. But Fuentes wasn't around, and then Rampas said the Doctor wanted him for a special job. Special my ass, fucking two hour ride out to the coast to find out he had to drive another five hours to make sure little Wayne got on his airplane.

That's what the Doctor told him, "Make sure he gets on the plane."

Yeah? Well just how the fuck's he supposed to make sure that happened? He couldn't get past security without a ticket. And that's even if he *wasn't* packing a Glock 19 with an illegal fifteen-shot magazine loaded with hollow point bullets. But forget about it, you could never explain anything like that to the Doctor. Anyways, it didn't get that far. What happened, Lon was staked out across from the New Zealand Airline counter when Wayne showed up with this other dude. And this motherfucker was a whole different story, six foot six, three-fifty at least. There they were, the two of them, gay boys at the ticket counter, screwing around, bumping into each other. Finally, the girl counted out some cash, and the two of them walked out with it. Well, it didn't take no rocket scientist to figure the kid wasn't getting on the airplane. Yeah? So, what was he supposed do about it? The Doctor never *said* nothing about that.

Lon tailed the two of them out to short-term parking, lost them for a while when he went to get the Yukon, then picked them up again headed into the City. Now, he'd been following them around, bar hopping, for a couple hours and still wasn't much closer to knowing what his next step should be. He *could* call the Doctor. There was a number, rang on a line supposed to be secure. But the whole point of getting Lon to drive out there this morning was, the Doctor didn't want to talk on the phone. So, when he thought about it, Lon figured there wasn't no way around it. It was up to him. He was gonna have to decide.

Sitting with Todd in a back booth at *Five Card Stud*, right after last call, really took Wayne back. This was where he first met Roger. Roger, who hooked him up with the Doctor, and ran interference between the Doctor and the world.

"The man's as mad as cut snake," Wayne said now. "He thinks it's a few hours on a plane to New Zealand. It's fucking time travel, fifty years in the wrong direction. Cherry blossoms along the Avon. Give me a break! … Four years, and he just blows me off? I'll tell you, if Roger was here, he wouldn't have let this happen."

Todd looked at him now, "Man, you're always talking about that guy. What were you, in love with him?" Sounding a little jealous.

Wayne shrugged. "Everybody was in love with him. But it was never serious."

Todd shrugged, took a sip of his drink. "So … that dude at the airport … you thought he was following us. What was that about?"

Wayne shook his head. "It's the Doctor. I dropped some Molly off to this dude in the East Bay, and when I went back to collect, the whacker was gone. We don't do business with fruit loops, you know. They're all checked out. But this guy, man, it's like he fell off a cliff. I figure he thinks

I could be part of it. So he put a tail on to see if I make a pickup, before I take off. Except I'm not taking off. I'm not going back to fucking Christchurch ."

Todd asked him, "How much money are we talking about?"

"A couple hundred large. But it's not my fault, right? I just make collections."

Todd said, "The guy at the airport, you think he'd make a move?"

"Against the two of us?" Wayne laughed. "I hope so. After all the riding around, I could use some exercise."

Quarter after two, Wayne and Todd left the bar and headed out to Wayne's car, parked across the street, a half block down Harrison. The street was deserted now, the wind calm and the fog settled in, so it wasn't completely freezing, just chilly. Wayne didn't like the fog. But he figured you couldn't have everything, and fog was about the only thing Wayne *didn't* like about San Francisco. The way Wayne looked at it, San Francisco was a land of opportunity. Not that it didn't take some work.

Like with Todd, all night long, he'd been trying to bring the conversation around to what he thought of as a million-dollar opportunity. So far, Todd had been focused on his short-term prospects, hypnotized by the fact that Doug Carmichael was down with a knee injury, and Todd was slated to start in Denver on Sunday. But Wayne saw that as short sighted.

"Suppose you go down yourself," he said.

Todd shrugged. "It's part of the game."

"What I'm saying," Wayne said, "Now that you're starting, it gives you a window. Think about it. How long do you have in the pros, even if you stay healthy? Ten or twelve years?"

Todd said, "I guess, maybe."

"My point is this. Pat Summerall. Remember him? You know how long he played?"

"Isn't he dead?"

"Yeah, he's dead, but it's not the point. The point is, he only played nine years, 1952 to 1961. But how long was he on the telly? *Forty* years, mate, see what I mean? You're set for life. If you come out, you'll be a cult hero. The first gay commentator? The sky's the limit. And you know what?"

"No, what?" Todd said, not sounding too enthusiastic about it.

Wayne gave him a butt bump. "*I* could be your manager."

Suddenly, a form stepped out of a doorway, maybe a dozen feet in front of them, dressed in fatigue pants and a tee shirt, with a field jacket over his arm. He just stood there, didn't move or say anything.

Wayne said, "Hey, mate, how ya goin'? I told Todd here, you were following us." He turned to Todd. "This here's Lon. He's a real bad ass, you have to watch out for him."

Todd said, "Yeah? He doesn't look that big to me?"

Wayne said, "Lon was in the Marine Corps. He's got a tat to prove it. Go on, turn around, Lon, show us your tattoo."

Lon watched the two men fucking with him, and felt his right hand under the field jacket, fingers curled around the pistol grip of an automatic Benelli 12-gauge. Five in the magazine, but it wouldn't take more than two to get the job done, plus two for insurance. May as well get her done. He dropped the jacket now, brought the gun up, stepped forward and gave them each a round, the big man first, then the one with the mouth. The blasts blew each of them back a half dozen feet. But he stepped forward, angled the weapon down, and gave them each another round, just to make sure. The big boys were quiet now. R.I.P, motherfuckers.

CHAPTER 18

THE CLOSING

Shanna decided to dress up for the occasion. A new lace camisole, hip length, raw silk bolero jacket over a very short black pencil skirt. The way she set it up, everyone was supposed to sign at her office, but not all at once. Eddie was supposed to come at 9:30 to sign a deed and a set of the trust documents. Dick was supposed to come an hour later, sign the trust documents and the downstream corporate stuff. The company lawyer would come a half hour after that, and they'd do the property sale. Then, the company lawyer would take off and they'd drink champagne. That was how it was *supposed* to go.

How it actually went, Dick swept into the room a little after nine, spinning like a paranoid ballroom dancer, checking for cameras hidden in her palm trees and parabolic microphones aimed at her windows from boats that might be moored somewhere in the harbor. Then, he gave her a smile, danced over for a kiss. "Ready to get rich?"

She accepted the kiss, but found it hard today to handle the cologne, a heavy Armani. "You're early," she said. Are you by yourself?"

He smiled, pointing to a carafe Donald had put out. "Is that coffee?"

She sat down at the conference table while he poured himself a cup. "I told Charlie to be here in an hour. I thought we'd need some time to … get through … our part of things first." He held up the carafe, but Shanna shook her head, already coffee'd out.

He poured in some cream, shook in some sugar, stirred it around. "You got the package from Winsett?"

"Yesterday."

He sat down across from her, sipping coffee. "Charlie's got the stuff on the land deal, it came in FedEx from New York."

"Any surprises?"

"He didn't mention any. Just the usual stuff." He took another sip of coffee, not saying anything for a minute. "I've been under a lot of pressure lately. Jennifer's outdone herself. She's beyond extravagant. Unfortunately, in addition to that, I've had some ... reverses...in the market. But I won't bore you with that. I'll get to the point. When this thing is finished, I'm going to need a place to land. I'm not looking to start over at this point in my career. And, when you step back and take a look at it, I think you'll have to agree, I'm assuming virtually all the risk. Quite frankly, babe, under the circumstances—" He smiled, but it didn't reach his eyes. "I don't see where I'm being adequately compensated."

Shanna smiled back at him slowly. "Why, Dick Duncan! If I didn't know you better, I'd think you were trying to hold me up. ... I thought we were partners."

He took another sip of coffee. "We are, babe, we are. ... But like somebody said, there are all kinds of partners."

She ran a hand through her hair. "Okay, Dick. For purposes of discussion, what are we talking about?"

"I want half."

"Half?" She looked at him. "Dick, Eddie Fuentes gets half. If you get half, what's in it for me?"

He shrugged. "Really not my problem. But my suggestion would be, don't give Eddie Fuentes half."

"Dick, baby, come on. That's what we *agreed* to."

"Agree to something else."

"I ... can't do that."

"Why? Because you're fucking him? ... You are, aren't you?"

She took a cigarette out of a pack on the table, and lit it. "That's none of your business."

He reached for her cigarettes, shook one out for himself. "You're right," he said, blowing smoke. "It's none of my business … as long as I get half. How you do it is up to you."

Shanna got up now, walked to the window, then turned to face him. "The thing is, Dickey, you don't know this guy. He's like his old man. If I try to change the deal at the last minute, he could walk."

Dick poured himself another cup of coffee. "Then, don't tell him you're changing it."

"The guy can read, Dick," she said. "How can I not tell him?"

"Mmm, probably the same way you didn't tell me about that little side letter you cooked up that makes you the trust protector." He finished adding his cream and sugar then, looking up, said, "You forget, Colin and I go back. Why do you think I picked him? He's the only one in this deal I can trust." He sipped his coffee. "Really, kiddo, given the way you've set things up, I don't see why Eddie Fuentes needs to get anything at all."

It hung there, an uncomfortable silence, until the intercom beeped.

"What is it, Donald?"

"Mr. Fuentes is here."

"Okay, bring him in." Then, turning to Dick, she said, "I'm not agreeing to this, Dick, you understand? It isn't over."

Shanna's assistant, Donald, brought Eddie in then. She introduced Dick; they shook hands, friendly enough. Eddie had coffee. Then, the fireworks began.

Eddie looked straight at Dick. "The thing is, Dick," he said, "I don't want to rain on your parade or anything. But I have a problem with this deal, the way it's structured."

Dick smiled. "What's wrong with it?"

"You know, Dick," Eddie said, "I've been wracking my brain, but I can't seem to find anything that guarantees I'm actually gonna get anything out of it."

Which meant, the three of them went over the structure again. When they were finished, Eddie said, "Okay, I get that. But what I hear you telling me is, everything depends on this guy in the Caymans, what's his name?"

"Colin Winsett," Dick said.

"Yeah, basically, this Winsett guy can do whatever he wants with the money. He can pay it out, not pay it out. Invest it, not invest it, keep it one place, move it around."

Dick said. "But Winsett works for us. He does what we tell him."

"Right, my problem is, nobody can seem to show me it *says* that anywhere."

"Well, it doesn't say that. For very good reasons, and I think we've been through what they are already."

Eddie took some time with it. "So, my guess is, you're pretty tight with this guy."

"Winsett?" Dick glanced at Shanna. "Very tight, right Shanna?"

"Yeah, that's right."

Eddie said, "Okay, but see here's the thing. I'm not. In fact, I don't know him at all and, no offense, Dick, but I don't know *you*, either." He looked at Shanna then, holding her with those frank, blue eyes. " I guess what it boils down to, I'm trusting *you*."

Her eyes on his, Shanna said, "That's right, Eddie. I'm the one who brought you in, and I'm the one you need to trust." Then shaking a cigarette out of a pack on the table, she added, "We can't do the deal without you, so there *is* no deal if you decide to walk. But before you do that, I think there's a question you need to ask yourself." Eyes on Eddie, she lit the cigarette, and blew out some smoke. "If you hold onto the land, what the fuck is it really worth?"

When it was over, when the documents were finally signed and notarized, and the lawyer from West Coast Lumber had come and gone, Dick wanted to take everybody to lunch. Shanna knew Dick Duncan like a book, which meant she also, knew she should not be leaving Eddie Fuentes alone with the son-of a bitch. But her head was splitting and her beautiful lace camisole was soaked with sweat. So, she begged off and, when they were gone, pulled a bottle of Stoli out of the bar freezer, collapsed on the sofa and poured herself a long, stiff drink.

Just as the pounding in her brain was beginning to back off, the intercom sounded and Donald's voice came over. "Murrelet Myers on one?"

"Who? … Take a message," then, " No, wait." She punched a button. "Hello?"

"Shanna? What do you think?"

"Who is this?"

"Murrelet. Myers. I mean, Rhonda. Murrelet's my handle. Like the bird. What do you think?"

Taking a drink, a bit weary, Shanna said, "Murrelet, sure, that's … great."

"Right, and the reason I'm calling, we got it together."

"I'm sorry …."

"You know, the equipment, everything. We brought a couple people from out of town, and we figured, hey, why wait? We're going in tonight if it's okay with you."

And Shanna was thinking, Jesus, there had to be an easier way to make a living.

* * *

The Waterfront Inn was a couple blocks from Shanna's office, a converted Victorian overlooking Redwood Bay, painted in shades of gray and cream and burgundy. There were Oriental rugs on the floor, white tablecloths, crystal stemware, fresh cut flowers. It had waiters who looked like they belonged on daytime TV shows. In a nutshell, it was exactly the kind of place Eddie would never go. The maître 'd greeted Dick Duncan like an old friend and told him he'd reserved his usual table, which turned out to be in a secluded nook with a view of the harbor. Redwood Bay wasn't a tourist destination, and the boat traffic on the harbor tended toward fishing trawlers, crabbers, and timber barges. But on a clear day like today, when the fog was out, it was still a beautiful view.

The table was set sideways to the windows. Duncan took the chair facing the entrance, leaving Eddie a seat facing the back of the room. Eddie had a feeling this was an old habit; Dick Duncan needed to see who was coming; he'd probably been in a thousand restaurants and bars either with women he wasn't married to, or scoping them out. Eddie found himself wondering how many times he'd been here with Shanna.

"You come here a lot?"

Duncan shrugged. "Often enough. It's convenient. The food's passable. I'd caution you about the Italian dishes, though, if you're going to be meeting people. The chef thinks Italian is synonymous with garlic."

A waiter came then; they ordered drinks, Eddie a Corona, Duncan a kir. When the waiter was gone, Duncan said. "Shanna tells me you grew up here."

Eddie said, "My father felled timber for West Coast Lumber for a while. Most of the kids I grew up with had relatives who worked for the company, one way or another."

"Does he still live in the area … your father?"

"He's dead. Didn't Shanna tell you?"

Duncan sipped his ice water. "I suppose she did. … That's right, and she said you lived in Oakland."

"I was a cop."

"But as I understand, not anymore." If Eddie was going to describe this guy, smooth would be the word for it. Tall, impeccably dressed, with a cologne you could smell across the table. A womanizer.

"So, how did you and Shanna get together?"

"Oh, I don't know; it was a couple of years ago. I think, through a mutual acquaintance."

"You mean the Doctor?"

Duncan hesitated. "Doctor? No, I don't believe so." He smiled slightly. "More likely, it was a lawyer."

Eddie said, "Roger Bachman."

Duncan didn't answer, saved by the waiter, who appeared with the drinks. When the waiter was gone, Duncan raised his glass. "Better days,"

He drank without waiting, not really a toast. Eddie watched him for a second, then drank himself.

"On the subject of lawyers," he said, "the one in the Caymans, what'd you say his name was?"

"Colin Winsett."

"Winsett, right. I don't know why I can't remember it. How long have you known him?"

He thought a moment. "Let me see. Actually, I met him when Harriman Saul took over the company, so that would make it three, four years, something like that."

"But, why the Cayman Islands? It's not exactly a center of the logging industry, is it?"

Duncan laughed. "It's a center of the tax shelter industry. Harriman Saul has an insurance company down there."

"You mind my asking why?"

"Taxes. It's all about taxes. Saul's companies buy insurance from a company in the Caymans that Saul happens to own. They deduct the premiums, but Saul's company doesn't pay taxes because the Caymans don't have a corporate income tax."

Eddie asked him what happened to the money.

"The company invests it. It doesn't have to pay taxes on the investment income, either. In fact, there's no tax at all until the money comes back to the United States."

"When does that happen?" Eddie asked.

Duncan said, "It doesn't."

"And I suppose all of this is legal."

"Let's say it's not *illegal*. The IRS could disallow the deduction, maybe try to force Saul to pay taxes on the offshore income, but Saul would take them to court. Eventually, even if the IRS won, which is far from certain, he'd only have to pay some back taxes, plus interest and penalties."

"A slap on the wrist."

Duncan smiled. "A *tap* on the wrist. The corporate world isn't the streets of Oakland, Eddie. Legal and illegal aren't nearly so ... clear cut."

"Funny, I never thought of the streets of Oakland as particularly clear cut." Eddie drank some beer. "So Winsett, he runs the insurance company, that's how you two met?"

"Truth be told, there isn't much to run; just a little paperwork. One of the perks of having an insurance company in a tropical setting is that you get to go there periodically to maintain the fiction that there's a board of directors that has genuine meetings. Since you can't bring the money back, you tend to spend it over there, buy houses, boats, airplanes maybe."

"Is that what you've got over there?"

Duncan laughed. "Don't I wish. I'll let you in on a dirty, little corporate secret, Eddie. They call me the President of West Coast Lumber, but truth be told, I'm a puppet. I click my heels, salute and do exactly what Harriman Saul tells me—for which, I earn a fairly respectable living."

"Is that why you're doing this?"

"You mean our little transaction? I suppose that's part of it."

"And you really think Saul won't find out you're on both sides."

"Why would he?"

"Because somebody would tell him." Eddie smiled. "Since you let me in on a dirty little secret, Dick, I'm going to let you in on one. Crimes don't get solved because somebody finds a missing clue, or has a brilliant flash of intuition and suddenly puts all the pieces together. They get solved because people drop a dime on each other. They piss each other off, or rip each other off, or sleep with each other's women. Or could be somebody they know finds out what they did and gets jealous. It's not the play that goes wrong, it's the people, The problem, Dick, is the fucking people."

CHAPTER 19

FLIGHT OF THE MURRELET

A little after midnight, Eric was standing in the woods watching seven kids dressed in black, kneeling in a circle, one of them holding a flashlight, all of them looking at a map. Eric was more or less sidelined by the Thomas collar, standing a little ways back. Somebody had decided they should all have code names for some unknown reason. Rhonda had become Murrelet—Mur-let, everybody was calling her, leaving out the second syllable, though Eric was still inclined to call her Rhonda. Then there was a big, square jawed local they elected team leader; they called her Ladyhawk. And four sherpas to carry the loads and do the climbing: Spiderman, Batman, Iron Man and X-Man. Jesus. And, of course, there was Eric, not involved in the operation, but somebody said he needed a name, so they decided to call him Neck Man, which everybody thought was so hilarious they spent an hour and a half laughing about it.

Looking at the map now, playing dumb, Rhonda asked, "What're all the little green lines?"

"Elevations, see the numbers?"

"Uh-huh."

"That's how many feet above sea level. See this here?"

"Where?" Rhonda leaned closer, if that was even possible.

Ladyhawk, a bull dyke Eric believed, traced the route on the map with her finger. "Next to where it says 263. That's Salamander Creek. We go in there. Snake through the creek bottom, up toward Green River, and it's right … about … here."

Rhonda said, "I was never that good with maps, actually." Jesus, that was the understatement of the decade, the girl got lost twice he knew of, going from Berkeley to Oakland.

But if Rhonda was clueless, everybody else seemed to know the drill. Spiderman and Batman were the climbers; Iron Man and X-Man did the ground ops. Ladyhawk was the local expert, supposed to know the trails, and Eric was hoping she did. It could be a real long night if she didn't. The last thing he'd recognized was a 7-Eleven, coming in off the freeway. After that, a couple turns, a long uphill grade, then what looked like logging roads. They drove a half hour in the dark, then pulled off and unloaded their gear near an old abandoned cabin. That's where they were now.

Getting ready to go, Ladyhawk said, "Okay, listen up. Keep close. And stay on the trail. They grow some serious weed back in here. You don't want to get lost up on the clearcuts, believe me. It's getting near harvest."

And off they went. Eric started in front, but they weren't more than a hundred yards past the cabin when things turned ugly. He said, "Jesus, you call this a trail?"

"Shhh!" They all said it together, like they held rehearsals.

Eric kept at it another twenty or thirty yards, then stepped aside to check out his shoe lace, let the sherpas go past, hoping they'd make it easier getting through the fucking vines. A hundred yards further though, totally unexpected, they broke into a creek bed that ran through a canyon, and things got easier. Until they didn't. All of a sudden, everything bunched up and came to a stop.

Eric said, "Hey, what're you guys doing up there?"

"Shhh!" In unison.

A guy in front of him motioned to what looked like a bunch of down logs clogging the bottom of the canyon. Up ahead, Iron Man was whispering something to Ladyhawk, and she was motioning to what might be a trail that led uphill to the left. She said, "Lemme check it out."

Rhonda said, "I'm going with you."

And off they went. The rest of them sat down and waited for fifteen minutes. Jesus.

When they came back, Ladyhawk gathered everybody around her. "There's an old clear cut up there," she said. "Follow me. Let's keep it to the tree line, okay? Stay close."

The "clear cut" she was talking about was like a scene from a Tim Burton movie. The moon was up now, turning everything blue and silver, stumps and snags looming up like ghosts. Plus, the ground was littered with logger shit—beer cans, chain oil containers, Styrofoam takeout cartons, rusty pieces of metal. The total effect was somewhere between eerie and disgusting.

Then, everything stopped again.

Eric muttered, "Jesus, now what?"

"Shhh!" The fucking Greek chorus.

Next thing he knew, they were moving again, faster now, on a diagonal, back toward the creek bottom. Somebody was whispering, "Go, go, go."

No Greek chorus now, everybody stumbling through stumps and brush and shit, more sliding than running down the hill. A few minutes later, they were back at the creek bottom, gasping for air.

Ladyhawk held her hand up, looking at Eric. "Shhh!"

"What?" He wasn't even going to say anything.

A minute later, they heard a ruckus somewhere up the hill. A sound like fireworks. POP! POP! POP-POP! POP! People shouting, a lot of people. Then, more fireworks. But by this time, Eric was getting the idea it probably wasn't fireworks. And also realizing the shouting wasn't in English. And it was coming closer, though hard to tell how close. Then, something whizzed past his ear!

"Shit!" Everybody hit the deck.

At first it seemed like the shots were getting closer, then he couldn't tell where they were, then they seemed to be getting further away. Then silence. And after what seemed like an hour, Ladyhawk finally whispered, "Let's go."

They tramped through the creek bed for another half hour, nobody saying a word. Then, the canyon widened. The guy next to him pointed up, and Eric realized they were in an old growth redwood forest, an awesome experience, even in the middle of the night. There was nothing like it, sort of an outdoor cathedral. Ladyhawk had a certain tree in mind, up a ways from the creek. It was set off by itself and looked old, scarred with fire at the bottom. And it was big. Everybody liked it right away. Bigger was better, right?

How they did it, Iron Man had something they called a "throw rope" with a weight at one end that he managed to get over the lowest branch. Once that was done, they tied on a bigger rope and hauled that over. Then, they went up, one at a time, and started hauling up the gear. The platform went up first. Then the tarps (red, white and blue, supposed to be like the American flag), sleeping bag, clothes, electronics, then the food and water packed in plastic buckets—even a little Port-a-Pottie. Then they put Rhonda in a climbing belt and hooked on the ropes.

Eric gave his parting words of advice, "Remember," he said. "Watch the four-letter words. And sound bites. Talk in sound bites."

Then, they hoisted her up in the tree and Rhonda was transformed, starting her fifteen minutes of fame as the Marvelous Murrelet.

*   *   *

Harry Saul's voice rattled the squawk box.

"I see a line item, a hundred thousand dollars. Every month I see this item. 'Private Security Services, one hundred thousand dollars. And this what I'm paying for? A teenage girl in a tree giving me the finger on national television?"

"It's YouTube, Harry," Dick said, "Not national television. And I don't think she's a teenager."

Not listening, as usual, Harry said, "I am looking at a teenage girl on my property with a tee shirt that says, 'Fuck Harriman Saul?' What did you just say?"

Standing by the telescope, slowly panning the cul-de-sac Dick said, "I said, I don't think she's a teenager."

"I don't care if she's in assisted living," Harry said, "Where's that moron in charge of security."

"On his way." Dick said. "You have to be realistic, Harry, we've got a hundred thousand acres. We can't patrol it all."

"I'm not saying patrol it all," Harry said. "I'm saying, use your head. The kids are screaming about old growth. It wouldn't take a rocket scientist to figure out that's where they make trouble. We need a strategy on this Dick. We're not in front of it. We're behind the curve, reacting. ... Dick, are you listening to me?

"I'm listening."

Harry said, "You sound like you're in the shower."

Through the telescope Lucia Hellman—Dick had pulled her name from Human Resources—was standing at the front door of the white frame house in a bathrobe, arms folded across her breasts, watching her husband, Walt, jog to his truck. The HR files revealed that Walter J. Hellman, retired at age 45 after twenty-three years in the military, and employed by West Coast Lumber as Director of Security for the past seven years, had been married a year ago to one Lucia Gonzalez Moreno, age 32, a native of Barranquilla Colombia. Hmm.

Harry was saying, "Do you have me on a speaker? Dick? ... Hello?"

"Right here, Harry."

"Is somebody there with you?"

"No, no, nobody else."

"Then pick up the goddamn phone."

The way Alan Michaels had explained it to Harriman Saul, it started when Connie Kurosawa sent out a tweet about her "Five Alive" segment, uploaded the compete interview to YouTube, posted a link to the interview on her Facebook page and emailed her agent. As it happened, CNN happened to use Channel 5, Redwood Bay, as a local news affiliate, so Connie's agent emailed a link to a CNN news producer and the producer picked it up. Why not? It was unique; it was visual. And, they worked it into the evening news, and eventually into the Headline News rotation, airing every half hour twenty-four seven, until the other networks had to pick up the story, if not the interview.

CONNIE: This thousand year old redwood tree is home to 21-year old Murrelet Myers, who is trying to save it from being chopped down by West Coast Lumber Company. Ms. Myers is with us live courtesy of Skype and the AT&T digital network. Also with us by telephone from West Coast Lumber headquarters in Liberty, California, is Company spokesperson, Brett Cox. Let's start with you, Murrelet. First of all, is that your real name?

MURRELET: Real enough, Connie. A way of calling attention to the plight of my new neighbors, the marbled murrelets, who live in the old growth redwood trees.

CONNIE: That's a bird.

MURRELET: Right. They nest right up here. They're an endangered species.

CONNIE: And is that why you're living?—and as I understand, you are actually living—up in the tree?

MURRELET: Right, well that's one reason. The other reason is the old growth trees.

CONNIE: You use the word, 'old growth,' can you explain what that means?

MURRELET: That's the original redwood forest before they cut it down. Some of these trees are two thousand years old, three hundred fifty feet tall. There used to be two million acres of them. They already cut 95% of it down. And now West Coast Lumber Company is trying to chop down more.

CONNIE: And that's why you decided to climb up the tree.

MURRELET: I'm here to protest the illegal actions of corporate racketeer Harriman Saul and West Coast Lumber, which he controls. In the last two years, this criminal enterprise has been cited for over six hundred violations of California forestry regulations, which is a violation for every single working day, for two years! They're trying to murder these trees so environmental crook Harriman Saul can complete some illegal airline takeover scheme he has going on that the SEC should really investigate.

And I'm inviting people all around the world who care about these beautiful trees, to let the government know that they aren't going to stand for it. And I'd also like to say that everybody can see me live twenty-four seven on our "tree-cam" and engage in live chat at www.TreeSitterGirl.com. That's Tree Sitter Girl, all one word, dot com.

There was another part of the interview, where Connie talked to a company spokesperson who said West Coast Lumber owned the land, and was entitled to earn a fair return on its investment, and a representative from the State Parks System, who admitted the State had tried to buy the land, but couldn't afford the asking price of a half billion dollars.

None of this sat real well with Harry, but he was particularly pissed off about the "illegal airline takeover" part, and wanted to know how a bunch of kids in the middle of nowhere found out about the Southeast Airline deal.

Dick asked him if he ever heard of the internet. "You filed a 13D. These kids know how to do a Google search. They aren't stupid, Harry," letting Harry know that Dick wasn't stupid either. The thing Dick was learning about Harry, he kept pushing until you pushed back. If you pushed back hard enough, he eventually stopped pushing. Or maybe he fired you, but every day that passed, that seemed to be less and less important.

Now, Harry was saying, "You picked up the phone? I'm not on the speaker?"

"You're not on the speaker."

"Good. Because I want to be clear about this, and I want to make sure you hear every word I have to say to you. Are you listening, Dick?"

"I'm listening."

"It's my fucking tree, Dick. So your options are, you can either get the girl out of there, or I'll find somebody else to do it."

*   *   *

"Harper, Stearns & Foster."

Seven o'clock Monday morning, Shanna still asleep, Eddie was standing on the deck outside Shanna's living room, talking on his cell.

He said, "Colin Winsett?"

"Mr. Winsett? One moment please."

Eddie glanced out at the water. The air was cold, a faint breeze blowing, the coastal evergreens appearing and disappearing in the fog.

"Colin Winsett speaking." There was a trace of a British accent.

"Colin—" Eddie said, "You don't know me. My name is ... Norville Petty. Dick Duncan and I are involved in a few business arrangements here in Redwood County, California. We were having lunch the other day, and your name came up."

He chuckled. "I certainly hope you weren't talking about golf."

Eddie chuckled back. "Actually, we were talking about money."

"I feel better already. Are you a lawyer, Mr. Petty?"

"No, why do you ask?"

"Well, it's just ... we're accustomed to dealing through attorneys stateside. The arrangements tend to be ... complex. I'd be happy to speak with your attorney if that would be preferable for you. "

Eddie found himself glancing in the direction of the bedroom, and tried a nervous laugh. "The thing is, Colin, I've gotten myself in a situation where my attorney is also ... call it a partner ... in a particular transaction. I believe you know her. Shanna Black?"

"Say no more. I understand completely. What can we do for you."

"Well, the way this came up ... you see, the truth is, I'm ... in a situation somewhat similar to Dick Duncan's."

"Not an entirely unpleasant situation."

"You could say that, but it also has its ...."

"Complexities, I understand. Did Dick explain to you the range of services we provide?"

"In a general way, but he didn't get into all the details."

"If you're interested, I'd be happy to put together a descriptive packet."

"That would be fine. But ... the thing is, the ... transaction ... is moving quickly, I'm in a bit of a hurry."

"All right. Well, as I'm sure Dick explained, we specialize in asset protection. As attorneys, we have the ability to create completely customized programs. Limited liability vehicles … sandwich structures …. here in the Caymans, or in other tax-advantaged locations … and I think, most appropriately, in your situation, discretionary trusts of various kinds …."

"Trusts, right, that's what Dick was saying. But I didn't really understand the particulars."

"That's not entirely surprising. Well—" Winsett paused. "—on a basic level, these structures are all tax driven. As Dick may have explained, the key from the perspective of the U.S. taxpayer is that he or she must be able to answer 'no' to the question on Form 1040 about ownership of a foreign trust. An affirmative answer to that question will almost certainly trigger an audit."

"He mentioned that."

"Right. Basically we create a trust in which you are not a beneficial owner, typically under the laws of St. Kitts and Nevis. You own nothing more than a certificate that permits you to share in distributions when and if made, in the sole discretion of the trustee. Another feature is the inclusion of an 'event of distress' clause. If a legal action is filed against the trust or the trustee—by one of your creditors for example—the trustee's powers are immediately terminated, so it becomes impossible for him to pay over the trust's assets in response to a court order."

"I think I get that part, Colin, but —can I be perfectly frank for a moment?

"Of course."

"What I don't understand, is how the person—I'm not sure what you call it—the person whose money we're really talking about."

"The certificate holder," Winsett said.

"Okay, the certificate holder. How he or she would know the trustee is actually going to do what he wants him to do, and not just, let's say, disappear with the money."

Winsett laughed. "And a reasonable question at that! I suppose the first answer is, our business comes exclusively by referral. We're delighted to provide references, and very much encourage prospective clients to check us out. Having said that, we also encourage our clients to consider establishing a 'trust protector'. Once we put that in place, the trustee is required to obtain the advice and consent of the protector before performing any discretionary action, such as making distributions. In addition, if an event of distress were to occur, terminating the trustee's powers, the trust protector could step in to, for example, move the trust assets to another jurisdiction."

Eddie was trying to figure this out. "You say, you 'create' the trust protector. How do you do that? Is that something you put in the trust agreement."

"No, no, no. You see, the Internal Revenue Service could treat the trust protector as a beneficial owner of the trust, which would make him or her taxable on trust income. It's generally considered better to handle the arrangements in a side letter."

"A side letter."

"Think of it as a letter of instructions to the trustee, that the trustee acknowledges."

"And this ... trust protector. Who would it be ... ordinarily?"

"Well, it could be anyone, of course. But, if you're as deeply concerned over the safety of your assets as most of our clients, you'd want it to be someone you trust implicitly. It needn't be an individual. It could be a corporation or limited liability company you control. It could be a trusted attorney—probably not in this case." Winsett laughed again. "Or, of course, it could always be ... yourself."

CHAPTER 20

AT THE RANCHERIA

"**W**hat did I say to you, Lon?" The Doctor was watching Lon, sitting now on the same stool where Wayne sat a few days ago.

Lon rubbed his face with his hand, bobbed his head up and down, but did not look at him. "You told me the Feds had the Salvadoran, and there was a good chance they'd pick up the Kiwi, and he'd roll over on us. So, you didn't want him hanging around."

"What did I say to you Lon? I want to know my exact words. What did I tell you to do?"

Lon blew out some air, his knee bobbing up and down now. Finally, he mumbled. "Make sure he got on the plane."

"I'm sorry, I didn't hear that."

Finally, Lon looked at him. "You said to make sure he got on the plane. … I *know* what the fuck you told me, but …."

"And did he *get* on the plane? … Lon? … Did he?"

Looking down now, Lon grinned, just a little. "Not unless they shipped him back there to get buried, I guess." He looked at the Doctor to get his reaction, smiling.

The Doctor shook his head, but didn't say anything.

"Well, I don't see what the big deal's about," Lon said now. "He ain't gonna testify, is he?"

The Doctor tapped a copy of the San Francisco *Chronicle*, lying on the counter. "Do you know who was with him? You killed the starting left tackle for the San Francisco 49ers."

Lon looked at the newspaper, shook his head, "That there's a mistake. The guy I shot was *gay*. I could tell by the way the two of them was acting together."

The Doctor started to say something, then didn't. Talking to Lon was like talking to Homer Simpson with a shotgun. Finally, he said, "Well, what's done is done." He was quiet a minute. "I think both of us are going to feel a whole lot better about your next assignment And on the brighter side, I didn't take the spread on the Niners."

First time Lon Odom met Norville Petty, he'd come back from Iraq looking for something to do, and put in a quarter acre of weed on some old clearcut land in the hills southeast of Manzanita. Around harvest time, Petty showed up with some deputies, and told Lon they was confiscating his crop on account of he hadn't paid his taxes. Lon told him he didn't pay taxes to no punk ass pork truckers and managed to take out a couple with a shovel before they busted his collar bone and hit him with a Taser. It wasn't long after that, Lon's old man had his accident and Big Billy had to go up to Canada. Lon would have done Petty then, except he took Big Billy's place working for the Doctor, and the Doctor told him he didn't want no one messing with the law enforcement situation. Well, those days was gone now, and Lon didn't see a reason to delay what Norville Petty had coming.

When the Doctor got done with his shit bitching, Lon drove the Yukon into Manzanita, stopped by a place called Ray-Lee's, sat down at the bar, and ordered himself a Coors light and a meatball sub. Ray-Lee's didn't serve much else but draft beer and meatball subs, and probably nobody went in there ordered anything different, but that didn't seem to bother the deputies from the South County Annex. They just about kept the place in business.

Waiting now, Lon picked up a paper, started in reading about the "double murder", they called it, down in San Francisco. There was a picture of the Kiwi, and a guy in a Forty-Niners uniform, big guy, Todd something or other, that could have been the one with him. Lon was trying to put it together in his mind how somebody played pro ball could wind up at a gay bar with a fucking butt muncher.

Dora brought him a beer, and a couple minutes later came back with the sub. Dora, a big woman with a solid build, was married to Ray— Leoni, Leonetti, something with a "lee" in it—he was the one owned the place. Lon was pretty hungry, and the sub was good, so he wasn't paying much attention to what was going on in the bar till a couple minutes later, he heard a voice behind him.

"Hey, Lon. What you doing around here?" He looked up, and there was Artie Stroh, a deputy worked at the jail, and one of the folks Lon was hoping he might run into.

Lon told him he wasn't doing much and motioned to a stool. "Sit down, take a load off."

Artie held back a minute. "You sure?"

Lon looked at him. "Why not?"

"You know, what happened to your brother. I hope there's no hard feelings about that."

Lon shrugged. "Billy was a fuck-up. Everybody knows that."

"You know what I mean, though," Barry slid one cheek onto the stool, but still wasn't looking that comfortable. "We didn't want to take him in. We had to do it on account of the TV. Then, Hellman—don't know if you know him, he's in charge of security over at West Coast Lumber—he was screaming at everybody how we was all gonna get sued if we didn't lock somebody up."

Lon said, "Billy was a fuck up, Barry. Like I told you, there's nothing to be sorry about."

"Yeah, I know, but your Mama, she must have took it pretty hard."

"Well you know Mama. She's got his ashes in a box right on top of the TV out at the trailer."

Barry looked at him.

Lon took a pull on his beer, nodding. "Keeps her in mind of the impermanence of human existence, is what she says about it."

Barry shook his head. "I don't know. I think that'd give me the creeps, having the ashes right there in the living room. ... Hey there, Dora."

Dora was there now with her order pad out, asking Barry what he wanted.

Barry pointed at Lon's plate. "That sub sure looks good. How about getting me one of those?"

"And to drink?"

Barry looked over at Lon's beer, but then he said. "Better make her a Coke, Dora."

She drew the Coke from the fountain, then took off with the food order.

Lon looked at the Coke, "Petty's got you on a short leash, huh?"

Barry checked behind him to see if anybody was listening, then he said, "I don't know how short his leash is," he said, looking down at his crotch, "But the rest of him's short enough."

Lon thought that was interesting. "So—what's this I hear, He's got himself a boat?"

Barry rolled his eyes. "Don't let *him* hear you call her that. No sir. What the Sheriff's got is a Magnum 44 Banzai—made by the people do the new Coast Guard interceptors. Had her trucked all the way from Florida."

"My oh my," Lon said, trying to sound impressed. "Where's she berthed?"

"Sanchez Landing." He smiled. "Yeah, damn thing looks like she come right out of *Miami Vice*, remember that? I don't know if the Sheriff thinks he's Jamie Foxx or Colin Farrell."

"Maybe he don't know the difference."

Barry laughed. "Maybe he don't. I'll tell you one thing, though, the man is nuts about that boat. Runs her up and down the coast every god-damn weekend. Calls her the High Life."

"The High Life. ... Well, I tell you one thing about running around in a boat like that, Barry. You don't know how to control all that power, it can get dangerous."

* * *

Friday morning, Danny Villa was sitting in the trailer down at the Liberty Mill, sexting a pretty hot waitress he met last night at a bar in Manzanita, but also wondering what the fuck was going on. First he thought it was the same old company bullshit, all the time starting and stopping again. Starting in at the Watershed show, then stopping when the girl goes up the tree and the thing gets on the news and in the papers . Then, this morning, he gets a call from Mr. Page. He says, there might be some work after all. Danny should go to Security, ask for Mr. Hellman. Then, Danny starting thinking. Hellman? Security? *Jesuchristo! Podría ser?*

First of all, the thing was over. He hadn't seen the woman in a couple weeks at least. Second, how could the guy even know about it? But, then thinking, the man was security. And there was even a sign in front of the house about video surveillance. Fuck, what was he even thinking?

Now, here was the man, dressed like a fucking *federale*, wearing a gun. "You Villa?" He said it so it rhymed with "Gorilla."

"Vee-ya," Danny said, "Like Pancho, you know? In Spanish, when there's two 'l's' together, you say that way 'y'. Vee-ya, you know?"

Danny didn't like the way the guy was looking at him. "Is that right? Okay, Pancho, why don't you come with me."

Danny went with the man into an office with a pretty good view of the big overhead crane at the mill. Danny's old man used to work there before he decided it was too fucking cold up here and went back to Guadalajara.

In the office now, the man said, "Sit down, Villa," not changing the way he said it.

While the guy read through some papers on his desk, Danny was trying to get in his mind how the woman took him home from the bar that time—showed him some positions he never seen before—could hook up with this dude. It was pretty hard to imagine. What she told him, she met the man back home, in Colombia, through some agency on the internet. She said, guys from the U.S. came down there looking for women who wanted a husband.

Danny asked her how it was working out. She didn't say anything right away, but then she told him, in a quiet way, that marrying this man was the worst thing she ever did in her life. He wouldn't call her by her name,

Lucia, but kept calling her Lucy. She told him the man was old, and had trouble getting it up. He could get rough sometimes, too, slap her around, when he couldn't do it. Danny asked her why she put up with it, she said, what could she do? Anyway, he didn't hit as hard as the guys in Colombia. What bothered her more was about the culture.

"I'm from Barranquilla," she said. "We have carnival. We like to party. This man, he don't even know how to dance. In the night, he goes downstairs in the basement, plays with his guns."

The last time Danny saw Lucia, she asked him what kind of work he did at the mill. Danny told her he didn't work at the mill. He was a topper, climbed the big trees in the woods. Usually, when Danny told that to a woman, she thought it was cool. Not Lucia.

"Oh," she said, "I thought you drove a forklift."

And that was the end of it. Within a week Danny heard she was fucking some dude drove a forklift at the mill. And not only was the dude married, he looked like he was taking ugly pills. Danny couldn't believe it. A woman who only did it with guys who worked where her husband did? Usually it was the other way around. But then, that was the thing with women. No matter how many times you got in bed with them, you still never knew where they were coming from.

Now, the man, Hellman, got up from his chair, and started walking back and forth with his hands behind his back, like he was playing a part in some old war movie. "Here it is, Villa. I asked your supervisor who was the best climber in his crew and he said it was you." He stopped, looked at Danny real hard. "Is that true, mister? Are you the best climber there is?"

Danny was wondering if it was a trick question. "The best?" He shrugged. "Hey, man, how would I know? There's a lot of climbers out there, you know? California. Oregon, Washington. Idaho, Colorado. Plus you got Canada. Probably some places I don't know. I'm pretty good, I guess."

The man didn't seem to like the answer. "I'm looking for a man able to undertake a difficult mission," he said. "I don't think 'pretty good' is going to cut it."

Danny was never in the Army, but he was pretty sure it would be something like this. But one good thing, this didn't seem to be about Lucia.

The man kept walking back and forth, talking to himself now, saying, "Tim Page is a good man. I'm not inclined to ignore his recommendation. Maybe it's a self-image problem."

Then he started in talking about the girl in the tree and how she was making a mockery of private property rights and how it was of vital importance to West Coast Lumber Company that these violations must be "brought to a halt at once". Then he started talking about the "mission" and how he was putting a "strike team" together and Danny could be the "point man, at the tip of the spear" and so on.

When it was over, Danny asked him if he was talking about the girl on TV.

"The girl on TV. That's right, mister."

Danny didn't much like the idea. First of all, it seemed stupid and, second, the girl on TV looked kind of cute. "So basically, what you're saying is, you want me to go up there, steal the girl's shit and monkey wrench her situation."

The man pulled out a piece of paper. "Actually, we made up a little list for you."

Danny read it. "Food, water …Video camera? Laptop computer? Cell phone, pager, walkie-talkie, solar powered battery charger?"

Hellman said, "You don't have to bring the stuff *down* with you. You can just toss it out of the tree. That's up to you."

Danny was quiet for a minute, thinking about the implications. Finally, he said, "Here's the thing. What I do, I go up and top the trees. With the weather, the fog and shit, it could get dangerous, but you get used to it, you know? But this thing, see, this is *completely* different."

"Different how?"

"Well for one thing, I never snuck up on a girl in a tree before. Suppose she comes after me or something. What if she has a gun?"

"She doesn't have a gun."

"Okay, you're saying. But you want me to take her shit. Wouldn't that be stealing?"

"She has no right to be there. She's trespassing."

Danny shook his head. "I don't know," he said, "It seems to me there's a lot of risk with this. It's not like ordinary climbing."

The man looked at him, arms folded, "What's your point?"

"What I'm thinking, if I'm gonna bring an end to a 'mockery of private property rights', and act as 'point man on a vitally important mission'—that could be worth a lot of money. "

*　*　*

Headed out to Juanita in the Cube, Eddie was thinking about the deal with Shanna. After he talked to the lawyer in the Caymans, he had the un-mistakable feeling he was getting had. He remembered what Russell said, if he walked away from the deal, he ought to have his head examined. He had nothing when he came back to Redwood County. So what did he have to lose? It was like going on a run in Vegas. You were playing with the house's money. If you lost it back, what did you really lose?

The trouble was, that way of looking at things didn't *feel* nearly as good as it *sounded*. Even if it *wasn't* his money, Eddie didn't like being conned.

Russell was at hard at it on the computer when Eddie walked into the tribal office in Juanita. As it turned out, he was looking at gambling equipment, doing comparison shopping.

"It's a revelation, dude," he said. "I had no idea."

"What's that?"

"SBX," Russell said. "Server based gaming. On-demand configuration control. The player can select any game he or she wants from a menu, without ever leaving the console. Totally eliminates the risk of unpopular game choice or obsolescence. Of course, you have to get a central system manager, which is considerably more up-front money, but in the long run? Shit, I'd spend the money. What do you think?"

Eddie told him, yeah, it sounded terrific. When they got through that, and Eddie finally told him why he came out there, Russell took a minute, looking out the window. Finally, he said, "Let's go for a ride." Then, glancing at Eddie's Cube through the window, said, "I'll drive."

They headed into the Rancheria in Russell's old truck, across that broad, coastal plain, dotted with scrub, dried the color of straw. They drove west, into the sun, passing faded wooden houses, tumble down fences, rusted tricycles, overturned trashcans, broken swing sets, and pickup trucks with faded paint parked on unwatered lawns.

Eddie said, "Hasn't changed much."

"You think it would?"

Eddie shook his head, "I thought it *never* would. That's why I took off. I couldn't wait to get out of this fucking place."

"Yeah, man," Russell said, "Me neither."

"Right, but, with you, it was different. I never felt like I belonged here."

"Cold Flats, are you kidding?" Russell laughed. "Nobody belongs here. It's a place of exile. The fucking wind, the fog. It's not...." He shook his head, not bothering to finish the thought. They drove in silence for a while.

Finally, he said, "I was at Berkeley when the old man passed. I came back for the funeral. I remember, the folks came by to see him off." He looked at Eddie now. "He was a fake, my old man. You know that? A drunken loud mouth phony. Scared as shit people would find out who he really was. The thing is, those people that came? They *knew* that, understand? He didn't fool anybody. But they came. 'Cause he had a *place* here. I don't mean Cold Flats. I mean ... ." His voice trailed off. "Maybe I don't know what I mean."

Eddie looked out the window for a while. Finally, he said, "I'm not sure what that would feel like."

"What?"

"To have a place somewhere."

They pulled to a stop on the old lighthouse bluff at the edge of the Redwood Bay, the bluff cleared now, nothing but some cypress trees left. The place used to belong to Jesus freaks back in the seventies, but had been abandoned, turned into a teenage hang out by the time they were growing up. Now, the lighthouse, the ranch buildings, the old redwood water tower, everything was gone.

Eddie said, "Damn, what happened?"

Russell shrugged. "Some Christian group bought it. Probably ten years ago now. They wound up giving it back to the Feds. No more souls to save, I guess."

"I guess."

They got out of the Ranger now, ambled toward the bluff edge, sat on a log, near where a narrow path led down to the beach. It was a clear day, the afternoon sun strong here, reflecting off the water, but the air still had a bite, and you could see the fog bank sitting offshore, waiting to come in when the sun went down.

Russell pulled out a baggie, waved it under Eddie's nose.

Eddie smiled, "Like the old days, huh?"

Russell rolled a joint, then turned away from the wind to light it with a match. He took a hit, handed it to Eddie. "Tell me what you think."

Eddie took a pretty good hit. The effect was quick. "Where'd you get *this* shit?"

Russell looked at him, but didn't say anything. Eddie took another hit, and the stone coming on now seemed to clear his head out, let him see things he couldn't quite see before. "It's from him? The Doctor?"

Russell lifted the joint out of Eddie's hand, took a hit. "You see that new Community Center driving in? Don't provide jobs, but it gives folks something to do, waiting for the eagle to shit, if you know what I'm talking about."

Eddie did understand. Eagle shit meant government checks. Russell handed him the joint again. "Remember that day, we were down in Liberty, what I said to you?"

Eddie took a hit. He said, "The whole thing was a show? So, what you're saying ..." Now, able to answer his own question. "The Doctor's running the demonstrations."

Russell smiled. "Call it crop insurance," he said. "He needs time to get his harvest in. We're helping him out."

"Why didn't you tell me that before?"

"I did tell you, a couple of times. I thought you'd figure it out."

Eddie thought a minute. "And with Duncan?"

Russell laughed. "Man, everybody's paying that dude off. He's an equal opportunity motherfucker."

There was still something Eddie was getting stuck on. He said, "But if the Doctor's running the whole thing ...,"

Russell took the joint back, shook his head. "Look at it this way, *hombre*. This is America. The land of opportunity. Everybody's an entrepreneur."

Eddie sat there a while, trying to see this thing. "So, with Matty's place ... how does that work? The Doctor's making payoffs 'cause he doesn't want the road. But the people getting paid off, they're buying up land to build the road. So I'm guessing ... what? He doesn't know?"

Russell laughed. "Oh yeah. He knows."

"You're sure about that."

Russell said, "I ought to be, *hombre*. I'm the one told him."

"When?"

"Right from the start. First time Shanna called me up, asked me about Matty."

"What did he say?"

Russell nodded. "Let me ask you a question. You've known Shanna, what, a couple months? How long did it take you to figure out you couldn't trust her?"

Eddie looked at him.

"Doctor's known her a hell of a lot longer. And he's not fucking her, either."

"But ... he wasn't pissed off?"

"Actually? He got a pretty good laugh. See you don't know the guy. He's got everybody running around like rats in a fucking maze. He's been doing this shit for years. It's a business. As far as the payoffs, think of it like rent."

"Rent."

"Yeah. He rents things—people, demonstrations, protection. That's what he says. It's temporary. Everything is. Part of the business. Long as he has time to get his crop in, what does he care if they build the road or not?"

Eddie took some time, until he felt like he had a handle on this. "Okay," he said, turning now so they were face to face, "I get it. Everybody's in business, making trades. Nobody doing favors. But there's still one thing I don't understand."

Raising his eyebrows, Russell said, "Which is?"

"All this shit you got going, hooking me up with Shanna, feeding information to the Doctor. What are *you* looking for?"

Russell gave him a slow smile. "Jesus, Fast Eddie Fuentes," he said. "I was beginning to think you'd never ask me that fucking question."

*   *   *

Danny told the man he'd get to the woods at sunrise. He'd climb for a thousand dollars, but no way in hell he was going up a three hundred foot tree in the dark. And he wouldn't do it at all if he hadn't blown the amp in his truck.

The way it worked, the security went in first to make sure nobody else was around, then Danny went in with his gear. It was easy getting his throw rope over, especially when they wouldn't let him use his gun. But after that, it was easy. Pull the climbing rope over, tie on a Blake hitch, and pull himself up.

He couldn't see the girl when he first got up there, or for that matter, 'till he got pretty near to where she was. You had to say, the kids that hauled the shit up there, did a hell of a lot of work. They had a platform made out of plywood probably three-quarter inch thick. There was even a tent on top of it, and all kinds of shit tied on the branches with ropes.

When Danny first saw the girl—dark hair, overalls, a little dirty looking, but still kind of cute, holding her little white plastic bucket—he said, "Hey girl, how you doing?"

She looked at him. "Hey *girl*, how you *doing*?"

He tried to smile, "Hey, okay … my name is Danny. And I'm thinking you probably don't get too many visitors up here, right?" The girl looked kind of mean. He said, "Right, so, I'm not looking to invade your space or nothing, but … you mind if I come up for a few minutes?"

She said, "You work for West Coast Lumber, don't you? What'd they do? Send you up here to monkey wrench my camp site? Is that it?"

Danny shook his head. "No, no. Why would I do something like that."

She said, "Hey, Danny? Look at me."

He looked up, and—

She tipped over the bucket she had in her hand, filled with piss. Fuck, poured it right on his head. Jesus, you know? It was hard to believe a person would do a *thing* like that.

He said, "Jesus, girl! What fucking zoo did you grow up in?"

Then, she started throwing shit at him, calling him names, and the next thing he knew, Danny sort of lost it. He was up in the branches now, tying his safety line on, then heading toward her, the girl backing away with a cell phone in one hand, this little thing looked like a pen in the other.

She said, "I'm warning you, this is a camera. You're *live* on the fucking Internet man, *right now.*"

"Oh yeah?" Moving toward her, Danny waved, "Hi, Mom." Then he started untying the girl's gear, throwing it out of the tree, working his way around the platform.

She held up the phone. "I've got the Five Alive News on speed dial, Connie Kurosawa's direct line. She's coming on the line. Hello … hello, Connie?"

Danny said, "Hi, Connie!" Tossing a plastic bucket of ramen noodles toward the camera.

The girl said, "This dickwad is from West Coast Lumber. He's in the branches now, coming toward me, I don't know what he's going to do …."

Moving across the platform now, Danny said, "I'll show you what I'm gonna do, you fucking skank."

The girl said into the phone, "Connie? Are you picking this up? ... Get it on tape if you can't go live."

"Put this on tape." Danny grabbed a battery charger, sailed it out of the tree.

The girl said, "Ass wipe! Don't you realize you're participating in the destruction of a sacred environmental monument? How much is West Coast Lumber paying you for this?"

Holding out the cell phone now, like she was doing an interview on television. Danny tried grabbing it, but she yanked it back.

"Get out of here, you prehistoric fudge bag!"

Danny moved toward the cell phone. "Give it to me."

The girl backed away. Danny tried again, the girl backed away more. Danny tried again. The girl backed up even more ... only now there wasn't nothing for the girl to back up *on*.

He thought, "Oh, shit."

"Aahh!"

The next thing he knew, the girl was falling toward the ground, backwards, cell phone in one hand, camera in the other. Down, down. Then, gracias Jesus, her overalls got caught up on a branch. Danny went to the edge and looked over. And there she was, hanging on the branch.

Danny called out, "You all right down there?"

And could hear her yell into her cell phone, "I've been saved by the tree! Terra has saved me!" Then she takes the cell phone away from her mouth and screams up at him, "You're going down for this, you douche bag! You hear me? You are going the fuck *down*."

CHAPTER 21

THE HIGH LIFE

Sanchez Marina was deserted early afternoon, just like Lon figured, the tuna fishers and crabbers not back quite yet. Lon knew right away which one she was, moored out toward the end of the pier, nothing else within a few slips of her. Forty-five feet of goddamn nautical thunder— clean lines, triple portholes, plus the one at the prow, kind of a wood grain finish. And sure enough, there it was, "High Life" painted on her stern. Figured to be a full stateroom below, with a stand-up head and shower. Should work out just about perfect.

The Doctor had a little Donzi 38 with twin 500 Mercs he kept out at the Costa Perdida to pick up stuff that fell off the occasional freighter, what he called "precursor chemicals"—used in his drug lab operation. Probably not a good idea for Petty's boat to wind up anywhere near where they kept the Donzi, so he ran her up to Fool's Cape, moored her in a cove. He set it up with Rampas to drive up from the garden and meet him there at noon, then drive him the twenty miles south to Sanchez. That's where he was now, gear in a gym bag, ready to rock 'n' roll.

Lon strolled out on the pier now, no hurry, like he was checking out the boats. When he got to where the High Life was moored, he looked around one last time to make sure no one was around, then hopped aboard. He had his picks, in case the cabin was locked, but it wasn't, the man figuring no one would have the balls to break into his boat. Yeah, well he'd find out he was wrong soon enough.

What they taught you in Force Recon, aside from the shot, the hardest part of the job was learning to wait. You'd get choppered in, middle of the night. Two man team, shooter and spotter. You'd generally have to pack-in, there could be some terrain, and some weight. Your M40A5 was fifteen pounds, plus your ammo, coms, additional weapons, rations, miscellaneous. You'd establish your base, stash your nonessentials, and move to your target to get set up. Then—you'd wait. How long? You'd have an idea, but wouldn't never exactly know. Lon was on assignment one time, the plan kept changing, wound up being the longest week of his life. You tried not to talk, learned to use hand signals. Lon liked that part. The part he never liked, the part nobody liked, was the wait.

*   *   *

Three-thirty Friday afternoon, Shanna told her assistant, Donald, sure, why not? Take off, have a nice weekend, have a nice life, whatever. Then, she kicked back on the couch, poured herself a Stoli out of the freezer, and tried to figure out what the fuck was going on.

She hadn't heard word one from Dick, or from Eddie, since they signed the documents. Now, the red flags were up. Her instinct was telling her something was going on. But what?

Eddie being predictably unpredictable, and Dick reliably unreliable, looking back, it was hard to believe she let them have lunch alone. They could have done what? Anything—worked a new split that cut her share down, or even cut her out. Dick was definitely capable of it—especially after he found out about the side agreement. She hadn't counted on that. On her last trip to the Caymans, she thought she and Colin had established a certain … rapport …. Apparently she underestimated Dick's money, or overestimated her own allure. Suppose Colin sent a copy of the agreement to Dick and Dick showed it to Eddie. It would look like she was trying to fuck them both. Maybe not a good use of words.

Shanna had been feeling lately, that things were slipping. Looking at her life objectively, she could see where someone might say she wasn't completely honest, or maybe not honest at all. But the truth of it was, all she'd ever been trying to was expand her options. Look at it. She grew up the daughter of a fundamentalist Christian horse rancher in Pinehurst, Wyoming. What were the options? Stay or go.

So, she got on a bus. All of a sudden, there were options. Hell, every place the bus stopped was an option. She picked the one that was as different from Pinehurst as she could get—Reno, Nevada—a town that billed itself as "The Biggest Little City in the World". A lot of options. But it wasn't long before she realized that, without money, most of them looked even worse than Pinehurst. The takeaway? Money equaled options.

Rex King equaled money. Then, she realized she didn't have to stay with Rex to get the money. So she filed for divorce. Even more options. But she got greedy, and lost most of it in an oil and gas play, when the promoter turned out to be a crook. She vowed she would never get taken again, took what was left, and put herself through school. When she got the job with Jimmy Kennan, she had reached the top of her game. But things started to unravel. Why? Lying on the couch now, Shanna took a long drink, then a deep breath, remembering those days, six years ago in Sacramento.

What happened? Analyze it. Bad luck? Bad decisions? An excess of ambition? A lack of self-control? Whatever it was, her world was reduced, her options narrowed. And then, be honest, she lost confidence. Ran away. Moved to Redwood County. Roger came along, a step in the right direction. But then, he was gone and she fell in with the Doctor, and that led to Dick. Dick Duncan, Jesus, the man was like Rex King without the fucking crown. But then, with the land, there was hope. A light at the end of the tunnel. A way out, except …. Eddie. He was different. Not a part of the calculation. Where the fuck did he fit into this? Honestly—if you could use that word in this kind of situation—he didn't.

With the land, her thinking was, if she told Dick that Eddie got half, and she told Eddie that Dick got half, she'd have room to negotiate. If either one of them pushed back, said they wanted more, she'd have options. With Winsett and the side letter, she'd have a *lot* more options. Did she have it in the back of her mind, that maybe she wouldn't have to split the money at all? Maybe. But she thought about that like she thought about everything else. It wasn't something she was definitely going to do. It was an option.

Now, with Eddie and Dick possibly scheming to cut her out, things had gone completely off track. And Shanna was starting to get this feeling— not a good feeling— like maybe there was something *she* was doing, or maybe *not* doing, that was getting her into this shit. Shanna had always figured *options* equaled *freedom*. Which meant she got nervous every time she had to make a decision, because *deciding* cut the *options* down. But what if options *weren't* freedom. What if they were only *options*, and freedom was something else altogether.

Her cell rang now. She looked at the caller ID. "Murrelet"? Jesus, Donald must have updated her contacts. It actually said Murrelet. Shanna let the call go to voicemail. Sorry, Murrelet, not ready to deal with your shit at the moment. She took a deep breath, finished off her drink, then happened to glance at the doorway, and saw a man standing there, arms folded, looking at her with gray blue eyes.

"Hasn't anybody ever told you it's not healthy to drink alone?"

* * *

Jennifer said, "Seven-thirty sharp, Dick. Your daughter is the star of the show, okay? So just this once, do think you could try not to spoil it for her?"

Standing at his telescope, Dick said, "Absolutely."

Jody was in a play at school, something about the Lewis and Clark Expedition. Little blonde Jody playing Sacagawea, the Shoshoni Indian guide. Apparently the Mainwaring School was dealing with a paucity of Native American enrollment.

"Oh, and *whatever* you do? Don't forget the bouquet at Dawes. I called the order in this afternoon and they promised to have it by five o'clock. Two dozen red roses. They're making a big presentation at the final curtain."

"*No problema,*" said Dick. And no sign of the Silverado at the white frame house across the freeway. But, wait a minute, what was this? A new Dodge Ram pickup, slowing down and now, stopping. A man getting out, dark complexion, early thirties, bigger than the guy with the Silverado, but not nearly as good looking. The lady of the house apparently switching from Chevrolet to Chrysler. Hmm.

"Don't forget what Dr. Rosen said. The children look to us as mirrors of their achievement. Every time we're there for them, appreciating their little triumphs, we lay another brick in the foundation of their self-confidence. So let's not *fuck it up,* shall we, *Dick*?"

Through the telescope ... the door was open now, the man going inside, but no lights on. Dick couldn't see much. The fog was headed in, the tops of the hills disappearing and reappearing, and the curtains on the master suite appeared to be drawn.

The intercom buzzed. "Mr. Duncan?"

"Yes?"

"Alan Michaels on two."

Dick had been waiting for the call all day, though not looking forward to it. "Jen?" he said, "Gotta run. See you later."

She said, "Seven-thirty, Dick. And don't forget about the ...."

He punched a button. "Alan. We're keeping you busy. The guys out there are calling it the 'flight of the Murrelet'. I wish I could have seen it."

"You really mean you haven't?"

"Haven't what?"

"Seen it. She recorded the whole thing. It's on YouTube. The guy coming toward her, the girl warning him to stay away, the guy coming closer, hitting her with the pepper spray, the girl screaming, the rush of leaves, branches breaking on the way down. Shaky hand-held shit, kind of like *The Blair Witch Project* only it's a lot clearer who the bad guy is."

Good thing he no longer gave a shit. Dick did a little Harry impersonation. "'Get the fucking girl out of the tree, Dick, or I'll get somebody who will.' Well, the asshole can't say he didn't get what he wanted."

"They're putting a march together for tomorrow."

"Tomorrow? Gee, that's too bad," Dick said mildly. "I'm pretty sure that would conflict with a field hockey game I have to attend. Or no, wait, maybe it's soccer."

"I talked to Harry, told him the way this thing is going, there's no way he can cut that tree down."

"Why not?"

"What's he going to do? Cut it down with the girl in it?"

Now Dick was surprised. "She's still up there?"

"She never left. They had a medical team go out there, but first they had to get her down. So they sent up a couple climbers, but she wouldn't come down. She wanted to go back up to her perch. Apparently, except for a couple bruises, she's none the worse for wear."

"Should I laugh or cry? I'm not sure which."

Alan said, "Don't decide yet. When I told Harry the girl was still in the tree, he said she could get married and raise a family up there for all he cared."

"He said that?"

"He said, he's going to leave her in the tree and log around her. I said, Harry, you're making a big mistake. People could get hurt. Not to mention, it would be a public relations disaster. You know what he said? He said, in his experience, public relations and disaster were synonymous. Oh, one more thing. He said, he's not in his office, so don't bother trying to call him."

After Dick hung up, he told his secretary to go home and poured himself a single malt Scotch. What the fuck was going on? The tree with girl in it was in the middle of the right of way. It was impossible to "log around it". Harry knew that. It's why the kids picked it. Harry knew that, too. Dick picked up the phone and tried Harry's private line. It went to voicemail. He was debating whether to call his cell when the intercom buzzed. "Mr. Saul on line one."

Dick said to his secretary, "Are you still here? Go home." Then, he hit an extension button, putting Harry on the speaker. "Harry," he said, "I just called your office."

"I'm not there," Harry said. "Write this down. Columbia Aviation ...." Then, Harry gave him a local number. "Talk to Chuck Halsey."

Dick said, "Talk to him about what?"

Harry said, "Helicopters,"

Dick couldn't believe it. "We're renting helicopters?"

"Not renting," Harry said. "Buying."

*   *   *

Friday night, just after closing, Lana Janich slid into the back booth at the Wharf Rat, next to Norv Petty, who was doing shooters with Harvey Cousins, the asshole that owned the place. Harvey was drunk, as usual, hitting on Betty Pogue, one of the girls that worked weekends. Betty wasn't interested—who would be?—trying to keep him off her without getting fired. Meanwhile, Lana was trying to tell Norville about the car, but he wasn't listening.

She said, "That's what he called it, Norville, the 'sun shell'. He said it's shot to shit, broke up into a million little pieces. He said, it needs a whole new transmission."

"Mmm hmm." Norville said, watching Harvey holding up a hundred dollar bill, telling Betty to come closer, he'd put it down in her stupid pirate girl blouse.

Lana said, "I asked him how much it was for a transmission, but you know what he did? He just shook his head, Norville. He said the car's got 127,000 miles, he don't see where it's worth fixing it."

Norville smiled, watching Harvey trying to get his hands on poor Betty's hooters. It sure was hard to get the man's attention. "And I believe what he *said*, Norville," Lana went on, "'Cause if we was to do the repairs? *He'd* be the one getting the business." Showing him she'd thought things through, and had his best interests at heart.

Norville was nodding vaguely, but still not saying anything. So Lana moved a little closer, her knee touching Norville's under the table now. She said, "But you know what? I was down at Iverson Ford last weekend, and they just happen to have the most adorable little Mustang convertible. Bright red with a black interior, two years old, only got 33,000 miles on it. The man over there said it belonged to a lady worked in the mortgage business, but she moved back to Chicago, and it's never been in a serious accident or had frame damage or anything."

Now, Norville had a kind of a frozen smile on his face, pretending he didn't hear what she was saying, so Lana spoke up a little louder. "What he *told* me, Norville, if I had a trade worth five thousand dollars? He could let me have the Mustang for $500 a month, which is a number I can live with. But the problem is, now the Camaro's ready for the junkyard, I don't have a trade anymore.. So, what I was thinking—" Lana moving a little closer, sliding her hand down there on his thigh. "Maybe we could work out a little arrangement …."

Norville Petty did not like the direction things with Lana Janich appeared to be taking. A week ago, for example, Lana asked him if it *bothered* him that she had to wear the skimpy pirate girl outfit, letting everybody look down her top and up her bottom, getting their hands in there every which way they could. Trying to keep it light, Norville said he didn't see a problem. Hell, if members of the opposite sex were trying to get in *his* pants, he'd take it as a goddamn compliment. Well, that didn't go over too well, so he said look-it, he was a married man, she knew that. The arrangement always was, neither one of them had a claim on the other. Far as he was concerned, she could play around all she wanted, and he wasn't going to get sideways about it. And that went over even worse, Lana started in crying like a two-year old, saying she never said she had a claim on him, but if he cared about her even a little bit, he'd want to have an honest relationship.

Well, Norv wasn't about to say it, but just about the *last* thing on earth he wanted at this point in his life was another goddamn honest relationship. As things stood, he was loaded down below the water line with honest relationships. Carla on him twenty-four seven trying to save his soul for Jesus; Becky with two kids and no husband, camped out behind the house in a trailer; Norville Junior, 26 years old, still living at home, working part time as a bicycle mechanic. And here he was, 58 years old, triple bypass surgery survivor, wearing a goddamn pacemaker. No, what Norville needed in his life right now was not an honest relationship. What he needed was a hot piece of ass, paid in cash, no questions asked or answered.

Honest or not, though, six months into the relationship, Lana had already worked him up from a C-note on the dresser to five hundred cash, each and every week, to "help out with expenses." Now, she had her hand down there in his private parts, telling him she needed five thousand dollars, whispering in his ear how *nice* she could be when she wanted.

He'd about had it. "Fuck *me*!" he said, pulling away now. "I don't believe this shit." He said to Harvey. "Hey, Harvey, Lana here wants five thousand dollars for a little pork snorkel. What do you think? Is she worth it or not?"

Drunk, as usual, Harvey laughed too loud. "Five thousand? Shit, I bet Betty here'll do it for five hundred and throw in a blow job. What do you say, Betty?"

Betty slapped him hard across the face, turned around, and walked out. But that didn't seem to bother Harvey. He was too busy laughing. "I guess she don't need the money." He called after her, "Come on back, you change your mind." Then, he stood up, kind of swaying, managed to peel some bills off a roll, and smacked them down on the table. "Okay, Lana. Here it is. My best offer. Five hundred cash, right now. You do us both right here on the table."

Lana sat there a second, then burst into tears, "Let me out! Let me out, goddamn it!" She pushed past Norville and rushed out toward the rest room in back. "You're disgusting!" she said. "Both of you."

Motherfucker! Norv had it in his mind he was gonna take Lana out, get laid on the boat tonight. Now *that* wasn't gonna happen, unless he went after her and apologized, which was about the last thing he wanted to do. But he did it.

"Hey, honey, come on. Harvey was drunk. We was only kidding."

At the bathroom door now, Lana turned around, looking like a raccoon, her eye makeup all messed up from crying. "How could you *do* that to me, Norville? For the love of Jesus. Everybody in the place heard what you said out there. Now they're gonna think I'm a whore or something."

"Aww, come on, baby. Most everybody's gone home. Besides, who cares what they think?" Norv put an arm around her shoulder. "Hey, I tell you what? How about you and me, we go out on the boat, have a little fun? Then, first thing tomorrow morning, I'll take you down to Iverson's, pick up that little Mustang you got your eye on."

Lana wiped her eyes with the back of her hand. "You're not nice to me, Norville," she said. "You're gonna have to treat me a whole lot better, and I mean it. Otherwise, one day you're gonna wake up and realize what a good thing you don't have anymore."

*   *   *

It had been pitch black a long time when Lon started to hear the noises—so long, in fact, he'd pretty much given up on getting the job done tonight, lounging on the couch with a glass of Wild Turkey. But hearing the sounds, he swung his legs down off the couch, and checked his watch. It was 2:21 a.m. Okay, fine. Bring her on. He sat and listened, letting the sounds come to him out of the silence, separating them from the sound of the water lapping against the hull of the boat. The sounds turning now into voices, two of them, a man and a woman, coming closer until they were very close, right next to him. For a moment, the voices stopped, and now he could feel the pitch and roll of the boat as they got aboard, a man and a woman, talking, and laughing. Not making a sound, Lon got up off the Naugahyde, smoothed the surface, picked up his drink, eased open the door to the head, and went inside.

Inside the head, he poured what was left of the whiskey into the sink, checked his Glock, racking the slide to chamber a round, slipping the gun inside the back of his fatigue pants. Then, he checked the gym bag he'd left in the shower. Inside there was an X26 Taser, able to deliver 50,000 volts at 15 feet, just the ticket to make things look like a boating accident. The only trouble was, you couldn't count on it against more than a single subject. Hmmm.

Lon was trying to figure out in his mind how the thing was going to work with two instead of just one, when he heard the engines roar to life.

* * *

It was clear and cold out on the water, everything black and silver in the harbor lights as Norv eased her out through the marina, past where the last crabbers were moored. As soon as he cleared the breakwater, though, he pulled back on the throttles, the part he liked best, the engines rising to thunder, the boat leaping forward, hydroplaning across the water at fifty knots. Lana was there beside him, jumping up and down in her little miniskirt, trying to hold her patent leather jacket closed against the wind.

She yelled over the engines, "It's cold out here!"

Norv grinned at her. "Get closer, then!"

She did, pressed against him, all over him, in fact, so he couldn't much see where he was at, not that it mattered, since they were the only ones out there in the middle of the night. Shit, this was what he wanted, wasn't it? To feel like a goddamn school boy, running blind, one hand on the wheel, the other one under a woman's skirt.

When she told him again, how cold she was, Norville said, "I don't know, seems pretty hot down there to me."

She gave him a smile, but also pulled away a little. "Well, it may be hot down there," she said, "but out here, it's goddamn freezing." Then she said, "Why don't you drop anchor someplace, honey, come on down to the cabin. I'll warm you up real good, I promise."

Then, she gave him a little wave, and disappeared down the compan-
ionway.

Norv ran the boat around a while, letting the cold air clear out his
head. He was ready to drop anchor, but then found himself thinking about
Carla. That was weird. Here he had that hot piece of ass down there waiting to give him whatever the hell he wanted, and his mind was on Carla.
How they fooled around in the back of the old '77 Chevy. And the night
she told him she was pregnant, how he felt— trapped like a coon in a
cage, but also more of a man in a way. Then, when Becky was born, Norv
still in the Army then, stationed at Fort Campbell, Kentucky. He remembered how Carla had to get a girlfriend to drive her to the hospital, on
account of they couldn't find Norv, out somewhere drunk and drinking.

Now thinking about Becky, when she got pregnant the first time and
Norv was after her to say who the father was, Norv telling her the bastard
would marry her or he'd make sure the sonuvabitch never knocked up
a girl up again. Then, Becky telling him he didn't get it; she didn't *want*
to marry the asshole, she just wanted to fuck him. Telling Norv, *he* of
all people ought to know *fucking* somebody didn't mean you wanted to
marry them. Seeing the look in her eye that night, the way she *saw* him,
and there was no way to fix it and nothing was ever going to change that
way she looked at him.

Then his mind went to Norv Junior but ... Jesus, what the hell was he
doing ... standing up there in the cold, thinking about all this shit, when
Lana was down there in the cabin, a goddamn expert at letting him forget
about it.

Norv had the High Life turned back in toward the harbor, running lights
on, but riding at anchor now, with the engines off. Coming down the com-
panionway, into the cabin, he said, "Hey, who turned out the lights?"

"Why don't you take your clothes off and find out?" Lana's voice came
at him from the bed. "I got a surprise for you in here, you're not gonna
believe it."

"A surprise, huh?" Norv getting his clothes off fast now. "Something hot or something cold?"

"A little bit of both." She laughed. "Come on, baby. I'm tired of waiting for you."

"Just a second," he said. "I gotta use the head."

Lana said, "Don't bother to put a rubber on, honey. I'll do it for you, that way you like so much."

That got him. Norv turned right around and jumped into bed.

And Lana said, "Surprise!"

*   *   *

Next morning, running the High Life up to Fool's Cape, Lon was remembering what they taught you in Force Recon training about improvisation. In general, it was discouraged. To the greatest extent possible, you were to follow orders, stick to the plan. Still, it was recognized there were times when this was impossible, when circumstances changed in an unexpected way, and the soldier was required to adjust, to alter tactics, while keeping the overall mission objective in mind. Lon felt more or less comfortable this was what he did last night, but still not a hundred percent sure he had made all the right decisions.

The overall mission objective was to eliminate Norville Petty while making it look like an accident. The tactic selected was simple: zap the man with a Taser, tie him up, run his boat up to Fool's Cape, zap him again, untie him, and dump his body over the side. When Lon saw Petty had the woman with him, the boating accident got harder to pull off. Who was going to believe two people fell out of a boat and drowned at the same time? Plus, two people was trouble with a Taser, reload being way too slow. That could mean a scuffle. Petty could be packing. People could get shot, and the accident was out the window.

Lon was considering all this while Petty was running the boat around the harbor. Then, the idea of Petty having a gun gave Lon an idea about another way to go. The man must be out with his mistress—sure as hell would not be out there with the wife. Say they got in a fight, Petty killed the woman, then he killed himself. It was stupid, but it was also simple. Which meant it let the fuzz wrap the case up quick. So that's what Lon figured. Zap Petty; use his weapon on the woman, then help old Norville use it on himself. But when he saw the woman, he knew pretty quick, the plan might need some modifications.

The way it happened, Lon was standing behind the door to the head, looking out the crack. The woman came down the stairs, turned the light on, then, turned right around and flipped Petty the bird. "Asshole!"

Then, she kicked off her shoes, flopped down on the bed, kind of rolling back and forth. "Christ almighty," she said. "How do I get myself into these shitty situations?"

Then she sat back up again, fiddling around in her handbag for a while. Then, the next thing he knew, the head door was open, and there she was, looking at him, the two of them face to face. She didn't scream, or seem like she was going to. She just stood there and looked at him.

Lon showed her the Glock, put a finger to his lips, and said, "I come for him. You understand? I ain't gonna hurt you if I don't have to."

She nodded her head, and didn't say a word.

He said, "You're not gonna scream, are you?"

She shook her head. "You gonna kill him?"

Lon took a few seconds, "Let's say I got a message for him that he don't want to hear."

She said, "You could kill him, you know," nodding her head. "I don't give a shit. He's an asshole, got it coming as far as I'm concerned." She took a few seconds, then she said, "You gotta be careful, though. He's got a gun. I never saw him, he didn't have one on him."

Lon said, "I figured he might."

Lana said, "I could help you with that. Make him take his clothes off, you know?"

Lon thought about it. "That would be helpful."

"But the only thing is, if I was in bed with him, I could get hurt. I mean, if you shot him through the covers."

Lon thought about that, "I could be in there with you," he said.

What Lon was thinking at this point, having the woman involved didn't have to change the situation. He could still zap Petty, then shoot the woman, same as before. So Lon got his X26, they turned out the light, and got under the covers with their clothes on. Then, they waited. Meanwhile the boat was still roaring along, Petty taking them for quite a ride, bouncing over the water, Lon right there next to the woman, up next to her butt in that little miniskirt, smelling her perfume.

Lon told her he'd never been in bed in a boat before.

She said, "It's a little bit like a waterbed. Not as good, though. Ever been in a waterbed?"

Lon told her he hadn't.

She giggled. "You oughta try it sometime. It's fun," kinda wiggling her bottom a little bit, "I mean, depending on the company." Then she said, "So, do you …? I mean, what you're doing with Petty … is that, like, for a living? I hope you don't mind my asking."

Lon never really thought about what he did as being "for a living". What he said was, "Basically, I'm a soldier."

She turned, ran her finger across his neck. "Is that what the tattoo's about?"

"Swift, Silent Deadly," Lon said "That's Force Recon. Marine Corps. Only there hasn't been any decent wars lately. All they got now is these goddamn insurgencies. You go in there, don't know who the enemy is. You're just as like to get shot in the back as in the front, if you know what I'm talking about. What I do now, is sort of, you know, military missions, only in the civilian sector."

She took a while, apparently absorbing the idea, then she said, "So you're, like, a soldier of fortune."

Lon never much thought about that term as it applied to himself, but he did like to pick up the magazine from time to time, and found quite a few items of interest. It kind of put some things together for him. He said, "Soldier of fortune. Yeah, I guess you could call it that."

"Wow," she said, "That's kinda awesome. I never thought I'd meet a genuine soldier of fortune. ... By the way, honey, I don't think I got your name."

They introduced themselves, Lana telling Lon she was presently working as a cocktail waitress, over at the Wharf Rat, though she didn't see herself doing it as a permanent occupation. Then, she said, "You know, I've got a tat of my own. Remind me sometime, I'll show it to you."

Suddenly, the engines died to idle, then went off, and Lon could feel the boat start to drift. A minute later, the anchor splashed, and Lon whispered, "Get ready."

"Oh, don't worry, honey," she said, "I am a ready teddy."

Lon had to admit, she was.

"Surprise!" She threw the covers back just right, and Petty stood there, buck naked, looking at the X26, eyes wide open, and scared to death.

"Don't!" he said. "I got money! Don't!"

But Lon did, and just like that, the man was on the floor. That was the thing about the EMD units, they didn't just screw the subject up, make him *think* he couldn't move. They sent a contraction command right to the muscles. As soon as those two darts hit old Norville in the chest, he froze up like a department store dummy; a second later he was face down on the cabin floor, naked and still as a corpse.

Lana went over, poked him with her toe. "Is he dead?"

Lon shook his head. "Just knocked out is all. He'll come to in a few minutes."

"What're you gonna do then?" She looked up at him. "You got to kill him, after what you done, don't you?"

Lon said, "I was thinking he could have a boating accident."

She said, "What about me?" looking right at him with these blue eyes she had.

Lon wasn't sure, but what he said right now was, "Suppose you was to help me with it?"

He went back in the head, got his gym bag out of the shower, put away the X26, and got out the duct tape. When he got back, Lana was leaning over the body.

"I don't know," she said. "I don't think he's breathing, honey. And he's got a kind of a blue color."

Lon walked over. "He do drugs? Cocaine, PCP, anything like that?"

"I don't know," she said. "He drank quite a bit."

"That wouldn't do it." Lon went over, leaned down, tried to get a pulse at the neck, but there wasn't nothing. Then, he rolled the body over. That's when he saw the incision in the man's chest. "You know if he had a heart condition?"

"If he did, he never told me about it."

"Well," Lon said, "If he didn't have one before, he's sure as hell got one now."

Headed up to Fools Cape next morning, Lon at the wheel, Lana next to him, she asked him again, what was he going to do. Last night, in bed, after he had sex with the woman, Lon was thinking quite a bit about that himself. He knew what he *ought* to do, which was stick to the plan. Shoot Petty with his own gun, then shoot the woman with the same gun, make it look like suicide. But he knew even then, *rigor* setting in, it was gonna be hard to get the man's hand around the gun. Not to mention, they cut him open, did their tests, the cause of death might not line up.

But for now, Lon was keeping it simple. When Lana asked what came next, he said, "I got a boat up to Fools Cape. I figure I'll set this one adrift."

Lana said, "I mean, what are you gonna do about me, baby?"

Lon knit his brow, but didn't say anything.

She said, "You know, Lon honey, I'm glad Norville's dead. He treated me like shit, and he got what he had coming. But you're different. You and me … when we's in bed together? You acted like a real gentleman."

"I'm a soldier." Lon said, "like I told you. A real soldier don't take advantage of a woman."

"It's a comfort to know that," Lana said, and moved closer now, Lon smelling that perfume again, the one he smelled when they was in bed together. "I guess maybe it's why I was always so fond of soldiers."

CHAPTER 22

END OF THE ROAD

Saturday morning, Eddie and Shanna met Russell at the Watershed Grove for the rally. It was Russell's idea. Eddie and Shanna would drive out to the cabin, then hike through the canyon to the tree where the Murrelet was assaulted—that's the word they were using. Russell said he had to make a stop but he'd meet them there. It was the weekend, and Shanna had never been out here, so they were treating it as an outing, a little hike along the route the road would take, winding up in the old growth redwood forest. Clearly, some work had been done ahead of time—weed whacking, fresh chainsaw cuts through tangles of down logs—the whole route neatly marked with yellow tape tied to low hanging branches. There were even laser printed signs, the kind Eddie had seen them use for movie shoots, with the word RALLY and an arrow, the same thing printed on the other side, upside down.

It was a made-for-media event, just enough people to fill the frame as the video camera captured the action. The setting was a steep, narrow canyon they were now calling the Watershed Gorge. Eddie didn't remember the place, though he was sure he must have been here, and he had forgotten how big the old growth trees really were—as tall as football fields, some of them—shading out most everything else, so the trees stood alone, except for the occasional patches of ferns and sorrel. It gave the place the quality of a church, a kind of silence that was so deep it drowned out everything else. Even now, with the speeches going on, the sound seemed small, it got lost in here. Also the people. Everything but the trees seemed incredibly small.

They had it arranged so the tree with the girl in it was the backdrop for the speeches. Eric, the victim in his Thomas collar, was talking in front of a couple dozen cheering demonstrators for the benefit of three different video cameras recording it for the news.

"This blatant corporate thuggery drags us back to the days of the Long Beach dockworkers' strike," Eric was saying, "The massacre at the Columbine mine, the Battle of the Overpass at River Rouge."

Standing with Shanna at the back of the crowd, Eddie wasn't sure what happened at the Columbine Mine or River Rouge, but he had a hunch the thing with the girl in the tree wasn't on the same order of magnitude.

Eric said, "We will not stand idly by and watch while a criminal conspiracy of corrupt local officials and callous corporations violates our fundamental human rights. We are calling on the State Police and the Department of Justice to launch an immediate investigation ...."

Coming in to stand next to them, Russell, dressed for the occasion in his deerskins and seashells said, "Dude has a way with words, you have to hand it to him." When Shanna asked him if he was going to make a statement. Russell said, "You mean, am I'm gonna compare the flight of the Murrelet to the Indian Island Massacre? I don't think so."

When they'd been there a few minutes, a half dozen men in orange hard hats appeared out of the canyon behind them, and headed straight for Eric and his microphone. Eddie recognized one of them right away as the head of security, dressed in his fatigue pants bloused over combat boots.

Shanna said, "You think we get pepper sprayed?"

Eddie smiled. "It would look pretty stupid out in the woods."

When the group got near the tree, the security detail hung back, and a clean cut guy in his mid-twenties walked up to Connie Kurosawa, there with the Five Alive News Team, and they talked for a few minutes. Then, ignoring Eric, who had stopped talking anyway, Connie motioned to her camera man and they set the new guy up for taping.

"Hi," he said with a friendly smile, "My name is Brett Cox, and I have a brief statement I'd like to make on behalf of West Coast Lumber." Then, reading from his notes, "While we need to make it clear that Ms. Rhonda Myers, also known as Murrelet, is trespassing on West Coast Lumber property—as you *all* are, by the way—and while we would be within our rights in removing her, the Company has no present intention of doing so. In fact, Ms. Myers is free to remain in the tree as long as she chooses. We would also like to announce that West Coast Lumber has amended its application for Timber Harvest Permit to reflect that we will not be building a road through the area known as Watershed Gorge. We are making other arrangements."

Back at her house on the coast, Shanna paced the living room with a glass of Pinot, trying to get Dick Duncan on the phone as the Five Alive News played on a flat screen with the sound turned down.

Redialing Dick's cell now for the third time, Shanna got the usual message.

She pressed the red button to end the call, and glanced out to the deck where Eddie was sitting with a bourbon over shaved ice, apparently doing nothing except maybe watching the sun go down. His attitude was hard to fathom. Either he didn't understand what just happened, or he was pretending he didn't care about it. Either way, it was annoying.

Suddenly, Shanna got the idea of calling Dick at the office and, amazingly, he answered. "Dick, it's Shanna."

"Well, hello Shanna." His voice had a flat, bemused tone.

"What are you doing in your office?"

He said, "Important work. If it weren't important, I'd have to be getting ready for the Friends of the Mainwaring School Faculty Awards Dinner."

She waited a few seconds. "Would you mind telling me what the fuck's going on?"

"You mean other than the Faculty Awards Dinner."

"I'm referring to the road, Dick. There's a kid by the name of Brett Cox running around telling people you're not going to build it."

His tone got more bemused than ever. "I guess that would be because we're not building it. You see, it turns out, I was wrong about

Harry, sweetheart. It isn't helicopters he hates. What he hates, is *renting* helicopters."

Shanna said, "I don't follow."

"Well then, let me lay it out for you. Harry just bought a company called Columbia Aviation. We're going into the fucking helicopter business."

"You're ... kidding."

"Does it sound like I'm kidding?"

"But... we signed the documents. We have a deal."

"Correction, babe. What we have is a lawsuit."

Shanna was having trouble catching her breath. "All right, then, we'll sue the bastard. I'm a lawyer ...." Shanna didn't care for the sound of her voice. Even to her, it sounded desperate.

Dick laughed, "You know what Harry's boys in New York said when I told them that? 'She wants to bring a lawsuit, tell her to get out her wallet. We'll bury her.' They weren't kidding. If you don't believe me, Google 'Harriman Saul litigation.' He's still fighting over landfill deals from back in the last millennium." Silence. "Then, there's the other part."

Shanna wasn't sure she wanted to know what other part, but Dick told her anyway.

"Think about it, babe, if we file a lawsuit? Who's going to sue. The California corporation? We're in discovery, they're going to see the documents, follow the paper trail. Who owns Shady Grove Enterprises? The Caymans corporation. Who owns that? The offshore trust. And who owns that? How would it look in court, do you suppose?"

Shanna glanced at Eddie through the plate glass, oblivious, drinking his drink, watching the sun go down, almost on the horizon now. She said, "So ... now what?"

Dick said, "That's up to you. For myself, I'm doing some housekeeping, shredding and such. Like I said, important work. Then, I'm leaning toward British Columbia. There's an interesting opportunity up there with Magnussen/Maginnis. By the way, you'd better call our ... agricultural clients ... tell them it's harvest time. When those helicopters go up, our little no fly zone will pass into history."

Shanna said, "How long?"

Dick said, "Depends on when the State issues the permits. I'd say, a week, more or less."

After she disconnected, Shanna turned to see Eddie, inside now, standing in front of the television. "Well," she said, "that's it. The deal's off." Eddie nodded absently, not looking over. So, she repeated it. "Did you hear what I said? The deal's off. There's no road. He's going to log the goddamn thing with helicopters."

Now, Eddie was nodding, pointing at the TV. "Look who's here. Your buddy, Jimmy Kennan."

And there he was, the Honorable Governor of the Great State of California, heavier now, hair shorter, and graying at the temples, but the same disingenuous, telegenic face.

"We've never made any secret that we'd like to see the Grove in public ownership," he was saying, "But, the fact is, it's *not* in public ownership, and with our present budgetary constraints, I don't see any realistic way to make that happen in the near future." Asked, now, to comment on the remarks of environmentalists, who were saying the episode was an example of corporate profiteering at its worst, Jimmy said, "Well, like it or not, this is America, and that means Mr. Saul has a right to earn a return on his investment."

"How about *our* investment?" Shanna muttered, muting the sound with a thrust of the remote.

She wandered over to the telephone base unit now, punched a button, playing back the last part of a recording. "You'd better call our agricultural clients, tell them it's harvest time. When those helicopters go up, our little no fly zone is history."

"Recording calls without consent. Isn't that illegal?"

"Not if you're doing it to provide evidence of a felony." She smiled, remembering it. "I researchedw that one a long time ago."

Eddie was quiet a minute, then changed the subject. "How much do you think it's really worth?"

She looked at him.

"The land. They said Saul wants half a billion dollars. You think it's worth that much?"

Shanna felt tired now. "What do I look like, an appraiser?" She clicked the picture off now, and turned to Eddie. "The deal's off, Eddie. Didn't you hear that? They're not building the road."

"Right, I got that."

"It doesn't bother you?"

He walked to the bar, poured a glass of wine, handed it to her. "Look at it this way. Now there's no money involved, you won't need to dream up tricky new ways to screw people out of it. Won't that be a relief."

She looked at him now, into those blue-gray eyes, but not getting much. "What are you talking about?"

"Colin Winsett. He sends his regards, by the way."

Her mind was racing. "You talked to Colin Winsett?"

Eddie smiled. "I used you as a reference, told him my name was Norville Petty. He's putting together a package for me. An asset protection trust, just like the one he did for you. I'm going to use a side letter to make myself the trust protector."

She began pacing. "Winsett's a complete liar. You can't believe a word he says."

"Shanna—"

"He and Dick are in this together. They're old golf buddies for Christ sake."

"Shanna!"

Shanna walked to the bar now, lit a cigarette. "What do you want me to say? All right, yes. There's an agreement. I admit it." She turned to him now. "But I didn't do it to screw you, Eddie, I hope you can believe that. I was trying to protect you—to protect us both. You don't know Dick. You can't trust him. You can't trust anybody in the Caymans. They're all connected down there. If we didn't have the side letter, they would have taken every last penny ...."

Eddie was watching her, still not saying anything.

"Who told you? I mean, in the beginning. It was Dick, wasn't it? He's such a shit. I knew something was going to happen when you two went to lunch together."

Eddie said, "Nobody told me." Shanna looked at him; Eddie shook his head. "I just took a guess." Shanna had a sinking feeling now, like she'd been had, the bastard smiling at her.

"So … just out of curiosity, how much did you tell Dick I was getting? Two-thirds or three quarters?"

Now, she sighed. "Three quarters is what I *should* have told him. I said half. The morning we signed the deal, he threatened not to go through with it unless *he* got half. I tried to tell him I couldn't give him half …."

"Because you already promised half to me."

"He wanted to cut you out altogether."

"And he knew that was a possibility, because—"

"Okay, Winsett told him about the side letter. But Eddie—" She moved to him now, putting her arms around his neck, looking into his eyes. "You have to believe me. What I just said was true. I was never going to cut you out. I was just trying to protect you. To protect us both. You believe me, don't you, Eddie?"

"I don't know, do you?" He was laughing now. She tried to punch him, but he caught her hand, drew her to him, kissed her on the mouth.

She felt herself melting in his arms, feeling a lot better than she rationally ought to. "You *never* believed me, did you?"

He kissed her again, "Not for a minute."

"And all that time, making love to me, you thought I was a cheap, conniving hustler."

He said, "I never thought you were cheap."

Kissing him, she said, "You're terrible, you know that?"

Kissing her, he said, "I know."

"Using me like that."

"Using you?"

"Sexually."

"Mmm."

"Playing along. Letting me seduce you. You figured I'd do anything to get my hands on that money, didn't you? Letting me do all the work. Waiting till we closed the deal. What were you going to do then? Cut Dick out? Tell him you'd go to Harriman Saul? Make some kind of a deal with Darryl? Maybe cut me out, too?"

He ran the tips of his fingers across her brow, along the line of her jaw, looking into her eyes, not saying anything.

She said, "Fast Eddie Fuentes. You fucking hustler," and pulled back a little now, looking at him. "You're not going to deny it, are you?"

He smiled a little, not admitting it, but not denying it, either.

CHAPTER 23

SHANNA AND EDDIE

Eddie and Shanna were still in bed two hours after they addressed their honesty issues. The love making was different this time. Better. More relaxed, with a different kind of closeness, making fun of things, of themselves, of each other. Now, it was dark outside, hard to say whether the fog was in or not, or if it mattered.

When the doorbell rang, they looked at each other.

"Expecting someone?"

Shanna shook her head. Eddie pulled on his jeans. Bare-foot, he padded across the living room and down the entry hall, looked out the view hole in the front door, then opened it. Darryl Waters was leaning against the door jamb, cool as Nicky Barnes, in a double breasted tan gabardine suit, over a black turtleneck.

"Eddie Fuentes. My *man*, my *man*. This is a coincidence. Though I guess you did tell me you was guarding the woman's *body* as I recall."

Eddie motioned. "Nice suit."

"You know," Darryl said, "I am so glad you mentioned that. On account of that barbecue McCutcheon got on my pin stripe Armani? The shit did not come out. So I figure, counting the cleaners, your ass into me thirteen hundred twelve dollars, fifty cents not counting the eight point seven five percent California sales tax."

"I didn't know you paid sales tax on stuff fell off the back of a truck."

Now, Shanna came out from the living room, wearing Eddie's faded work shirt and bare feet. She looked at Darryl. "What the fuck do *you* want?"

"Damn! What kind of attitude is that? What do I want?" Darryl adopted a hurt tone. "Here I come all the way down from the morgue see you folks, special trip, twenty miles out the way. Common courtesy, you ought to invite me in, see what important news I got to share with you, might impact your future plans and shit."

Inside, Darryl wandered around, doing his number, commenting on the two story living room, Oriental rugs, abstract oils "Mmm *hmmm*. Mmm *hmmm*. How you drug attorneys live. Now see, that time I was over your office in Redwood Bay? I thought *that* was your home, had your residence upstairs. Now I see I was wrong as could be. Show you how naïve I am, my level of ignorance, coming from the inner city."

"I'm glad you like it." Shanna took a seat on the couch, watching him.

"Oh, yes, I do." Darryl sat down, still looking around. "Very much, indeed. You mind my asking how much a place like this might cost?"

"Still trying to tally up your point totals?" Shanna turned to Eddie, "Darryl's boss is giving him a point for every dollar he manages to seize under the forfeiture laws. The guy with the most points goes to Hawaii."

Darryl said, "No, now, see you behind the times on that." Darryl was nodding now. "Yeah, old Darryl be moving on. First of November, I am out of drug enforcement altogether."

Eddie started to smile. "You passed the Bar."

"Working with the U.S. Attorney now, Special Investigation Team, looking into public corruption." He glanced at Shanna. "Money laundering, that kind of thing."

Shanna shook her head, "The U.S.A.? I don't know, Darryl. I saw you more in the criminal defense arena."

Darryl chuckled, "Well, you know how it is. That's a long road. Open up an office, stay awake nights wondering how you gonna pay the bills. What happens, you wind up scraping up anything happen to crawl through the door. On the other hand," he was smiling now, "you get a reputation being a bad ass prosecutor, your *name* could get around. Then say, you switch sides, people accused of crime see you could be connected on the inside."

Shanna looked at him. "So, Darryl … is that why you came out here? Run your career plans by us?"

"Shit, girl," Darryl said. "You just don't know how to be polite, do you? No, see this is *business*, why I came down here. On account of a body they got up there at the morgue, the deceased happen to be someone you had business dealings with. Someone you might even have a reason to want out of the way, come to think about it."

"You gonna give us the name?" Eddie asked him.

"Name?" Darryl looked at him. "Oh, certainly. Norville E. Petty, Jr. Man's dead. Thought the Counselor here might have something she want to tell me about it."

Glancing at Shanna, Eddie said, "Why would you think that?"

Darryl shrugged. "Put it together. Counselor paying the man off, old Norville under investigation. Kind of convenient the man pass away and all."

"You're saying he was murdered?"

Darryl took some time with that. "Coroner's not saying, one way or the other. Seem like a crab fisherman found old Norville in his cigarette boat up the coast, place called Fool's Cape—I do like that name, don't you? Fool's Cape?—Man lying in his bed, buck naked, and deader than disco."

"They have a cause of death?"

Darryl shook his head. "Awaiting toxicology, you know how it is. Like to take their time with it." Darryl looked at Shanna. "Maybe you already guessed, but old Norville, rolled on you, agreed to wear a wire. Got it all cued up for you. Norville's greatest hits." Darryl took a little recorder out of his pocket, pushed a button.

SHANNA: "The Doctor doesn't like people changing the rules in the middle of the game. He thinks it's cheating."

PETTY: [laughing] Tell him to call the cops. I got a boat to pay for. He wants to bring in a crop this year, it's five grand a week."

SHANNA: I'll pass it along. But it's your funeral.

Darryl punched a button, looking at Shanna.

She said, "It was a figure of speech."

"You could explain that to the grand jury." Darryl took a second, then smiled, shaking his head. "Always cracks me up, that line about calling the cops. Man had a sense of humor. ... We got about an hour of this shit on tape."

"Maybe you can use it at parties," Shanna said. "You sure as hell won't get it in evidence."

"Meaning now old Norville's gone, we can't authenticate it." Darryl chuckled. "You could be right about that. But what I was thinking, old Norville ain't the only one might have tax problems, say we start looking into where all these fancy houses and shit come from."

"The office was a gift, and I have a deed to prove it."

"How about *this* place? That a gift, too."

Eddie said, "What happened to the guy you busted down in Oakland? I thought you were gonna roll him over, use *him* to get to the Doctor."

Darryl looked at Shanna. "You didn't tell him?" Then back to Eddie, "We did flip him over. He fingered a dude by the name of Wayne Mehana. But that man's dead. Found a week ago in San Francisco, outside a gay bar South of Market. Him and a friend, tackle for the Niners, shot with a twelve gauge, execution style. Makes you wonder, don't it? Maybe the Doctor heard what was going on, decided to take the man out." He looked at Eddie. "But I'm sure neither one of you would might happen to how he could have found that out."

Eddie said, "No, we wouldn't."

Darryl looked at Shanna now. "Think about it, the whole thing puts me in mind of your friend, Roger Bachman. Like I told old Eddie here, Petty gave him up, too. Now, Roger and Petty are both gone, and Wayne Mehana, too. Could be house cleaning time. I'd watch my back, if I was you."

After Eddie let Darryl out, he came back into the living room and stood there, arms folded, looking at Shanna.

She said, "What?"

"The dead guy, Mehana."

"You're asking, did I set him up, tell the Doctor about him? No."

"Why didn't you tell me he was dead?"

It was a good question. Why didn't she? The truth was, ever since the first time Roger took her out to the Costa Perdida, she always thought of the Doctor as an amusing character, maybe dangerous in an abstract sort of way, but never dangerous … actually … never a genuine killer. When Eddie told her the Feds had been trying to get Roger to wear a wire, it stopped her, but she put it out of her mind. The Doctor was in love with Roger. He would never have had him killed. But after Wayne, she had to reconsider.

Now, she tried to explain it. "I suppose I didn't tell you," she said, "Because I didn't want it to be true. Because it means he's getting rid of everyone who could testify against him. If he killed Wayne, it means he could have killed Roger. And it means he's probably going to kill me, too." Looking at Eddie now.

His eyes on hers, he said, "Not necessarily. With Petty dead, the Feds don't have anything on you. Maybe he thinks you're not a threat. Maybe he thinks you're useful." He smiled. "Maybe he thinks you're cute."

She said, "That's a lot of maybe's. And Roger was pretty cute." Standing against the living room wall now, arms folded, she slowly slid down the wall, saying, "Fuck, fuck, fuck, fuck, fuck, fuck, fuck," all the way down.

Now, Eddie sat down beside her, the two of them sitting with their backs against the living room wall, facing her print of the big, abstract De Kooning, bought at the museum in San Francisco. He said, "Ready to hear what your problem is?"

She said, "No, I'm not."

"You don't want to hear the truth."

"Why on earth would I want that? The truth hurts. Haven't you heard? No news is good news. Ignorance is bliss."

Eddie said, "See, there it is in a nutshell. You can't handle the truth."

"No," Shanna said, "I don't *want* to handle the truth. The there's a difference. You know what the truth is?" Shanna turned now, facing him, "It's a comprehensive collection of all the things you can never have, and all the things you're not allowed to do—wrapped up in a neat little package of undeniable reasons you'll never get out of the fucking strait jacket that's who you are and what you were born into."

Shanna could see Eddie was surprised, and found herself wondering where the hell all *that* came from. Then, there it was, in real time, right in front of her. The ranch in Pinehurst. Her old man, terrifying, with huge, heavy hands and his raging fundamentalist Christian bullshit. Her brothers snorting crank behind the barn, practicing quick draw moves on unsuspecting jack rabbits. Her mother, hard eyed, head down and hopeless. Remembering the feeling of it, looking at her mother, realizing that's what *she* was going to be. She, Rose-of-Sharon Blackmon, her given name referring to an Old Testament verse. And remembering how it could have been her, except for what happened that one day, the day she got it into her head she was going to ride her old man's prize stud horse, a big roan stallion, strictly off limits.

She heard herself now, telling Eddie the story, how her father took her brothers to Thermopolis for a quarter horse auction while she stayed home with her mom. How she went down to the barn and took that stallion out, rode the living shit out of him, bareback, across the prairie. And how sometimes she still had dreams about it.

Then, telling him the rest of the story. "When my old man got home, he asked me if I'd been a good little girl. I looked at my mom, then I looked at him, square in the eye, and I said, 'Yes, Daddy.' And he said, 'That's good.' And he gave me a candy bar, Hershey's with almonds. I remember like it was yesterday. 'Cause I realized he didn't have any power over me. He wasn't God after all 'cause he had no fucking idea if I was lying or not. And I also realized, my mom wasn't going to say anything different."

When she was through with the story, Eddie said, "That must have felt good. Figuring how to get what you wanted."

"Yeah," she said, feeling it again now. " It did. It felt good."

"But the thing is, you're not a kid anymore, and the people you're dealing with, they're not your father."

"Yeah, so?"

"I'm saying, there's another way to get what you want. You could always just come out and ask for it."

Shanna smiled. "What if they say, no?"

"Then you deal with it. But the thing is, Rose-of-Sharon, if you start out expecting *no*, then, when the dust settles, *no* is pretty likely where you're going to be." Eddie took a minute. "There's this trick. ... It's like when I used to hustle pool. I'd always have to make it look like I was losing. Game after game, sometimes, till the mark got greedy. I'd get him to double down, give me a chance to get even. Then, I'd turn it on, just enough to win. But the thing was, that whole time it looked like I was losing, inside I'd have to *know* I was winning. Otherwise, when it came time to win, I wouldn't be able to do it."

"Yeah …. How the hell did you do *that*?"

He laughed. "*That's* the trick. In your head, you need to make it so there's nothing to lose. Like you already won. Like winning is who you are. Not something you need to do. Start with the picture of who you are. What you want to be."

She shook her head now. "That sounds great, but the only thing I know right now is what I *don't* want to be."

"Okay?" he said, "What's that?"

"Dead."

"Well," Eddie said, "I guess we could call that a start."

CHAPTER 24

THE ACID TEST

Working in the deep red glow of darkroom lights, the Doctor was getting ready to open the vacuum evaporator in his specially equipped lab at the Costa Perdida.

Watching from behind him, his new assistant, Désiré said, "*Alors, thees ees very difficult, no?*"

The Doctor looked up. Jacques Désiré Renaud, a native of the island of Mauritius (which he called, Maurice) was gorgeously built and incredibly exotic—skin the color of cappuccino, long dreadlocks, almond eyes. He spoke with a lilting French accent and, if that weren't enough, had astonishing facility with a butterfly knife.

Answering his question, the Doctor said, "Well, I wouldn't recommend trying it at home. Hydrazine can be nasty. And the molecule itself is unstable. It needs cool, dark places. But, if you know some organic chemistry and have the right lab equipment, it's simple enough." He thought a minute. "If you're serious about doing it, though, I need to warn you that the precursor chemicals are on a watch list, so you either have to synthesize them, or bring them in from somewhere with less prying eyes. … Lucky for me, I have a friend who makes migraine medications in Costa Rica. Have you ever been to Costa Rica?"

Désiré shook his head.

The Doctor smiled. "Beautiful country. Maybe one day, you'll take a trip—no pun intended."

"Do you go there?"

The Doctor sighed. "We used to go, sometimes, in the winter. Guanacaste—Playa San Miguel, Playa Samara. Or the Caribbean sometimes. They grow coffee in the interior."

And it all came back now, in a flood of memories—bouncing over the washboard roads in a rented SUV, the howler monkeys at night, the sound of the jungle in the rain—and he felt, what? Old, wondering if he would ever see any of it again. In his mind, he was in the rental car now, Roger beside him, both of them stoned on acid, Roger smoking up the remnants of some weed he bought in Puerto Viejo. They were looking for the airport in San Jose, going around and around on a ring road carrying a kilogram of ergotamine tartrate packed in Café Britt export coffee bags. The Doctor was driving, Roger in the passenger seat. Roger, with a deep tan and a two week beard, dressed in a Hawaiian shirt and sunglasses, doing his imitation of a Latina Dionne Warwick—

Do ju know de way to San Jose?
I bean away so long
I may go wrong and lose my way

Both of them breaking up. Somehow they made the flight, then flash forward, hours later, the Doctor coming down, but still high, practicing Jedi mind tricks on the customs agent in Houston, suggesting there was nothing amiss here, another gay couple returning to San Francisco from a sun and sand vacation. And watching it work! How much younger he was then.

As if reading his thought, Désiré asked him, "So, you have been doeeng thees a long time."

"A long time, yes." The Doctor took a deep breath and wished away the waves of nostalgia, letting them dissolve back into the cosmic Jell-O from which they had emerged. Such a mystery it was—where these waves came from, and where they went— waves of the future, condensing into waves of the present, fading into waves of the past.

In the beginning, the Doctor was as confused about drugs as anyone. To those around him, they were just the second leg in the triple crown: sex, drugs and rock 'n' roll. But the Doctor's father was a pharmacist, so he had a broader view. To say a drug was either "good" or "bad" was ridiculous, because all of them were both. Innocuous aspirin could cause ulcers; acetaminophen was a good substitute, but a fairly small overdose caused liver failure. Used externally, alcohol was a good antiseptic; taken internally, it could be either a mild intoxicant or a deadly poison, depending on the dose. Opiates were the ultimate down rush, the gold standard of pain relief, but physically addictive, and poisonous. Vinca alkaloids were also poisonous, yet widely used in chemotherapy. Good or bad wasn't an either-or thing. It depended.

Drugs differed widely in their effects. Some were primarily physical, others mental or emotional, and a small number, at least potentially, spiritual. From a rational standpoint, comparing cocaine or methamphetamines with mescaline or LSD was like comparing masturbation with meditation. Throwing stimulants, depressants, and hallucinogens together into a mash up called "controlled substances" made about as much sense as throwing Roman history, organic chemistry and French literature on a transcript and calling it an education. Of course, the powers that be had done both. Not an accident, in the Doctor's opinion.

To the Doctor, drugs were a door—either to hell, or to a beautiful inner world of consciousness, a world far more entertaining and far less constrained than the dim shadow dance of so-called reality. They also made him a pretty good living. As he grew older, he understood better the complex interplay of the inner and outer worlds—not at all the one science assumed. Far from being the effect of matter, thought was its cause. This realization was at once liberating, isolating and depressing. Liberating because it explained many things and conveyed a certain power. Isolating, because it was impossible to communicate, and had to be experienced to be understood. And finally, depressing, because it meant that the drugs that had been so much a part of his life, would one day have to be discarded. As a part of matter, they were only a crutch.

The phone rang now. Not the black one, which he never answered, but the red one he sometimes did. He motioned to Désiré, who picked it up, and said what he'd been trained to. "General hospital. *Oui*, yes ... I will see if he is in." He covered the mouthpiece, turned to the Doctor. "It is a woman, Shanna Black. ... You wish to speak with him?"

The Doctor said, "Do I wish to speak with *her*," and reached out to take the phone, wondering what on earth she'd want.

*   *   *

The next day driving in the Rover with Eddie, headed down the 101, Shanna said, "Yeah, it's *like* the other one, but .... For one thing, I'm not at the Bellagio."

"Where are you this time?"

"A casino, but I don't think I've ever been there before."

"Yeah ...." Eddie noncommittal, not really into further dream analysis.

The plan was, Eddie and Shanna would pick Russell up in Juanita and the three of them would drive out to the Costa Perdida in the Rover. The trip would take over an hour, so Russell figured they'd have time to run through the deal with the Doctor and, hopefully, get Shanna's buy-in. Eddie thought he'd lay some groundwork on the trip up to Juanita, but Shanna was into her dream routine.

"It starts out the same. I'm rolling passes, I have a big pile of chips, there's a crowd pushing in, trying to get a better look."

"How about the wardrobe?"

"Use your imagination. ... So, I've got the dice in my hand, and I'm about to roll, and remember before, there was a gun?"

He played along. "The blue steel revolver."

"Right. A guy slaps it on the pass line. Only this time, I get to turn around and see who it is."

"Want me to guess?"

"No, smart ass. And I don't want you to tell me what it means, either. I'll tell you."

There were two stories people told, why they called it the Costa Perdida. The first was, because the engineers who built the coast highway didn't have the technology to hug the Pacific through the Rey de la Paz mountains, so they turned the road inland to meet Highway 101 south of Manzanita and left part of the coast without a road. The second story was, the engineers mapping the coast got lost in the fog.

No fog today, though. It was one of those clear, crisp October days, the wind blowing from the east, keeping the fog offshore, the air cool, but the sun strong. They picked Russell up in Juanita, headed south to Manzanita, then caught the little two-lane road that wound west through hills covered with Douglas fir, twenty-odd miles to the coast. Along the way, Russell laid out the play. When he was done, Shanna said, "And the Doctor, is willing to do this … why, exactly?"

Russell hunched his shoulders. "Globalization. Legalization. How long does he have? A year? Maybe two? The Mexicans are all in. The wholesale price is headed down. … And corporate America, man when that wave breaks, his life is history. … To tell you the truth, I think, he'd like a last hurrah. Take that motherfucker down."

Shanna seemed to be thinking it through, "It would get the government off my back."

"And clear the air with the Doctor," Eddie said.

Shanna was nodding, then looking at Eddie, "You gonna tell me what it does for you?"

Eddie and Russell looked at each other, Eddie said. "Yeah, I'll let you know when I figure it out."

When a milky white fog bank appeared in the distance, high above the trees, they turned off the main road onto an unmarked dirt track, crossed a bridge, climbed a hill, and pulled in next to a dark green Tesla parked in a grove of cypress trees on top of a knoll that overlooked the Pacific.

Eddie said, "Where's the house?"

They walked through the trees to what looked like an elevator door, set in a small concrete vault. That was all you could see. Before they could ring a bell or, for that matter, find a bell to ring, the door slid open, and it was an elevator. Inside, there was guy, smiling at them, looking a little like

Johnny Depp in *Pirates of the Caribbean,* only this guy was younger, had a better build and dreadlocks with blonde streaks.

"*Bienvenue! Entrez, entrez!*" The pirate motioned them in, pushed a button, and they were going down. After a moment, the blank wall behind them opened into an expansive ocean view and Eddie realized they were in an elevator shaft made of glass, passing through two different levels, and finally arriving at a third, where the elevator stopped, and they got out.

He could see now that the elevator was at one corner of a house that had been built into a bluff facing the Pacific, with the entrance at the top, and the rest of the house underneath. Coming out of the elevator, they were in a massive living room with a wall of windows looking out at the water, still a few stories above a rocky beach. Looking at the view, the impression you got was that the whole house was made of glass. But looking more closely, you could see that the side facing away from the water had no glass at all, and though you couldn't see what was in there, behind closed doors, down private halls, you had to assume it was an underground concrete bunker, with no windows at all.

The view today took your breath away, though there was still a bank of puffy white fog far offshore. Eddie was still trying to figure out how they built the place, or what they'd do if the elevator broke down, when a tall, heavy set man swept into the room. It was hard to tell how old he was. He looked like a character out of a movie—Star Wars, maybe—a big man, with rounded features, fair complexion, and a mass of reddish curls worn long. He was dressed in a white laboratory coat, silky green hospital scrubs and sandals. He could have been Orson Welles, except for the hair.

"Well," he said, gesturing with a cocktail glass full of some foamy green liquid, "The gang's all here." He greeted the people he knew, then turned to Eddie, "And, last but not least, the infamous Fast Eddie Fuentes."

He offered a somewhat limp hand; Eddie took it, saying, "I probably lost a couple steps since they called me that."

"Don't hustle me, Eddie." The Doctor winked, then gesturing to the pirate, like he would take the orders, said, "What can we get you all to drink?"

After they got the refreshments squared away, Coronas all around, in crystal goblets, except for the Doctor, who stuck with the foamy green liquid. Eddie turned, "Before we get down to business, Shanna has something she wants to say to you."

The Doctor looked at Shanna, raising heavy eyebrows. "Okay...."

They talked about it in the car, coming clean about the land, but Shanna was definitely not without a queasy feeling about it. You never knew which way the Doctor would go.

She took a deep breath. "Philip," she said finally, "I need to tell you something ... about the road."

And she did, trying to read his reaction along the way, but not getting much. How she knew he was financing the demonstrations, the girl in the tree, and so on. And she understood the objective was to slow down the road.

Shanna said, "Of course, as your attorney, I followed your instructions. But early on, it became obvious to me that Harriman Saul was going to log the Watershed with helicopters if he didn't build a road."

The Doctor tilted his head. "How prescient of you."

"Yes, well I did have the benefit of Mr. Duncan's insight on the matter. In any event, as you can appreciate it was a 'lesser of two evils' situation, helicopters or a road, And I determined at a certain point in the process, that it would be in your best interest, if I ... participated ... to a degree in the transaction, so as to better monitor and perhaps even control the timing and so on."

"I'm sorry, the 'transaction'?"

"Related to the land. You know, that the company needed for the road."

"Ahhh," the Doctor was nodding.

Shanna took a breath. "By taking a position .... You see, Dick ... Mr. Duncan .... had come up with a scheme to make a profit selling the land to the company ... and I felt, in your interest, it would be prudent to pretend to participate so as to better ... control the situation."

"Yes, participate. You used that word before. But I wasn't sure what you meant by it. Were you going to tell me you acted as his attorney? That you were also his business partner? That at some point, you came up with the idea of cutting him out of the deal? Or how about the fact that you were fucking him? Were you going to tell me that part, too?"

The Doctor raised his eyebrows, waiting for an answer, but Shanna had become suspended in space, and had lost the ability to talk.

"Shanna, Shanna, let me tell you, as a career criminal who has pitched and caught all manner of bullshit, you are one of the least accomplished bull shitters I've ever come across. You're like the lawyer in the joke."

The Doctor turned to Russell. "How can you tell when Shanna's lying?"

"Her lips are moving," Russell said.

"Her lips are moving!" The Doctor clapped his hands. "Now you see why I love this woman. She is utterly and hopelessly *predictable*. Don't ever play poker, Shanna darling. You have a horrible tell."

"You knew ... everything," Shanna managed.

The Doctor smiled. "Well, I didn't know he was going to buy the he-licopter company till Russell told me. Good old Harry! I hope you learn something from all this. It's the twenty-first century. You should have taken an option on the helicopters, instead of fooling around with a road." Now, he was quiet a minute. "How much time do we have?"

Russell said, "Saturday, I'm told."

"Mmm." The Doctor sipped his drink thoughtfully, the strange, green liquid almost seeming to come alive in his glass. Now, looking at Shanna again, he said, "Needless to say, my dear, your actions have violated every known rule of professional conduct. However, what you lack in ethics you more than make up for in a certain *je ne sais quoi*—"

He dipped his fingers in his green liquid and sprinkled it on her head, like holy water. "*Deinde, ego te absolvo a peccatis tuis in nomine Patris, et Filii, et Spiritus Sancti. Amen.*"

His words seemed to echo oddly now. "*Patris, et Filii, et Spiritus Sancti. Patris, et Filii, et Spiritus Sancti.* "

Eddie nudged her.

"Hmm?" Shanna looked at the Doctor, his head seemed larger now, almost disembodied, floating in his laboratory coat. "You want me to tell him about Darryl, too?"

And she did, telling the story start to finish.

"A trip to Hawaii!" The Doctor clapped his hands. "Who said bureaucrats had no imagination? I assume he wanted you to wear a wire."

She said, yeah, he did, but she never agreed to do it. And now that Petty and Wayne were both gone, she didn't see where the Feds would have a case.

Meanwhile, the Doctor was watching her, nodding. When she was through, he was quiet a minute. "Poor little Shanna," he said finally, "Afraid of going to the Doctor. I should have given you a lollipop. Isn't that what doctors do? ... Maybe we can find you one." He called out the pirate. "Désiré? Go up to the kitchen. See if you can find a lollipop."

Now, the Doctor was putting an arm around her shoulder consolingly, and Shanna felt a wave of emotion overtake her, almost as if she wanted to cry. And suddenly, she was crying! Bitter tears, but feeling so much better!

"There, there," the Doctor was saying, "Everything feels all right now, doesn't it?" Then, looking around the room, at each of the people in turn, studying their faces. "How is everyone feeling now? Is everyone feeling all right?"

Even before the Doctor asked the question, Russell knew he put acid in the fucking Corona. There were sensory distortions; distances dissolving; the geometry of the room changing; words hanging in the air like balloons. For that matter, the beer itself was a trip if you got into it, the bubbles were a universe floating in liquid amber space. The room was a glistening pastel dream, floating in some invisible, but very real substance; the people were magnetic star groupings, connected by mysterious electrical waves. This wasn't Russell's first trip. He knew the best thing to do was relax and enjoy the show. The Doctor had done this sort of thing before. He called it his "acid test". Acid was a mirror, he said. People who couldn't handle it, couldn't handle a mirror. There was bad acid, and there were bad people, but on pure acid there was never a bad trip.

"Russell? Everything okay?" The Doctor's face seemed inches away now, studying him with milky blue eyes.

And Russell was giving him a thumbs up, but the Doctor wasn't there anymore, transported by light waves far across the universe to the other side of the room, saying something to Eddie now, a quiet murmur Russell couldn't quite make out. But what he *could* hear, all of a sudden, was the ocean. It was amazing he hadn't heard it before, right outside the window, this vast, rolling, conscious presence, the sun glistening on its surface in a hundred billion sparkling lights. Lights that were waving to him, beckoning for him to come closer, to dissolve himself, rest a while inside its glistening, radiant rays ….

The Doctor was sitting by the coffee table now, and the sun seemed lower in the sky. Russell checked his watch. It was almost six o'clock. He was trying to remember what time they came. Two o'clock? Three? He couldn't remember.

"Why don't we see where things stand?" The Doctor was taking a set of yarrow stalks from a tall, crystal vase on the coffee table now, starting to divide them, casting the *I ching* as he talked.

He glanced around the room, looking at each person, one at a time, all the time dividing and re-dividing the stalks. "Everyone knows why we're here … Russell, Shanna? Fast Eddie? We know the relationship we're proposing? We know the situation, the question we have in our minds about it."

Russell moved his head up and down, finding it easier to nod than talk.

Shanna's lips moved, but no sound seemed to come out.

The Doctor nodded, dividing the stalks.

"Fast Eddie …."

Russell looked at Eddie, who seemed far away, then suddenly very close, his eyes fixed on the Doctor, seeming to nod, but not saying anything.

"Good, good. Good enough."

Dividing, dividing the stalks, and now, the Doctor was looking down at the yarrow. "Well, this *is* interesting," he said, studying the pattern. "Fire over water. The final hexagram, sixty-four."

He took his *Book of Changes* from a shelf, paged through it to the end, then started to read, " The end of the journey is near. The situation is incomplete, but the chaos of the past slowly gives way to order. The goal is in sight, the way ahead is unobstructed, but the superior man treads, like the aged fox on thinning ice, at the edge of the pond, with caution."

Eddie remembered watching the Doctor, picking up the yarrow, looking from one of them to the other, nodding to each, in turn, as though he was concluding a conference.

He heard himself say, "One thing."

The Doctor looked at him.

"This is a game to you."

The hint of a smile, seeing the world in his eyes.

"My father. He was part of the game, too?"

The Doctor took a minute, watching him, unblinking. "Oh, *that's* it. You think —" He sighed, shaking his head.

Eddie was getting a sense of something, but not completely.

The Doctor went on. "A gentleman likes to drink. Your mission, should you decide to accept it, is to keep this gentleman from meeting with an attorney to sign some documents. How do you do it?"

Eddie was thinking, "Get him drunk," but he didn't actually say anything.

"And suppose someone worked for you, and you asked him to do that. How would you expect him to accomplish it? Pour a bottle of whiskey down his throat, or offer to buy him a drink?"

Eddie saw the Doctor's gaze shift. He seemed to be looking past Eddie now, at something behind him. Some new presence that had entered the room.

"Well, speak of the devil," he said. "Hello, Lon."

CHAPTER 25

THE TROUBLE WITH LANA

L on recognized the Counselor's car coming in, but didn't expect to see all the people in there. And he couldn't quite figure the situation out. Kind of like you walk into a movie in the middle of it. Everybody else knows what's was going on, but you don't. Then, the Doctor saying, "speak of the devil," when he came in, like they was *talking* about him. It didn't feel real good, especially the man the Doctor was talking to, staring at him with cop eyes, like maybe he knew something he shouldn't know.

"Lon, you know the Counselor, of course; and Russell George. But I don't think you've met Mr. Fast Eddie Fuentes—he's the one Little Billy tried to run off the road in a stolen tow truck before he turned himself into a human pancake. Which reminds me," he turned to Shanna. "They should be releasing the bail money we lent to Lon, shouldn't they? Now that the defendant has moved on to greener pastures?"

"Any day now," the Counselor said, for some reason looking at Fuentes.

And Lon was thinking, so that's who it is, the guy looking a little like the picture that was in the papers, but not much like an Indian.

Still looking at Lon, Fuentes said, "You knew my father."

Lon took some time, keeping his eyes on the guy, but not giving it much, trying to figure out what he was doing here. "Did I?" he said, "I don't remember."

"Lon has memory issues." The Doctor said, giving it an edge. "Even simple instructions are a challenge for him."

Jesus Christ, when was he gonna let the damn thing go? First it was the old man, "What did I *say* to you, Lon? What were my exact *words*?" Then it was the Kiwi. "Did he *get* on the plane, Lon? What did I tell you to *do*?" For the love of Christ, you'd think he'd give him credit once in a while. What about Petty? That one worked out, didn't it?

But now they were on their way out, this Fuentes still looking at him. "I guess I'll be seeing you, Lon," he said.

Lon shrugged, "If you say so."

Truth was, he wasn't thinking about Fuentes right now. Where his mind was, he was thinking about the five grand he needed for Lana's Mustang.

The trouble with Lana started up that morning. They was sitting in the Yukon outside the trailer park in Tobago, Lon trying to explain the situation, but Lana not having any of it.

"I heard what you *said*, Lonny," she told him, "but you and me's moving *in* together. You can't keep a thing like that secret from your Mama, even if you'd want to." She turned, looking at him now. "Are you ashamed of me? Is that what it is?"

"No, no, nothing like that. It's just ... Mama ... you know, she's kind of set in her ways. It could take her some time to get used to the situation."

"Well," Lana seemed to consider it, "you wouldn't need to tell her we was moving in all at once. You could start out, saying I was your girlfriend, you know, we've been going together ... something like that."

Lon said, "I'm walking in there, taking my clothes, Lana, Mama's not stupid. She's gonna put two and two together. ... You don't know her. Mama's sharp. And she's not shy, either. She'll come right at you, probably ask you a lot of questions you might not wanna answer."

"I don't mind." Lana moved a little closer. "I'm not all that shy, myself, Lonny, in case you didn't notice."

Lon wiped a hand over his forehead, starting to feel the heat, and not even in the trailer. "Okay, I tell you what, baby. Let me just go in there first, kind of break the ice, okay? Then, if everything's going on all right, I'll come out and get you. How does that sound?"

"It *sounds* like you're afraid of your own goddamn Mama is how it sounds, honey." Lana bounced back over to the other side of her seat "This whole thing is pretty weird, if you don't mind my saying, Lonny. You say I can't move in with you 'cause you're out in the field 'maintaining a perimeter'—whatever *that* means. I say all right, if I can't move in with you, you can move in with *me*. Then, you tell me you got your stuff at your Mama's. A soldier of fortune living with his Mama, I don't mind telling you, Lonny, that's a pretty hard thing to put together."

Lon took a minute, getting things straight in his mind. "No, I told you, the thing with Mama, that's just temporary," he said, "In between assignments. Provides a base of operations. The work I do, sometimes you have to move fast, in and out of various locations."

"Well, I hope you're not planning on moving too fast in and out of *my* location." She thought a second. "I mean …. Well, you know what I mean."

Getting an empty duffle from behind the seat, Lon said, "Okay, now look, I'm not gonna be in there more than a couple minutes. You just wait right here, and it's gonna make matters a whole lot simpler, you can trust me on that part, okay honey?"

After that, Lon got out of the Yukon, eased the door closed, and headed around the corner with the duffle. When he got to the trailer, he knocked on the screen door a couple of times. "Mama? Are you decent? It's Lonny. I'm coming in."

It was dark inside, shades drawn, the TV going like always, *Bold and the Beautiful* by the look of it. Mama's voice come out from the bathroom. "Lonny? Is that you? Come on in, sweetheart. I'm just getting out of the shower."

"Take your time, Mama." Lon tiptoed past the shower over to the Mama's bedroom. Jesus, one o'clock in the afternoon, when the hell *wasn't* she taking a shower?

Mama's voice came out from the bathroom again, "There's some beers in the fridge, hon. Why don't you be a sweetheart and go get us a couple?"

Lon picked up a couple boxes out of Mama's closet, dropped them in the duffle. "Right," he called out.

"Where you been at, anyways? ... You take care of the fella that done Little Billy, yet? I ain't seen nothing about it on television."

Lon was back out in the hallway now, double timing for the bedroom where he had his stuff. He said, "Not yet, Ma, I been real busy. Had to go down to San Francisco." In the other bedroom, he tossed the duffle on the bed, started going through the drawers. "I just come by to pick up some stuff. I'm in a kind of a hurry."

"Well, don't run off. I'll be out in a minute."

"Shit," Lon muttered, stuffing clothes in the duffle fast as he could. It didn't make any sense, but it seemed like if he could just get his shit packed up before Mama got out here, everything would be all right somehow.

"What you doing, Lon, honey? You going somewhere?"

Uh-oh. He turned around and there she was. Mama leaning against the door frame with her arms folded in that short little robe of hers.

"Hey, Mama," he said, going over to give her a kiss.

She tilted her head up to get the kiss. Then all of a sudden, she went stiff as a corpse, holding on to him, with her hand on his neck, not moving a muscle.

"Who's the woman?"

"What woman?"

"The woman that belongs to the perfume. I may not have much education, but I know perfume when I smell it."

"Mama...." Lon tried to pull back, but she wouldn't let go of him, the woman a lot stronger than she looked, holding him in a kinduva headlock.

Then she yelled, right in his ear, "Tell me who it is or I'll bite your goddamn ear off!"

She could do it, too. "Okay, Ma! Jesus! Her name's Lana."

"Lana." She let go of him then, kind of pushed him off of her. "Lon and Lana. Well, if that ain't the cutest damn thing I ever heard of."

She went over to the bed, started going through the duffle, pulling stuff out, one item at a time.

"Socks. Pants. Underwear. Where's the toothpaste? Don't want halitosis, porking little Lana. You got to have that in there."

"Mama ...." Lon tried to get the duffle away, but she had hold of it like a bulldog. She took out a pair of underpants, started twirling them around.

"She pretty good in bed, is she? Know all the tricks of the trade? I'll bet she does. Enough tricks, she's got you sliding around here packing your boxers while your Mama's in the shower. What were you gonna do, slip out the back?"

"Mama ...."

"Don't you 'mama' me, you worthless pecker head. Men! You're all alike. You think where you piss, is your problem. Do anything some little girl wants if she sits on it for you. ... So, where is your little Lana? ... No, don't tell me. Out in the car?" Mama laughed kind of a hard laugh. "That's right, ain't it? Out in the car, waiting 'cause she don 't have the *guts* to come in here and tell me she's taking my son away from me."

"Oh, I got the guts all right!" Lana's voice came from the hallway. And now, she was standing in the door, leaning against the frame, arms folded, just like Mama was a couple minutes ago. "Lemme tell you something, Grandma, the place I was raised in makes *this* dump look like a suite in Las Vegas. I got guts you wouldn't even dream of."

Lana marched in, stood there, hands on her hips, looking down at Mama. "I thought something like this might be going on in here. What a performance! You oughta get a goddamn Academy Award!"

She pointed at Lon. "Take a good look. This here is a grown man, Granny. He's not sucking on your tit any more, you got that? He's with me now. ... You asked him, am I good in bed? Lady, you got no idea how good I am. I'm giving him all he can handle and a whole lot more."

She took hold of Lon by the arm, now. "Come on, baby. You can pick up some things in town. You don't want any of this old rat shit anyways."

Lon just managed to get a hand on the duffle as Lana dragged him out the door.

Now, Mama was screaming at him. "You're gonna let that whore drag you out of here? You feeble minded fairy," then, "Nobody walks out on me. You understand? Nobody!"

Uh-oh, something was coming now, Lon just knew it. And sure enough, they wasn't halfway through the living room when Mama came out of the bedroom swinging Little Billy's red metal baseball bat from high school, not all that easy inside the trailer.

"Take her easy, Mama," Lon was saying over his shoulder, heading out the door.

Wham! Little Billy's ashes went flying through the air, coming down like a snowstorm.

"We're family, remember?"

Wham! She smashed the pole lamp.

Outside now, more or less breaking into a run, Lon called back over his shoulder, "Come on, settle down now Mama."

"I'll see you in hell, you pussy-fogged shit fritter."

Lon turned, ducked in the nick of time, as the bat whizzed past his ear.

Getting in the Yukon a minute later, Lana said, "Your Mama's pretty good with that baseball bat."

"Yeah." Lon fired her up, threw her in gear, and laid rubber. "But she's a whole lot better with a shotgun," he said, pointing at his duffle bag, "Good thing I took her ammunition."

CHAPTER 26

DARRYL PAYS A CALL

Darryl had himself a window booth at Ken's Killer Krabs, place right on the water in Redwood Bay, recommended by the girl at the Best Western where Darryl was staying. As a ruled, Darryl preferred his crab made up in the cakes, but took a chance this time, going with the Killer Kombo, consisting of the crab, done up with Ken's secret garlic butter sauce, served up with the mixed grilled vegetables and the vinegar garlic fries. The Kombo was a little heavy on the secret sauce in Darryl's opinion, but overall, the experience wasn't that bad. Then, some unexpected company showed up.

"My man Darryl. What a coincidence. Mind if we join you?"

Darryl looked up and there they were, grinning, like somebody just told a joke and Darryl wasn't in on it. There was three of them. Fuentes, the Counselor and a tall, interesting sort of dude Darryl hadn't seen before, a little color to the man, thick head of long black hair pulled into a pony tail. Fuentes motioned and they all piled into the booth, Fuentes and the Counselor sitting across, the tall dude next to him.

The dude was nodding now, looking at Darryl's plate. He said, "Killer Kombo, huh? Next time, tell them to give you the sauce on the side. Otherwise, they bury the shit in it."

Darryl took a second, then looked at Fuentes, "I want you all to know, I'm packing tonight. If any of this goddamn sauce gets on my suit, I'm 'a pop a cap in the ass of the motherfucker does it."

Looking at the tall dude, Shanna said, "Darryl has a clothing fetish."

Fuentes said, "Your suit's safe with us, Darryl. We're doing career counseling tonight." He turned to the Counselor.

"Okay. Reality check, Darryl," she said. "You have a plan, I respect that. Work for the Justice Department, build your reputation. Then, switch sides. Problem is, a thing like that takes time. A few years with Justice at least. Doing paperwork—warrant applications, motions, bullshit. And we both know, the salary's not terrific."

"You got somewhere you going with this?"

"You look at the career of any big time trial lawyer, Darryl, what do you see?"

Darryl picked up a crab leg. "Money. What do you think I see?"

"I'm talking before that. How they got there. Five, ten years kissing ass, know what I mean? Working for the government or an associate in some office. Finally, they're on their own, they scrape by, barely making the rent, paying cappers for slip-and-falls, taking phony rear end accident cases. But then, Darryl—one day—something happens. Something that turns everything around. Know what it is?"

"Yeah," Darryl said, "Aunt Sadie dies, leaves them a property in Sausalito. Why don't you get to the point?"

"The big case, Darryl, that's the point. The big motherfucking case. The game changer, makes you a household name. That's what every-body's waiting for, Darryl, that big case that maybe one day just happens to walk through the door."

"Yeah, all right. Like Johnny with O. J. I feel you."

"Except, Darryl, they don't all have O. J.'s money. Sometimes it's more like Erin Brockovich. Remember the movie?"

Darryl did remember it, Julia Roberts in her push-up bra, working as an assistant in a rundown law office, scrambling to make a few dollars.

"But that didn't really tell the story," Shanna said. "How Ed Masry had to lay out expense money, pay for experts, investigators, work the case for years, not getting paid a nickel. Sure, when they won, they won big, but believe me, they earned it. And sometimes, Darryl—a lot of times—they don't even win. A lot of times, they lose."

"Yeah, I got that. What's your point?"

"My point, Darryl, is when an opportunity presents itself that's a virtual ticket to the big time, a no lose proposition with no financial risk that's guaranteed to turn you into a household name, someone in your position would have to be a horse's ass not to jump on it."

Darryl glanced at Eddie Fuentes now, then back at Shanna. "All right, now I'm gonna go ahead and take a wild ass motherfucking leap here. You all —" pointing back and forth between them, "just *happen* to have the kind of motherfucking case you been talking about, and you're thinking you *might* just let me in on it, on account of we all being so *tight* with one another."

The three of them were all looking at each other now, grinning, nodding their heads up and down. Finally, the Counselor said, "That about covers it."

"Uh-huh," Darryl said, "but see now the thing is, I look around the table here, I don't see nothing reminds me even remotely of the big time. So, why don't you tell me what we talking about. You ready to give up the Doctor?"

The three of them were still looking at each other, grinning even more now. Eddie Fuentes shook his head, "The Doctor is *small* time, Darryl. We're talking *big* time."

"Big time. Uh-huh. Is that right?"

The Counselor said, "That *is* right, Darryl. Two words. You ready? Two words that are going to change your life forever. First word, Harriman; second word, Saul."

*   *   *

Eleven-thirty East Coast time, Harriman Saul was sitting in his Citation X, en route New York to Tampa, surrounded by a half dozen flat screens. But he wasn't watching the talking heads on CNBC or the tape crawls on his Bloomberg Terminal, what he was watching was the live feed coming off the Tree Girl's website. The girl, Murrelet, a nice looking brunette, was taking a sponge bath, washing her unshaved underarms for a worldwide audience.

Harry said to Dick Duncan on the speaker, "I see the girl is still in the tree."

Dick said, "She's still in the tree, Harry."

"Is she suing us yet, our little Mangled Murrelet?"

"Not yet."

"Michaels said she's getting a hundred thousand hits a day on her website."

"True, but it skews heavily male, high school age, plus some dirty old men. Not what you'd call a politically active audience."

"I don't get it," Harry said now, looking at the screen. "What kind of life is that? Tweeting over a cell phone, eating Ramen noodles. When she has kids someday, and they ask her, Mommy, what did you do when you were our age, what's she gonna tell them? I sat in a tree and pissed in a bucket?"

Dick said, "I don't think she's having kids, Harry."

"She's a good looking girl. How do you know?"

"Know what?"

"She isn't having children."

Sitting in his office, watching the same live feed, Dick Duncan said, "Cause she's gay, Harry. She has a girlfriend. That's what the security people tell us."

There was a long silence on the other end of the line. Finally, Harry said, "Maybe I should introduce her to my daughter." Then, he changed the subject. "The reason I called, I'm on my way to Tampa. When Crawford heard I was logging with helicopters, he wanted to know what *kind* of helicopters."

"Sikorskys, tell him. Sky Cranes for the big stuff. Something they call "Shortskys" for smaller stuff. You can tell him, it's a 61 with part of the middle cut out."

"A 61 with the middle cut out, he'll love it. He said he'd 'like to be there when the big birds split the sky.' 'Big birds split the sky.' Jesus. ... I said, 'Sure thing, Trace, no way I'd miss it.' So I guess we'll be seeing you there first thing Saturday morning."

Dick said, "We'll all look forward to it, Harry."

Harry said, "I'm sure you will."

Dick hung up, slumped back in his chair, glanced out the window. No activity at the little white frame house across the freeway. The end of an era. He picked up an account statement from Standard Charter Bank in the Caymans, showing a balance of $473,237. Where had all the money gone, he wondered. Here he was, at an age when he should be looking forward an indiscreet liaison and a messy divorce, and he didn't even have a pot to piss in.

The intercom buzzed. "Mr. Duncan? There's a man here to see you. He says he's with the Drug Enforcement Administration?"

"Dick Duncan, my man, my man. How you doing?" Darryl looked the man over now, sitting there behind the oversize desk. Hickey-Freeman sort of suit, olive nail head tweed, woven silk tie, custom broadcloth shirt with French cuffs, script initials on the pocket. Darryl gave him a big smile. "You know, I have heard *so* much about you."

"I'm afraid I can't say the same, Mr.—?"

"Waters. Darryl Waters." Darryl handed him a card. "Drug Enforcement Administration."

Duncan looked at the card for a second, "Mr. Waters. Sorry, I'm ... incredibly busy, today. What can I do for you?"

"Yeah, I know how that is." Darryl chuckled, wandering around the room, taking in the antique hand carved desk, dark wood paneling, antique Oriental carpet. "Go for weeks, months, could be years sometimes, sitting behind a desk, not much happens, till that one day, the shit-storm come down, and you realize your custom made English umbrella is back home in the closet."

He got up and wandered around. "Very nice office, Dick, I must say. Traditional, but tasteful. ... Telescope's an unusual touch. What do you see through that, anyway?" He leaned over the telescope, but couldn't quite figure out how to focus.

"I don't mean to be rude," An edge coming into Duncan's voice now, "but would you mind stating your business."

Darryl looked over. "My business?" Darryl chuckled again. "Absolutely. Happy to do it. In fact, that's why I'm here, Dick, strictly business. Let you know that you, and your company, West Coast Lumber, are targets of a federal criminal investigation for drug trafficking. Conspiracy to violate Section 841(a), Title 21, United States Code."

"What is this, some kind of a joke?"

"Joke? I don't think so. Ever heard of an attorney by the name of Shanna Black?"

"What about her?"

"Ms. Black entered into an agreement, says she willing to go before a grand jury, testify under oath that you directly involved in several large scale marijuana growing operations on West Coast Lumber Company property."

"Shanna. So *that's* it." The man took some time, nodding now, like he was feeling relieved, getting some clarity on the thing. "I'm sorry, Mr. Waters, I've been under a lot of pressure lately. Why don't we sit down and talk about this. Can I have my assistant get you something to drink? Coke? Mineral water? Cup of coffee?"

Darryl smiled. "How about a Perrier? You think your ... assistant ... could dig up one of those?"

A few minutes later, now sitting in armchairs with their drinks, Duncan gave Darryl an embarrassed sort of smile. "I really don't know how to begin this. The whole thing is ... terribly embarrassing. The truth is, Ms. Black and I ... have been having an affair."

"Oh my," Darryl said. "You don't say so?"

"Are you married, Mr. Waters?"

"No," Darryl said, shaking his head. "Sadly, I've had to put that on hold."

"Yes, well, I am married, you see … happily, I'm proud to say. Two wonderful children. And this thing with Shanna, it was … well, it just … it should never have happened. It was a weakness on my part. I take full responsibility." He sighed. "In any case, a couple weeks ago, I finally summoned the courage to … break it off. And … what can I say? Shanna didn't take it very well."

"Ah *hah*!" Darryl said. "So, Dick, I don't want to put words in your mouth or anything, but what I think I hear you saying, the Counselor … Ms. Black … is on a revenge mission. Dealing with feelings of rejection, something of that nature."

"Well, you know what they say about the fury of a woman scorned." Duncan was shaking his head now. "I don't blame her, of course. Shanna's a beautiful woman, intelligent … exceptionally talented. As I said before, it was all my fault."

"Make sense to me, Dick. Make sense to me." Darryl was nodding again. "I mean, as a strategy. My guess is, you figure it would be more or less, your word against hers. Upstanding corporate executive on the one side, disreputable drug attorney on the other. Who's the grand jury to believe? You or her? … All except for one thing, Dick. Seems like Ms. Black? She had a … kind of a nasty habit, you might say … where she recorded all her conversations." He chuckled. "And I don't mean just on the telephone, either. Sort of wore her own wire, if you can believe it. I mean, think of the class of people the woman had to be dealing with to even think of a thing like that."

The man swallowed so hard at this point you could just about hear the gulp, but he recovered quickly. "And …what if I told you Shanna was also my … attorney … so our conversations were privileged?"

Now Darryl smiled. "I'd ask you to produce a written fee agreement, documenting the relationship, as required by California law."

Duncan looked at him a few seconds, cleared his throat, then got up and walked back to his desk, real slow, and sank down into his big, executive leather chair.

Darryl said, "Yeah, what Ms. Black told me? Being a criminal lawyer like she is, and knowing how the system works, she figured, if she ever got busted, she was gonna need something to trade." Darryl took a pause. "Looks like that was you."

Darryl got up now, walked over to the window, looking out on the little logging town, the wood frame houses, the tree covered mountains. Then he turned back to the president of the corporation. "Conspiracy to possess a controlled substance with intent to distribute. I can lock your ass away twenty years, Dick. That's first offense, and no priors." He let it sink in, before he went on. "Now, Ms. Black, I'd say she was on the right track. Came up with something to trade. I told her, if she gave you up, I'd cut her a deal. Now it's your turn. If you got anything you want to give me, now would be the time to tell me what it is. Otherwise, I'd say you looking at a serious change of lifestyle, Dick."

CHAPTER 27

HARVEST MOON

Ten a.m. on a foggy Thursday morning, Sarah Breckinridge studied her reflection in the window of her corner office on the eleventh floor of the Federal Courthouse Building in San Francisco. Not bad for a woman her age—forty-five last April—regular features, strong jaw, clear blue eyes, a full head of hair worn short, the natural gray enhanced with some platinum highlights. She liked the look. It suited her. A hard-nosed career litigator like her Dad, never wanted to be anything else. A year ago, after a five year stint at Stone Webster pulling down a million a year defending corporate scumbags, she gave it up to accept an appointment as U. S. Attorney, returning to the job she loved best —tough ass federal prosecutor.

But now, a disturbing realization was staring her in the face. In the face literally, because she was reading over the copy an assistant had just emailed her, updating her Wikipedia page. And disturbing, because the only major call-out in the whole damn piece dealt with medical marijuana. It read, "Ms. Breckinridge has aggressively closed large state-approved medical marijuana dispensaries, including efforts to seize the property of landlords." Why mention they were *state-approved*? It was true, but seemed to invite the question, if they were state approved, why bother to raid them? And *efforts to seize*? It sounded weak, calling attention to the fact that they hadn't been completely successful. A few more victories were collected under a catch-all called "The Work of the Attorney General". These included a settlement with UPS over shipments from unlicensed pharmacies, a case against a Johnson & Johnson subsidiary dealing with health care fraud, and a settlement with Wal-Mart about hazardous waste disposal. Really? Wasn't there anything better to put in there?

Launching her browser now, she pulled up the Northern District of California page on the DOJ website and started reading the recent case headlines. *San Jose CPA Sentenced For Tax Fraud.* Yawn. *Oakland Man Charged In Identity Theft Scheme.* Snooze. *San Leandro Woman Sentenced For Assaulting Federal Courthouse Security Guard?* Hmmm.

Just out of curiosity—or maybe it was masochism—Sarah Googled Preet Bharara, and clicked the Wikipedia link. After running through his early life and career, his victories were organized in neat little categories. *Financial Fraud*—Oversaw funds recovery from the Bernie Madoff Ponzi scheme; investigated and prosecuted Galleon Trading Group, SAC Capital Advisors; eighty convictions for insider trading without a single loss. *National Security Cases*—Life sentences for the Times Square Bomber and the guy responsible for the U.S. Embassy bombings in Kenya and Tanzania; thirty-three year sentence for Somali pirate, Abduwali Muse, the first piracy conviction in modern times. There were also call-outs for *Public Corruption* and *Organized Crime*, the latter including a multi-state organized crime takedown, charging twenty-six members of the Gambino crime family with racketeering, murder, and narcotics charges. And there was more.

Sarah Breckinridge leaned back in her swivel chair and sighed. Preet Bharara had haunted her ever since college—they both went to Harvard and Columbia Law—and Sarah got better grades. But that was where their paths diverged. Being a San Francisco girl, Sarah came back to California. Preet, on the other hand, went to Washington, and wound up chief counsel to Senator Chuck Schumer. From there, it was a hop, skip and a jump to an appointment as U.S. Attorney for the Southern District of New York—where all the action is. Coming back to Justice, Sarah had hoped to turn things around. So far, well, Wikipedia told the score.

The intercom buzzed. "Ms. Breckinridge? Michelle Thomas to see you."

Uh-oh.

Sarah said, "Tell her to come in."

Michelle had been a fifth year litigation associate at Stone Webster. When Sarah got the U.S. Attorney appointment, she convinced Michelle to come with her as an AUSA. Michelle was an able and attractive young woman. African American, a native of the East Bay, Walnut Creek as Sarah recalled, she attended Berkeley and Boalt Hall, graduating with honors. As Sarah understood it, she was the daughter of an optometrist who had expanded to three locations before retiring to Coto de Caza. She was intelligent, hard-working and loyal. But having said that, she seemed to lack the indispensable quality that set apart top notch litigators—the killer instinct.

As she came in now and took a seat, Sarah said, "So?"

Michelle shook her head. "Move to discharge. All we can do."

"You're saying, without indictment."

"Witness is dead. Testimony can't be used as evidence or leverage. We got nothing left."

Sarah looked out the window, not wanting to let it go. If there was one thing she hated *almost* as much as losing a case, it was discharging a grand jury without issuing indictments. "You're sure. There's nothing. Nothing at all."

Michelle took some time. "Well," she said, starting to smile just a little. "There is *one* thing. You remember the *attorney* assigned to the task force by DEA, now moving over to join us here at Justice."

Sarah ran a hand over her face. "Darryl Waters."

"Mmm hmm."

"Okay."

Imitating Darryl, Michelle said, "Darryl say, he got something *big.*"

"Something big."

"The *big case*, he says. The one's gonna make us all household names."

"Like Ajax Cleanser."

"Like Johnnie Cochran."

"He said that? Johnnie Cochran?"

"Mmm. He said he'd give me the case in two words. 'Two words gonna change our lives forever. First word, Harriman. Second word, Saul.'"

It stopped Sarah, actually took her breath away. She assumed Michelle knew who Harriman Saul was. But what she didn't know—could not have known—was that the SEC and the DOJ had both been after the bastard for *years*—during three different administrations. And even now were rumors swirling about stock manipulation connected to some airline merger he was involved in. So far, he'd been too slippery— and too well connected— to even receive a target letter. Could the time be ripe for the weasel to take a fall?

Sarah's first reaction, after Michelle ran her through the case, wasn't overly positive. "I don't see probable cause," she said.

But then, after they talked it through, figuring a way to back up a warrant, she started to consider it more seriously. "I hope you made it clear to our friend, Darryl, I'm the only one in the office who grants immunity," she said.

"I told him."

"As far as the lawyer," Sarah said, "I guess we need her to give us the other guy. But he's the one I'm interested in. What did you say his name was?"

"Dick Duncan."

"Duncan, right. It's a narrow window, but—you think he'd wear a wire?"

Michelle shrugged. "One way to find out."

Sarah thought a minute. "Set up a meeting. Let's see just what Mr. Dick Duncan thinks he can deliver."

When Michelle was gone, Sarah turned to the window, where the sun seemed to be breaking through the fog, and caught her reflection, smiling. Preet Bharara, eat your heart out. What wouldn't you give for a wire on Harriman Saul?

How the thing got started with Michelle, Darryl got hold of her while she was food shopping at the Safeway in Emeryville, told her he needed to see her about urgent business.

She said, "Yeah? What's that, Darryl? You got another dead witness you want to tell me about?"

He told her no more dead witnesses. What he had was a major drug bust, conspiracy to distribute. She asked him, was it the Doctor? He said it was bigger than that, and complicated, so he didn't want to talk on the phone. Michelle said she couldn't see him now, on account of she had to pick up her daughter at daycare before six o'clock, and it was already five-forty seven.

"Serena? Suppose I pick up her up? She at the Montessori on University, right?"

It stopped her, the woman not aware Darryl knew her daughter's name or where she went to school. She said, "What are you doing, stalking me?"

Darryl said, "What we do, girl. We detectives. Didn't nobody tell you that?"

They worked it out so Michelle picked up Serena, and Darryl waited in line getting pizza someplace Michelle told him about. She was already home, changed into blue jeans by the time Darryl got there, a little past seven.

Coming in, he said, "Rough out there, yo. Like my mama said, you can pick up jailbait in this town easier than pizza."

Standing next to her mother, little Serena said, "What's jailbait, Mama?"

Looking at Darryl, Michelle said, "Never mind that, Serena."

Darryl had never been to Michelle's before, but he knew where it was—on the bay in Emeryville, a condo just off the 580. She said she was renting, but Darryl wasn't so sure. The word on Michelle was, she came from money. Had a daughter while she was still in college, married at the time to a rich white boy studying medicine. The marriage didn't stick, and the white boy flew back home to Illinois, or it could have been Michigan— but he was still paying child support. Whatever the facts of the matter, this place was not too shabby: bright white walls, hardwood floors, tile baths, stainless steel kitchen. Whether the girl was owning or renting, one thing was for sure: no way she was hurting.

The apartment was set up with a dining "L" off the kitchen, fronting on a terrace that looked out on a swimming pool. They ate the pizza looking out at the view, making small talk with little Serena, both of them asking her questions about school. She was a cute kid, eight years old, curly brown hair, blue eyes and a light colored skin. She had a mouth on her, though.

When Darryl asked her what she thought about her mommy being a big time attorney, little Serena said, "Mommy says her job's bullshit."

Michelle tried to interrupt, "Serena—"

"Mommy says, the legal system is a joke, and the people *running* the country are the ones who belong in prison. She says Obama's an empty suit—"

"Serena!" Michelle told her that was enough, and it was time to go do her homework.

When she was gone, Darryl said, "You think he's an empty suit, huh? First African American President. The most powerful person in the world."

And Michelle said, "He says he's African American all right, but I'd like you to tell me one single thing he's actually done for black people."

*   *   *

Sitting at a back corner table at the Delta Belle, halfway through her second straight up vodka martini, Shanna watched Jimmy Kennan sweep into the room. Surrounded by a discreet phalanx of security personnel, the Governor was smiling genially, waving to whoever happened to be in the room, shaking hands, kissing cheeks, eventually getting around to Shanna's. The Delta Belle was not an unfamiliar venue to Shanna. The old sternwheeler, docked on the Sacramento River at Front Street, was kind of a tourist trap. Jimmy knew the owners, who had been known to comp him a suite upstairs called the Captain's Berth when the need arose. Shanna met him there a few times when, as she had overheard him tell his wife, things were running late at the office. Meeting here tonight, returning to the scene of the crime, as it were, was Shanna's idea, part of what she called Plan B, and what Eddie called the "nuclear option".

At first, she was somewhat reluctant to call the Governor—understatement of the millennium—and told Eddie she didn't see what it had to do with getting immunity from prosecution. But Eddie said, this was how the Doctor set it up. It was a package deal, all or nothing, take it or leave it. Besides, he told her, smiling, it would be good for her self-esteem.

Self-esteem, really? Jimmy Kennan had abused her, fucked her, and dumped her. He had his reasons, sure. He was married to a woman with boatloads of money for one thing. For another thing, it was his nature. He was an opportunist, incapable of shame or remorse. But even knowing all that, their prior relationship hadn't exactly been a confidence builder, and Shanna didn't see where reviving it was likely to do much in that area either. But what happened when she finally called the prick genuinely surprised her.

James G. Kennan, Shanna's former employer and one time sex partner, now Governor of the State of California, returned her call in less than twenty-four hours. When he did, *mirabile dictu*, the asshole literally fell all over himself telling her how *sorry* he was for what happened, how he thought about her all the time, how he wondered how she was doing, and why she never called or asked if she could use him as a reference. A reference? What was this? Did he genuinely not remember what he'd done to her? Or, was it something else?

Shanna played along, told him she was fine, she'd been practicing law, but was branching out and, in fact had a public relations idea she was dying to discuss with him. Public relations? He said it with a nervous little laugh. He was intrigued. What was it? Shanna was going to give him her pitch at the time, tell him how she had an idea that could help him reconcile a couple difficult constituencies, but for some reason, she didn't. Instead, she told him she didn't want to talk on the phone, but she guaranteed he'd find the idea well-nigh irresistible.

He laughed again and asked how much it was going to cost him?

Shanna said, "How about dinner for starters?"

Now, in the restaurant, as he kissed her on the cheek, she slid into her sexy smile. "Jimmy, you haven't changed a bit." He was still a sleazy jerk, so it wasn't a lie. On the appearance front, he'd put on a good twenty pounds (if there *was* such a thing as a good twenty pounds). And he still had the same game show host looks, the same fast laugh, the same quick, blue eyes that darted around the room like dragonflies, incapable of resting on any one object for more a couple seconds at a time.

He ordered a bottle of wine, and sitting there, sipping $300 Pinot Grigio, Shanna began to realize Jimmy Kennan was scared, playing defense, sparring like a fighter in the opening rounds, dancing, using the ring, trying to avoid the corners.

"I had to cut it off," he said, a half bottle in. "Meg didn't give me a choice. I told myself you understood. That you understood, those were the rules from the start."

Where was he going with this? Shanna had a recording queued up in her pocket. She could use it anytime she wanted. But what was the hurry? She heard herself say, "You always told me you two were partners. That you had an arrangement, an understanding. It was politics."

Drinking wine, he said, "And at the time, I believed it. But it was always about her. Her version of the 'arrangement' was, nothing could never get serious. It could never threaten her hold on me, because if it did, that would mean she might lose. Meg could never let me leave her. Not because she cared about me, but because she cared too much about herself."

This was interesting. Shanna rolled the wine glass back and forth between her palms. "How *is* Megan?" she asked.

"How is Megan?" He repeated the question, drinking more wine. "What can I say? Megan is ... the bed I lie in. It was always *her* money, *her* family, *her* connections. I am, in a sense, the instrument of her ambition. I always said she was a better politician than I am."

"Maybe she ought to run for office."

"Maybe she will. It wouldn't surprise me if she's thinking about it. Not that she'd tell me, unless she thinks she could benefit from an endorsement or figures a way to turn a divorce into a bump in her poll numbers." He gave her his pathetic, game show smile, and Shanna felt ... what *did* she feel? *Sorry* for him?

He looked at her now. "You know, when you got canned, you could have made something out of it. I'm sure she left a trail. It would have been worth plenty, too. She would have paid. She would have had to. But you didn't go that way I always thought it showed a lot of class."

"Well, you know me, Jimmy. I'm a classy girl."

He smiled. "When you ... called me up, I thought maybe you changed your mind about that."

Shanna started to smile.

"Well, you know, what you said about getting back into public relations, I thought—"

She raised an eyebrow. "Really."

He hesitated. "When, you left, there were rumors. You know how people talk. I heard you ... might have recordings, possibly even ... video."

Shanna raised her head to glance up toward the Captain's Berth. "Now that you mention it, some of that stuff really could be damaging, couldn't it? Like, remember that time in your office, you were talking to Megan on the phone while you had me ...." She smiled. "Well you remember. Imagine that one on YouTube."

Their eyes met.

"Or right upstairs, remember that time? .... It sure is a good thing I'm a classy girl, right Jimmy?"

He looked at her carefully now. "Like I said before, I always appreciated the way you handled the situation. I'm ... deeply, deeply ... grateful."

Shanna gave him a smile she didn't exactly feel, saying, "That's good, Jimmy. Real good. What we need to talk about now, is *how* grateful."

*   *   *

Nine o'clock, Eddie finished watching one of the *Oceans* movies on pay-per-view at the Hyatt Regency—amazed they'd charge money to see a movie as old as that—and decided he needed to go for a walk. No destination, not really knowing the town, he wandered past the State House, up to the Vietnam Memorial, back down the Mall toward the river. Meanwhile, he was thinking about the movie—about movies in general— how you could end the story anywhere you wanted. You picked a spot where the hustle was over, they got away with it, they're riding off into the sunset, or drinking *mai tai's*, making love on a sailboat, whatever, then you fade to black, and roll the credits. The problem with real life was, the hustle might be over, maybe you got away with it, maybe you rode off into the sunset, but that wasn't the end of it. The sun went down, but then it came up again. There was no such thing as happily ever after.

Without exactly knowing how he got there, Eddie was down on Front Street, kind of a tourist area with wooden sidewalks, restaurants, cafes, old buildings fixed up to look like they did back in the Gold Rush. On an impulse, he wandered into a little hole in the wall called River City Books bought himself something to read, then started back to the hotel.

He was standing outside a place called the Old Town Saloon, tempted to go in, but turned off because it looked crowded. He glanced across the street, and there was the Delta Belle, where Shanna was supposed to be having dinner with Jimmy Kennan. He stood a minute, wondering if she was still in there. Thinking about Jimmy Kennan, how he looked on TV, the guy reminding him of Dick Duncan, both of them big men, blonde, smooth operators. And thinking how Shanna made it with both those guys, kind of using them, probably everybody using everybody else. And wondering how she felt about that, or *if* she felt about it, and then, wondering how she felt about him.

He glanced back to the bar then—jammed with conventioneers— and caught his reflection in the window. He found himself wondering what a woman like Shanna would think of the guy he saw there. Kind of a dark complexion that set off the blue eyes, a rumpled look with the wiry hair and a two day growth of beard. Not exactly Jimmy Kennan.

Two hours later, Eddie was reading his book back at the hotel, when Shanna walked in, carrying a bottle of champagne.

"Hey, sailor. How about a drink?"

She was standing in the doorway, swaying a little on spike heels, a knockout in her sexy black outfit with a very short skirt.

He said, "How's the Governor?"

She shook her head, kicking off her shoes. "Not good. Nearing the end of his political career. Doesn't know what he's going to do with the rest of his life. No legacy to speak of." She held up the champagne bottle. "You have something to open this with?"

Eddie held out his hand. "Here, I'll do it."

She handed it to him and went on. "He's got problems with immigration, education, budget deficits, unemployment. Doesn't know his kids, his wife never loved him, and he thinks she's positioning herself to run against his record in the next election. What else do you want to know?"

Eddie popped the cork, and went to the bathroom to find a couple glasses. "What happened?"

"Yeah, well...." Shanna thought a minute. "I really wanted to smoke that asshole, you know? Rake him over the coals? I had the fucking Penal Code memorized. 288a. 'Oral copulation by means of force, violence, duress or menace. I had the video queued up on my phone."

Eddie poured champagne into a water glass and handed one to her. "Okay."

"I'm a classy girl, Eddie. What can I tell you?"

Eddie poured himself a glass, and raised it, "You're classy enough," he said.

*   *   *

Finishing a late dinner of oysters *rouille* with French baguettes that would almost certainly give him heartburn, the Doctor asked Désiré whether he had heard back from Alex's about the reservations.

"Ah, *oui*, yes. The man he say, they are very busy this week, but you are a good customer, so they must fit you in."

"And the discount?"

"Fifty per cent, *comme vous avez dit.* "

The Doctor's farmer, Ike Rampas, was a big Neil Young fan. Alex's was a code they worked out, taken from a restaurant in Woodside where Neil's wife, Peg, used to work. The name showed up in a video of one of his songs called Harvest Moon. So, a reservation at Alex's meant it was time to pull the crop. Fifty off meant, pull half the crop and leave half in the ground.

So, as the *I ching* declared, things were beginning to fall into place. Wayne gone to his ancestors; now, the sheriff as well. Lon was in the arms of his *nouvelle amie* as Désiré might say, though who knew for how long … which reminded him, it was time to make a call.

The Doctor found out about Lana Janich more or less by accident. When Lon asked for five thousand dollars to buy a car, the Doctor asked him what kind of a car you could buy for five thousand dollars. Lon said he was helping somebody out, and it was just a down payment. The Doctor asked if it was his mother. He knew Lon lived with his mother, though he didn't like to talk about it.

"Unh-uh," Lon said, "Somebody else."

Finally, the Doctor dragged it out of him. How he met the girl on Petty's boat, and decided he could trust her because she was involved— got Petty to take off his clothes, helped with the body— and because she hated Petty anyway and said she wanted to see him taken care of. Also, given the financial request, it was obvious to the Doctor that Lon had, to some extent, tempered his filial allegiance.

The Doctor could trust Lon, he knew, because Lon was bound by his self-imposed warrior code. The woman was another matter. She hadn't demonstrated much loyalty to Petty—not that he deserved it—but what was going to happen when she got tired of Lon, his body odor, for example, or his choice of tattoos? The situation seemed … well, precarious.

So, he asked Lon, "What about your Mama? How does she feel about Lana?"

Lon looked away. "Mama's mama," he said. "She'll get used to it."

But having heard his share of Mama stories, and knowing his own mother, the Doctor suspected this was rank optimism. Considering all this now, he walked to a wall phone, picked it up, and punched in some numbers.

The operator said, "Directory assistance for what city?"

"Tobago, California, I think. I need a listing for Odom, O-D-O-M. I'm not sure of the first name."

The operator said, "There's a charge of $1.99. Would you like to continue?"

"$1.99?" The Doctor repeated it in disbelief.

"That's correct. Would you like to continue?"

Would he like to continue? How the hell else was he going to get the number? He said, "Absolutely."

"One moment." The phone went dead for quite a bit longer that, then the Operator was back on. "I have a Marilyn Odom on Sleepy Hollow Drive. Would you like me to connect you?"

Putting on his best illiterate accent now, the Doctor asked if there was an extra charge for that service. When the Operator assured him there was not, the Doctor said, "Well, in that case, yes ma'am, I would. I mean, if it wouldn't be too much trouble for you."

A tri-tone played, then a recorded woman's voice thanked him for using AT& T—as if he had any choice about it.

After a second, the phone rang, and a woman picked up. "Hello?"

The Doctor got in character. This was going to be fun. "Lana? Hell you at, anyways?"

"What'd you say?"

"I *said* where the hell you at. You's supposed to be here at six. I just got down here, the girls told me you never showed. I got goddamn tables to cover."

The voice was suspicious now. "Who *is* this?"

"Who is it? Harvey. At the Wharf Rat. Who the hell else is it gonna be?"

"Harvey who?"

"Don't give me that Harvey who. You're on six to two. Hey, wait a minute. What number did I dial? Is this Lana?"

"There ain't no Lana here."

"Is this eight-eight-seven, eleven oh six, Lon Odom's place?"

"He don't live here anymore."

"Well, shit," the Doctor said now, "I just *got* the damn number from a friend of his a few minutes ago. I called up her place behind Marty Stroh's, ain't no answer."

She said, "You talking about Marty Stroh up at Sanchez Landing?"

"That's right."

"Well, you got the wrong number. You're talking to Lon's Mama in Tobago."

"Well suck my tit with a vacuum cleaner—sorry for the language, ma'am. But hey… has he got a cell I could call? What I hear you, can't get the two of them off each other with a paint scraper, so if I get hold of *him*—"

Click! The line went dead.

The Doctor belched unexpectedly, and went to the refrigerator, poured himself some carrot juice to settle his stomach. Ahhh! He smiled in relief, then broke into song. A little snippet from the old Neil Young number—

Because I'm still in love with you
I want to see you dance again
Because I'm still in love with you
On this harvest moon.

CHAPTER 28

BY THE BOOK

Saturday morning, Darryl was on the headset, feet up on the desk in the little office he shared with three other dudes just off a bullpen at DEA headquarters, Oakland. Darryl was talking to Eddie Fuentes, no one else around at the moment.

He said, "But what I'm saying, you didn't *see* anything that you could swear to of your own personal knowledge."

Fuentes said, "You mean as far as the warrant."

"Uh huh, see what Michelle says, it's got to be bullet proof, you see where I'm going with this."

Hung on the wall across from Darryl was a whiteboard with the case map, the Doctor's name at the top with a box around it. Connected to that box were boxes for Roger Bachman, Wayne Mehana and Shanna Black. The boxes for Roger Bachman and Wayne Mehana had X's through them. Connected to the Shanna Black box there was a Norville Petty box and a Dick Duncan box. The Norville Petty box also had an X through it.

Looking at the board now, Darryl said, "We got the Counselor saying she paid Duncan off, and we got Duncan saying he got *paid* off. But who do we have saying the weed is actually growing in the ground out there?"

Fuentes said, "You guys have drones, don't you? Why not do a flyover, take some pictures?"

Darryl grinned. "No, see we don't use the "D" word around here, on account of we not authorized to do domestic surveillance. Anyway, the boys around here a bit gun shy on account of that situation down Malibu a few years back. Place called the Trails End Ranch. They got a warrant based on aerial recon, went in, somebody started shooting and a rancher wound up dead."

"So?"

"Wasn't nothing there. Good size settlement on a wrongful death suit, though."

Silence on the line, finally Fuentes said, "What do you want?"

"We thinking, you go in there, take some close-ups you can text us from your cell phone, maybe bring out a sample for backup. Boys think it should be a piece of cake, seeing you know the area."

"That's what the boys think, huh?" More silence, then. "I don't know."

"You got a cell phone, don't you?"

Fuentes said, "I got a cell phone, Darryl. I'm talking on it."

"So, what's the problem?"

"You mean, besides I could get my fucking head shot off?"

Darryl said, "Yeah, besides that."

Sitting in the passenger seat of the Rover, headed from Sacramento back up to Redwood County, Eddie punched the disconnect on his cell phone, seemed to think a minute, then went back to reading his book.

At the wheel, Shanna looked over. "What did your friend, Darryl, want?"

"Not Darryl. It's the A.U.S.A., Michelle something or other." He looked up now. "She says there's no probable cause for a warrant on account of nobody can swear the weed's actually out there. She wants pictures with enough detail to show the leaf serrations. And a physical sample, if we can get it, in case the warrant gets challenged."

"Oh, it'll get challenged all right. They'll have the best lawyers in North America trying to poke holes in the damn thing. 'Cause if they can't, it's *hasta la vista*, baby." She looked over. "When do they want you to go in?"

"Tonight. They wanted me to leave my cell phone in there, so they could triangulate the location off the GPS, but I told them I'm going to have to bring the phone out to send the pictures because the service up there's so shitty."

"Why can't they get the location off the pictures? Doesn't your phone geotag with the location?"

"I don't know. Maybe, or maybe not, 'cause of the signal. Anyway, they want me to go back in when they do the raid." He thought a minute. "But, uhhh, about going in there tonight, what would you think about giving your buddy the Doctor a call, so he can let the boys know I'm coming."

"You're kidding, right?" She looked over. "If I even tried to talk to him about this shit on the phone, he'd think it was a setup."

Eddie took a few seconds now. "So, about that, they figure the Doctor could be hard to find after the raid goes off. "

She smiled. "Is *that* what they figure?"

"Yeah, they're going with coordinated raids. And since you're the only one knows where he lives—"

"Russell knows."

"Russell's not getting immunity."

She sighed, thinking about it. Getting into Ukiah now, the oak dotted hills were giving way to distant mountain ranges. She said, "What about Odom?"

"What about him?"

"What *about* him? He's a killer. A pro. He does it for a living."

"I'm not sure what that means." His voice was strange, flat, matter of fact.

She said, "It means, he gets paid to kill people."

"A lot of people do. You know that picture, American Sniper? Chris Kyle? What do you think he was doing? With Lon, you know the tattoo? It's Force Recon. Marine Corps snipers. No battle lines, no questions asked. He got paid for that, too."

"That's the *military*."

"Right, the military. Then you get out, and all of a sudden, they change the rules. They tell you how to kill, but they don't tell you how to make a living." She watched him, staring out the window. Finally, he said, "Well, I wouldn't worry about it. They'll probably pick him up in the sweep."

"What if they don't?"

"If they don't? He'll probably kill some people, unless somebody kills him first."

There was something about the way he said it that brought back that feeling again—the one she had when she found out Wayne was dead—the feeling that danger wasn't hypothetical, that it was close, that it was possible. And with it, she was also realizing that men like Eddie Fuentes lived with that danger, that it didn't bother them, or they learned to live with it, if it did.

She said, "You make it sound like a cowboy movie."

He shrugged, "Well, you're a cowgirl, right? Grew up in the wild, wild west?"

She said, "When I got to Reno, Eddie, I threw that fucking cowgirl under the bus." Shanna glanced at the paperback he had in his hand, obviously a western, the cover image, a man in a straight brim Stetson, reversed out in silhouette, with a title that said, *Hombre*. Now, she motioned to it, "I don't even see how you can *read* that shit."

He said, "This one's not bad."

"It's not, huh?"

He shook his head. "They made a movie out of it a long time ago. I saw it when I was a kid. But the thing is, when they made the movie, they changed it. See I always thought it was about an Indian, a half-breed Apache raised by white men, who goes back to living with the Indians. But in the book, it's the other way around. The guy's a white man, raised by Apaches, who goes back to living with the Indians."

"What's the difference?"

"The difference? I guess … he didn't have to be an Indian, so…." He paused, apparently thinking it through. "But maybe there *isn't* a difference. Either way, he had a choice. He decided what he wanted to be, and it turned out to be an Indian."

*   *   *

Later that night, lying next to Shanna in the loft at the cabin, Eddie was thinking about the Rancheria. Not anything in particular, just scenes from the life out there—standing by the side of the road waiting for the school bus in the morning, feeling the bite of the wind blowing across the plain, playing football, running through grass the color of straw, shielding his eyes against the pale yellow sun coming through the fog. Did it mean anything to him, growing up there? Being an Indian? Was it part of him? Was he proud of it? Ashamed of it? Was it something he wanted? Or something he didn't want?

Three o'clock in the morning, he touched Shanna on the shoulder, and told her it was time to go.

Eddie had found the way into the garden earlier that night. On a hunch, he had Shanna drive past the turn-off to the cabin, heading south toward the Watershed, toward the point where the ridgeline turned sharply to the east. He knew there had to be a way in somewhere off that road, because it would be too hard to pack shit in and out through the canyon. And sure enough, thirty yards before the bend in the road, he saw a stretch of chaparral that didn't look right. After the long, dry summer, *all* the brush up there looked dead, covered with dust. But this chaparral *was* dead. It had been cut and tied with wire, so it could be moved. On the other side of it, an old logging track headed down a southwest facing slope. Fifty yards down, the track ended in a small clearing, where loggers had bulldozed a truck landing years ago. Eddie couldn't see much in the fading light, but it looked like somebody had put up a shack down there, under a canopy of tanoak, at the edge of the clearing.

Now, the sky dark, the moon already set, the sun not up yet, Eddie sat with Shanna in the Rover, doing a final equipment check—cell phone, flashlight, Spyderco knife, the load in Matty's Colt automatic. He could feel Shanna watching him.

"What?"

She nodded in the direction of the gun.

"It's a guy thing."

"Mmm." She changed the subject. "So, the U. S. Attorney, she'd be happy with the pictures? Or, they definitely want the physical evidence?"

"She *needs* pictures. She *wants* physical evidence. I'm supposed to text Darryl if I get it; he'll arrange for a deputy to fly it down to San Francisco. He says they want it in the evidence locker in case the warrant gets challenged, but they don't need it to issue the warrant."

She said, "You know, when the Feds go in there, they'll seize some of the product for evidence, but mostly, they'll burn it." He looked at her. She said, "It's the best field grown weed in north America. You know that, right?"

He said, "That's what I've heard."

"I don't know if this occurred to you, but ... since they're *telling* you to bring out the weed, that would constitute official authorization to possess a controlled substance. I mean, there's no way they could prosecute you for it."

"In your considered legal opinion."

Shanna shrugged. "Just ... wanted to throw it out there."

CHAPTER 29

IN THE GARDEN

On the eleventh floor of the Federal Courthouse Building, San Francisco, California, Michelle was reading over Darryl's warrant affidavit while they waited for the pictures to come in from his confidential informant.

"I, Darryl Waters, being duly sworn, declare and state that I am a law enforcement officer of the United States, empowered to conduct investigations of offenses enumerated in Titles 18 and 21, blah-blah-blah. I have been a Special Agent of the Drug Enforcement Administration for— thirty-seven months?" Her voice having a question in it.

Darryl said, "I had a couple years before that as a state fraud investigator," noticing Michelle's long, delicate fingers with red polished nails as she turned the pages, the polish matching the dark red suit she wore today. It was the first time he'd seen her in the color, ordinarily wearing blue, brown, black or beige. The suit she was wearing now looked like a wool crepe, showing off her figure. Darryl had to admit, she was a fine looking woman, even if she did have some personality issues.

Michelle went on reading. "I am currently assigned to the District Office in Oakland, California, blah-blah-blah. Have received sixteen weeks of specialized training in Quantico, Virginia in a variety of investigative techniques and resources, including physical and electronic *surveillance*, analysis of *telephone* records, and the use of various types of informants and cooperating sources." She looked up. "That how you found out where I live?"

"What I told you, I'm a detective."

"Mmm. ... I have assisted in undercover operations ... executed arrest and search warrants ... debriefed informants ... have become familiar with the methods used by narcotics traffickers to smuggle safeguard and distribute narcotics and collect and launder proceeds related thereto. I am familiar with the methods employed by large-scale narcotics organizations to thwart detection, including counter-surveillance techniques, false or fictitious identities, and coded communications and conversations." She looked up from the affidavit. "You're really into this, huh?"

"Into what?"

"This." She tapped the papers. "Surveillance, busts, plea deals, asset seizures, all that drug enforcement bullshit."

Darryl looked at her now. "Michelle, where I come from, you either on *one* side of the law, or you on the *other.*"

She looked back at him, a little different now. "The thing is, Darryl, where *I* come from, it's not like that. There's a whole other world of people just living their lives, not *on* one side or the other."

"What're you doing here then, working for the government? How come you didn't stay where you were at? Stone Webster. Pulling down the big bucks?"

She looked away. "It's not what you think."

"How do you know what I think?"

"'Cause I know men like you looking at the thing from outside of it. You think a job like that's about being a big shot, sitting in a high rise office in San Francisco wearing a two thousand dollar suit."

Darryl laughed. "You got that right. That is *exactly* what I think."

"That suit, Darryl? Listen to me now. That suit is a strait jacket. Twenty-two hundred hours a year, minimum. That's what you have to bill, Darryl. Works out to eight and a half hours a day. But understand, that's *billable* time. You can't *bill* for when you're checking your mail or hanging with your homeboys on the telephone. Running errands, eating lunch, going to the bathroom, whatever else you have to do, that doesn't count. Get what I'm saying? You've got to *bill* eight and a half hours a day, and if you want to do that, you have to be *in* the office eleven, twelve hours at least.

You want some kind of personal life? Spend time with your daughter? No way you can do that."

Darryl tried to lighten things up. "All right, I feel you. That wasn't the life for you. You better off this way." Smiling now "Plus which, now you get to run with the bad boys. The big time drug busters."

She smiled back, "Bad boys, yeah."

A text alert went off on Darryl's phone, he looked at it for a minute, scrolled through some photos, then broke into a grin. "Check it out. Photos just provided by Mr. Edward F. Fuentes, former member of the Oakland city police department, a confidential informant known to the undersigned to be reliable. We can print these up, use them as an exhibit to my affidavit."

Michelle took some time, looking at the pictures carefully. "And what does Mr. Fuentes say about the physical evidence. Is he able to bring some of that out, or not?"

Darryl looked at her.

She gave him a slow smile, "You know, just asking ..."

Darryl was thinking, hmm, maybe he could get to like the woman after all.

* * *

Sitting at the kitchen table in her house at the coast, Shanna took a hit off the jay and passed it back to Eddie. "How much do they want for evidence?"

Eddie took a hit, talking with a squeaky voice. "You tell me, how much do they need? You're the lawyer."

Shanna glanced at the forty gallon black plastic trash bag on the table. "Not one whole helluva lot Eddie!"

They looked at each other, and burst out laughing.

The way it started out, Eddie didn't think he'd be able to get any weed at all. In fact, he thought, he'd be lucky to get out alive. After all, he was going in blind. The one thing he was sure of, if an ex-Marine was providing security, the place would be rigged with SID's—seismic intrusion devices— like the kind they used to protect base perimeters in the military. He'd seen how they set them up in Iraq, an array of sensors rigged to trigger an alarm at a central location. There would be a display somewhere with a bunch LEDs on it, laid out to mirror the layout of the sensors. When the alarm sounded, they could tell where the intrusion was by seeing which LEDs were lit. Eddie figured the central location was probably the shack he saw earlier that night. But knowing the location didn't tell him where the sensors were. All it told him was the direction the gunfire would be coming from if he tripped one.

What he tried to do, lying in bed last night, was figure out how he'd set it up if he was designing the perimeter. And his idea, if he was doing it, would be load up the sensors where the intrusion would likely come from, down in the canyon, and not worry too much about putting sensors where the firepower was, up by the shack. So Eddie figured where he'd go first, was the shack. The only problem was, if he did trip a sensor, he'd be tripping it right next to the guys with the guns.

Explaining this to Shanna now, sitting in the kitchen, she said, "What is it with you boys and your guns?"

Eddie ignored the remark, and went on, telling her how, as he got down toward the shack, he heard mariachi music in the distance. He assumed it was coming from a radio, but couldn't tell where the radio was. Moving closer, he saw green tarpaulins stretched between tanoak trees, with string lines run underneath. The music, louder now, seemed to be coming from the trees. Closer still, he could see bud stalks tied on the strings, which meant they had already pulled the weed, or anyway, some of it.

"So you just walked in and walked out?"

"Well, not exactly," Eddie said.

He remembered growing up, how people got high picking weed, absorbing the THC through their skin, He hoped that was going on here; everybody got stoned, and fell asleep. Except, what was the deal with the music? As he moved closer to the tarps, he saw a light, and even closer, what looked like a card table set up with a lantern and a radio on it, but no people. It wasn't till he was nearly on top of the table that he almost tripped over the men—two of them, lying on the ground, fast asleep. So, he moved back, circled under the tarp, and started picking.

Telling it now, Eddie laughed. "But I tell you what, growing *this* shit, they're lucky I *didn't* trip any sensors. They probably would have wound up shooting each other."

* * *

Out at the garden, Ike Rampas was scratching his head, looking at the bud drying on the line. He thought the rows was full, but now it looked like a couple had some stalks missing. Hmmm. Probably the *braceros*.

He pulled a stalk down—looking at it close, under a 10X glass, focusing in on the white hairs, a few of them starting to turn golden. There was a lot of tricks to growing primo Hawaiian Sativa hybrid weed, but the one where the Doctor went his own way, was when he cropped it. Most growers would let the hairs turn first, 'cause it meant there'd be more resin in the pods. More resin meant more weight, sure, but that didn't tell you what was in it. You cropped later, you got more CBDs in there with the CBNs. You cropped earlier, you got less weight, but purer, THC—less body stone and a clearer head. That was the Doctor's difference.

When the message came in about the reservations at Alex's, Ike wasn't too sure the girls was ready to go, but rolling one out, and flaring her up now, he was reconsidering. Oh yeah, these girls was ready to party!

* * *

At the wheel of the Yukon, headed over to Iverson's, Lon said, "Look, I told you, Lana, I can't go in there with you. I got somewheres else I need to be."

She said, "Come on now, baby. It's not gonna take more than a few minutes."

A few minutes? In a car dealer? Lon shook his head. "Unh-uh. No way I should even be here at all. This time of year, after the product's been, you know, consolidated, it's cops and robbers, honey, twenty-four seven."

"But ... suppose they ask ... questions."

"Who? The dealer? What's he gonna ask?"

"You know, about the money What am I supposed to say?"

"I don't know, say it was tips. Look, they're not gonna ask no questions, Lana. Trust me on that. Lots of people use cash around in here. Ain't no law against it. They don't report it to the feds unless it's over ten grand, and we're not talking that much money."

Lana didn't say anything, but she was wishing they *were* talking about that kind of money. The payments would be a lot lower if she could put down another five grand, that was for sure. The way things stood, she wasn't going to have a lot of breathing room, even with the 0.9% APR financing.

Right now, though, she thought it was better to change the subject. She said, "You know, Betty Pogue, baby? Works at the Rat. She told me, your Mama was around there asking questions."

That got his attention. "What kind of questions?"

She shrugged. "About me."

He looked over. "When was that?"

"Yesterday afternoon."

Lon seemed to think a minute. "What did she want to know?"

Lana shrugged. "Nothing. Just wanted to see me, I guess. Maybe she wanted to patch things up. She knew we was living together. Even knew where it was, more or less."

"Your friend, she give her the address?"

"Betty wouldn't know, even if she asked her for it. But, honey, it's not that hard to find the place. Everybody know I live behind Marty Stroh, and Marty's got his wrecker out front half the time, says 'Stroh Brothers' right on it."

Lon didn't say anything much after that, eyes on the road, but you could tell his mind was on something. When they got down to Iverson's, after he parked in the lot, he opened up the glove box, took out an envelope, and handed it to her.

"Here's the cash. If there's any questions, you can get me on my cell the next half hour or so. There's no service where I'm going after that, and I'll be out of touch the next day or two."

She said, "Okay," and was getting ready to ask him if maybe he could put a little more in the envelope, but he was already pulling something out of his boot, and handing it to her.

"You know how to use one of these?" handing her the coolest little gun Lana had ever seen.

Lana took hold of it, like she seen on TV, aiming with two hands, trying to look professional. Lon pushed the barrel to one side, so it wasn't pointed at him, then took it back, held it up so she could see what he was doing.

"This here's a Beretta Nano," he said. "Made for concealed carry. Nine millimeter cartridge; six shot magazine." He demonstrated, hitting a button so the magazine dropped out of the handle, then snapping it back in again. Then, he pulled the slide back to chamber a round, and let it snap forward with a click. "The gun's loaded right now, ready to fire. This here's the safety, see? To fire the weapon, all you need to do is flip it off, like this, and pull the trigger."

She looked at him. "I know how to use a gun, honey. My Mama taught me that much. What I don't see is why I need it. I'm gonna *finance* the car, not *steal* it."

Lon said, "It ain't about the car, honey. It's about Mama. You met her once, but you don't really know her. Okay, so let's say, you see her around? If she's got something, maybe under a coat, looks like it might be a shotgun? I wouldn't get in any polite conversations with her, okay? Just take out that little gun, pull the trigger, and keep on pulling till you're out of ammunition."

* * *

Rasta John's was a little hole in the wall, shoe-horned in between Arsham's Custom Upholstery and Keondra's Beauty Kingdom down there on Fourteenth Street, San Leandro. Hard to miss it, though, painted red, yellow and green, kind of a rainbow effect, the sign out front decorated with big green marijuana leaves on it.

Darryl pulled up in front with Michelle in the DEA car, a cream Crown Vic with cop lights in the back window. Michelle shook her head. "Darryl, are you crazy?" She pointed down the block. "Pull down there. You park this thing here, you'll put the place out of business."

After the warrant got issued, Darryl asked Michelle where she liked to go for dinner—not asking *if* she wanted to go, you know, just *where* she liked to go, keeping it indefinite, but positive. She thought a minute, and told him she knew a little Jamaican place she thought could be interesting.

Darryl said, "Interesting good, or interesting how exactly?"

Michelle said, "Interesting as in, how you react to it."

They went around a little bit then, Michelle finally telling him, yeah, interesting meant interesting enough to go out with him, but she was a mom, and that meant she'd need to get home early, and arrange a sitter. Darryl said, sure, no problem, then, remembering, asked her if she'd mind stopping off in Oakland cause he had a package he needed to drop off at the DEA on Clay Street.

Michelle said, "That wouldn't happen to be the evidence that came in, would it?"

Rasta John's was smoky inside, candles on the tables, the place fixed up to look like a shack, bamboo on the ceiling, walls painted with banana leaves and various kinds of flowers. Bob Marley floating in from speakers somewhere or other.

> *Don't you look at me so smug*
> *And say I'm going bad*
> *Who are you to judge me*
> *And the life that I live*

I know that I'm not perfect
And that I don't claim to be
So before you point your fingers
Be sure that your hands are clean

A brother ambled over, grooving to the music, hair in dreads, tie died T-shirt over drawstring pants. He looked at Michelle. "Yow, me sistah, long time nuh see."

"What's happening, Johnny?'

"Gawn bout me business, ya know."

She smiled. "Monkey business."

"Ya know, ya know." The guy motioned to Darryl. "Speakin' a de monkey, wha dat in de stripe suit, der?"

Michelle said to Darryl, "He's just kidding, right John?"

The guy gave Darryl a loopy smile. "Dege dege, mon. Jus' kiddin'." Then, said to Michelle, "Yuh wunna eat something, dawtah? Gut a table far yuh. Bes' in di house tonight."

He led them to a table in back, left a couple of menus. Darryl picked one up, found himself looking at stew chicken, banana fritters, pigeon peas—he never heard of any of it.

Darryl looked up. "I'm not stupid, you understand. I *see* where you going with this."

She said, "Mmm hmm."

"Little experimentation, analyze how I do in regard to the unfamiliar. See if I got to control the situation, if I can go with the flow of things or not."

She said, "Extremely perceptive, Darryl. Here's the thing. You gonna let me order for you? Yes or no?"

She ordered something they called jerk chicken, kind of a deep fry, with some peppers and onions on top of it. Fried bananas, they called plantains, and pigeon peas, kind of a bean he never had before, but good.

She said, "The food's natural. Rastas don't believe in chemicals, nothing in cans. Don't believe in alcohol or soft drinks, either."

"Just the *ganja*, huh?"

"Well, that goes back to the Bible. 'Thou shalt eat the herb of the field.'"

"Herb of the field, huh?" Darryl took a minute with it. "That part of the experiment? Get me down with the 'herb of the field', see how I do with it?"

Michelle said, "Here it is, Darryl. You're ambitious. Want to make it in the big wide wonderful world. I understand that. But that's a white world, Darryl, see what I'm saying? I was married to a white boy once, and I'm not going that way again. I'm a black woman, and what I'd like to know, is there a real live black man down there inside of you?"

As it turned out, Darryl never did stop off at Clay Street on the way to Rasta John's, the 980 jammed coming in off the bridge. Now, after dinner, back in the Crown Vic, Darryl reached over, took a manila envelope out of the glove box, and handed it to Michelle.

"Go ahead," he said, "Open it."

When she had it open, she looked at him. "I'm not stupid, Darryl. I *see* where you going with this."

"Is that right?"

She said, "Mmm hmm. Get me into a law enforcement environment, see how I deal with it." He looked at her. She pointed. "That's backup for the warrant, am I right? On its way to the evidence locker?"

Darryl shrugged "Mmm, yeah. But what I was thinking, an informant give me a package, has some dried up herb in it, how would I know for sure it's marijuana? You know, far as probable cause is concerned."

"Have to take it to the lab."

Darryl shook his head. "No time for that. Raid going down first light tomorrow. Emergency situation I'm thinking, best we can do is firsthand experience."

Michelle looked inside the envelope, and pulled out two perfectly rolled jays. She said, "Well, I don't know who this confidential informant of yours is, but it looks like he thought about that ahead of time."

Darryl was nodding, some more of Marley's words going through his head right now.

The road of life is rocky
And you may stumble too
So while you talk about me
Someone else is judging you

CHAPTER 30

BEFORE SUN-UP

Shanna was riding that big roan stallion bareback, holding on for dear life, hands wrapped in his mane, feeling powerful muscles working against her naked body, her loins, her thighs, the insides of her knees. Feeling him rise and fall beneath her, the rolling asymmetry of his gait. She was racing down a narrow wooded trail, wind in her hair, the world rushing past at a breakneck pace. She was jumping streams now, brushing the low-hanging branches of trees. She had no idea where she was going, the stallion racing on its own, wild, out of control. No way to stop and no way to let go—

"Shanna?"

"Hmmm?" She opened her eyes; it was still dark. "Whoa .... Jesus. What time is it?"

She heard Eddie's voice above her. "Four-thirty. I'm headed out. They'll pick you up in an hour. Here, take this." He handed her a snub nose revolver. "Be careful, it's loaded."

Shanna was suddenly awake, feeling the cold, hard weight of the gun. "Tell me why I need this."

"You don't. It's just—"

She said, "A guy thing?"

He leaned over and kissed her. "I gotta go."

Shanna lay there, watching him head to the door, then stopped him. "Yo, Fast Eddie—" He turned. "Your buddy, Russell, told me back when you hustled pool, he never saw you lose."

"Is that what he told you?"

"That's what he told me."

Eddie said, "How we'd work it back then, was like the Texas road gamblers—Johnny Moss, Sailor Roberts, Amarillo Slim. They were our heroes. And see, with those guys?" He shook his head. "The problem wasn't winning the money. It was doing it without getting fucking shot."

Eddie took the Cube south from Shanna's, toward the cabin. What the hell, it was insured. Not only that, he charged it on his fucking Amex, so the collision damage waiver was included at no additional cost.

When he hit the freeway—no traffic at this hour, the sky pitch black, the moon already down—he called Darryl on his cell.

"Yo, this Darryl."

"It's Fuentes."

"Where you at?"

"On the freeway maybe a half hour out. I picked up a flare gun at Wal-Mart, in case I see you guys flying around in circles." Then, "You get the package?"

"The eagle has landed."

"You open it?"

"Mmm hmm."

"What did you think?"

"As a law enforcement officer with sixteen weeks specialized training in narcotics trafficking at Quantico, Virginia, I'd say it was some goddamn exceptional shit."

The idea was, Eddie would go in and hide out with the cell phone on, so they could triangulate the location or, if they couldn't pick up the signal, use the flares, give them the location that way. None of that was the tricky part—not the getting in, the hiding out, not even firing the flares, if he had to. The tricky part was not getting shot. Eddie had seen it with drug busts in Oakland. Running a risk didn't necessarily mean primary through the door. It meant being anywhere in range when the adrenaline kicked in. All bets were off then. In a situation where people started shooting, it was even odds—getting shot by a perp, or getting shot by a cop.

It was still dark when he got to the top of the grade, passing the dead chaparral they used to hide the entrance to the garden. He didn't like leaving the car, but this time didn't have a choice. He drove a couple hundred yards east along the ridge, found a place that could pass for a turnout, and parked the Cube along the road.

It was a quarter mile from the road down to the shack. It sat on what must have been an old landing bulldozed out of the woods, a place to buck and truck the redwood they felled off the hillside and hauled up the slope. Now, the woods had grown back to tan oak and madrone—and, of course, marijuana. The scene hadn't changed much from the night before, except he didn't hear music. The shack was quiet and dark, bud stalks strung up to dry under the tarpaulins. Only now, there was a new addition: a large van pulled up next to the shack.

Eddie stopped, stood still for a minute, letting the sounds come to him, separate themselves out of the silence. Except for the coyotes and the occasional hoot of an owl, there was nothing. No movement, no sound. Now, checking his cell phone, he saw there was no signal either. The raid wasn't set to go off till sunrise, so Eddie decided to hike back up to the road where he could text Darryl, let him know the weed was still here, but triangulation probably wasn't going to work, and he'd need to look for a flare.

He was on his way back down when he heard a sound—the low rumble of a truck exhaust in the distance. The sound got loud, incredibly loud, against the background of silence, like a herd of animals crashing through the brush. Eddie fell back from the road, drifting into the woods, until finally, headlights appeared, then a black SUV, raising a cloud of dust as it bounced past, and Eddie caught a glimpse of a shaved blonde head behind the wheel. That would be Odom.

*   *   *

Ike was fast asleep inside the cabin when he felt something poking him in the gut. "Wha—" Ike sat up, "What the *fuck?*" He'd have shit his pants—if he was wearing any. There was Odom with a fucking shotgun.

"Whattya think you're doing?"

"Any SIDs fire off up here? You see anything?"

"I's asleep goddamn it, can't you see that? How's I gonna see some-thing?" Ike sat up now, trying to clear his head out. This time of year, the resin under your nails, in your nose, buzzing around your brain, you never did come down off it. "Fuck you doing, poking me with a shotgun? I thought you's supposed to be out there guarding the perimeter."

Odom didn't exactly answer the question. "There's a car out there, past the turn-off, little shit cruiser, looks new, kind of a blue color. You know who belongs to it?"

"How the hell would I know? It ain't mine and it sure as hell don't be-long to the sombreros. Kids probably."

Odom took a minute. "Next year, I'm setting that perimeter back up, around the cabin."

"And have you blow my balls off every time I take a piss? The hell you say!"

Odom seemed to think about that. Finally, he said, "You hear a sensor fire, call me on the radio. I'm going out and have another look."

It was still dark outside, coyotes yipping like they did just before dawn, but otherwise quiet. Rampas was right about the shit cruiser. It wasn't Mexicans. No serious bud hound was gonna drive around in a thing like that. And it sure as hell wasn't connected to law enforcement. It was kids—screwing in the woods, maybe ripping off some weed, maybe a little bit of both. Best thing, teach them a lesson they wouldn't forget. Something they'd tell their friends about. So what he did, he drove back out to where the thing was parked, got his bull bar up against the rear bumper, gave the shit cruiser a nudge, and watched the fucker bounce down the hill and disappear out of sight.

KEEE-RRASSH!

*   *   *

Not yet dawn, thirty agents of the Drug Enforcement Administration, in logo raid jackets and Kevlar vests were hanging around the Redwood

County Municipal Airport, drinking bad coffee out of Styrofoam cups. They had the little DEA copters lined up, ready to go, but the big birds out of Columbia Aviation were late, supposed to be there fifteen minutes ago.

Vanowen looked at his watch. "These clowns know what time we're set to go?"

Darryl said, "Chill, man. I told you, they'll show." Then, watching Vanowen shake a cigarette out of a pack, said, "Those things gonna kill you. You know that."

"Life is gonna kill me," Vanowen said, "Ain't you heard? Nobody gets out alive." He lit the cigarette, took a drag, and blew out a stream of smoke. "This guy, Fuentes. You know they kicked him off the force down in Oakland."

Darryl said, "Mmm, heard about that. Bounced his ass, excessive use a' force. Man working vice same time, same as yourself, I understand it."

"We didn't work together," Vanowen said.

"You left pretty much the same time, though."

"Here's the difference. I walked out with a pension and he didn't."

Darryl smiled now, the beat of rotors coming up as two big Sikorsky's came into view.

"Yeah, see but what I heard, the brass let you and the lieutenant finish out your twenty, 'cause it was easier than busting your ass for that pussy tax y'all took off the pimps on the West Side. So what I'm wondering now is just how much cash the Doctor paid, when you told him we flipped over the Salvadoran."

*　*　*

A little before seven o'clock, three unmarked Ford sedans pulled to a stop at the turnoff to the Doctor's house at the Costa Perdida. Shanna sat with Russell, keeping her company in the back seat of the lead car, with two DEA agents in front. There were two cars behind them with four agents each. Comic overkill, in Shanna's opinion, but then, she knew a few things the DEA didn't.

Up front, the lead agent, a serious, buffed out redhead by the name of Miller, turned around in his seat and said, "How far from here?"

Shanna said, "I'm not good with distances," and looked at Russell.

He said, "Quarter mile, maybe less. I think he's got motion sensors in the road, I don't know where, you could have tripped one already. And there's cameras, like I told you. I've seen the video."

"Yeah, you told me that already." Miller didn't look pleased. He got out of the car, went to talk to the other agents.

When he was gone, Shanna tapped a manila folder Russell had on his lap. "You going to tell me what's in the folder?"

Russell opened it up, and handed her a four-color flyer that said,

Development Opportunity—160 Acres
$48,000,000

Below that, there was a picture of some vacant land that didn't look like much.

She said, "Where is it?"

He pointed to a little map in the bottom right hand corner. "You know the exit off the 101 where you head out to the Watershed? There's a 7-Eleven?"

"Not exactly."

"It doesn't matter."

Tapping the folder, she said, "What do you want me to do with this?"

Russell said, "Pass it along to your friends at the U.S. Attorney's office and tell them it's our price for cooperating in a joint law enforcement operation."

*   *   *

Dick Duncan looked out the window of the no-frills Bell 206, heading south toward the Watershed. The sun wasn't quite over the horizon, just beginning to hit the mountaintops, the valleys still plunged in darkness. Fifteen minutes ago, still dark outside, Harry's new Citation had touched down at Redwood County Municipal, depositing Harry and Trace Crawford on the tarmac, the two billionaires having left Tampa-St. Pete at something like four o'clock in the morning East Coast time to watch a goddamn logging operation. Dick was sure of one thing. If he could write a check for ten percent of what either one of these bozos could, he wouldn't be within a thousand miles of here.

But here they were, Saul, the little swindler, worth in the mid ten figures, yelling in Trace Crawford's oversized ear, struggling to be heard over the roar of the uninsulated engines, no doubt telling Crawford how they could make even more money by breaking some law or other. Crawford, the famous aviation pioneer, a big John Wayne type, worth nearly as much as Saul, looking out the window, nodding distractedly, not apparently all that interested. Dick edged closer now, trying to pick up the conversation. The truth was, he wouldn't be all that interested either, except for the little mini-digital recorder he was carrying pursuant to a Deferred Prosecution Agreement he had entered into with the U.S. Attorney for the Northern District of California. The FBI agent who fixed him up with the wire, told him, as a general rule, he should assume the recorder would be able to pick up about as much as he could, though they could clean up the tape to some extent, to take out extraneous background noise.

It was weird, the way it worked out with the Feds. When Dick's lawyer, Harley Rosenfeld, set up a meeting with the U.S. Attorney in San Francisco, Harley and Dick both thought the Feds would want to hear about the dope operation, how it worked, how long it had been going on, how much Dick got paid, and so on. As it turned out, they didn't seem to give a shit. Weren't they after the Doctor? Yeah, sure, but the way they saw it, Dick didn't have anything to give them on that. He never had direct contact with the Doctor; there was always someone in between. What they *were* interested in, though, was Harriman Saul. Apparently, they had been for years. Now, with the Southeast Air transaction, they were building a case.

Harley finally worked out a deferred prosecution deal where Dick agreed to cooperate in what they called an "ongoing investigation of illegal activity involving West Coast Lumber, its officers, directors and shareholders"—which mainly meant Harry—so Dick was in the clear. What was keeping him awake nights, though, was a certain clause in the agreement. The clause said the government could revoke Dick's immunity if he "committed or attempted to commit any acts punishable as felonies under federal, state or local law, in addition to those set forth in this Agreement." Dick was wondering, did "in addition to" mean "subsequent to" or did it include stuff he'd already done, but nobody had found out about yet? Because that could be a long list. Take money from the Mexicans, for example, or double billing expenses, or taking kickbacks from the truckers. He wasn't sure if those would be "punishable as felonies" though. It was worth a call to his lawyer.

Then, there was the clause about the immunity being revoked if he gave "materially false, misleading, or incomplete information." As the helicopter headed south to view what the titans of industry sitting across from him thought was going to be a logging operation, Dick was wondering, how incomplete were they talking about?

*   *   *

Sitting outside the shack, Ike blazed up, taking a little morning moment while he watched the boys stumble around, trying to get the van loaded. Hard not to laugh, kind of like a comedy movie, the *braceros* grinning at each other like gorillas. Who gave a shit, you know? What could be better than the fucking harvest?

Ike was feeling it now, man, that shifty rush. Sneaky but freaky, like the Doctor's weed always was. And light, man, you swear to God there's nothing going on, and the next thing you knew, boom! You was somewheres else altogether. Doctor knew his herb, seed to weed. But there was another part to it he didn't get, and nobody could if they wasn't out there dancing with the damsels day to day. Yeah, there was that personal part, that extrasensory thing. No science to that. You had to feel it.

It was an art, growing the *sinsemilla*, an art. And Ike was the fucking *artiste*, man. The Dali of dope. The Monet of maryjane. The Rembrandt of reefer.

*   *   *

Just before sunrise, a dozen helicopters headed south toward the Watershed Grove—eight from the DEA, two from the FBI, and two Sikorsky sky cranes commandeered from Columbia Aviation. The Sky Cranes were Darryl's idea, the problem being, they needed boots on the ground, and most of the DEA birds were the MDs, smaller units used for observation.

The Sky Crane boys thought they were going to haul logs today, but when they got to the airport, Darryl had a surprise for them. Jogging out through the downwash, a square jawed kid, built like an ice hockey player, met him at the door. "What's going on, man?"

Darryl said, "We shooting a reality TV show. Real Dope Growers of Redwood County. This is your chance to be a star."

CHAPTER 31

THE RAID

Sun-up now, sitting next to Trace Crawford in the cabin of the Bell 206, Harriman Saul said, "Here's what I'm thinking. If you break the interior southeast out as a separate region, and look at the numbers, you're running load factors in the fifty-five to sixty range. In a good month, sixty three or four. What would you think of adding another hub, say in Nashville or Memphis?"

Crawford said "Hat's off to your pilot, Harry. He's doing a great job with this little bird in the crosswinds."

Harry said, "Right."

Crawford said, "Hard as hell flying these goddamn things even in good conditions. I know; I've tried. Like fucking a woman on a balance beam, if you get my meaning." Nudging him with an elbow.

Harry pursed his lips, not sure if he understood or not.

Crawford motioned with big, beefy hands. "An airplane *wants* to fly, see? Air flows under the wings, holds her aloft. A helicopter does *not* want to fly. You can't *glide* in a goddamn helicopter. You're under power or you're going down. Can't wait to see how they haul logs with the goddamn things." Crawford thought a second. "Now on these hubs, I'll tell you my opinion."

"That's—"

"You financial guys are idiots. Sure, I saw what you did with the options, ride the stock down, ride it up on inside information. You make money playing the market. Your problem is, you don't know about anything about what you're buying and selling. Like with the hubs, you all do the same damn thing. You build up the load factor, and think you'll make more money. But you don't look at the fuel you waste or the frequent flyer costs, get me?"

Harry looked at him. "I'm not—"

"Of course you don't. What I'm talking about is all these flights in and out of the hubs, they double your fuel consumption and the miles in your FFP. Then, when you finally realize what it's costing you, what do you do?" He looked at Harry. "You change the program rules to wipe out the frequent flyer miles. Right?"

Harry managed a nod.

"Then, what happens? I mean, in addition to the class action lawsuits." Crawford looked at Harry like he was expecting an answer, but Harry couldn't think of one. "It destroys your goddamn brand! That's what." Crawford said.

Harry managed another nod.

"You guys don't understand this, but ask yourself, who *made* your goddamn brand to begin with? The frequent flyers! They're your core customers. Piss them off, they'll go somewhere else if they have the option. I tell you, you bean counters don't know the first goddamn thing about running an airline." He looked at Harry now. "Well, you'll buy the company, do whatever the hell you want with it. I got mine; I guess I ought to shut up about it."

He looked out the window. "But I'll tell you, if I was a young man, starting out, what I'd do? Buy me a bunch of hub busters, charge a premium for direct flights, and peel off your customers." Glancing over now, Crawford said, "I'll tell you something else, my friend. You may be able to make *money* doing what everybody else does, but you don't make *history* that way, if it means anything to you." He paused for a second, then pointed out the window. "Now what the hell do you suppose they're up to?"

"Hmmm." Harry looked out the window, then jumped back as a sort of missile flew past.

Crawford laughed, "It ain't live fire, Harry. It's a flare. ... Probably marking a location." He pointed. "Sure, see, there's your S-61s. Isn't that the outfit you just bought? Columbia Aviation?"

Harry looked out the window, puzzled, then turned to Duncan, pointed toward the cockpit. "The Grove's *that* way, isn't it?" Then, pointing to the right. "Why are they going *that* way?" And saw the rest of them—a swarm of smaller helicopters, it seemed like a dozen of them, headed in the same direction. "What's going on out there? Dick?"

Duncan looked over, grinning like there was some kind of inside joke, only Harry wasn't in on it. He said, "Little detour, Harry."

*   *   *

Murrelet Myers was sitting in her redwood tree when she heard the helicopters in the distance, but not paying any attention to that, as she was talking on her cell to Harriet Nathan about her book proposal.

"I'm sorry?" she said, "But it *hasn't* been done."

"*Up a Tree*? Hasn't been done? What about the girl, what's her name, was in the tree a few years ago?"

"It's not the same thing. This is *Up a Tree: A Woman's Journey of Self-Discovery*. It's a different genre. "

"*Mmm* hmm."

"Ecology doesn't sell. Okay, I get that. But this isn't ecology. It has a different focus."

"*Mmm* hmm." The reception up in the tree was good enough that Murrelet could hear the boredom in the woman's voice. "Isn't it interesting, I can't remember her name. . ."

The beat of helicopter rotors was getting louder now. THWAP! THWAP! THWAP!

POOM! A flare arched into the sky. Then, POOM! Another flare. Murrelet reached for her binoculars.

Harriet was saying, "The girl in the tree, she was up there over a year as I remember."

"Seven hundred thirty eight days."

"Really, seven hundred thirty eight. That *is* an accomplishment. But I still can't seem to remember—"

"Her name? Butterfly Hill."

"You're missing the point, darling. What's interesting isn't her name, what's interesting is that I can't *remember* it."

Finally, Murrelet lost it. "You can't *remember* it because she wasn't a *lesbian*, you fucking bimbo. How many times do I have to tell you? This isn't ecology. It's a different genre."

She punched "end" in disgust, and jammed the phone into her overall pocket. Selling a book wasn't as easy as Murrelet had thought. A sample chapter and an outline didn't get the job done, even if you did have a website with a hundred thousand hits a day. Self-publishing was definitely the way to go. They only problem with that was, you didn't see a nickel till you actually had a manuscript.

POOM! Another flare. She picked up the binoculars now and, sure enough, there they were. Big red and white helicopters, some smaller ones buzzing around. And close, too. Pretty soon, the whole thing was going to be over, and what did she have to show for it? No talk shows, no endorsements, no book deals, no nothing.

It could be time to rethink her whole life trajectory.

POOM!

* * *

Ike heard it, sitting on a log watching them load the van, the sound close, but not like a gun, sort of muffled, like when they shot off fireworks at some distance. POOM! … . Then a few minutes later … POOM! Ike looked up, half expecting to see lights in the sky, but he couldn't see nothing through the tanoak canopy.

Then, the next thing, he heard rotors whipping up over the rise. THWAP! THWAP! THWAP! Not the little Robinsons or Bell Jets you heard out here from time to time. These were big, military motherfuckers. Like the Hueys in Nam, or maybe bigger. But he still couldn't see nothing.

Then, Odom was there with an HK. "You see that?"

"See what?"

"Flares, asshole."

The Mexicans was all standing around by then, looking at the two of them, trying to figure out what was going on. Odom fired a burst into the ground. "Load the truck!" He was yelling at 'em, "Load the truck, god-damn it!" He fired another burst, but the Mexicans just stood there, look-ing at him, like he was crazy.

"I'll be back," he said, sounding like Arnold Schwarzenegger, crash-ing off into the brush. Man, the guy must have lost it, giving orders to Mexicans in English like they was supposed to understand what he was talking about.

Ike motioned. *"Darse prisa! Darse prisa!"* But they still didn't move, just stood there, looking at him, half stubborn, he was guessing, and half stoned. Then suddenly, Carlos, the *jefe*, jumped down off the truck, and lit out into the bushes, just like that. Didn't say a word. The other ones looked at Ike for half a second or so, probably waiting to see if he was gonna shoot they guy or not, and when he didn't, shit, those motherfuck-ers took off too, scattered like the cockroaches in grandma's kitchen.

Now, Ike stood there a few seconds, considering the situation. Flares, helicopters, automatic weapons—it didn't feel like old Norville Petty and his Fairy Pranksters. And come to think of it, he was dead anyway. Now, this was the Feds, dude. The fucking Feds. Shit, with those mandatory minimums. Fuck *this* shit! Time to get outta here! Stuff some bud in your pockets, and take the *fuck* off!

* * *

Out at the Costa Perdida, the three unmarked DEA cars rolled into the parking area under the cypress trees at the Doctor's house, the lead car near the elevator door and the other two cars behind. The lead agent, Miller, turned around, looking at Russell and Shanna in the back seat. "You two wait here."

Russell pointed behind them, through the back window. "If it's okay with you, dude, how about we wait over there in the rocks. That way, we won't get in the way of the action."

Miller looked to where Russell was pointing, then shrugged. "Whatever." He motioned to the agent beside him. "You go with them."

From a safe distance now, Russell watched as Miller motioned three agents past the elevator door toward the bluff edge and three others to the door. Two stood back, giving cover to the third guy, who rang the bell. Once. Twice. Nothing happened.

Miller motioned. An agent with some kind of a special breaching gun moved up to blow the door. But before he could fire a shot, a low rumbling sound came from deep underground, like an earthquake, followed by a muffled explosion. Poom! Then another one. Poom!

Miller yelled, "Get back!"

The agents scrambled behind the cars, as the explosions went on. Poom! Pa-Poom! Poom-Poom! Pa- Pa-Poom! interspersed with a distant sound like shattering glass.

A few seconds of silence. Then, a bigger explosion. . Pa-Poooom!

And slowly, Err-Eeek! With a massive groaning sound, the whole damn thing collapsed, and the entire area—bluff top, cypress trees and DEA cars, tumbled right down to the beach.

* * *

When, Lon got back down to the landing, what he saw was the van, parked next to the bud, half loaded, cargo door open, and not a soul in sight. And through the trees, you could see two big Sikorskys hovering fifty feet above the top of the rise, DEA at the doors, set to rappel down on climbing ropes. Lon could get out of here no problem, pack out on a trail he knew through the canyon. And he wasn't worried about the van; that was rented on a phony ID. The problem was the fucking Yukon. They got hold of that, they could put him at the scene. Anyway, it never felt right running.

Now, they was coming down the ropes. What Lon needed was a diversion, something to give him time while he got out of here. He raised the HK, aimed, and fired off a short burst, then another. Ta-Tat! Ta-Ta-Tat! Two agents fell off the rope. He lined up another shot. TA-TA-TAT-TA! Another agent went down, falling into the weeds.

Piece of cake plinking them off their ropes. Like target practice, but with the assholes wearing vests, best you could hope, they'd break something coming down. And there were dozens more coming after. Take out the pilot would be better. Bring the bird down, or at least make 'em pull back, give him time to get the Yukon out of here. Lon set up, braced against the van and took his time, lining up the shot, pulling the front window into the ghost ring. Then, he squeezed off a burst. TA-TA-TAT-TA!

Paint flew off the nose, and the 'copter pulled up, gave the DEA boys on those ropes quite a ride! But then—

TA-A-TAT-A-TA-A-TAT! TA-A-TAT-A-TA-A-TAT!

A fucking blizzard of incoming shredded the canopy, bud flying everywhere, rounds thudding into the van, the jerk-offs firing blind, not knowing what they was shooting at. But shit, they could get lucky. Lon double-timed to the bunkhouse, set up against the wall, and pulled the front window of the second 'copter into the ghost ring, his finger tightening on the trigger, when—

CHICK-CHICK! A pump action shotgun chambered a round somewhere behind him. A voice said, "Drop it."

Lon stood still.

The voice said, "Three seconds. One."

Best Lon could figure, the man was eight feet behind him and slightly to the right. Dive and roll could work, come up with the knife. But there was something in the voice.

"Two."

Against the scattergun, he didn't like the odds. He raised the HK above his head, tossed her in the weeds.

"Now the Glock. With your left hand. Two fingers. Take it out." He did. "Throw it down." He did that, too. "Hands on your head."

Lon moved his hands up slowly, wishing he still had that Nano, but feeling the weight of the Scarab in his sleeve pocket, knowing he still had a play. Not yet, though. He needed to see the man before he made his move.

"Now turn around."

As he turned, Lon's eyes found the Mossberg first, the gun held waist high, aimed just above his midsection. Then, his gaze came up to the man. Lon remembered him from that one time at the Doctor's, but never really looked at him good, till now. Six feet, decent build, dark skin, un-shaved, and blue eyes that watched him, but didn't seem to move. No hesitation in the eyes. The man behind those eyes would pull the trigger. Three seconds, give him three seconds and he could take this man. Dive and roll into a leg sweep, drop the Scarab out of his sleeve and cut the man's throat. Three seconds. But with a shell chambered in that scatter-gun, three seconds was two seconds too long.

* * *

Eddie stood six feet off now, holding Odom with the Mossberg. He was a big man, six-three, two thirty, solid, and looked fast. His complexion was fair, head shaved clean, his face showing reddish blonde stubble. Eddie had seen the neck tattoo, coming up behind him: A skull with wings, and under it, the words, Swift, Silent Deadly. That about covered it.

Odom seemed to be measuring him now, with dead blue eyes. "You ... serve in the military?"

Eddie watched him, not saying anything.

"Where at?"

"Anbar, mostly."

"Took out some Hajji's, huh? How many, you guess?"

"I forget."

Odom seemed to smile. "You gonna pull that trigger, you might as well get her done."

Eddie said, "Why? You in a hurry to die?" A second passed, the two of them looking at each other." He said, "Tell me about my father. What happened? The night he died."

Odom seemed to think about it. "He was supposed to meet the lawyer. The woman. You know her. Doctor didn't want it to happen, so he told
me to go up there."

"What did he tell you to do?"

"He said, get him high, get him drunk, whatever it took."

"Then what?"

He shrugged. "It was a waste of time. I got up there, he was high
enough."

"But you had your orders. So what did you do, pour a bottle of whiskey down his throat just to make sure?"

Odom shook his head. "Didn't have to. He did that all by himself." He
took some time now, bringing back the memory. "I run into him outside
the Chain Saw. You know, up at Wild River. He was weaving down the
street, headed out of town, toward that old railroad bridge they got up
there, has the steel truss on top of it. I went with him."

"You gave him a bottle."

"I ain't gonna deny it. Doctor wanted to know, was he gonna sell his
land to the lawyer, so I asked him."

"What did he say?"

Odom shook his head. "No offense, but the man was out of his mind.
First, he said he wasn't gonna sell the land 'cause he gave it away already.
Then, I asked him who'd he give it to, he said, he never owned it. Didn't
make any damn sense."

"Then what?"

"Then nothing. I got tired, fucking around with him, so I left him there
sitting on the bridge with the bottle, headed back to town." He seemed
to be remembering it. " I seen what happened, though."

Eddie waited, letting Odom take his time with it.

"I was maybe fifteen, twenty yards down the road, I heard sounds, like
whooping and hollering. There was a moon that night, but I couldn't see
nothing at first 'cause of the trees, so I took a few steps back out toward
the bridge. And I'll be goddamned if the crazy som'bitch wasn't up on the
top of it—the steel part—way up in the air, whirling around, high stepping,

clapping his hands. Doctor wouldn't believe me when I told it to him, but I got no reason to lie about it."

Eddie tried to visualize it, get the picture in his mind, Matty up there twirling around with his long hair flying, and he could just about see it. He said, "So, you're saying what? He fell?"

Odom hesitated, finally shrugged. "I wouldn't say he fell, no, or jumped, neither. It was more like he just … stopped dancing, then I didn't see him no more."

They stood a second, looking at each other, then—

TA-A-TAT-A-TA-A-TAT! Automatic weapons opened up from somewhere in the trees, plowing into the shack.

Then, PA- POOM! A propane tank must have blown, sending flaming debris flying. Eddie and Odom dove dove in opposite directions.

Coming up, Eddie looked around, caught a glimpse of Odom crashing into the brush. And he was right; that man was fast! A second later the automatic fire seemed to come from everywhere.

TA-A-TAT-A-TA-A-TAT!

Eddie rolled under the half-loaded van. He called out, "DEA! Hold your fire!"

They didn't. TA-A-TAT-A-TA-A-TAT! TA-A-TAT-A-TA-A-TAT!

Eddie hunkered under the van, trying not to get shot, as a dozen agents broke from the woods into the clearing. Somebody called to him from above the van. "Government agents. Throw out your weapon."

"Law enforcement." Eddie said. "I'm not armed."

"Out here! Right now! Hands first. Let me see your hands!"

Crawling out, military style, Eddie said, "Look at the jacket? I'm one of you, you dumb fuck."

"Right there! Stay on the ground! Don't move! Hands behind your head."

He could feel somebody fumbling around, trying to cuff him. "I told you, my name's Fuentes, Eddie Fuentes. I'm working with Darryl Waters. Go get him, you can ask him yourself."

Then, he heard a familiar voice. "What we got over here? Look like one of them bad ass perps must 'a stole a vest."

"He said he's with you."

"He did, huh."

Eddie said, "It's Fuentes, you asshole."

"Fuentes? Hmmm. Not sure I recognize the name. Go on, get him up. Nice and slow."

They did, and there was Darryl, laughing his fucking head off.

* * *

Russell was standing there, arms folded, thinking how beautiful it was today, this clear fall morning at the Costa Perdida. It flashed him back to the day they had their little acid test out here, everybody drinking the spiked Corona. Only today, the fog was nowhere in sight, sun shining down, the view clear to the horizon. "Beautiful, huh?"

Standing next to him, Shanna was nodding, looking out at the big, blue Pacific, where the Doctor's house used to be.

After a minute, Agent Miller, walked up to them, and said, "Looks like your friend had plenty of warning."

Russell looked at Shanna. "Really."

Miller took shook his head sadly. "Shaped charges placed at stress points, the use of accelerants—or I assume it was accelerants—somebody took his time. And probably knew engineering. The whole thing … it's just … gone. Forensics will have to go over it, but my bet is, the place is going to come up clean as a whistle."

* * *

Eleven a.m., Lana was sitting in the trailer up at Sanchez Landing, watching *The Price is Right* on TV, Amber showing off a Chevy Cruze while the announcer explained the rules of the Lucky Seven—how the contestant could drive home in the car if she guessed the price without giving back all the dollar bills—when the door banged open.

Without looking up from the TV, Lana said, "Lon, is that you? I didn't hear you drive up, honey."

Lon flopped down on the sofa, started taking his boot off without saying anything.

Lana said, "What happened to the Yukon?"

"Ditched it. ... Jesus Christ. You got any liquor around here? Rubbing alcohol?"

"Baby, you can't drink rubbing alcohol. Anyway, it's eleven o'clock in the morning."

"I ain't *gonna* drink it."

She looked over then, saw his sock was covered with blood.

Lana said, "Jesus, how did *that* happen?" and ran into the kitchen, got a dish towel. "Here ... try not to get it on the carpet. I just got it cleaned, okay, honey?"

Lon ripped off his sock. "Can you get some damn liquor? And something bigger for the blood—a sheet or something."

She didn't move. "I'm not going anywhere till you tell me what happened."

He looked at her. "I got *shot*, okay? Must have been a ricochet. Now for the love of Christ, would you do what I tell ya?"

She did. Got him some whiskey and an old bath towel. He got shot in the heel, as it turned out. The bullet came out clean, but did some damage, is what he told her. He washed it with the whiskey, then drank some of it, and Lana gave him some Advil she had in the cabinet.

When that was done, he told her people would be coming, and he was going to have to take off for a while. He said, "I'm sorry, honey, but I'm gonna need the keys to that Mustang."

She said, "Lonny, I told you, I can't go without transportation. If you take the Mustang, how am I gonna get to work? Or go shopping? It's the middle of nowhere up here, you know that baby."

Lonny pointed to a black plastic trash bag sitting by the door he must have dropped on his way in. "There's your wheels, right in there. You better get it somewhere out of sight though, before the cops show up."

Lana went over and looked inside. There had to be a couple dozen pounds of high grade bud inside there, and when she saw it, Lana couldn't help herself, she just burst out crying.

Lon said, "What're you crying about?"

She said, "I'm sorry, baby, it's just … you know, here you are, all shot up, on the run, got to ditch the Yukon …. And in the middle of all that, you were still worried about me, thinking of my best interest." She threw her arms around his neck and kissed him then. "Lonny, I really do love you, baby."

So, there they were, the two of them kissing in front of the screen door, and it was a rare and beautiful moment in a cruel and indifferent world, but then all of a sudden, Lon kind of stiffened up in her arms. She said, "What's the matter, baby."

And Lonny said, "Hello there, Mama."

CHICK-CHICK! That's what she heard, a shotgun pump, a round going into the chamber. And the next thing she knew Lon's big arm grabbed her, and she was flying across the room toward the kitchen, and right after that—

POOM! There was this huge explosion and, looking up from the kitchen floor, she saw Lonny fly back across the room, land on the sofa with blood all over, the screen door on top of him. Then, POOM! Another explosion. Lana couldn't remember much of what happened after that, just little pieces of things. Like she remembered she was on the linoleum floor, opening the kitchen drawer, seeing that cute little automatic Lon give her in there. And she remembered the gun in her hands, holding it out in front of her like they do on TV. She remembered a dark kind of a silhouette at the front door, the light pouring in behind, the silhouette turning this way and that, holding a long gun. And she remembered that little automatic jump in her hands, Lana pulling the trigger again and again, until she pulled the trigger and nothing happened 'cause the bullets run out.

CHAPTER 32

MEMORIAL DAY

Memorial Day weekend, two years after the bust, Eddie and Darryl were cruising up the 101 in Darryl's new black-on-black 5-Series Beemer, headed into Redwood County. It was a nice day, the sun shining, the fog bank somewhere offshore where you couldn't see it. But it was there, giving you hints—a little bite in the air, wispy clouds blowing in from the West through gaps in the hills.

Darryl drove, Eddie thumbing through the latest issue of *Time* magazine. There was a great shot on the cover, United States Attorney, Sarah Breckinridge, sitting on a pallet load of bank wrapped hundred dollar bills, looking tough, arms folded. The headline read:

TOP OF THE HEAP:
Inside the Largest Drug-Related Asset Seizure in U.S. History

Eddie turned to Darryl, holding up the magazine. "You *read* this thing?"

"Not yet," Darryl said. "Michelle says it's a puff piece. Sarah hired some P.R. dude's got an in with the editor. But what it's really about, Sarah's trying to impress her daddy, used to be a big time litigator. He's in assisted living now, but every time Sarah goes to see him, he throws it in her face how she went to school with Preet Bharara. Know who he is?"

"I do now." Eddie said. "It's how they spin the whole piece. How they went to school together and now they're battling it out for the hard ass federal prosecutor award. It says Sarah 'made it her mission to target corporate corruption on the West Coast.' Like it was her idea, she *went after* Harriman Saul, nobody else even involved with it."

Darryl frowned. "You saying I'm not in there at *all*?"

"Nobody is," Eddie told him.

Back around the time of the bust, there was a ton of media coverage—they had segments on *Dateline*, most of the cable shows. Darryl's appearances weren't exactly Johnnie Cochran caliber, but good enough, so he decided to skip the government job and open a law office in San Francisco. Eddie was back in the Bay Area at the time, trying to unravel the mess with Karen—open a new bank account, pick up the credit cards that never got forwarded. Man, what a mess. Figure out the car lease, what to do with the apartment and, of course, file for divorce.

The divorce was how Eddie and Darryl got together, Darryl hungry for business with his new office. He didn't have much experience, but Eddie figured, what the fuck? Eddie living on unemployment, waiting for his P.I. license to come through, how much experience did he need? There was the land, yeah, but Karen couldn't get her hands on that 'cause Eddie inherited it from his old man, so it wasn't community property.

Now, Darryl said, "How about Michelle, she in there?"

Eddie shook his head, paging through the magazine. "What we got here," he said, "is Sarah Breckinridge. Where she grew up, where she went to school, where she worked, how many kids she's got, and who she's married to."

"That's it?"

"They're big into irony. You know, now that Prop 64's coming up, and it looks like weed's gonna be legal."

"There is that," Darryl said. "Any more, they just not busting for weed."

Eddie flipped through the pages. "They got a box on the ten biggest drug busts of all time, if you're interested. They say we came in number five."

"Who's number one?"

"Juarez Cartel. Warehouse outside L.A., 1989. Ready for this? Thirteen tons of coke. Enough to cut five lines for everyone in America. Worth $21 billion."

"Coke's high value. Gonna beat your weed every time."

"In terms of drugs, yeah. What we got is the record for a 'drug-related asset seizure'. According to the Guinness Book of World Records, the largest one before us was $180 million, they took it off a Colombian in 1998. They're putting the value of the land they took from West Coast Lumber at $550 million."

"So it says we got the record," Darryl said. "But it don't say who the we is."

There wasn't much on the actual bust, altogether, a couple short paragraphs. Two raids, it said, less than a week apart, conducted by a joint federal-state task force, netting a quarter million marijuana plants with a street value of half a billion dollars. The first raid was small, part of the crop already harvested. The second raid was bigger, and resulted in the arrest of twenty-seven Mexican nationals, including two mid-level soldiers linked to the Sinaloa cartel, according to Justice Department sources.

The common denominator of the raids was that they occurred on land belonging to West Coast Lumber. According to U. S. Attorney Sarah Breckinridge, the drug operations were conducted with the knowledge and participation of company president, Richard R. Duncan, who agreed to cooperate with the investigation in return for a grant of immunity pursuant to a deferred prosecution agreement negotiated by none other than Sarah Breckinridge.

"I guess she don't need the DEA or the FBI," Darryl said, "She just do the whole thing by herself. What else it say?"

It said that, faced with the possibility of treble damages under the Racketeering Influence and Corrupt Organizations Act, better known as RICO, the Company agreed not to contest the civil forfeiture of about 8200 acres of old growth redwood and related property, neither admitting nor denying guilt in connection with the arrangement. The interesting thing, from Eddie's point of view? No one in the whole fucking deal was charged with a crime. Shanna walked for giving up Duncan. Duncan walked for giving up the dope, and maybe his boss. As for the Doctor, there was evidence he paid Duncan off, but nothing that tied him to the dope. There was talk of charging him with arson for blowing up his house, but nothing came of it. No one was injured and, if it was a crime, it wasn't federal.

The story did note, in passing, that the case had originally been brought to the attention of California state officials by the Mynot Indian tribal authority and that, under "equitable sharing arrangements" authorized by federal law, the state and the tribe would be receiving portions of the seized property in return for their cooperation. The state lands would be used for a new Watershed State Park, it said, and the land transferred to the Indians would be used for "economic development".

"I like that," Darryl grinned, looking over now. "Economic development. ... What's it say about Saul? Now that was a scene in a motherfucking movie."

It was. Twenty people sitting around a conference table in federal courthouse building with another forty sitting behind them. Saul came marching in with an army of New York lawyers, saying he wouldn't stand for it. Then, he found out the whole thing was a setup to take his land for a park! The pounded the table so hard he broke his little finger, or that's what Eddie heard, whether it was true or not. "I ate dinner at the White House," he said. "I slept in the Lincoln Bedroom—twice!"

"That was a scene all right," Eddie said. "It's not in here though."

What *was* in *Time* appeared in a green shaded box that ran across half of two facing pages titled, *When a Tree Falls in the Forest*. It started out, how loggers will tell you, when you cut a tree down in a forest, surprising things can happen. One tree can bring down another tree, creating a domino effect, with unpredictable consequences. And that's what seems to have happened with Harriman Saul.

The stock in Saul's holding company, known as HASCO, took a huge hit when rumors leaked about the drug forfeiture and a possible RICO indictment, falling from $49 to a low of $17, before it rallied when the settlement was announced. But that was just the first tree in the forest. Without the Watershed Grove, Saul couldn't get the financing to buy Southeast Air. The deal fell through, and Southeast's stock took a dive. That was tree number two. Tree three was Dick Duncan. Based on information he provided under his plea agreement, along with information later obtained from Ina Jaffe, described in the article as Saul's longtime confidante and assistant, the SEC launched an investigation into trading in Southeast Airlines stock, which led to Harriman Saul's indictment for insider trading conducted through a trust in the Bahamas.

"He'll make some kind of deal," Darryl said. "That's what happens."

The story noted that the investigation had originally included suspicious trading in HASCO put options ahead of the drug raid, but that Saul didn't seem to be involved in the trading, because the bets were made *against* the stock at a time when Saul had no apparent knowledge the raid was coming.

Eddie looked up. "The bets against Saul's stock— you know who that was, don't you?"

Darryl took a minute. "God *damn*," he said, "I *wondered* how the man was gonna get back that money he lost, giving up his own weed."

"*More* than got it back is what Russell said. He said that was the idea from the start, beat Saul at his own game. And it wasn't even illegal cause the tips didn't come from the company. So you couldn't say he traded on inside information."

They drove in silence for a while. Finally, Eddie asked Darryl what was going on with Michelle. Darryl had to think about it. "You mean why she didn't come?"

"Start with that."

"She *said*, account of Serena."

"Okay. It's a long drive."

Darryl shook his head. "What she meant, it's not a good *environment*. I said, baby, you been to Las Vegas, right? Kids all over the damn place. She said, 'not *my* kids'. See, she don't like Vegas, either."

"You were with her last weekend, though."

"Mmm."

"And the weekend before that."

"You're point being?"

"I was thinking, it might be getting serious."

"Serious?" Darryl shook his head. "Man, I don't know. Michelle, she's a fine woman, don't get me wrong. But she got some baggage, you understand my meaning."

"You mean Serena?"

"Could be, part of it. Serena, she's a cute kid, but what I'm seeing, you know, going out to the zoo, the wax museum, movie shows—that's just one part of the thing. Being there, day in, day out, worrying when she get sick, going to the doctor for her ear infection, making sure she do good in school, man, that's something else altogether. ... Shit, then, she get to her teens, the dudes start hanging around, I don't know if I could *handle* that." He thought a minute. "Even if I could, there's the other part."

Eddie looked over.

"See, Michelle, she don't like I'm representing 'the criminal element' how she puts it. She said she volunteered with the public defenders going to law school, so she know how it works. Man go to a lawyer charged with armed robbery, say he done a liquor store. The lawyer tell him he got to get a retainer first, otherwise how's he gonna get paid if he lose the case?"

"Sounds about right."

"Michelle say, suppose the man don't have the money?"

Eddie said, "I guess the lawyer says, 'Come back when you do.'"

"Yeah. Michelle say, here's the choice. Man go with the public pretender, he know that dude ain't got time to do nothing but plead the case. Now the truth is, nine out of ten conviction's on plea deals anyway but, going in, perps all think they gonna walk. So let's say next day, the perp come back with the cash, Michelle say, where you think he got it from?"

Eddie said, "He did another liquor store."

"I told her, you *know* that's the system. What do you expect? Lawyer can't work for nothing. He got bills to pay, expenses."

"So, what did she say?"

"Not a goddamn word. Just look at me like I'm some bitch ass motherfucker, you know?" He thought a minute. "See, that's the thing with Michelle. Way she looks at things, the shit's all wound up together. Don't matter if a man *got* to do a thing or the thing's *legal*. All she sees is, what kind of *example* would it make for her little girl? What kind of *role model* would I be for little Serena?"

Eddie thought a minute, "That's the one good thing with Karen. She didn't want kids. If we had kids, it would have been a fucking disaster."

Darryl drove awhile, not saying anything, then looked over. "You see her?"

"Who, Karen?" Eddie shook his head. "I was down at C.I.D., getting my experience certified, you know, for the P.I. application? This Asian chick down there, she's a friend of Karen's. She goes, 'You *know*, she's not with Bluestein anymore.' Waiting for me to ask where she is, how I can get hold of her, like I give a shit."

After a pause, Darryl said, "What about Shanna?"

"Shanna? … She's—" He was nodding, then shaking his head, finally he said, "What I wonder, if a man and a woman can be *too much* alike."

The Ellendale ramp was slammed, CHP directing traffic, sheriffs' cars at the bottom, lights flashing, a line of cars a half a mile long waiting to get in the parking lot entrance. Across the street, an old, flatbed truck was parked in a vacant lot next to the 7-Eleven. The truck was set up like a stage, with sound equipment, a microphone, speaker stacks. A sign on top of the cab said:

STOP THE REDWOOD CASINO

In front of the truck, they were hawking tee shirts. A scrawny kid with shoulder-length hair was dressed up like a redwood tree; a fat brunette in a shabby bird suit was holding a sign that said, "Marbled Murrelet."

Darryl said, "Seem like kind of a low rent operation."

Eddie nodded, "They don't seem to have their hearts in it."

Darryl said, "Not that it matter. How they gonna compete with that?" He pointed across the street, where a gigantic computer controlled, multi-colored, digital electronic sign was screaming:

**** REDWOOD CASINO ****
$$$ MILLION DOLLAR JACKPOTS $$$
$50,000 PAYOUT ANY SLOT
POKER * BLACKJACK * ROULETTE
LIVE ENTERTAINMENT NIGHTLY

Behind the sign, across the parking lot, you could see the building. It had a mountain lodge look to it, only bigger, four story entrance, granite on either side supporting giant redwood beams and behind that, an eight-story hotel tower. Off to one side, there was a sign that said, "Redwood Nature Center" with a neon flashing arrow. Walking up from the lot now, they followed the path to a little stand of two-year-old saplings that might be redwood trees one day. Next to the trees, was a little redwood kiosk, complete with a good looking brunette in a form fitting park ranger uniform.

"How you doing?" Darryl said to the girl, and when they were past, "Nice touch."

"You didn't recognize her."

Darryl looked over his shoulder, "She does look familiar."

"The girl in the tree."

"The … girl … in … the … tree!" Darryl repeated it slowly, nodding. "Yeah. Dudes at DEA used to sit around watching her wash under her armpits. I wondered what happened to her."

Inside, they wandered past rows of slot machines, roulette, table games. There was a familiar face dealing blackjack at one of the tables, a well-built blonde.

Darryl said, "Damn, Lana Janich. Like old home week around here. I lost track, after they let her go. Self-defense, I recall."

"They never filed charges. Shanna said if you were a defense lawyer, it was an impossible case to lose. A mother shoots her own son, a jury won't see her as much of a victim."

What they were looking for was on the far side of the casino floor, a bar with a glassed in dining area called the Redwood Lounge. Russell was standing at the entrance, watching them, a good looking brunette with him, a tall, Latina, with a great figure.

Eddie shook his head, "Jesus, look at you." Russell was decked out today in a deerskin fringe jacket with snakeskin inlays, set off with some nice, new necklaces made out of what looked like abalone shells.

Russell said, "Everybody got to have a look, *hombre*. You need to work on it. Like our man Darryl here, with his suits. Tell him how it is, Darryl."

Darryl laughed, but didn't say anything, eyeing the brunette.

"Oh yeah," Russell motioned. "This is our new hostess, Lucia Moreno. Lucia's Latina from Colombia, but it's okay 'cause she's half Indian."

The woman, Lucia, said, "We call it *mestizo*. In Colombia, everybody is *mestizo*."

"Lucia's teaching me *cumbia*," Russell demonstrated, shifting his hips in some funky moves. "She says where she comes from, everybody's gotta dance." He turned. "Babe, this is Darryl Waters, he's a lawyer. And Eddie Fuentes. Eddie's gonna be in charge of security, if he ever gets his fucking license."

Lucia smiled at Darryl briefly, then turned to Eddie, holding out her hand, "Russell told me so much about ju. My hawsband was involved with security, before he pass on. With West Coast Lumber. Maybe juw knew heem."

"What was his name?"

"Walter Hellman."

"He was your *husband*?" Eddie was surprised, the woman at least twenty years younger, then caught himself. "I'm sorry," he said, "I didn't know he passed away."

She spoke thoughtfully. "It was very sudden. A forklift driver drop a load of on his head. They said, he never knew what happen."

Russell had a table set up by a row of floor-to-ceiling windows that looked out on the hills. He told Eddie the idea was a kind of a reunion of the folks involved in getting the casino together, bring them up for the opening. He said he invited the U.S. Attorney, people from the DEA, the BNE, even the Governor. Hey, no hard feelings, man, he even invited Harriman Saul.

Not that he expected them to show up. The ones who did were already through their first round of drinks by the time Shanna came in. And man, she could walk into a room. That long red hair she had, the cropped leather jacket, skintight jeans, the hand-tooled cowboy boots—the same outfit she wore the day they first met.

She turned to Eddie, "Like the look?"

He smiled slightly, "Compared to what?"

She gave him the same slight smile. "Ask me later, I'll give you the options." Then, turning to Russell. "So, who *was* that out there?"

"Out where?"

"On Ellendale. You know. Save the Redwoods?"

"Oh yeah." He shrugged. "What can I tell you? A couple tribes don't like the competition."

She made a face. "Who are they using for P.R.?"

"Right." Russell laughed, "Somebody ought to tell them, you can't go green against the Indians, even if you're a fucking Indian yourself."

Later, at dinner, Darryl asked Russell about a rumor he heard, the tribe turned down a deal with the boys from Las Vegas, and was running the place itself. Russell told him, yeah, Caesar's wanted thirty percent for the financing, *plus* three percent of the gross *and* five percent of the net for running the place. It was pretty much what the casinos all wanted, so they decided to make other arrangements.

Darryl said, "Other arrangements?"

Russell said, "There's a lot of money in Redwood County," he said, "if you know where to look."

After they finished eating, Eddie and Shanna wound up at the bar. They hadn't seen much of each other since Eddie moved back to the Bay Area. But sitting next to her now, in the fog of her perfume, it didn't seem to matter.

"So, Eddie," Shanna said, taking a drag on one of the e-cigarettes she'd taken to smoking, "Your buddy, Darryl, tells me he's representing you, going after the city."

It was true. Eddie being a drug-bust hero, a reporter for the East Bay papers started poking into his situation with the Oakland Police, asking why the Department forced him out, and coming up with some interesting possibilities.

"He talked me into it," Eddie admitted, feeling a little guilty about it. "I told him it wasn't like the Department didn't have reasons for kicking my ass out of there, you know? The lieutenant was taking money from De Marius, sure. But maybe Al Whitaker was giving him a hard time, too. I said, I didn't see how he could prove motivation."

"What did he say?"

"It wouldn't get that far. He said, the City would look at two things. How much it cost to try the case, and how much it was worth to keep it out of the media. Add up the two figures, and that was the settlement.

"Darryl's a natural born lawyer. ... He took it on a contingency?"

"He was hungry. Just starting out. You know how it is."

"I do. " She took a drag, blew out a cloud of smoke, then smiled. "Actually, I'm getting out of the business."

Eddie looked at her, surprised.

She shrugged. "Prop 64. The Doctor was right. Times are changing. Pretty soon, *nothing* will be illegal anymore. Speaking of which ..." she chucked a thumb behind her to the casino floor, packed with losers playing the slots, "... it looks like you guys are gonna do okay with the place."

Eddie smiled. "Russell says the problem's the split. He's got people coming out of the woodwork wanting to be Indians."

"I was considering it myself." Shanna ran a hand through her long, red hair now, brushing it back from her face. "Or not." She paused. "Tell me about the land. You still own any of it?"

"The hillsides and the cabin. The state took a right-of way through the bottom land; they needed it for a road into the park."

"How'd you make out?"

"They don't pay above appraised value, but even so ... . Acre for acre, they still paid more than you offered my father."

She let that one go by like she didn't even hear it. "So, how much did you get? A couple hundred grand?"

He glanced at her, but didn't answer, waiting for the play to come to him.

"The reason I ask," she said, "I was thinking you could have something you might want to invest."

"You mean we could be, like ... partners . . ."

Shanna played with her e-cigarette. "I'm closing my law office. Converting it to a more relevant, twenty-first century enterprise. And I could use a little cash for ... inventory ... you know, get things going."

"What kind of inventory are we talking about?"

Shanna smiled, "Dope, what else? Prop 64. Democrats are behind it. The NAACP, the doctors. Christ, I heard even the Republicans are behind it. It'll pass for sure."

Eddie nodded. "I heard prices are down."

"Gimme a break. Twelve hundred an ounce? They're down, but it's not exactly alfalfa. Besides, I'm not fucking around. Strictly high end. Finest cannabis on the North Coast. Set it up like a cigar emporium. ...You could get in on the ground floor."

It got him thinking.

"It's a cash business," she said, picking up on his interest. "We'll need security. We could grow the stuff too, maybe out at your father's place. Right on the way to the park? What's wrong with that. I got a farmer, used to work for the Doctor. Think about it. Set it up like a winery, knock down the cabin and put in a tasting room."

Shanna leaned closer now, her knee brushing his. "It's a new world out there, Eddie," she said, holding out her e-cigarette. "Go ahead. Try it."

He turned, and their eyes locked. Eddie felt the cigarette in his hand, and now he was inhaling, taking a drag. "Jesus," he said after a minute, "What's *in* this thing?"

She shrugged. "A little hash oil. But really, Eddie, it can be anything. Extracts—that's the name of the game. Designer drugs, custom highs. ... The Doctor's on the cutting edge when it comes to chemistry, but his marketing methods are strictly last millennium." A thought seemed to cross her mind. "Hey, I want to show you something. It isn't open yet, but I don't think Russell would mind." She held out her hand. "Come on."

The room was in back. Not big, but classy—a half dozen brand new Brunswick Golden Crown tables, a cue rack and a row of spectator chairs.

"The idea is to host high stakes games," Shanna said.

Eddie had to smile. "What's the rake?"

Shanna took a couple cues down, handed one to Eddie. "No rake." Moving now to a table, she started magic-racking a game of 9-ball. "Russell said he'd make money on the side bets."

"If I know Russell, he will."

Now, Shanna ran long, graceful fingers over the velvety green felt, tilting her head up to look at him. "What do you say, Fast Eddie? You ready to go?"

Eddie took some time, finally shook his head slowly. "Gee, I don't know, Shanna," he said. "I haven't played in a while. Everybody knows, you're pretty tough …. You might need to give me some weight, you know, even up the game."

Shanna gave him a sideways look. "How much *weight* are we talking about?"

"Well—" Eddie examined the cue Shanna had given him, then put it back and took a heavier one. "I'll tell you what." He crossed to the table, chalked up, placed the cue ball half way between the bottom center spot and the left hand rail, then looked over.

"You spot me the break, we'll play it straight up from there. How would that be?"

Shanna smiled, just a little, holding him with those gorgeous green eyes of hers. "Show me what you got."

Eddie lined up the shot, took a few practice strokes—and hammered it. The balls flew around the table like birds flushed from cover, all except for the nine. It rolled from the center of the rack straight into the right top corner pocket.

Shanna looked at him, arms folded. "Well," she said, "I guess I can't spot you the *break*, can I?"

"Yeah, you can." Eddie put his cue on the table and walked over, close to her now, catching a whiff of her perfume. "You can spot me whatever you want. As long as we split the take, and I know which way you're betting."

Shanna thought a second, smiling slightly. "How you it played it with Russell …."

"We were partners."

"You said you were like the Texas road gamblers. But now I'm thinking Texas highway robbers is more like it."

"What makes you think there's a difference? Remember I was telling you about that book with the white man who decided to be an Indian?"

"You were reading it in the car."

"I'm thinking it's the same as what Russell told me one time. You are what you *say* you are. Like, I'm an Indian, if I say I'm an Indian."

"Your point being?"

"If we *say* we're partners …."

She gave him a slow smile now. Slipping her arms around his neck, she said, "I like it, Eddie. You and me, blowing smoke together."

"Sure," Eddie said, caught up again in that subtle scent she wore. "Only this time, not at each other."

But he wasn't exactly sure he believed it.

www.ingramcontent.com/pod-product-compliance
Lightning Source LLC
Chambersburg PA
CBHW071241170626
46809CB00001B/46